The Room Beyond

Stephanie Elmas

To Christelle
With Love From,

Stephanie Elmas

For Alpaslan and Jarmila

SERENA'S STORY

I gazed at the door. It seemed impolite to invade the slumbering air by knocking, so instead I watched my reflection in its glossy black paint: a medley of curves, as if a stone had unsettled the waters of a well. And then I checked the two brass numbers at the top again: 36.

The heat had made a mess of me. My new linen suit clung to my hips and ribs as if it had shrunk a size, and the lining glued itself against my white shirt underneath. To make matters worse the buds of blisters were now rising up beneath the soles of my feet and at the sides of my toes.

Inching back I peered up at the façade of the building, the last in a long grand terrace of almost identical houses. I had to crane my neck just to take in the full complement of storeys that seemed to sprout up and out of each other like the layers of a wedding cake.

In the corner of my left eye the terrace stretched out into the distance; a fortress of sparkling whiteness. It brought back a distant memory of standing, dwarfed by the wall of a moored luxury cruise ship. And yet to my right, only a few steps away, the road was entirely cut off by an old wall, held together mostly by wild plants and a prodigious climbing rose. That's what made it so quiet here, this unexpected slice of nature forcing the road into a dead end. Almost as if it was trying to fool me into thinking that I wasn't actually in London at all.

The front door seemed to be growing in size, as impenetrable as a castle gate. I forced a few lungfuls of air in, tried to blow some of it up onto my baking cheeks, and then I caught sight of a stucco moulding just above the door. It was a little blurred, distorted by more than a century of polluted air and numerous coats of paint no doubt, but it was still possible to see the outline of a garden in it, with a blossoming tree at the centre. There were two figures in the scene as well, Adam and Eve perhaps, entwined lovingly and yet half hidden by the tree.

'Can I help you at all?'

I jumped at the sight of a man standing before me; the door suddenly and miraculously open. He was in his late fifties perhaps:

tall and lean-faced, his limbs protruding from starched tennis whites.

'I'm here for the interview?'

His brow wrinkled. 'I'm afraid I don't know anything about an interview, are you sure you've got the correct address?'

'Yes I have, but it's funny you should say that because just now I got slightly confused by the numbering on your street. The houses, they jumped from 32 to 36...' His wide eyes looked patient if not a little perplexed. 'I was expecting this one to be 34 you see, although I'm sure everyone says the same thing... Do they?'

'Some do.' He heaved a sports bag across his shoulder and then looked back at me. 'Just a bit of war damage. May I ask, for what position are you expecting to be interviewed?'

'Oh, yes of course. The nanny position.'

His eyes narrowed and his brow wrinkled up even more. 'Are you quite sure?'

'Yes. I have an appointment with Arabella Hartreve.'

'Well that's my wife. I suppose you'd better come in. She's somewhere in the house, just have a rummage around.'

He squeezed his long limbs past me and strode out into the street.

'Oh, and if you find her could you let her know that the Portuguese Ambassador is coming for drinks tonight? Nice to meet you.'

The first thing I heard inside the house was music, the soft tones of a piano drifting across the hallway. And the air smelt delicious: baking and wood polish mixed up together. Exactly how a home should smell.

The music seemed to be coming from a room to the right, just before the bottom step of a great curving staircase. A teenage boy was sitting in there, at a grand piano. He seemed to have come to the end of his piece but was now striking three or four notes repeatedly, his eyes half closed in the deepest concentration. His long slim build was similar to that of the man I'd just met at the front door, but his skin was peppered with spots and he had that awkward teenage appearance of a face that hadn't quite filled in yet.

Suddenly he looked up at me.

'Hello. I'm looking for Arabella Hartreve. Do you know where she is?'

'Upstairs. Second door on your left.'

'Thank you.'

He stretched his fingers across the keys again and launched into a fresh piece of music.

Climbing up the grand staircase of the house felt a little like entering a museum. The air was cool but weighed down by the presence of so much polished wood; definitely not the sort of place where you could shout, or perch on a step to chat on the phone, or walk about in a dressing gown. And yet in spite of its grandeur, there was also something rather faded and weary about the place. The walls were positively crammed with photos, prints and paintings and the carpet on the stairs was tatty at the edges, crushed thin in places.

You see I am a home. A real home, it seemed to say.

I breathed in the atmosphere with the same enthusiasm as city dwellers do the country air. And I ran my fingers up the winding wooden banister, swept to a shine by a century of hands.

Upstairs the patchwork of prints and paintings continued. The second door on the left had a stained glass panel in the upper half depicting a scene of Grecian revellers drinking wine and feeding grapes to one another. All seemed quiet inside, but as soon as I knocked, a silhouette moved towards me through the glass. The door swung open and a man looked up at me. He was small and round with twitchy, bird-like features.

'Hello. I'm here for the interview...'

He crossed his arms impatiently and frowned.

'... I'm here to see Arabella Hartreve?'

'Serena, is that you?' exclaimed a female voice from inside the room. 'You've caught me unawares! I'm awfully behind with things today.'

'I'm so sorry Mrs Hartreve,' I called back over the man's shoulder. 'You don't have to see me now. I can wait downstairs if you prefer.'

'No, that's fine. Sasha was just leaving, weren't you?'

He made a reluctant bow and then brushed past me, his face crunched up like a fist.

'Now do come in.' And the woman herself suddenly materialized before me with a sort of conjurer's flourish.

I swallowed hard at the sight of her. She was beautiful, just like someone with a name like Arabella Hartreve should be. But it was the sort of beauty that instinctively made me want to take a step back.

It was her skin that caught my attention first; almost too perfectly smooth to be real. How old was she? Thirties... forties... fifties? And although her face was quite angular, it was dominated by large eyes and rather thick, sensual lips. Like the sort of mannequin you see behind an expensive shop window.

'Come on in. You look awfully hot, is it steaming out there?'

'Yes it is. Lovely and cool in here though.'

The room was a spacious, shady office with shutters at the windows keeping the blazing sun at bay. And she too was coolness personified. The soft scent of patchouli wafted around her as she moved and she was wearing a floor-length chiffon dress that would have fitted in rather well with the Bacchanalian scene in the room's door.

'Would you like a drink? I do recommend water, with a hint of lime.'

She waved a hand towards a decanter on a nearby dresser. Above it hung a framed black and white photograph of a young dark-haired man with his face turned back towards the camera as if he'd suddenly been caught out. He had long, thoughtful features, the centre of his eyebrows raised in a questioning arc; very handsome in an old-fashioned film star sort of way, or maybe that was just because the photo was in black and white.

'Ah now that's my son Raphael,' said Arabella.

'It's a good picture.'

'Yes I can see you like it... did you want a drink?'

'Oh, yes please,' I scooped up a glass. The decanter was deliciously cool, covered in tiny spheres of condensation. 'Um... as my aunt explained to your friend, I don't really have much experience of looking after children. I hope she made that clear to you.'

'Now how did I get your details again, please remind me. I've had several agencies on my back and they're all so ridiculously pushy: wanting me to make hundreds of phone calls and fill in thousands of forms. It's simply not my way. I'm far too busy for all of that with my Africa work.'

'Africa work?'

'Yes. And my arthritis,' she added, drawing her long and rather nimble looking fingers through ringlets of ash-blonde hair.

'Well my aunt, Jessica Eustace, is a member of an amateur

dramatics group with a friend of yours, Susan Norris? It was Susan who said you were looking for a nanny. That's why I wrote to you.'

'Susan Norris, Susan Norris...' she swished the name about in her mouth as if she were tasting a new wine. 'Yes, I have a vague recollection. I meet so many charity people, she must be on one of my boards.'

'Oh I see. Anyway, as I said, I'm not an experienced nanny. But I really love children and am quick to learn. I was actually wondering whether I could meet your daughter?'

'Of course you can, but I couldn't possibly tell you where she is right now. Probably in a bar, or at her club.'

'But isn't she... four years old?'

Arabella drew her eyebrows up into her hairline and suddenly exploded into tinkling laughter.

'Oh, you mean my granddaughter!' she cried out. 'You've been mistaken, Beth is my granddaughter.'

'Really? I'm so sorry, I didn't realize. It's just that you look so young.'

'On the contrary, you've made my day.'

My cheeks were burning again. 'So, would it be possible to meet your granddaughter then? Beth? I didn't see her when I came in.'

'Oh my dear, I don't have a clue where she is either. Don't ask me. No, I don't watch over her. As I said earlier I have my Africa work.'

'And your arthritis.'

'Yes. Now Serena,' and she clapped her palms firmly down on her knees. 'Fascinate me!'

I stared back into her expectant face.

'What, what would you like to know?'

'Gosh, I'm not sure really. What does one reveal in these sorts of interviews? Perhaps you could tell me something interesting about your upbringing.'

'My upbringing? It wasn't all that fascinating I'm afraid,' I laughed.

But she said nothing in response. I searched for some words as her long fingers began to fiddle with the edge of a tablecloth. She raised her other hand to her mouth for a moment, as if she were stifling a yawn.

'Um, well my aunt, who I just mentioned, brought me up...' I began. 'My parents died when I was young. But I suppose what's most interesting about me is my love of art. Ever since I was a child I've wanted to draw and paint and I've had bits and pieces of success so far. I'd love to show you some of it, perhaps... it wouldn't interfere with my work here of course. Actually I was fascinated to see the large collection of art you have in this house.'

'What happened to them?'

'To who?'

'Your parents.'

A flicker of interest seemed to have sparked up in her eyes. Her fingers had stopped fiddling with the tablecloth.

'Tell me about it,' she said in a hushed voice.

'I really don't think... It was a long time ago.'

She raised her shoulders in a little shrug. 'Well it's up to you of course, I wouldn't want to pry.'

A breeze drifted through the room and across my face, the sunlight winking at me through the gaps in the shutters. I'd never been in a home like this before, with grand pianos and winding staircases. And yet there was still something familiar about it; the smell of baking perhaps, bringing back old childhood memories.

'Such a long time ago.'

She raised her eyebrows encouragingly.

'There was an accident. A group of them were in a clapped-out old minibus on their way into London.'

I glanced into her eager face. Somewhere a clock was chiming.

'Something snapped in its engine along a busy shopping street. The driver lost control and the bus veered into a shop window. So... I went to live with my aunt and there I stayed.'

The shafts of light sneaking through the shutters merged for a moment into a single golden puddle.

Arabella gazed back at me.

'And do you believe that they are now with God?' she murmured. A silvery scarf had found its way into her hands and she drew it around her neck, running its tassels through her fingers.

'No. No I don't think so.'

She raised her eyebrows. 'Why not? Surely in your circumstances you would find it of some comfort to believe in life after death?'

'I find it hard to believe in things that I can't see.'

'But what if you were blind?'

There was no tinkling laughter now, and those luscious lips of hers had become rather thin and drawn. The heat of the day suddenly flooded back over me and a trickle of sweat slithered down between my shoulder blades.

'Then I'd probably be too angry with God to believe in him anyway.'

She smiled. 'Are you always so straightforward Serena?'

There was a sharp tap on the door.

'I'll be with you in a minute!' she called out. 'You'll find coffee in the drawing room!'

The sound of footsteps retreated down the corridor. I'd never even heard their approach.

'One of my academics,' she beamed. 'Now, these nanny agencies with all their forms and questions and whatnot. As I said I really don't have time for such trivia. We come from an old family, and we have our own ways as I'm sure you understand.'

I nodded, slowly.

'Beth is a special little girl, and as a family we won't be dictated to. All we're looking for is an agreeable companion for her with a wise and sensible head on their shoulders.'

'OK.'

She glanced at her watch. 'Gosh, I am in rather a hurry now. Such a busy, hectic life I lead! So, when would you like to start?'

My jaw must have fallen open and then the words just seemed to trip out on their own. 'As soon as you like.'

'Shall we say Monday week?'

'Yes, that's perfect.'

'I think I'll let some of that splendid sunlight into the room now,' she cried, throwing open one of the shutters.

I could see now that the room looked down over the wall at the end of the road, just where I'd been standing and sweating anxiously only a short time ago. From this angle you could see deep into the climbing rose. It was covered in swarms of pink buds; perfumed presents waiting to explode.

'I hope you'll be happy living with us.'

'I'm sure I will, you have such a wonderful home. I was so disappointed when I thought I'd got the wrong road.'

'The wrong road?'

'Yes, when I saw that number 32 was the second from last house on the road. I just assumed for a moment that 36 didn't exist...'

'Oh that. It's a long story, silly really. There was a mix up when the houses were first built. Now, did you have a coat or something?'

She was striding over to the door.

'No, nothing. Oh! I nearly forgot to tell you. Your husband asked me to let you know that the Portuguese Ambassador is coming for drinks tonight.'

Arabella came to a sudden halt and whipped her face towards me.

'Tonight? That's absolutely out of the question! Edward knows that I always have a migraine on Thursday evenings.'

'But, it's Wednesday.'

'Really? Oh yes, of course. I shall look forward to seeing him again then.'

Back outside I peeled off my jacket and let my body slowly deflate. I felt myself smiling; it was like that feeling of euphoria at the end of a successful first date. I began to hobble away on my blisters, but after leaving 36 behind me I couldn't help but pause outside number 32 next door. Why had Edward and Arabella Hartreve both fed me different stories about the missing number? And neither of them had really seemed to want to talk about it either.

I peered over to the other side of the road, but there was no similar discrepancy in the numbering: 33 and 35 were very much there, although the style of the houses on that side was slightly different, upsetting the symmetry of the road. No, for some reason number 34 had definitely been left out.

I limped along a little further down the road and dug out my phone.

'Serena?' came Jessica's familiar low voice at the end of the line.

'Yes it's me. And I got the job.'

'Congratulations! Are you going to take it? I know you didn't really see yourself as a nanny.'

The topiary hedges and chandeliered ceilings glided past me along the road.

'Yes, but I think it'll do. Might be slumming it a bit though...'

'Oh really? In Kensington? Now that does surprise me.'

'No, I'm only joking. It almost feels like a filmset here; loads of stuff to get my creative juices flowing.'

And it was true. I could actually feel my fingers twitching for the touch of a pencil, my heart beating with the urgency to get it all down on paper whilst the image was still fresh: the doorway with its stucco details, Arabella Hartreve's faultless skin, the snake-like curve of the banister.

'You know what, I think I might do a bit of sketching in the park before I get the train back. You haven't planned anything have you?'

She chuckled softly down the phone. 'No no darling, you take your time. I haven't heard you sound so jolly in ages. I'm glad you've found some new inspiration.'

Back at the beginning of the road again I turned for a final look at the place that was going to be my new home. The rose covered wall at the end had shrunk to the size of a postcard and the houses that framed it seemed to heave with history and grandeur. I could barely blink.

A montage of all the crummy bedsits and flat-shares I'd lived in over the years flashed through my mind; one place so small that it had been easy enough to make a reasonable meal from the comfort of my own bed.

'Convenient though,' Jessica had said on her visit and we'd both hugged our sides with laughter.

A black car with darkened windows edged round me and purred down the road. Could that be the Portuguese Ambassador arriving early? I would draw him thin and sleek with a little black moustache, perhaps kissing Arabella's long fingers whilst she twisted a scarf about with her other hand.

'Come up to my room and tell me about your childhood,' she'd whisper through confiding lips.

Just the idea of it sent little cooling thrills up my spine.

Marguerite Avenue. That's what it was called. I paused at the signpost and tried to stop myself from touching it. Even the name felt like poetry. Closing my eyes I drew in a deep breath of freshly cut grass and honeysuckle. Yes, Marguerite Avenue was already in my bones.

1892

Miranda skirted around the corner and walked the length of the road with brisk strides. The new rose was settling in nicely, already spurting out fresh green shoots across that eyesore of a wall at the end. She let her front door float past her for a closer inspection. Yes, masses of new tendrils gripping at those dusty bricks and some tiny pink buds.

Her eyes swept across number 36, the last house in the road, and in an upstairs window the silhouette of a woman flinched away. It was enough to take the warmth out of the air for a moment. She hurried back past her neighbour's door, snatching a glance at its chipped yellow paint. Jane would be getting fractious.

'Hello there. I think I just caught Mrs Eden staring at me through an upstairs window.'

'Is that so?'

'Yes. Is everything alright dear?'

Tristan seemed to be hovering half in, half out of the library and he had something of the startled rabbit expression about him. Her eyes slipped down his arm and found a large glass of brandy cupped in his hand.

'Of course it is. It was just rather hot in the office, that's all. Thought I'd make an early afternoon of it.'

A ray of sunlight caught at his blue eyes, made him seem years younger than he was for a moment, like a handsome cheeky boy.

'That sounds like a good idea. Perhaps we could do something. I've just been to the park and it's...'

'I have to go out again soon, something at the club,' and his lips tugged themselves up at the corners into an uncomfortable smile, filling his cheekbones with shadows. 'I won't be back for dinner. Another time, maybe. Sorry.'

Jane was sitting in her usual place in the drawing room with a cup of tea perched in her hand.

'You've been gone a long time,' she murmured.

'Yes, I met the Jamesons in the park; I've invited them to dinner tomorrow night along with Reverend Farthing.'

'How dull.'

Miranda tried to smile patiently at her sister. The sunshine was still running through her veins.

'You know I think I just spotted our neighbour Mrs Eden staring at me through her window.'

Jane sipped her tea and nibbled at a crumbly biscuit which began to disintegrate in her lap.

'Why not invite her around as well?' she said with a sudden playful smirk.

'Don't be ridiculous, she's far too scandalous for our lot!'

'I think it sounds like fun; might stir things up a bit. This Eden woman intrigues me. It's astonishing that in the three weeks since I've been here she hasn't called or passed me by in the road once.'

'Well that's not surprising, Marguerite Avenue is a dead end after all. And anyway, I don't think she really leaves the house after... after what happened.'

The muscles in Miranda's neck were starting to grind together again, all that freshness suddenly draining away. And when her neck hurt it always made her want to hunch up, which gave Jane yet another thing to complain about.

'Sit up!' she always barked. 'You look as if you're hugging something secretive to yourself.'

She tried to force her chest up and out but the sensation of her spine crushing in on itself actually made her wince. Outside on the hot road a small gust of wind played games with the dust. Silly mistake to have invited the Jamesons. Jane found them dull and goodness knows what Tristan would have to say about it. It must have been the sunshine that had made her so flippant. She could already picture Tristan, pulling faces across the dining table at her and Jane being deliberately caustic.

She felt her shoulders collapse into a hunch.

'Sit up! You look...'

'Yes, I know I know! Very well then, I'll ask Mrs Eden to come too. As you said, she might stir things up...'

'Oh good. I've heard so much about the woman it would be a shame not to be able to return home without a story or two to tell about her.'

'How could you even think about gossiping about our neighbour like that? The poor woman's been jilted by her husband.'

'Poor woman? They're theatre people, you loathe her!' Jane cried.

'Music hall people to be precise and anyway that's too strong. I have never *loathed* anyone in my life.' And yet she could still feel a deep flush of red guilt rising up her neck. 'I've been wrong to avoid her, I know that. It's just that something keeps stopping me; perhaps it's all the rubbish in the gossip columns.'

Jane eyed her up and down, her shrivelled lips defiant. 'I doubt whether it's that,' she murmured. 'She's hit a raw nerve with you, somewhere along the way. Now, I must get on. Can't sit around drinking tea all day. I'm dining out tonight so don't concern yourself about feeding me.'

When her sister had gone Miranda drew her knees up tightly against her chest. Outside thunder clouds had moved in, tinged blue and black like bruises punched into the sky. She wrapped a blanket around her shoulders as a long shadow fell across the room. Soon it would probably rain.

As everyone was out she spent the afternoon writing letters, which included an invitation to Mrs Eden, and making several aborted attempts to grapple with the garden between hot, sticky showers. The jasmine she'd planted by the dining room window was beginning to bloom; she loved its sweet scent, even if Tristan found it too sickly. And the rain brought the perfume out even more. She rubbed some of the flowers against the dip at the base of her neck.

She sat alone at the dining table for supper, but although the chops smelt delicious enough when Mrs Hubbard brought them through, the thought of actually eating them made her throat want to cave in. She hacked the meat off the bones and ferreted it away in her napkin to avoid comments.

At about midnight a slamming door shocked her out of sleep. Footsteps clattered across the hallway downstairs. Tristan, home at last, probably heading to the dining room for a smoke before bed. She threw a shawl around her shoulders.

The dimmed lights in the hallway filled the air with an amber glow. She'd learned how to move almost noiselessly through the house now, with only her shadow anticipating her approach. Downstairs something small and white was lying on the floor near the front door: a crumpled piece of paper. Tristan must have unknowingly stepped on it on his way in. It seemed to be a note, written in a scrawled, impatient hand on what looked like a page torn out from a magazine.

To dear Mrs Whitestone at number 34. I think I'll probably come tomorrow although I desperately need some sleep before I see anyone. Lucinda Eden.

On the other side of the piece of paper was the remains of what must have been a table of contents: *p.24 French wig making for the stage*, it read.

The dining room was empty; the chairs uniformly pushed in beneath the swirling sheen of the long mahogany table. This room had been such a source of pride to her in the early days, so spacious and tranquil. What marvellous dinner parties she'd planned for then, with friends and family, little feet running about perhaps.

From above the mantelpiece the portrait of herself and Tristan glowered down at her. The painter had captured Tristan's likeness so well. In just a matter of minutes he'd teased the oils into such an uncanny replica of his features. His expression was demure, princely even, his eyes so commanding.

And yet the construction of Miranda's likeness had consumed countless hours of humiliation. The painter had attempted to flatter her: to add a little chin where it failed to exist, to widen the eyes, add plumpness to the lips. The resulting image was of a woman of some beauty, but with features that had little relation to her own. She could barely bring herself to look at it.

Back in the hallway the scent of cigar smoke met her nostrils and she noticed that one of the drawing room doors was ajar. She stood perfectly still. The rest of the house was so silent that she could just hear him: his lips sucking at the sides of the cigar, his mouth drawing in the smoke. His hair would be tousled now, his eyelids getting a little lazy. She took a step towards the room, raising her hand softly against the door. Her breathing had suddenly quickened into short, sharp little gasps. And then her hand fell away, collapsing limply against her side.

'No,' she murmured under her breath and, just as deftly as before, retreated back upstairs to her bedroom, pulling the blankets tightly up beneath her chin.

The following day was warm again and quite humid by the evening. Mrs Hubbard's joint of beef for the dinner party had filled the house with an oily aroma that sent Miranda racing about the house opening windows.

The dining table had been set beautifully with the new linen table cloth she'd bought and their wedding cutlery. She pushed the window open as wide as it would go and let out a gasp. The jasmine was radiant. Just in the last few hours it had exploded with even more blooms. She closed her eyes and hugged her arms around her body, breathing in great lungfuls of its scent.

'Are you alright? Shall I close the window? Those flowers...'

'Oh,' she felt herself start at Tristan's voice. 'No, please don't. It's actually rather hot in here, don't you think?'

He was wearing a new suit that particularly flattered his tall slim build and his wide shoulders. His eyes were startling in the evening light; so intensely blue, the exact shade of the Italian sea where they'd spent their honeymoon. Perhaps she should tell him that, surprise him a little. He couldn't have forgotten how in love she'd been with the view from their hotel window.

'The Jamesons are here, as well as that odious preacher.'

'Gracious, when did they arrive?'

'About ten minutes ago I think.'

'Why on earth didn't you find me sooner?' she patted at her hair with nervous fingers, rushing at top speed towards the door.

'I thought you would have heard them. I went to take cover in the kitchen.'

'Oh you mustn't be like that. These are our guests after all!'

'Your guests, Miranda, your guests.'

'Please do at least try dear.'

He looked down at the floor. 'Yes, of course.'

'And we do have another guest coming tonight: Mrs Eden from next door.' He raised his eyebrows in surprise. 'Perhaps she'll brighten things up for you a little.'

The three of them were sitting in a neat row on one of the drawing room sofas.

'Reverend Farthing, Mr and Mrs Jameson, how lovely to have you here! Please do excuse my delay; I was needed in the kitchen for some moments. Is Jane not here yet? She's been busy packing but I know she's dying to see you all.'

Mrs Jameson flashed a demure smile at her. 'We were just commenting on how awfully close it is tonight. The air. So close! Weren't we Reverend?'

'Close?' The ancient man blinked slowly like a toad emerging from a puddle. 'Yes the air. Storm's brewing.'

'Oh dear, shall I open the window a little more then? Ah Jane, there you are. Have you been busy packing?'

Her sister collapsed rather heavily into a chair. 'No, I was just finishing an excellent novel.'

'How interesting, was it a romance?' Mrs Jameson asked.

'No, a murder mystery actually. Quite riveting.'

Mr Jameson made a small grunt. A bead of sweat rolled down the side of his neck, blotting itself on his shirt collar. 'Then you have a far stronger stomach than we do my dear,' he murmured.

'There's no denying its strength,' said Tristan, ambling into the room. 'But will it be able to withstand Mrs Hubbard's roast beef tonight?'

Jane gulped back a laugh. Why were the two of them always so cruel about Mrs Hubbard's cooking? Of all the things in the world which they could have agreed on, why should this be the only one?

'Tristan does make fun of our poor wonderful Mrs Hubbard. We're so lucky to have her though.'

'But she has been with you rather a long time,' said Jane.

'Two years. She joined us shortly after we moved in. I'm awfully fond of her.'

'And yet I've warned you about this time and time again, haven't I?' There was a sudden spark of fire in Jane's eye. 'You will insist on getting close to staff. She's done it from childhood; remember how ridiculously attached you became to the gardener and his wife?'

'Mr and Mrs Yates? They were very kind actually.'

And they really had been, smiling and trying to include her when no one else would. He'd grown prize onions as big as her head and Mrs Yates, well she couldn't quite recall her face but she'd had the most marvellous arms, like succulent sausages.

'And where are they now? Where are they?' Jane was frowning at her in a way that brought her eyes startlingly close together.

There was so much rage behind that expression. It made her feel as if she were shrinking in its shadow, just like something she'd once read in a book about a person shutting up like a telescope.

'A THOUSAND apologies for my lateness! Am I late?'

The new voice seemed to hurl itself across the room at them. It came from a figure standing in the doorway. A woman. She was wearing a sapphire blue dress and her hair had been adorned with peacock feathers.

'And which of you is my hostess?'

The woman's voice had such a deep velvety resonance that Miranda's answer seemed to dry up in her own throat. And when she did speak her voice shook appallingly.

'Hello Mrs Eden,' she rattled. 'I'm so glad you were able to come. Please, sit down.'

'Lucinda! Call me Lucinda! Do you have any champagne? I'm incredibly thirsty.'

'Um...' She scanned the room for help. Jane and Mrs Jameson were gaping open mouthed at the woman. Reverend Farthing fiddled with his wig.

'Of course we have champagne.' Tristan stepped forward. 'If you will allow me a moment, I'll take care of it myself.'

'Thank you,' she replied, fixing her almond eyes on him. 'You are Tristan Whitestone?'

'Yes, although we have met briefly before.'

'Before? I remember very little from *before* I'm afraid. I have been reincarnated you see, burnt on my husband's funeral pyre and resurrected, a shadow of my former self.'

'Your husband has passed away my dear?' asked Mrs Jameson.

Lucinda's lips parted in a grin which revealed a flash of her white teeth. 'No, madam, but I wish he would.'

Alice in Wonderland.

Yes, it had been Alice, the little girl in the story, who'd found herself shutting up like a telescope.

Tristan disappeared from the room and the cold shiver of having been left stranded in a dark lonely place ran up Miranda's spine.

'We were commenting just now on how close the air is tonight,' she faltered. 'Reverend Farthing thinks that there's going to be a storm.'

But Lucinda only widened her great eyes in astonishment, as if she'd just been spoken to in an exotic language.

'Really?' she replied. 'I rarely notice the weather.'

How was it possible that someone swathed in such gaudy apparel could still appear so frustratingly beautiful? Miranda could barely take her eyes off her. Her neighbour's face had suffered a little in the last year, that was quite evident. Her cheeks had grown lean and there were small lines forming at the corners of her eyes, but it was still the sort of face that could command an entire room to look at it and enough to make Miranda feel smaller and paler than ever.

'I hope you are managing quite well on your own now,' said Jane. 'It was only the other day that I raised some concern at not having seen you since arriving at my sister's house.'

'I rarely leave my home,' replied Lucinda. 'It's been quite miserable; there are so many wagging tongues out there you see. People with nothing better to do. No, I prefer to stay in my house for now, where I feel safe.'

She drew her fingers through some loose locks of hair which had fallen over her shoulder between the feathers and Miranda's hand darted instinctively to her own nest of hair, all wispy mousiness; quite impossible to coax into anything more than the drabbest of styles.

Tristan swept back into the room, the butler following with champagne.

'How long have you lived in Marguerite Avenue dear?' asked Mrs Jameson.

Lucinda smiled. 'Since the buildings were first constructed. My father gave me my house as a wedding present.'

'What a kind thing to do!'

She raised an eyebrow in response.

'It seems that our guest would disagree with you there,' said Tristan. He hardly blinked as he looked at her and Lucinda met him straight on, her eyes twinkling.

'Yes, he's right,' she nodded. 'You see my father only bought the house to get rid of me, and my vulgar gypsy husband.'

Silence.

'Shall we go through to dinner?' said Jane.

In spite of all the open windows, the dining room was so hot that Miranda's thighs glued themselves together and her body began to slide inside her clothing. The roast beef stared up at her from her plate like a ghoulish mouth. The smell of jasmine now only curdled in the heat of the room, turning everything sickly. Tristan had been right after all, she really shouldn't have planted the thing by the window.

Lucinda yawned through the small talk and toyed idly with the stem of her wineglass. Miranda watched Tristan's eyes simmer across the woman in the candlelight. He began with her fingers that were stroking and fawning at the glass, and then he moved on up the pale flesh of her arm and across her shoulder, which was glistening slightly in the heat.

'I see you've had your portrait done,' said Lucinda suddenly, interrupting whatever it was that Reverend Farthing had been talking about. He brought his conversation to a close by coughing into his napkin.

'Yes, a wedding present from Miranda's father. An Italian did it for us I think, what was his name?'

Miranda felt her face flush as the entire room turned to stare at the ghastly portrait of the two of them.

'Berlotti maybe,' she stammered. 'Something like that.'

Lucinda cocked her head at it. 'That's an excellent likeness of you Mr Whitestone.'

'Thank you.'

But she then cast a quizzical eye across Miranda before staring back at the painting again. 'The mind of an artist can work in such extraordinary ways; don't you think Mrs Whitestone?'

Tristan flashed a sardonic smile at them all. 'Surely you must find yourself at less of a disadvantage now,' he said to Lucinda. 'You after all received a house as your wedding gift; we on the other hand have had to make do with that picture.'

Lucinda threw her head back in laughter, her breasts rising up in her tight bodice. 'But you don't know my father; you can have him if you like!' she cried, raising her glass at the same time. 'There, it's settled. I happily bequeath you my father!'

'You do not have a good relationship with your family?' asked Jane.

'They are idiotic, unimaginative people, don't you think?' Lucinda replied.

'I'm afraid we don't know them,' answered Mrs Jameson.

'Oh, I thought everyone did.'

'I think I know,' said Jane. 'Are they not the Hartreves? They have an estate in Wiltshire.'

'Spot on! Let us toast those fine, horse loving people!'

And Lucinda slammed her glass vigorously against Reverend Farthing's.

Miranda rose to her feet. 'Anyone for water?' She could feel her neck coming out in blotches, like hot welts on her skin. 'It's getting awfully hot in here, the beginning of a fine summer I imagine.'

Out in the hallway the air was cooler and blissfully quiet. She was actually panting, as if she'd just run a great distance.

'Are you alright?'

It was Mrs Hubbard.

'Yes, fine thank you. Just in search of some water for the guests.'

The cook knitted her brow a little, the corners of her mouth turned down in a sad crescent moon. Miranda knew that look quite well. It was protective, motherly, enough to unleash the torrent of tears she was trying to restrain.

'The food was marvellous, thank you so much. I'm sure you'll be wanting to get home to your family soon.'

Mrs Hubbard brushed her apron smooth and shook her head. Her hair was almost completely grey and tied back in a no-nonsense sort of way from her high forehead.

'Oh I wouldn't worry about them; it's not the same once you're widowed and my boys are all old enough to look after themselves. I'll get the girl to bring your water.'

Miranda nodded silently and let her eyes rest on the apron knot in the centre of Mrs Hubbard's back as she hurried away.

Back inside the dining room Mrs Eden now appeared to be humming to the tune of a popular music hall song as Reverend Farthing talked with the Jamesons. Jane threw her a glance, her jaw clenched as tight as a ship's bolt. 'Sort this out Miranda,' her expression seemed to say. Tristan's eyes were radiant, and his shoulders shook with amusement.

'Don't you agree, Reverend, that this city is falling into degeneracy?' asked Mrs Jameson suddenly across the noise. 'That the politicians who govern us, the people of commerce, the artists, the musicians, all of them, are turning their backs too readily on God? I know of no other place so destitute.'

The humming stopped.

'It is one of the many dilemmas of our modern decadent society, Mrs Jameson, and is at the forefront of so many of my sermons...'

'May I interrupt?' asked Lucinda. She reached over to an arrangement of fruit on the dresser behind her and plucked a grape, raising the green orb up to the candlelight. Miranda held her breath.

'Why of course my dear,' said the Reverend. 'Is there a point you wish to add?'

'Yes, you see I'm a little muddled. Surely society as a whole is turning away from religion because people are finally beginning to accept the fact that there is no God. We are almost at the dawn of the twentieth century! Surely we've now reached a point where as human beings we can not only recognize but embrace our jungle heritage.'

She placed the grape in her mouth and crushed it, loudly, between her teeth.

Miranda gripped the edge of the table, her heart pounding in her ears. But then a sudden unexpected clamour of what sounded like applause and laughter broke through: Tristan, clapping and bellowing loudly.

'Bravo!' he cried repeatedly. 'Bravo!'

Slowly the room's tense shoulders softened around her.

'Have you ever acted before?' he asked her. 'You'd make a first-class actress.'

'A little, but that was my husband Alfonso's territory. I haven't so much as stepped inside a theatre in months.'

'Then you must come with us, next week. What is it we're going to see dear?'

'Hamlet.'

'Ah yes, Hamlet. Go on, say you'll join us.'

Lucinda brushed her fingers across her forehead. 'Perhaps, but unfortunately I have to leave you now; I'm afraid I've developed one of my headaches. They plague me nowadays. I hope you won't think me rude. What a divine evening!'

Miranda forced herself up. 'It's been a pleasure, I'm so sorry about your poor health. Perhaps a good physician...' But Lucinda was already half way out of the room. 'Let me show you to the door!'

'Not at all, I can manage quite well. Good night,' she cried without a backwards glance.

And then she was gone. All that glimmering blueness just suddenly vanished. Miranda collapsed back into her chair again; her joints stiff and tired. It had been even worse than she'd imagined and yet her sudden absence now felt surprisingly menacing. The table had turned into an arid plain. Tristan already looked glum again. He filled his wine to the top of the glass and embraced it towards himself. The rest of the party politely peered at their plates and toyed with their napkins.

'Reverend, do please tell us what we have to look forward to from your next sermon,' she said quietly.

The Reverend looked pleased. He opened his mouth and began to speak, but the sound of his voice barely touched her. She smiled and nodded from afar as if she were drifting gently away. And then the image of those glistening peacock feathers came back to her, entwined in all that hair.

What colour was Mrs Eden's hair exactly? Chestnut? It was hard to tell. Yes, chestnut, with sparks of red running through it. And all that flesh on display, ripe and fruity, good enough to sink your teeth into. No. It was quite simply out of the question. She'd have to cancel Hamlet. They'd move house if necessary. On absolutely no account would she ever let Tristan into the company of that woman again.

SERENA'S STORY

'It'll rain,' said Jessica. She was twisting her head back owl-like whilst gripping the steering wheel with one hand and the back of my headrest with the other.

'You'll never get in. There's a much larger space over there,' I said.

'Yes, but that's on the wrong side of the road. You should take an umbrella; I've got one in the boot.'

The sky was yellowish and soupy, but I could just about spot some blue patches in the distance.

'I don't need it. It won't rain, and I've got enough stuff to get onto the train as it is.'

She snapped off the engine with a triumphant flourish. 'Did it! Now I've got something for you, a sort of good luck in your new job present.' She grabbed her handbag from the back and rummaged about in it. 'I thought of you as soon as I saw it in the shop. There you go.'

She handed me a red velvet jewellery box and inside there was a small brooch, watery pink and gold in colour and finely crafted to replicate the feathery petals of a peony. Tears instantly sparked up in the corners of my eyes.

'It's beautiful Jess. It makes me think of her.'

'Yes I know, she did love them.'

The image of Mum kneeling in the garden instantly came back to me. I could still just about recall the sickled curve of her back under her old T-shirt as she patted down fresh soil, petals brushing against her face. I fixed the brooch to my top and kissed Jessica on the cheek.

'Thank you.'

'Good luck darling, not that you need it.'

My pile of bags billowed up out of the back seat, pressing themselves tightly against the window. They looked a lot heavier now than when they'd sat in the corridor at home. I dragged them out hotly.

'Are you really going to be alright?' Jessica craned her neck from her place behind the wheel.

'Of course. What could go wrong looking after a four year

old? Bye, and thanks for the brooch.'

'Serena, the umbrella!'

The train was stuffy; it smelt of synthetic fast food and coffee breath. It was only a short half hour journey into Paddington, but I felt as if I were plunging headlong into a different world and ribbons of expectation tangled themselves up into a tight knot at the pit of my stomach.

I prayed that Beth would like me. I'd read enough books about parenting and caring for children in the last few days to try and blag my way through bedtime routines, descriptive praise and learning through play. Hopefully it would be enough.

When I dropped my heavy bags down on the Hartreves' doorstep the sky was still heavy and foreboding, but it hadn't rained and I glared at Jessica's huge umbrella neatly folded up on the top of the pile.

This time a small, neat-looking woman opened the door with a little girl right beside her. Beth. She eyed me curiously from the threshold, delicate arms hanging against her cotton dress and fine blonde hair tied up to one side. She had an intelligent, impish face and intense blue eyes with which she regarded me with deep seriousness.

In spite of her littleness she was really quite intimidating. The few children I'd come across in my limited experience had been the sort of individuals who liked running around in muddy gardens, playing rough and tumble and pulling funny faces. Beth didn't look like that sort of child at all.

'Hello. I'm your new nanny.'

'I like your brooch, what sort of flower is that?'

'It's a peony.' I bent down so that she could have a better look. She touched it tentatively with her fingertips as if the petals were real.

'Do you like shells?' she asked solemnly.

'Um... well, yes!'

'I'll show you my shell collection then.'

She took me by the hand, tugging me inside, and I followed her up several flights of stairs to a cool cream corridor.

'This is my room, yours is up there.'

I followed the direction of her nod and to my surprise discovered another much narrower flight of stairs directly opposite her door.

Beth's room was spacious and sunny, with two bay windows overlooking the street, but the walls and floor were more cluttered than an old forgotten junk shop. Shelves overflowed and mounds of nick-nacks, old toys, books and boxes of strange and unexplained objects covered almost every inch of carpet.

'Here you will find my collections,' she said with an encompassing wave of an arm. 'One day I would like to work in the Victoria and Albert Museum. I've been there forty-seven times. Now let me find those shells.'

We climbed over to a precarious looking tower of boxes in the corner. The top one was an open biscuit tin containing an assortment of rusty springs.

'They're just under here!' she said, heaving it away with surprising strength. Underneath, in yet another box, the shells glinted up at us like of row of pink coiled snakes. 'They're from Morocco, very rare indeed.'

Beth had that concentrated look on her face of an expert basking in the knowledge of her profession. And suddenly I could picture her on *The Antiques Roadshow*, offering her informed opinion about people's ancient wardrobes and bits of jewellery. She cradled a particularly beautiful pink specimen in her hands.

'This is my favourite shell, it's the same colour as that peony,' and again she looked admiringly at my brooch.

'Is pink your favourite colour? It was mine when I was a little girl; I used to have a pink bedroom.'

'It was for a while, but now I prefer turquoise and anything sparkly.'

She picked up two more shells, more serious than ever. 'These shells look like they should come from fairyland.'

'Have you been to fairyland?'

'Of course not, it doesn't really exist.'

'Who told you that?'

'Eva.'

'And who's Eva when she's at home?'

'Don't you know?' and the little girl blinked at me. 'Eva's my Mummy.'

'So you're already showing off your kingdom to her then,' said a voice.

The woman from downstairs was now standing in the

doorway.

'Oh I'm so sorry, I didn't introduce myself properly to you,' I stumbled across the cluttered floor towards her with my hand stretched out. 'I'm Serena, Beth just whisked me away I'm afraid.'

The woman peered at me with startled eyes. She looked me up and down and then exchanged a questioning sort of look with Beth.

'I'm Gladys, the housekeeper,' she said, her voice quivering slightly as if she was shy. She cleared her throat. 'And before you ask I do try and clean this room, but little lady guards it like you wouldn't believe.' She coughed again and glanced about her a little awkwardly. 'Now, would you like to come and see your room?'

The three of us puffed our way up the narrow flight of stairs together.

'It's a bit of a hike, but very private,' said Gladys, pushing open the single door that occupied the small landing at the summit. Bright daylight instantly beamed across our faces.

The room was dominated by two glass panelled doors leading onto a balcony, and the view through them made me gasp with pleasure: fresh green leaves on gnarled branches and glimpses of tiled roofs and chimney pots beyond. My room was like a nest perched amidst London's rooftops. It felt like being at the top of a tower, or in a turret.

'This is the first thing I'll draw here,' I exclaimed. 'The chimney pots poking up through the leaves.'

'Are you an artist?' asked Beth.

'Yes. When I'm not being your nanny!'

The room itself was fairly small, with pale blue walls and not much furniture, but I was far more interested in the view and the balcony which, on further inspection, looked just large enough for a chair and perhaps a couple of plants. It was home already.

'You open the doors like this,' said Gladys. She undid a small catch and they opened effortlessly. 'Nice view. In the winter you can see Holland Park through the bare branches.'

I grasped the balcony railings and inhaled. The air smelt cooler, cleaner from up here.

'If you grew your hair longer you'd be like Rapunzel,' came Beth's voice from somewhere behind me. She was curled up quite contentedly on my bed. It was good to see that she already felt so comfortable in my company.

I gazed across the higgledy landscape of roofs and foliage and a warm smile filled my face. The distance buzz of the city beyond rang gently in my ears. To my right I could see the blunt corner of where the house finished; the final frontier of Marguerite Avenue. To my left I could see two or three similar balconies to my own on other houses belonging to the terrace, but the majority had clearly been removed to make way for decades of alterations and modernizations to the grand homes.

There was no balcony on the back of the house next door. I could still see the mark on the wall where it had once been right next to mine, but it must have been taken away to make way for a flat roofed extension that jutted out just below. I turned away but then something instinctively made me look back again. It was a feeling more than anything, a strange sort of hollowness that made me peer through the still empty air. I grasped the railing and swallowed. Funny, but I'd never suffered from heights before and this certainly wasn't the place to start.

Back in the room Gladys had gone, and my bags had miraculously arrived.

'Would you like to meet Eva, she's downstairs in the drawing room,' said Beth, tilting her small face up at me from the bed. 'With Seb,' she murmured, as if it was a sort of afterthought.

We floated down through the house; past a thousand paintings, photographs, rustic looking jars of flowers on antique kidney-shaped tables. In the hallway at the bottom, the door to the room with the piano in it was half open again. I craned my neck to see inside but no one was there this time.

'That's the library,' Beth said, catching my glance. 'But it doesn't have any books in it and no one ever reads in there. Robert uses it more than anyone.'

'Robert?'

'My younger uncle. He's a musical genius you know.'

'Is he indeed? Actually, I think it must have been him playing here last time I came.'

'Yes probably. He plays the piano mostly, but he also has an outstanding flair for the flute, violin and harp.'

'Did you hear someone say that once?'

'No. Come on, this is the drawing room over here.'

Beth grasped my hand, pulling me across the hallway through a door with a bulbous doorknob like a paperweight. The drawing room was expansive and high-ceilinged and was the perfect realization of warm wallowing comfort that I must have craved for at a thousand dreary bus stops. It had the exact chair I'd always wanted to curl up and hide in and the sort of all-encompassing sofas for which most people would trade in their beds.

The room ran along the full depth of the house, with a bay window looking out over the street in the front and an ornate raised conservatory at the back. It had wooden panelling on the walls and a Turkish carpet on the floor. In the middle two huge sofas sat opposite each other like basking hippos, with a table between them and piles of books, newspapers and magazines all around. I watched Beth walk over to the sofas and then realized that two heads were lolling and half buried in the cushions there. One of them rested against the back of the sofa facing away from me and revealed nothing more than a mop of dark blonde hair. The other, which belonged to a woman on the sofa opposite, was only just discernible from the nose up.

Both figures were slumped so low that there was something almost secretive about their intimacy. It felt as if we'd caught them in the act of disclosing confidences across the coffee table between them, and I immediately felt awkward. An instinctive urge made me pull back, but Beth grabbed me by the hand and drew me further into the room.

As we came closer I caught sight of her properly, the woman in the sofa opposite. She had an attractive, doe-eyed sort of face, but it was so cold and so thin. The corners of her mouth and her eyes sloped downwards at the edges in perfect parallel, like two rainbows, making it one of the saddest expressions I'd ever seen.

I felt myself staring at her, rudely perhaps, but her face was a riddle, and as approachable as a shard of broken glass. And beneath all of this her fingers ran repeatedly along a string of pink pearls she was wearing around her neck. The action reminded me of Arabella, although these hands were much bonier.

'Bethany, come and give me some of your big fat kisses,' she said in a quiet and considered voice. But Beth ignored the request and tucked her legs up in a leather-bound armchair close by instead. I was left alone in the middle of the room, not even sure whether she had noticed my presence at all.

'What should I do?' Eva continued. 'Daddy wants me to go to university, but where on earth am I meant to go with two Es and an F?'

'I don't know. What about Cambridge?' Beth replied.

'No sweetie, you've got to be clever to go there.'

'What if you pay them?'

'Um, maybe, I'll ask Daddy,' she mused, toying with her pink pearls with renewed vigour.

So, Eva was young, barely out of her teens. In my naivety I'd never made a connection before between underage sex, teenage pregnancies and the privileged upper classes. And now it all fell into place: why Arabella had taken the responsibility for interviewing me, Beth calling Eva by her name, the reason for the whole family living under one roof. She threw a glance in my direction.

'You must be the new nanny.'

'Yes... my name's Serena; it's nice to meet you.'

I moved towards her a little, but she didn't move an inch.

'We had a nanny when I was small,' she continued, her attention back on Beth. She stole one of my bracelets so Daddy sacked her.'

'Was it an antique?'

'I don't know, probably.'

Beth screwed up her nose. 'Disgraceful.'

It was hard to believe that Beth was really only four years old. In contrast to her mother she appeared like a little wizened old soul. There was some similarity between the two faces: Beth was far blonder, her eyes much bluer, but they both had the same beautiful fair skin, faultless like spilt wax.

Eva lit a cigarette, inhaled deeply and began to smooth out the ruffles in the silky slip of a garment she was wearing. It was just long enough to pass for a dress and yet suitably short to reveal the infinite length of her slender legs; just like the legs on my old Barbie doll, even down to the pointy feet.

Something suddenly moved in the corner of my eye. It came from the other sofa. I'd completely forgotten that someone else had been present all along, and I now turned to find a male figure there, slouched as comfortably as a cat.

The deep cushions obscured his face from where I was standing, but his body was long and lean and although he was dressed only in scruffy jeans and a faded old T-shirt, his lolling posture suggested that he was totally at ease in this place. He moved again, this time with a dramatic stretch and the sigh of a long waking-up yawn.

Who was he? What was the name Beth had murmured when we'd been up in my room? Seb. He shifted forwards and his profile came into view. It was lithe and high cheeked, in need of a shave and framed by unruly dark blonde hair.

'Shouldn't you be at nursery Beth?'

His voice was still drowsy although tinged with playfulness.

'I tried it a few times, but I've decided not to go anymore,' she replied softly.

'Oh, didn't know you could do that.'

'Neither did I,' I added.

The corner of his mouth curled up into a smile at the sound of my voice and, slowly, he turned to face me.

His eyes were glacial; so translucent that they barely passed for blue. And in that first brief moment when they met mine, they seemed to sear right through something deep inside me. It made me want to draw my stomach up into my chest. I wavered a little, betrayed an anxious laugh and the eyes instantly softened in response; all that lucid blueness mellowing into a more apologetic grey.

But the side of my cheek felt the onslaught of yet more eyes: Eva watching me like a hawk, her face wide with interest, astonishment even. Her mouth was actually gaping open a little.

'This is Serena, she's my new nanny.'

Beth's voice sounded cautious, as if she were testing tricky waters.

'Well thank God you're here. We've been waiting for someone like you for ages, haven't we?'

Beth didn't reply.

He shook my hand and his skin felt cool against mine. 'I'm Sebastian White, friend of the family.'

'But we all call him Seb, and he's always hanging around here,' said Beth.

He hurled a cushion from behind his back in her direction. 'I'm a big favourite of hers, as you can see.'

His eyes met mine again and then he scanned my body up and down. I felt my face turn scarlet.

'So how did Arabella find you?'

'Oh, a friend of hers does amateur dramatics with my aunt.'

'How very straightforward!'

'You know what Mummy's like,' interrupted Eva.

'Oh yes, and we love her for it. Have you been a nanny long?'

Somewhere on the periphery I could still feel Eva's stare boring into my skull like a series of cold, grey bullets.

'No, actually this is my first job as a nanny,' I shrugged and tried to smile beneath the onslaught. 'Not really selling myself here, am I?'

'Don't worry, you don't need to,' he beamed. 'You'll be fine.'

'You think so?'

'Of course, and if you find Beth too difficult just tell us and we'll swap her for a Labrador.'

The cushion instantly came hurtling back in Seb's direction, but this time Beth did betray a giggle.

'What *did* you do before this then? I mean, you must have done something?' asked Eva, cutting the merriment with the precision of a scalpel. Although her mother had already employed me, it was quite obvious that for Eva my interview had barely begun.

'Yes, I'm an artist, although I've always had to work to keep myself going. I've brought my materials, perhaps Beth might be interested in some lessons...' Eva blinked but said nothing. 'I'm always looking for inspiration... actually I've just been to Thailand on a sort journey of discovery.'

'And what did you discover?' asked Beth, wrinkling up her forehead.

'Oh, not much in the end,' I laughed. 'How to live on ten dollars a day I suppose, how to avoid a lot of other tourists attempting to do exactly the same thing. But you could say that a pretty vile stomach infection discovered me, so I came home.'

'How remarkable.' Seb seemed as wide-eyed and innocent as a little boy. 'Why on earth did you do it?'

'Do what?'

'You know, go so far away by yourself? Where did you live?'

'In a hut on a beach for most of the time.'

'Everyone does it Seb,' said Eva, wryly. 'It's the thing to do nowadays.'

'Well anyway, I'm in awe,' he answered, standing up and stretching his body to its full height. As he raised his arms I caught a glimpse of flesh above the top of his trousers. 'Eva's just come back from Morocco, haven't you darling?'

He brushed his hand softly against her cheek and my heart sank. So that's why she'd been glaring at me.

'Do you... live here?' I asked.

He unleashed an enigmatic grin. 'No, I just spend A LOT of time here. It's the best place in London after all, don't you agree?'

'It seems beautiful, although I just arrived this morning. I haven't even unpacked yet.'

'Oh you'll love it, you'll just love it. It's paradise here isn't it?' he exclaimed, attempting to encompass both Beth and Eva in his enthusiasm with a wave of the hand. Beth ignored him completely, and Eva just raised her eyebrows until they formed two perfectly plucked half-moons.

'And you simply can't beat the Hartreve women for their unfettered energy and enthusiasm.'

I burst out laughing and then swallowed hard to stop myself as Eva actually turned her face away despondently.

'I'm bored. Can we go to the park?' said Beth.

'Yes, although shouldn't you be having some lunch?'

I looked at my watch, it was nearly one o'clock.

'I don't like lunch.'

'What does Beth usually eat for lunch?' I asked Eva.

'I don't know,' she replied with a blank look. 'I thought she just said that she didn't like it?'

Beth slipped out of her chair and dragged me away by the hand. I felt a warm, grateful rush at her acceptance of me.

'Have fun!' said Seb.

'We will.'

I felt his eyes watch me leave and fought hard not to return the glance. Eva Hartreve was quite clearly the last person I wanted to get on the wrong side of.

I took Beth to Holland Park. We went to the playground first but she only looked bored there, kicking her heels around in the sand nonchalantly and eventually sitting down on a bench by herself.

'What would you rather do?'

'I'd like to go over there and look for insects.'

We flopped down under the large tree she'd singled out at the edge of the park. It was a secluded spot, cloaked in mottled sunlight that filtered down through the canopy of the tree. A subtle breeze teased the leaves above our heads.

'Sounds like silver foil, or new clothes wrapped in pink tissue paper,' she said. I looked at her face and noticed that her eyes were closed, tightly wrinkled up in fact. She seemed to be feeling the sounds around her, tuning herself to the environment. A dog whined in the distance.

'What does that sound like?' I asked.

'A bear in a cave, or maybe an unhappy ghost.'

She opened her eyes and they lit up suddenly.

'Look Serena, there's a ladybird on your arm!'

We placed it carefully on a leaf and counted its spots as it waved its antennae furiously at us: a small conductor with two batons. And when eventually it flew away, scooping pools of sunlight up into its wings, Beth's face was a picture of delighted fascination.

'Does Eva bring you to this park?'

'No, she doesn't really do parks. Raphael does sometimes.'

'Ah yes, I saw a photograph of him.'

'He's Eva's twin brother,' she added, pulling her dress over her knees and resting her chin on them. 'Grandma and Grandpa have three children: Eva and Raphael, and then Robert, the musician I told you about. Oh and then there's Seb, who's like a sort of family member. Raphael's not around very much, he lives abroad mainly.'

'You must miss him.'

'I do. He buys me nice presents, beautiful interesting things. And he tells good stories about his travels.'

Yes, stories. I'd forgotten how important they were to childhood. My parents must have told me stories when I was a little girl but I couldn't remember a single instance. I blinked hard at the sky: didn't all children have some sort of memory of sitting on their mother's lap being read to? I could remember Jessica reading to me, from a large hard backed edition of *Alice in Wonderland*, her favourite book as a child. Perhaps she'd wanted to share her feelings of nostalgia for it with me. But as a ten year old I'd found it rather juvenile and actually quite distressing. I couldn't really grasp the charm of a small girl all alone, constantly changing size and running into weird characters who wanted to chop her head off.

'What sorts of stories do you like?'

'Spooky ones.'

'What, ghost stories?'

'Yes. I have a large collection of them at home.'

Was this normal for a four year old? But this was Beth, and although my knowledge of young children was limited even I could tell that she was unusual for her age; a small eccentric in the making.

'Have you ever seen a ghost?' she asked, cautiously.

She'd picked up an ant and was watching him circumnavigate her bent knee.

'Not really. I might have heard one once, though.'

She looked up.

'Tell me about it.'

'OK then. It's a silly thing really, probably not half as impressive as your stories at home.'

'That doesn't matter.'

'Well, when I was a little girl, probably about seven or eight years old, I went for a sleepover at my friend's house. Her name was Sally, Sally Davies. She lived on a farm in a big old squeaky house that I was a little bit scared of. That night we stayed awake in her bedroom talking for ages until we got really tired and closed our eyes to go to sleep. Suddenly I heard whispering, so quiet that I couldn't understand the words. "What did you say?" I asked Sally, but when I listened to her breathing I knew she was fast asleep. I heard the whispering again and again. It scared me so much that eventually I pulled my covers over my head to block it out. The next day I told Sally about it, thinking she'd probably laugh at me. "Oh don't worry," she said instead, "that was just the ghost." I never stayed at Sally's house again after that.'

Beth brushed her fingers through the long spears of grass around her feet. Her forehead had wrinkled up. She'd clearly taken my story quite seriously, maybe I should have kept it to myself.

'It's a bit of a rubbish ghost story.' I stroked her shoulder. 'And it was such a long time ago, I don't really remember it properly.'

'I liked it.' A cloud had momentarily obscured the sun and her eyes darkened.

'I hear voices all the time,' she murmured.

A flurry of cool air rose up my arms, like a flock of birds

swooping over the horizon.

'Where do you hear them?'

'In my room.'

I pictured the scruffy walls of Beth's room and its endless piles of collected artefacts.

'Are you sure you're not imagining things?'

'Oh yes. I hear this one woman crying mostly. She just cries and cries and cries and cries.'

I shuddered inside. I couldn't help myself, even though it felt so foolish to be freaked out by a young child's colourful imagination.

'And when do you hear her?'

'Usually during the day when I play there on my own. I just tell her to stop crying; sometimes she does, sometimes she doesn't.'

'I think you're making things up.'

'Think it if you like, but it's true.'

Her face looked open, sincere. She wasn't challenging me or trying to get a reaction of some sort. That was the problem.

'Come on Beth, you must be hungry by now. Let's go home and find ourselves something to eat.'

She put her small hand in mine, and together we prowled back through the grass towards Marguerite Avenue.

1892

Lucinda planted herself firmly in the middle of the bench. It was in a perfect spot: set back under a large shady tree and away from the throng of the pathway. A ladybird landed on her knee, a droplet of blood against her violet skirt.

'Where did you come from?'

It crawled onto her finger and then suddenly spread its wings and hurled itself back into the sky.

'Goodbye little man.'

She closed her eyes against the world and let the orange sunlight wash coaxingly against her lids. How long had it been since she'd last ventured so far? A month or two perhaps, it was difficult to tell. Her senses gradually softened, like taut strings being unhooked one at a time. The noises in the park merged into a gentle hum and the glow of the sunlight spread about her.

Tristan Whitestone.

That name just kept coming back to her again and again and every time her lips automatically curled into a smile. How on earth had that chinless fidgety woman found such a husband for herself? Yet he was cruel enough; he'd enjoyed her bad behaviour a little too much the other night.

But gosh, those blue eyes of his... like fire and ice at war with each other. She could recall them so easily; the way they'd laughed with hers. If only she could open her eyes right now and find them watching her again.

Suddenly she was falling. Bumping to and fro against the walls of a deep well lined with black velvet. Down. Down. And then an enormous jolt. She snapped her eyes back open and gripped the edge of the bench to steady herself. The scene in the park came back to her in a mass of colour and jagged edges. Had she been asleep?

Her throat tightened up. Already she could sense the whispers, seeping from between the fingers of raised gloves: *Did you see Lucinda Eden in the park? Fast asleep on a bench and lolling about like a drunk! She's let herself go since Alfonso left her for that dancer you know. Have you seen the lines on her face?*

Someone somewhere was laughing. *Look at that jilted woman,* it seemed to cry out. She peered through the haze but found no one she even vaguely recognized. Her throat loosened a little and as soon as she felt the rhythm of her breathing coming back, she raised herself on unsteady legs.

It was slow going back on the pathway. People were bumping into each other, and a myriad of strange faces swarmed at her like flies. A few months ago she would have adored it here; hanging onto Alfonso's arm, laughing in the sunshine.

'I'm going to get married Daddy. To Alfonso Eden.'

It felt like only yesterday. Father down at the stables, his face still pinched and sallow after mother's death.

'If you do Lucinda, it will be the worst mistake of your life.'

'But I love him!'

'No you don't. You love the idea of him, you love his degenerate ways, you love being able to think of yourself as a rebel by marrying him.'

'How dare you insult me like that!'

He'd turned his back to her; impenetrable, a fortress of resistance.

'First your brother leaves us for Africa, then your mother... Am I to be the only Hartreve left? The only one to cherish all that we have here?'

'No, of course not. And Alfonso is a huge admirer of yours; he simply adores the prospect of entering the family.'

'I'm sure he does.'

She'd placed her hands on his shoulders, pressed her cheek against his back.

'He's a good man Daddy.'

'And do the whores who dance on his stage for him agree?'

The path had got too frantic, she stopped for breath by the sparkling pond. What was that across the water? Something bright and blue and familiar.

How right her father had been all those years ago. But to keep sending that damned servant of his, week after miserable week to spy on her, as if her pitiful circumstances were too repugnant for him to face her by himself...

She touched her face. Her anger had caught at her skin. And there was that thing across the water again. What was it over there? A silvery blue pattern, like dolphins swimming upwards, emerging and then disappearing within the crowd.

'My Venetian Duchess!', 'My alabaster bride!'

Silly things for a man to have called his wife, and yet there was a hollow place now inside her where the luxurious touch of Alfonso's flattery had once been.

A group of young men rowed towards her on the water; trim and handsome with limbs much too long for the small vessel they'd hired. They splashed water in each other's' faces, laughing at the hilarity of their cramped postures.

She eased an inch or two forwards, but the boat sailed past and they jeered and whooped and fought over the oars without a second glance at her.

Tears flooded her eyes. Her lips twitched with the urge to cry. And through her blurred vision she could see that blue thing again. It was quite close by the water's edge now, directly across from her. She brushed the tears away. Alfonso.

She must have gasped rather loudly because several passers-by paused to offer her their puzzled glances. And of course, he was wearing the blue and silver waistcoat she'd given him last year for their anniversary.

Something made her want to grin suddenly. He really was the most outrageous looking man, getting fatter by the day it seemed and hardly a hair left on his head. But he had such a comical, amiable face, like a big over-fed baby. The sort of cheeks that women loved to kiss and knead fondly at with their fingers.

It made her think of the first time they'd met, at Sally Feversham's party for which she'd told her father all manner of lies to get to. She'd never been to anything like it: lights dimmed to virtual darkness, half dressed women perched on men's laps and a sweet smoky flavour to the air which left her completely light-headed.

'May I introduce myself princess?'

Even the voice had been round and jovial.

'Alfonso Eden, manager of The Empress Theatre Soho. But I'm afraid you'll have to leave soon as I'm already rapidly falling in love with you.'

He was a little slimmer then of course, never handsome but fuelled with enough charm to more than compensate for his lack of physical prowess.

He was looking back at her now, open mouthed with surprise from across the water. He raised his hand in a small wave. And then from the midst of the crowd another figure joined him. Petite and feminine, dressed in canary yellow. Betsey. She put her arm through his and then gave him one of her insipid smiles, all sweetness and vulnerability like a little lost fawn. He seemed flustered, looking back and forth at the two of them with coy snatched glances.

'Stupid fool,' she murmured under her breath.

'There's a note here for you ma'am.'

'Not now Sarah,' she said, marching past the maid and into Alfonso's old office. 'I'm not to be disturbed for the rest of the afternoon.'

She threw herself into the arms of the deep leather chair, lit a cigarette and watched the curious fingers of smoke rise up into the air. It wasn't dark enough in the room, even with its heavy wooden shutters firmly closed. The blasted sunshine had found ways of wheedling itself in through the small joints in the slats, bouncing impishly against the angles of the furniture and lighting up the painted faces in the stained glass panel of the door.

'Idiotic man,' she spat out at the gaudy display of glass; a crude rendition of a Bacchanalian feast that Alfonso had had commissioned. 'Ridiculous thing for an office door, really.'

She rested her head against the side of the chair and waited for the last sliver of burnt tobacco to fall from her cigarette before lighting another. There was a knock at the door. Sarah again.

'There's someone here to see you, it's Mr Burke from the grocer.'

'What, again? Wasn't he here yesterday?'

'I know ma'am, but he's getting awful persistent that you pay him.'

'Tell him to go away. I don't have time for visitors at the moment.'

But Sarah peered around the room instead, squinting in the semi-light.

'I know what you're doing and the money simply isn't in here. Please just leave.'

Sarah crossed her wiry arms and stayed exactly where she was.

'Ma'am I hate to say this but sooner or later you're gonna have the law on you. You've got to pay your bills and Mr Burke, well he's been coming day after day. We're getting a bad name for ourselves.'

Lucinda forced her fingers through her hair, tugging at it aggressively until her scalp hurt. 'Am I never to be left alone? Am I to be bombarded, constantly? All I have asked for is peace. Am I to be denied that again and again?'

She pressed her fingers to her temples; a dull tribal thud had started to resonate deep within her skull. 'Take the money from the box. It's over there on the second shelf, behind the vase. Found it? Good. Now, please, for mercy's sake, make sure I'm not bothered again today.'

'Thank you Mrs Eden. Oh, and here's what came through the door for you this morning.'

An envelope fell into her lap, and she cast her eyes quickly across the note inside.

Dear Mrs Eden,

We so enjoyed having you to dinner the other night. I do hope your head is better. I owe you an apology I'm afraid with regard to our planned trip to the theatre next week to see Hamlet. Unfortunately a charitable event which I foolishly overlooked has clashed with the outing and I am much relied upon to man the tombola. Although I adore the theatre I'm sure you will understand where my duty lies. Perhaps instead we should have tea together one day?

Yours sincerely
Mrs Whitestone

The headache turned into one of the worst yet: a grotesque kaleidoscope of garish colour and cruel confrontations. She curled herself up as tightly as she could in the armchair, but nothing could stop that miserable hollow thud, endlessly approaching, louder and louder all the time until she longed for it to just take hold of her and complete whatever it had set out to do.

Snatches of her childhood came back to her. Things she hadn't thought about for years. Her father proudly leading her along on a new pony. Her mother, cold and far away. And then that time when she'd walloped nanny clean across the face with her old doll Amelia. How she'd cried after that; having to watch Amelia dying on a bonfire, her face disintegrating into ash.

And yet between those flames dolphins suddenly appeared,

blue and silvery, swimming up into the sky towards something garish, canary yellow. Betsey with her insipid smile. And then the whole world was laughing at her: people in restaurants, passers-by on the street, Hamlet in the midst of a soliloquy pausing to hunt her down in the audience, his face wrinkling up in hilarity. *Thud thud thud.*

When she woke up it was pitch black in the room. The headache had gone, but in its wake had left her with a strange hollow feeling, as if a part of her brain had been removed. It was eleven o'clock. Downstairs the house was empty, but Sarah had left her a meal. She took it to the library.

Funny that they'd called it the library, because it didn't have much in the way of books. There were an awful lot of shelves, filled mainly with old theatre programmes from The Empress. She stroked her hand along the grand piano, the best bit of the room. It felt so sleek and glossy, like patting the flank of a prized racehorse.

The air was stuffy. She raised the window to let in the night, but with it came the pungent smell of a cigar. She leaned out and there was Tristan Whitestone, smoking idly in the street. He was lounging against the railings; such an elegant figure, so perfectly proportioned.

She glanced at herself in a mirror on the opposite wall and pinched her cheeks. The evening shadows had smoothed out her skin a little and her hair still looked good at least, unadorned and hanging loosely down her back.

Heart galloping, she tip-toed to the front door and, with just enough of a click to make sure that the still night air was only a little disturbed, she unfastened the latch. The door yawned open an inch or two so that a thin sliver of light poured out onto the street from inside.

Back in the library she drank whiskey and waited. The smell of the cigar slowly faded away but nothing happened. Not a sound, not one ripple of movement in the air. The minutes passed and soon her pounding heart smothered itself in disappointment. The bottom of her glass peered mockingly up at her.

'You have a funny way of inviting people into your home, Mrs Eden.'

Her eyes darted up and there he was, leaning against the doorframe.

'I didn't. But now that you're here you might as well help yourself to a drink.'

Tristan Whitestone undid the top button of his shirt and found the whisky.

'Nice piano.'

'Thank you. It was given to me by a rich American.'

'Why?'

'Because he liked my husband's theatre and our old piano caved in when an opera singer sat on it.'

'I owe you an apology,' he said.

'How strange, your wife said exactly the same thing in her note.'

He looked confused.

'Cancelling Hamlet?'

'Now that doesn't surprise me.'

She could see the annoyance shifting across his features.

'So, what do you feel the urge to apologize for?' she asked.

'For the tedious company of my wife and her friends last night.'

'That's quite unnecessary, I enjoyed myself heartily.'

'For all the wrong reasons.'

Her eyes lingered on his lips as he pressed the glass to them. He was more dishevelled than when she saw him last and clearly a little intoxicated by that pungent cigar he'd been smoking outside. His eyes were heavy, black rather than blue in this light, and hungry.

'I find it very strange that you should be married to that woman. Is there a good explanation?'

'Our fathers came to an agreement. It got me out of a... a situation during my time in India.'

'And what did she stand to gain?'

'A husband.'

'How romantic.'

'And what about you? Why did your husband run off with a younger woman?'

She felt her face twitch. 'Because his brain has rotted away.'

She'd been right about him; there was cruelty there, like playing with a dangerous toy.

They both said nothing and the minutes rolled by until she thought she might scream. And yet he seemed perfectly relaxed, languid even, sitting back with his glass balanced against his chest.

Finally he drew towards her.

'I didn't come here just to sit in silence,' he said.

'Is that so? May I ask the genuine intention of your visit then?'

He clasped her hand between his, pressing his lips gently to her arm. She held her breath and then raised her other hand to his face, following his cheekbones with the tips of her fingers. He pulled her closer towards him, but she drew back.

'Not yet.'

He let his face fall against her breast. 'When?'

'When the time is right.'

'You smell of ripe peaches.'

'Go home to your wife.'

'Must I?'

'Yes.'

He raised himself up but pulled her against him, greedily kissing her on the mouth.

'Don't leave it too long,' he murmured.

'I doubt whether you'll allow me.'

'Send for me, at work.'

'And where might that be?'

'The Whitestone Shipping Company, Bolter's Way. How am I supposed to forget about you tonight?'

'Don't. Think about me all the time.'

When the front door had closed again with a soft thud she drew her hands up to her hot cheeks. From somewhere in the room there came a gentle tapping sound. It was a moth, fluttering around the lamp on the table. It beat itself ungracefully against the glass, its dusty wings crinkled and distorted.

'Stop that now.'

She cupped it in her hands, moved swiftly towards the open window but then stopped herself.

'No. You'll only do it again silly thing.'

And instead she pushed her palms tightly together, crushing the moth between them.

After a deep luxurious sleep she awoke to bright sunshine streaming through her bedroom curtains. She pulled down the top sash of one of the windows to let yet more sunshine in, perching herself on the only chair in the sparsely furnished room to brush her hair.

This room had none of the comforts of the one she'd shared with Alfonso downstairs, but the idea of sleeping there again still made her feel sick. She'd even toyed with the idea of using the room at the very top of the house, with the small balcony looking out over the park, although it was really just a servant's room.

She put on a white dress, wrapped her hair in an amber scarf and treated herself to a long satisfied gaze in the mirror. She felt so light today, almost skipping down the stairs like a young girl, sliding her fingers down the cool banister as thoughts of hot tea with toast and honey swam through her mind.

Sarah was standing in the hallway below. The girl looked distraught, wringing her hands and padding from one foot to the other.

'What on earth's the matter girl?'

'You've got visitors ma'am.'

'Oh damn it. I thought you'd paid Mr Burke. He can't possibly be wanting yet more money.'

'No, much worse than that. It's your husband with his... lady friend, in the drawing room. I couldn't stop them coming in, he's still got his key.'

Lucinda felt her fingers form into a tight grip around the banister.

'Thank you. Perhaps you should go out, do a little shopping.'

'Yes ma'am.'

The two of them were perched unnaturally close together on a large chair.

'Get out of my house, immediately!'

'Lucinda Lucinda, just calm down my cherub.'

He rose up, gesturing with outstretched hands in that way he always did, as if trying to coax her into submission.

'*My cherub*? Is it really appropriate to jest at this present moment? Get out and take that slut with you. I never want to see either of your faces again. Do you hear me?'

Betsey shot past her, sprinting out into the hallway, Alfonso in her wake, but she clutched at their heels like a tidal wave. Betsey was wearing a lime green ensemble. She gave the outfit a deprecating glare and the girl let out a small scream.

'Betsey my dear, I think you had better go and sit in the carriage.'

'Sit in it? She'd be better suited to pulling the blasted thing,' Lucinda exclaimed.

Betsey burst into tears and the door slammed shut behind her. Alfonso gulped, letting the silence settle. There were dark shadows under his eyes. He looked weary.

'Can we... talk, like adults?' he asked.

He touched the side of her arm with his hand, but she flinched back and his face screwed itself up into a wince. He looked so pathetic that she almost felt sorry for him. There was a stain on his waistcoat, a brownish mark like tea just next to the top button. Something must surely be wrong with her proud, vain husband.

'Darling, what can I do to make things better?'

She pretended to think for a moment. 'You could die. That would be a start.'

'Come now, you don't really mean that do you?'

'My dear dear man, if I were to read of your death in a newspaper tomorrow, I would dance barefoot down this road and throw a riotous party to celebrate.'

A cloud swept across his face, acknowledging his forty-six years.

'She's not doing you any good, is she?'

He didn't answer.

'Is it not quite what you imagined it to be? Is that young, flighty little thing too much for you, or perhaps not enough? Have you found that she is, in fact, a little bored by her rich gentleman, or has she realized that you're not quite as rich as she thought?'

He peered at his feet. But when she walked away to the drawing room he followed her submissively.

'Does she know that the business barely pays for itself and that your wife has always propped you up with her fading bits of inheritance?'

'Please stop.'

'Oh, I apologize! I must have touched a nerve. Why did you come here?'

'Merely to pick up a few odds and ends and, to see you.'

'And did you have to bring the whore?'

'Betsey is not a whore. I had hoped that by putting the two of you in the same room, well, it might just make things a little easier.'

'Easier for whom? For your guilty conscience? *Goodness, how marvellous, Lucinda and the little dancer girl are such good friends! They had afternoon tea together today and...*'

'Stop it, please! Easier, if you must know, to see the true error of my ways.'

Alfonso pulled a handkerchief from out of his pocket and mopped his brow.

'I miss this house. I'm so... tired.'

He dragged his feet over to the window.

'There's a young woman waiting out there in that carriage for me and quite frankly, however hard I try, I cannot even picture her face. All I see is you, Lucinda. I forced the two of you together and she lasted no more than a few seconds. You're a magnificent woman and I have been an awful fool.'

'Running out of money?'

'Don't, please don't...'

He raised his hand as if to ward off the attack and she paused. How wretched and alone he looked over there by the window, with his stained old waistcoat and the beginnings of a stoop. She joined him and he drew her even closer by the hand, stroking it repeatedly as if she were a pampered cat.

It made her smile and his face immediately turned into a soft sponge of relief; a spark of his old self already glinting in his eyes. And suddenly they were back at the theatre again, ten years younger, she waiting for him backstage whilst the crowd roared on. Ready to dance all night long at the after-show party.

But then two blue eyes suddenly blinked back at her, as if from nowhere, sending a deep, dangerous thrill up her spine. *You smell of ripe peaches.* The words washed over her again like treacle.

She freed her hand from Alfonso's clasp.

'I have a lover.'

He started, his eyes round and huge. 'Who?'

'The man next door, Tristan Whitestone.'

'I... I could tell his wife this moment,' he spluttered. He clutched at his shirt collar.

'Do whatever you like, it doesn't bother me.'

'He will never leave his wife for you, they are decent people.'

'And we aren't?'

'We come from a different world!'

'No, you come from a different world which I have nothing to do with anymore. You've had your pleasure and now you want Lucinda back. Well you can go to hell. You're a self-proclaimed fool. I have a beautiful man in my bed now and I wouldn't take you back for all the money in the world. Now get out of my house, take your slut with you and never, under any circumstance, visit me again.'

When the sound of the departing carriage had finally melted away, she ripped the amber scarf from her hair, tearing it to shreds as she flew back up to her room. The tears poured out relentlessly; her pillow and even her dress were soon drenched.

And yet all the time, as the tears kept flooding out of her, she could hear something in her distant mind, a child's voice imploring her to stop.

'I'll try,' she told it eventually, biting at the pillow. 'Who are you?'

But the voice disappeared and she was left alone again.

When at last she knew that she couldn't cry any longer she changed her dress, smoothed her hair and checked her face.

'Sarah, are you back? I'm going out now!' she called.

She raced downstairs and scribbled the word *NOW* across a piece of paper, addressing it to *Mr Tristan Whitestone, The Whitestone Shipping Company, Bolter's Way.*

Sarah came bustling in with her things.

'Quickly please. I have an extremely urgent letter to deliver,' she told the maid, glancing at herself in the mirror just one more time. Her eyes were resolute, her chin a little raised. 'And I'll buy a new hat whilst I'm at it.'

SERENA'S STORY

'You're invited to dine with the family tonight.'

Gladys was pounding a spoon into a beige substance in a metal bowl. I raised my chin a little to try and see what it was, but she suddenly spun round to attend to something in a pan at the same time.

I allowed my jaw to drop behind her turned back. The kitchen appeared to be heaving under the weight of its production: pans frothed and sizzled on the rings of two separate ovens, the work surfaces overflowed with vegetable laden chopping boards and clusters of ingredients, nestled by yet more bowls, ramekins and saucepans, patiently awaited their turn. It felt more like the kitchen of a smart restaurant than a family home.

'Is it going to be a large dinner party?'

'No.' She turned the metal bowl out onto a baking tray and a large mushroom of dough appeared. 'Just the family.'

I retreated to my room to get changed, although my sketchbook found me first. I began trying to recreate the view from my window, just as I'd intended, but for some reason my pencil wasn't behaving itself and I tore the page off, scrunching it up into a tight ball before hurling it into the bin.

I began to scribble again on the next page, thinking about what to put on. Did the Hartreves dress for dinner? The scribble started to take shape, my hand now moving effortlessly across the page. Within a few short minutes I had the beginnings of a face.

Portraits had never really been my forte, particularly from imagination. But this face, with its high-cheeked slender lines just fell off the tip of my pencil. I watched with stunned fascination as Seb unfolded in front of me. I'd caught his image perfectly: the soft sweep of his lips and those beckoning eyes. It was only a small thing but probably the best and most accurate drawing I'd ever done. I actually found myself grinning proudly at it.

Finally I put the drawing to one side and threw on a dress. It was a blue one with small pink flowers on it that I'd had for years and was nothing particularly special, but it fitted well and showed off my legs; the only part of my boyish figure I was prepared to forgive. I peered at myself in the mirror.

'Good evening everyone,' I said in clipped English, the corners of my eyes wrinkling up at my reflection. 'I've been at my club all day and I'm afraid I've had one too many Margaritas...'

'Who are you talking to?'

I jumped round to find Beth lying on my bed. She was all limbs, like a small white kitten.

'Beth! How did you get here? You really should knock before coming into people's rooms.'

'Really? Oh. But I was sent up to get you because dinner's ready. This is a really good drawing.'

I snatched the sketchbook from her feeling my face turning scarlet.

'And you shouldn't go through people's things!'

Her chin dropped down so that I could only see the top of her head. 'Sorry,' she muttered.

'Oh don't worry,' I said, ruffling her soft hair. 'I'm sorry I snapped.'

She beamed up at me. 'What's a Margarita?'

Edward Hartreve was already in the dining room when we entered, reading a newspaper at the head of the table. His hair looked freshly combed, and he was wearing a crisp white shirt that was open at the neck; just as trim and dapper as when he'd opened the door to me in his tennis whites on the morning of my interview.

'Good evening,' he said, eyeing me over his newspaper for a little longer than felt comfortable. His eyebrows were arched high. 'We meet again.'

'Yes... it's very nice to be back.'

He seemed about to answer but the clatter of approaching footsteps made him hesitate and suddenly Eva, Seb and Robert were in the room. I instantly felt the urge to melt into the wall; just like being the new girl at school.

Seb's blue eyes captured me instantly in their frame, intense yet full of humour. I looked away, but he pulled out the chair directly opposite mine. Eva sat down at the other end of the table without offering me a single glance.

I tried again to avoid Seb's gaze and in response he leaned towards me, even closer, his elbows comfortably resting on the white tablecloth and his chin in his hands.

'Hello, glad you've joined us tonight,' he said. 'How was your first day? I've noticed that Beth hasn't eaten you yet – a good sign.'

'Took a week for her to digest the last nanny,' murmured Edward from the end of the table. His eyebrows were still unnervingly high.

'Well she did say she wasn't hungry today,' I replied. 'Although we're both looking forward to dinner, perhaps with some pickled ex-nanny on the side.'

Beth took no notice. She was busy folding her napkin into a complex series of folds, tongue poked out in concentration. But Seb's face filled with laughter and I began to giggle infectiously. And then I met his eyes head on, their blueness lapping me up in a millisecond. My mind turned somersaults in the sky.

Who are you? I thought to myself. *Why do you look at me like that? Just trying to get to know you better.*

The door flew open with the crash of a trolley and I physically jumped, upsetting the cutlery at my place-setting. Beth leaned over to set it straight, and suddenly the room was full of Gladys and her trolley, napkins on laps and, 'Don't touch the plate, it's hot.'

Had Seb actually answered me out loud just then? I tried to recall the act of him opening his mouth and forming those words, but got nothing.

'I thought you'd like them,' said Gladys, as a plate of noodles suddenly materialized in front of me. 'Considering your recent Asian tour.'

'Which gave her a dodgy tummy, didn't you know?' came Eva's voice. She was picking away at a small plate of canapés.

The colour drained out of Gladys's face. 'Oh I'm so sorry.'

'No please don't be! I'm fine now. I love Thai food.'

I peered back again at the dainty plate of canapés.

'She had to come home in the end Grandpa, because of her stomach. Didn't you?' added Beth.

'Yes, but I really am fine now.'

A plate of fish and chips landed in front of Beth as Edward regarded me, hawk-eyed, from the head of the table.

'Some kind of worm in the gut perhaps? Happens abroad,' he said.

I turned to Seb, hoping that he might change the subject of my intestine, but he seemed to be too absorbed by the arrival of his soup.

'Delicious, thank you so much.'

'It's a pleasure my boy, there's freshly baked bread as well,' Gladys murmured back.

'Robert now Gladys, give my son his food!' Edward bellowed, finally discarding his newspaper. 'Feed the children first, that's what I always say.'

Robert didn't look very much like a child, but he did seem like someone who needed feeding up.

'Now you didn't add salt did you?' he stammered, poking at a bowl of what looked like brown mushy peas.

'No, I've done your lentils just the way you like them.'

A different meal for everyone. So, that explained all those pots and pans I'd seen bubbling in the kitchen earlier.

'And now for me!' Edward grasped his knife and fork in anticipation as Gladys wheeled the trolley round.

'Roast beef with all the trimmings just the way you like it,' she said.

'Exactly what I was hoping for. Delicious!'

The door flew open again, and Arabella floated into the room. She was wearing an electric blue kimono style dress that made her look remarkably like an exotic bird.

'Darlings! And we have Serena with us tonight I see.'

She enveloped me in a long, searching gaze and then smiled briefly. But by the time I managed to smile back she'd flourished around the table, enveloping us all with the heady scent of patchouli whilst brandishing something in her hand.

'You must all listen to this, it's hysterically funny!'

It was an old cassette tape and she slid it into an ancient looking tape recorder on the sideboard. There was something so fluid about the way she moved. One action simply seemed to retune itself into the next, and before I knew it she'd clicked a button and was meandering back towards the door.

'I'll have my chicken salad upstairs Gladys. Africa work to be done!'

The tape made a loud belching sound and then exploded into brass band music.

'Enjoy!'

And she disappeared with a chiffony flourish and a final whiff of patchouli.

We raised our knives and forks to the reverberations of the

brass band music. But before I'd swallowed my first mouthful of noodles, the music came to an abrupt halt and two men started to talk to each other - in German. Immediately the faces of everyone around me, including Beth, began to crease up with hilarity. Edward exploded into raucous laughter every time one of the men made a joke, Seb and Eva exchanged mirthful glances and even Robert spluttered out some of his lentils mid-snigger, which made everyone laugh even louder.

I swallowed hard. Why had I given German up at school in favour of dance and drama? Peering round at the sniggering faces I felt a stab of loneliness. I hadn't been that bad at the drama though... I'd actually pulled off a pretty mean Lady Macbeth at the end of year show.

The German men were singing a comic song now, and Edward was actually guffawing into his roast dinner. Seb was gripping his sides. There was nothing else for it but to put my fork down, throw my head back and laugh hysterically. It wasn't hard at all and as soon as I started it seemed to spur the others on even more. I scooped the noodles up into my mouth between outbursts and before I knew it the play was thankfully over. All I had to do was pray every night that none of them would ever attempt to address me in German.

'How are the plans for the party going?' Edward asked Eva afterwards, wiping his tears of laughter away with the corner of a napkin.

'Well, I think. Are you coming?'

'Me? Oh no,' replied Edward. 'Your mother might put her head round the door, but I'll leave you lot to it. When's he arriving?'

'Not sure. He's been rather busy out there.'

Edward looked down at his empty plate, a momentary cloud crossing his face, and then he glanced up at Beth with a large smile.

'Now I'm pretty sure I know someone who can't wait for her Uncle Raphael to come home.'

By the time dinner was over it was almost dark outside. It was Beth's bedtime and our shadows accompanied us up the stairs as we went; mine long and dark and Beth's a little lighter and more scattered with her flitting about. Up in her room I tried to find some bedtime reading, but the bookshelf was mostly crammed with a lot of grim looking spines embellished with gothic writing.

'You do have quite a collection of ghost stories here,' I said.

I managed to tug out an abridged edition of *Peter Pan* from between them, and she listened to the opening pages with unblinking concentration.

'Who's your favourite in the book?' she asked after I'd finished reading.

'Um, I don't know. Tinker Bell probably. Now get into bed, do you like your lamp on or off?'

'Off. My favourite's Peter.'

'He is fun, isn't he? It's a shame we can't all be young like him forever.'

'Some people can. I know that for a fact.'

'Yes, of course you do! Now, sweet dreams.'

I kissed her cool forehead, and she seemed content to be left.

It really was dark now. I couldn't find a light switch so had to feel my way up the narrow stairs to my room. My shoulders started to relax; it was so quiet and peaceful up here. I closed the curtains but opened the balcony door behind them just a little to let in the cool evening air. It carried the scent of flowers with it, jasmine maybe.

Now, Jessica. I didn't really feel like ringing her yet. She'd probably start to worry if I attempted to describe all the German comedy and guffawing to her, so I sent her a text instead:

Am fine. House still lovely. Hartreves unusual but nice. Will ring in a few days when settled. Love Serena

I tossed the phone onto my bed; it was time to unpack properly, but then a sudden sound from the balcony stopped me in my tracks. What was it? A shoe scuffing against the floor? The closed curtains rippled gently with the breeze. No. Nothing more than a deranged cat would have braved a jump like that.

The noise came again and I could feel the whirr of blood start to rise up in my ears. I tiptoed over to the windows and, with one sharp tug, pulled the curtains back to scare whatever it was away. Instead I came face to face with Seb.

'Fancy a smoke?' he said, offering me a crumpled pack of cigarettes whilst lighting one for himself.

'Oh my God! How the hell did you get up here?'

'Ah, now that would be telling.'

I pushed past him and peered over the balcony at the spine-crunching drop to the garden. Even the flat roof of next door's extension seemed dangerously out of reach, although not impossible.

'How did you do it?'

'Come on, relax. I practically grew up in this house,' he said and then he rolled his eyes mysteriously. 'I know its ways.'

He sat down on the balcony step, exhaled an impressive array of smoke rings into the night sky and then beamed at me in a way that made me want to giggle like a schoolgirl. I perched next to him and we smoked in silence, my first cigarette in ages. I was supposed to have given up the habit.

It seemed surreal sitting up there high above the rooftops with him, as if we'd been picked up and placed into an alcove in the night sky. Seb's body was tantalisingly close and a pleasant shiver ran through me.

'Who are you, really?' I asked.

'Well that's a very good question. Some say that an itinerant group of cockle gatherers found me on a beach one day...'

'No, seriously, although I see that seriousness might not count as one of your major pastimes.' He flashed me a delicious smile. 'You're not one of the family, I know. I thought you were Eva's boyfriend, but you don't seem to be that either... are you? I mean I... I just don't really understand where you fit in.'

The muscles around his jawbone tensed up and shifted about.

'I went to school with Eva's brother Raphael,' he said slowly. 'I got to know the family, and they sort of accepted me as one of their own.'

'Where do you live?'

'Just... somewhere.'

'Right.'

His face softened apologetically. 'Sorry, you just don't want to see where I live. It's not very nice, that's all. I only use it for sleeping and a lot of the time I stay over here anyway.'

'I've lived in a few places like that. Pretty lonely eh?'

'Yes, pretty lonely.' He tossed the stub of his cigarette over the balcony and turned to face me, a smirk tugging at the corner of his mouth. 'How did you enjoy your meal with the family?'

'Um... very pleasant: charming, interesting... eclectic... German.' He frothed up with laughter. 'Can you all really speak German?'

'Yes of course. And French. Doesn't everyone?' he asked, laughing even more.

'OK then.'

My legs had gone slightly numb and I shifted sideways, pressing my spine flat against the door frame. He gazed back at me, his eyes suddenly more sober and almost purple in the half-light.

'You look very beautiful like that,' he said.

'Like what?'

'Sitting stretched up like that in the shadows. You look mythical, like an elf or something.'

'My father used to call me his little elf. It's because I was all scrawny like a boy, with wispy hair and pointy features.'

'But did he tell you that you were beautiful as well?'

'Oh God no!'

'I thought so.'

'Why?'

'Because you have absolutely no idea how to take a compliment.'

His fingers knitted themselves together with mine; they felt so long and elegant.

Let me stay with you tonight.

It was just like before, over dinner. I heard his voice, and yet he hadn't said a thing.

Not yet.

He seemed to nod his head as if he'd actually heard my reply, but his hand remained firmly in mine.

'Can I ask you something?'

'Go on,' he replied.

'What is the situation between you and Eva?'

Maybe I was imagining it but his cool fingers seemed to tense up a little in my hand.

'There is no situation, why ask?'

'It's nothing really. I shouldn't have asked. Sorry. It's just that this morning, when Beth brought me into the drawing room... I think that Eva was watching you sleep.'

'Oh don't worry about her. She's a great thinker, that's all, she feels things very deeply. They would have called her poetic a

58

hundred years ago, or something like that I suppose.'

'It was a bit of an icy reception that she gave me.'

Seb made as if to speak but then hesitated; he seemed to be choosing his words carefully.

'She does things her own way, she's unconventional,' he shrugged.

'I can see that. To be honest I was a bit surprised when I found out that Beth's mother was so young. Who is Beth's father?'

My throat went dry as soon as I said it, as if bereft of the words that should have stayed firmly tucked inside. Seb took his hand from mine to light another cigarette.

'No one knows, she's always refused to let on,' he answered in a deep, hushed voice. 'But everyone seems to have a theory about it. What do you think?'

It sounded like a test. And was that the hint of something bitter in his voice? Whatever it was it didn't suit him.

'I don't have a clue. I knew nothing about the Hartreves until this job came up.'

'What, you haven't even read about them, they're in the press sometimes?'

I shook my head.

He looked thoughtful. 'Well, I supposed it's been awhile and it's only really Eva doing the whole society bit now.'

'In that case I better start buying the right magazines!'

His shoulders softened a bit and the corners of his mouth turned up.

'So tell me about your family; where do your parents live?' he asked.

'Hmm, do you really want to know?'

'Yeah, why not?'

'Let's talk about it some other time.'

'No,' he said, as if suddenly spurred on by my reluctance. 'I want to know.'

'OK. My parents both died when I was young.'

'How?'

'They were in an accident... their bus veered into a shop window. I was brought up by my aunt instead.'

He didn't respond and the moment died. This time I reached for his hand. 'Look, let's just change the subject. We're bound to fall on a good one if we try hard enough.'

Seb squeezed my hand back gratefully and then a spark of light came back into his eyes.

'Do you want to come to the party this weekend? Raphael's coming home for a bit after a stint abroad and we thought we'd celebrate.'

'I wouldn't want to intrude. Where is it?'

'Here in the house. And no you wouldn't be intruding, you'd be my guest.'

'Alright then.'

'Hey, I better leave you to it.' He pulled me up from the step with both hands and we faced each other. 'Thank you for letting me into your room tonight.'

'I didn't have much choice!'

He linked his arms around my body and gathered me close to him. In a second my cheek was pressed against his chest and my eyes tightly shut.

The last person who'd held me like that had been my father. I'd forgotten all about it until that point, but the memory suddenly came back so powerfully that I could even smell the musty scent of his jumper as it had scratched slightly at my face.

I'd been playing in the garden and had fallen badly with a loud scream. Dad had come running out of the house, his face etched with concern and before I knew it I was in his arms, the safest place on earth.

I felt Seb's face smile above me.

'What is it?' I murmured.

'We're breathing at the same time, like soldiers falling into step.'

He released me and a deep sigh unleashed itself from my chest. I felt the brush of his lips against my mouth and before I even realized it, he'd gone.

For a moment I could barely tell where I was. Around me everything seemed askew, as if I'd walked into a macabre crooked house in a fairground somewhere.

The curtains against my balcony door had been closed. I walked over to the window and peered between them, half expecting, hoping, to see Seb standing there again. But only the dark silhouettes of chimney pots and branches remained.

Before I fell into bed I snatched up a pencil and within minutes a near perfect likeness of Seb's face was laughing up at me from my sketchbook. His eyes bubbled with good humour, just like they had done over dinner. Next time I would try to catch their sober side, the serious part of him. Because it was there, whether he liked it or not.

I spent the night lost in a heavy dreamless sleep and, when my alarm clock proceeded to yell at me the next morning, the journey to switching it off was no worse than clawing my way out of a deep blackened pit. I rolled out of bed and threw on some clothes. Beth wasn't in her room, so I carried on downstairs.

'Hello,' she said from behind a large bowl of cornflakes. She was sitting at the kitchen table, legs tucked up under her on her chair. Gladys was making tea.

'Hello. How are you this morning?' I replied.

'Fine. Shall we go to the museum today?'

'OK.'

I obeyed Gladys's nod to sit down.

'I'll put some toast on,' she said.

'Thank you, that's very kind, but look I'll make it.'

'No that's alright.'

Her lips were pursed as if to say, 'This is my kitchen. Leave it well alone please.'

Beth helped herself to more cornflakes, tongue poking out in concentration at the side. She was wearing a pale yellow gingham dress with a matching ribbon in her hair.

'Raphael's coming home soon.'

'Yes I know.'

She munched on and eyed me over her spoon. 'He's an artist like you know. Raphael sees magic in everything. He loves beauty, that's why he's an artist. He says he could never work in an office like Grandpa.'

'Here's your toast, would you like tea with that?' Gladys asked.

'Yes please, thank you so much.'

I half got up from my chair to help, but a sharp look from Gladys forced me right back down again.

'Would you like milk or lemon with your tea?'

'Milk please. But I can...'

'Brown sugar, white sugar or sweetener?'

'Nothing, thanks. Um, would it be alright if I ate in the kitchen with you tonight? I don't really want to get in the way of the family too much.'

She nodded her head as if the question came as no surprise to her.

'I've got a nice bit of salmon for Mr Hartreve tonight; should be enough for us too.'

Before leaving for the museum I raced upstairs to grab my bag from my room. It was a workout in itself running to the top of the house, and I was panting breathlessly by the time I pushed my door open. Eva was standing in there, holding my sketchbook in her bony hands. I spluttered in surprise.

'Are you... alright?' she asked, scanning me up and down.

'Yes,' I panted. 'You just shocked me a bit.'

'I'm sorry. I imagine I should have knocked, although you weren't here anyway.'

She held the sketchbook towards me, and then all at once her face seemed to melt into an expression I wouldn't have thought possible. For the first time I saw real gentle beauty in her features.

'Beth told me about your drawing. These pictures of Seb are very skillful. Extraordinary. You have a good eye. I never thought...' she trailed off and her eyes flitted across me again, differently this time, like a frightened little deer.

I took the sketchbook from her. 'Thank you, that's very kind. Would you like me to draw something for you? I love it when people enjoy my work, it's the main reason I do it I think.'

As soon as the sketchbook had left her hands she seemed to stiffen, hold back again. The angular bones of her face regrouped.

'No that's fine. I have to go now,' she swept past me but paused to take a final glance around her. 'Funny little room, this. Isn't it?'

Beth seemed to be in her element at the Victoria and Albert Museum, springing from one exhibit to the next like a small excited lamb. She led me around the four-poster beds and grand castle furniture first, saving her cherished costume exhibits for the grand finale.

'Isn't it beautiful?' she whispered, gazing with loving eyes at a Victorian wedding gown.

'Would you like to wear something like that one day?'

'Oh yes!'

We ate sandwiches in the museum's sunny courtyard, peeling our shoes off afterwards to have a quick paddle in the ornamental pond. It was a gorgeous day, and this was a perfect oasis from the city beyond. We skidded about in the water, pink and giggling with the sunshine. But then quite suddenly, just as she was scooping a cup of the water up into her hands, Beth staggered, as if she were about to pass out. I caught her elbow, her face was white as a sheet.

'Are you alright?'

'Hmmm, I think I'm getting one of my headaches.'

'Headaches? I didn't know you got those.'

Her cheeks felt cool and clammy.

'Come on let's take you home.'

Beth didn't utter a word for most of the journey back. Her hand felt small and limp, and she rested against me in the bus like a wilting flower, so vulnerable that I clung on to protect her from being crushed. But by the time we got to Marguerite Avenue, her hand began to respond to my grasp again. It felt warmer, more full of blood too. When we were just a few houses away, she released herself altogether and galloped past the last few houses to her own.

'Number 30!' she squealed back at me.

'Well done, you are good at reading your door numbers.'

'32!'

'Even better! How did you get to be so clever?'

'34!'

The ribbon in her hair had untied itself so that the two ends streamed behind her like tails on a kite.

'No Beth! There isn't a 34, it's missing. You're nearly right, but your house is actually...'

'36! Yes I know that!'

She was still running, the ribbons skirmishing behind her in the breeze. She must have made a mistake although my feet began to move faster nonetheless. Number 30, yes. Then 32. And after that... only one house left, 36.

Beth swung herself to a stop on the last corner railing of the terrace, the ribbons finally deflating. The extreme paleness had gone from her face and there was now the faintest blush of rosiness again across each small cheek.

'We're home now,' she gasped. 'Let's go in, I'm thirsty!'

1892

The brougham clattered to a halt outside the railings and a tatty-looking boy hopped down. Jane's cases were already waiting at the bottom of the stairs.

'Jane, your carriage is here!'

'I'm coming.'

Miranda crossed her arms and then uncrossed them again. Her foot tapped with a life of its own against the floor tiles.

'I think I've got everything,' said Jane, clutching a handkerchief to the side of her face as she descended the stairs shakily. 'Ah it still hurts; my whole face feels as if it's been trampled on.'

She did look a little wan and her hair had been tied back rather shoddily, but her eyes glimmered brightly enough.

'Well then perhaps you shouldn't travel. Not yet anyway,' said Miranda.

'No no, I've overstayed my welcome with this illness as it is. You must be keen to get rid of me.'

'Don't be silly. I'll call the boy in to get your bags.'

'Yes do, but before I leave I'd rather like to have a word with you please.'

Jane swept her eyes from one end of the hallway to the other as if in search of spies and then craned her neck towards her.

'Now, as our own mother is dead I feel it my obligation as a woman, and of course as your sister, to talk about what happened at that dinner party last week. As you know I've been far too ill to discuss this with you until now.'

The handkerchief had disappeared, and suddenly Jane was looking awfully healthy.

'Yes,' Miranda replied. 'It's quite extraordinary how quickly your cold came on after that night...'

'But you have been at the forefront of my mind, and I have to tell you that I'm extremely concerned.'

'Concerned? About what?'

Jane pulled a pair of grey gloves out of her pocket and carefully drew them over her fingers.

'I think that Mr Whitestone, your husband, enjoyed Mrs

Eden's dining room antics a little too much the other evening.'

'What are you suggesting?'

'I'm not suggesting anything. I'm telling you that Tristan has a roving eye, and I think that as his wife you need to learn how to rein him in a little better. There, I've said it. Now come on! Help me with my things.'

Miranda clenched her fists so tightly that her fingernails dug into the palms of her hands.

'No.'

Her voice felt dry and husky. Jane paused and turned back round.

'I'm sorry dear? Come, surely you're not upset. I've given you my opinion, that's all I have to say on the subject.'

'Yes and that is all you will say on this subject and on any other for that matter.'

'Are you alright my dear?'

'Not really. I'm afraid I don't take too kindly to being insulted in my own home.'

Her sister's eyes bulged so forcefully back at her that they seemed in danger of breaking free from her face, and Miranda fought back a sudden irresistible urge to laugh.

'Are you... sniggering at me?' Jane stammered.

'I have to ask, do you really have a cold or was it something you just made up so that you could stay and witness the aftermath of that hideous dinner party?'

'Have you gone mad?'

'I don't really blame you because, after all, Mrs Eden behaved like a Soho slut and my husband, as you noticed, seemed to enjoy every minute of it.'

'Miranda!'

'But not much has happened since, has it? I have to applaud your patience; five whole days of waiting for nothing in return. You must have been awfully bored.'

Jane screwed up her face in a way that brought back Miranda's worst childhood memories of being a younger sister.

'You say nothing's happened!' she spat. 'So tell me, why has your husband moved his desk up to that empty servants' room at the top of the house? What does he do up there all day? Why hasn't he been going to work? The two of you have barely exchanged a sentence since that night although I wonder whether that's anything new from what I've seen.'

'So you have been spying on me.'

'Oh my dear sister. I don't have to spy on you to see that your marriage is a disaster.'

'Better than no marriage at all, don't you think?'

Jane's face turned pale and all at once that puffed up lividness seemed to drain out of her. Miranda felt the cold shudder of regret.

'I think you give marriage a little too much credit.' Her voice, no longer indignant, seemed to tremble under the weight of some great burden. 'All that I have seen of marriage is misery and deceit.'

'But mother and father...'

'Oh stop wrapping things up in this great fairy tale in your mind. You have no idea what went on between them, and it seems you have little clue about your own state of affairs.' She hesitated for a moment. 'Do you know about what your husband really got up to in India?'

Miranda arched her back to pull away a little.

'Your Tristan got into so much trouble out there that he had to leave. Yes, you see I listen to the talk.'

'Stop now.'

'You think he married you out of love? Well either you're a fool or he's a jolly good actor.'

'Enough!' Miranda unpeeled herself from her sister's shadow and lunged for the door. 'Why are you doing this? Why? Stop blaming me. Stop... punishing me. Because that's what you're doing, still doing, isn't it? You have no sisterly concern for me, please don't pretend. We both know where all of this is coming from. Now leave, please. Leave me alone.'

She kept her eyes lowered but felt a rustle of air as Jane passed by her.

'You always have to bring it up, don't you?' came her sister's icy voice. 'If you'd only stopped dwelling on the past then you might be better equipped to conduct yourself properly now.'

Miranda closed her eyes and pictured Jane climbing into the carriage; her chin set determinedly, a few tendrils of her grey hair come loose. And then she listened to the carriage wheels start up their clatter along Marguerite Avenue until they merged into the noise of the city beyond.

The clock in the hallway began to chime. Ten strokes; he'd be here soon. She waited for her hands to stop shaking and then took up her sewing, seating herself in the usual place by the window to wait for him. It was overcast outside; spots of rain were starting to make black blotches on the pavement.

Rain's bad luck on a wedding day.

The servants had whispered it outside her bedroom door on that very morning. She'd heard their words as she stood peering at the reflection of herself in all her finery, flowers in her hair.

It had rained all day; not quite torrential but in a grim determined manner like a factory machine at work. June weddings were supposed to be full of sunshine and flowers, not row upon row of grim faces in a damp old church.

She looked up from her sewing and spotted him only a few houses away. Even after two years of watching him come and go, the man's extraordinary physique still made her want to gape open-mouthed.

He approached swiftly as always, with those huge rhythmic strides of his. Six foot five at least, with the physique of a crane fly; the oddest looking man that she and perhaps anyone else had ever seen. Today he wore a scarlet velvet suit and a long cloak of some deep purple cloth, the usual medley of charms and bottles hanging about his neck.

She lowered her eyes, studying his approach from under her lashes, and just at the last second looked up to greet the whisper of his smile and the subtle nod of his head. He strode on and she waited, as she always did, for the sound of his three sharp knocks on the door of number 36. Perhaps this time Mrs Eden would let him in.

The door opened. She heard the muffled sound of his voice, anxious but never pleading and then the sound of the closing latch. Rejected again. One, two, three, and there he was... striding back down Marguerite Avenue once more. No time for a nod or a smile now; his emaciated features set in a frown and then nothing but the back of his head with its long thinning mesh of hair.

'Who are you, strange man?' she whispered against the window pane. 'What brings you back to this place week after week?'

Mrs Hubbard was far from pleased with the recipe.

'It'll turn thick, like plaster,' she said, with a wary shake of the head.

But Miranda felt the flutter of triumph. 'It's just the most perfect cauliflower soup; exactly as I remember it. Father loved this! It was his favourite, and mine.'

They ladled it out, but Tristan was nowhere to be seen.

'Oh dear. And I thought *we* were running late.'

'I can go up myself to knock for him,' suggested the cook.

'No that's alright. He doesn't like being disturbed as it is, so it's probably better if I go.'

Miranda skimmed the tips of her fingers up the coils of banister. Up and up. It was like living in a lighthouse, or climbing up a helter-skelter in a fairground. She hardly ever went beyond her own bedroom now. So many rooms and nothing much to put in them. And then at last the little door right at the top: a bleak maid's door, not even painted.

'Tristan, supper's ready!'

There was no reply. A cold chill brushed against her face.

'Are you alright?'

She tried the handle but the door was locked. And there was that chill again.

'Come down when you're ready.'

She retreated back downstairs to the concerned lines of Mrs Hubbard's face.

'It's setting already ma'am. You won't be able to get a knife through it if it's not eaten in the next five minutes.'

'Mr Whitestone has been delayed I'm afraid. Try the best you can to water it down, I've no doubt he'll be here soon.'

Forty minutes later Tristan loped into the dining room. His shirt collar was rather disheveled, and he had an absent look in his face.

'What's that smell?'

'The jasmine plant outside.'

'Close the window. You know I hate it.'

'It is closed, it's very pungent that's all. How was your day dear?'

He slumped down at the table without an answer and Mrs Hubbard bustled in, the lines on her face now resembling contours on a map.

The soup had gone badly wrong: one part grey dishwater to

two parts gelatinous lumps. It now gave off a putrid smell that made Miranda's stomach lurch.

Tristan lifted his spoon and then tossed it back down again. He hadn't combed his hair and she could smell the liquor on him.

'I've been rather concerned about you this past week,' she said. 'It can't be good for your health being stuck up there in that poky little room all day, especially when you have such a lovely library down here. And are they not missing you at work? Surely you must have meetings to attend? How is the office able to function adequately without you there?'

He shot her a smile as cold as blunt glass. 'Please don't meddle,' he said.

'Oh, no my dear, don't interpret my words wrongly. It's only natural that I should care.'

Tristan prodded curiously at his soup. 'What is this in my bowl?'

'Cauliflower soup. I do hope you like it; it was cook's recipe when I was a little girl.'

He prodded it again and then tasted a morsel with the tip of his tongue.

'I read in *The Times* today that there have been all sorts of troubles at the docks. Perhaps you're the person they need, darling, to go and sort it all out. Oh!'

One sharp strike of his hand and his bowl skimmed across the table, spewing the soup all over the cloth. Little grey hillocks of cauliflower steamed everywhere.

'Perhaps I'm mistaken but I thought I asked you not to meddle in my affairs.'

'I'm sorry, I...'

'On and on and on. I seem to hear nothing but the grating whine of your voice. You have a house, a husband, your ridiculous circle of friends. What more do you want of me? I permit myself one small space in this vast house of ours; one small corner for my own private use. *Surely I can call this space my own*, I told myself. But no. Oh no! You choose to grumble and whine even about that.'

He pressed his thumb down against his nose, pushing it into his face until it went white.

'You have a snout Miranda. Not pretty is it? Now get it out of my affairs!'

A long sliver of saliva clung to his bottom lip and he brushed it away with the back of his hand.

The soiled tablecloth sneered up at her. She tried to rub away at the soup with her napkin, but the oily stains just got larger and larger.

'Stop that,' he muttered.

Her hand collided with a glass and a sticky puddle of wine now merged cloudily with the spilt food.

'Stop!' He slammed his hand down over hers.

She froze, her eyes now fixed on his. A hazy film had set across the blueness, as if he were blind.

'I am going upstairs now and will probably sleep in my office tonight. Under no account will you disturb me or badger me about my business again.' He withdrew his hand from hers and stood up. 'Oh and get that Hubbard woman to clear up this revolting mess. It's nothing short of a pigsty in here.'

The door was almost noiseless now: loud enough for her to hear the promise of its click but without all that dreadful scraping and grating. Lucinda threw a shawl around her shoulders and found Tristan half way over the narrow cast iron railing between their two balconies.

'Hello... be careful. How was your meal?'

'Disgusting.'

And then his lips were caressing her neck.

'I accused her of having a snout.'

'Goodness. What did she feed you?'

They fell into the small room together and she watched him peel off his shirt.

'We could go downstairs into the house, it's empty now.'

'No, I like it here. Come to bed.'

During his short absence she'd ached for the warm hard certainty of his body against hers and now it felt as comforting as moonlight in a dark forest. She turned on her side and glided her finger in circular movements over the skin just beneath his ear.

'I love this part of you the most. I love it so much I want to eat it. Can I eat it darling?'

'No you cannot.'

His eyes were smiling under their lids.

'Spoil sport. Shall we have some wine?'

'Go on then.'

She glugged some wine into the smudged and dirty glass they shared. Tristan balanced two cigarettes on his lower lip and lit them.

'I was going to ask you something, Lucy. This morning I heard someone knocking on your front door. Must have been loud for me to have heard it from all the way up here. You were still asleep; I was a bit worried it might have been your dastardly husband, so I crept downstairs and had a look out of the window...'

He paused to smoke, his eyebrows raised in a bemused arc.

'And was it?'

'Well, either old Alfonso's grown two foot and dressed himself as a court jester or you've got some vagrant witch-doctor knocking on your door.'

'Oh! What day of the week is it?'

'Tuesday, I think.'

'Yes. That'll be Walter Balanchine.'

His eyes narrowed. Oh good, she'd caught his interest, and with a surprising helping of jealousy thrown into the pot.

'And who is he?'

'Just an old lover of mine.'

He lurched towards her, catching her by the hair and she heard herself explode with laughter. But she could feel the blood draining from her face at the same time.

'Say you are joking,' he whispered, his face so close that she could see small pearls of sweat forming on his brow. His body pressed down on her, she could barely breathe.

'I never thought that being grappled by an enraged lion would be so exciting.'

'Say you are joking.'

She dug her elbows into his chest and pushed him sharply away, but the sudden loss of his touch gnawed straight back at her and she pressed herself hard against him, greedy for his skin.

'Do you really think I'd get into bed with a man like that? Of course not. Walter Balanchine is a freakish and abhorrent man who works as a sort of assistant to my father. He arrives at the same time every week to try and bribe me back home.'

'And what do you tell him?'

'Nothing. The servants are under strict instructions never to let him in.'

'And yet he still comes?'

'Religiously.'

He flopped back against the pillows, his eyes glassy, staring straight past her through the window.

She waited for her heart to stop pounding in her ears. Perhaps she should try and make him angry again, just to see if it was always quite so easy. But then her groaning stomach interrupted her thoughts instead.

'I'm starving. Sarah should have left a tray by the door.'

Outside she found a platter of ham, bread and grapes and a bottle of wine. They picked away at it together on the bed.

'Does defying your father's wishes ever upset you?' he asked.

'A little. I adored him when I was young, but he is so controlling. He hated Alfonso, wanted me to marry a man with, well, a little more to his name.'

'Perhaps he was right. You didn't make the wisest of choices did you darling?'

'Not really, but anything seemed better than dying of boredom like my mother in a damp country house.'

She filled her mouth with wine and let its velvety bitterness lap against her teeth and down her throat. 'I could have done the same as you, married some ghastly halfwit and then conduct myself exactly as I pleased.'

'There was no other way; I couldn't have gone back to soldiering, and my father would only let me join the company if I married. Not easy when most families in our circle wouldn't let me within a mile of their daughters.'

'I don't blame them!'

He pinched her cheek and pulled her towards him, her head locked neatly under his chin.

'So how then did you hunt poor old Miranda down?'

'Oh, her father was parish priest to a family acquaintance. So tucked away in rural Shropshire that they knew nothing of me.'

'Good heavens darling, you married a daughter of the cloth!'

'My father-in-law was an avaricious baboon of a man who used God only as means of getting everything he wanted for as little work as possible.'

'And did his daughter regard him in the same light?'

'Miranda? Of course not, she worshipped the old sod; never even suspected that he spent most of his time fornicating with one of the servants.'

'You discovered them together? Was she a silly young thing?'

'Yes I did and no *he* wasn't particularly. It was a little gem of information that served me rather well.'

'In what way?'

'Well, news of my reputation arrived in the village just days before the wedding. He wanted to shy away, save his daughter from my wicked clutches, but I soon put him back on track, stupid old brute.'

His eyes seemed smaller suddenly, pinched with cruelty.

'Did Miranda find out?'

'God no. They kept it all as quiet as possible, although I think the ghoul-faced sister had her suspicions.'

She wriggled out of his arms and took his face between her hands. Every inch of his flesh was so lean; she could feel each sinew tighten beneath her fingers. She could even trace the warm veins of racing blood beneath his skin.

'Darling, will you promise me something?' she asked. 'Let's not talk of our past lives. They're over now, something to be packed away and forgotten about. Do you promise? And you will never be cruel to me, will you? Can you promise me that as well?'

His eyes filled with tears and she felt as if she should turn away, but couldn't. He began to stroke her hair, over and over again.

'I promise,' he said.

'Me too.'

'You're my saviour Lucy,' his breath felt wet and urgent against her face. 'All my folly, everything I've done wrong in my life has served only as a way of getting me to you.'

'Then let's not talk of it anymore. Let's enjoy what is now, the two of us locked together. Like this, see.'

She wrapped herself around him and he clutched her back so tightly that his fingers cast deep grooves into her skin. Her body trembled. His mouth was by her ear, his confiding whispers probing softly in.

'Does this feel like cruelty?' he murmured.

She yelped; the cry of someone she barely knew.

'Don't ever leave me.'

'No.'

She closed her eyes and found that she was falling again; just like in that dream she'd had in the park. But this time she landed against forest earth: rich and black and all-consuming. She thrust herself in, plunging her fingers into its darkness. And then she let herself disperse; let it take hold of her, laugh and cry out with the pleasure of it. How could there ever have been a time before this man? How could she ever not have known him?

Morning arrived with barely a moment passing. Outside the treetops looked grey. In a few hours the mist would clear and the leaves would polish up emerald green. She dragged a filthy sheet over her naked body.

Tristan was still asleep, his long eyelashes curled together in a kiss. If only they could go out, to the park perhaps, and roam about in the dew.

There were a few dregs of wine left in the bottle; they splashed meekly into the glass. Tristan stirred.

'Save some for me.'

'Alright.'

The small clock on the mantelpiece began to chime the hour. He stretched and peered over at it.

'I should really go to work today.'

Those were the words she'd been dreading. She squeezed the glass hard in her hand until it snapped. One swoop of her right arm and the rest of the glass exploded in the clock's face. It was a good aim; the clock landed on the floor in a flurry of tinny sounding chirps followed by silence.

Tristan glared at the red splattered sheets. 'Is any of that your blood?'

'No, just wine.'

'Damn it darling. You've broken our only glass.'

'I'll get another... Why don't we go to Italy together?'

He didn't reply.

Her lungs felt dry and gritty.

'I have to go outside,' she murmured.

Out on the balcony the morning breeze brushed her hair away from her face. In the distance London would slowly be waking up. All that chaos: armies of men weaving their way to work, the shouts of market traders and the clatter of hooves filling the air.

Somewhere in the midst of it was Alfonso, still fast asleep like a big baby no doubt.

Had it only been a week since the first time Tristan had climbed over these railings? The door on his side squeaking so loudly, making them both cringe in the darkness and then into bed within a minute, drowning out each other's laughter with their kisses.

His hand fell softly on her shoulder and drew her back into the room.

'You've fixed the door, it didn't make a sound last night... I was serious you know.'

'About what?'

'About going to Italy.'

His face was empty.

'Don't you want to go away with me darling?'

'I'm happy here.'

'Well so am I, but we can't remain in this room forever. Do you realize that we've been almost constantly drunk in here for an entire week?'

'And you wish to throw this paradise away?'

'Of course not. I just thought that it might be quite nice to be drunk together somewhere else. People will start to suspect if we stay here. Your wife will start to suspect, if she hasn't already. Wouldn't you just love to run away from it all?'

'We'd be outcasts.'

'Well that's nothing new to either of us.'

'And we'd have no money.'

'I have a little and I could sell the house. It would last us for a while.'

He turned away. 'I have to show my face at work.'

'Tristan, please. Just think about it. Imagine us in a beautiful exotic place.'

'Full of exotic admirers to take you away from me.'

She poured herself against his back and he pulled her arms around him. Rays of sunshine had started to flood into the room and beyond them the mist was rising.

'We really could be anywhere up here in the trees, couldn't we?' he said.

'How long will you be at work?'

Her heart was pounding like an angry jealous child.

'Not long I hope. I'll show my face, make a few noises. I don't do much in that place as it is; it bores the hell out of me.'

'Come back soon then. I'll get us a nice meal: oysters and quails eggs and masses of chocolate. Oh and lots more wine of course.'

'Stop talking or I won't be able to leave!'

His eyes flashed. And then they were kissing each other again: eyes, cheeks, arms, falling out together in a scrambled mess onto the balcony.

'Watch this!' he cried, suddenly grasping the railings with one hand and jumping over sideways.

'Be careful, you might fall!'

'But I didn't.'

'Fine. If you do that again, then I'll follow you, in a dress.'

His white teeth glistened in the sunshine. 'And I'll be there to catch you my princess. I'll meet you for oysters, later.'

The emptiness returned as soon as she lost sight of him, as if her soul had clambered out of her on that balcony and scurried across the railings too.

Downstairs Sarah was busy polishing the banisters. The servant girl didn't look up or move out of the way for her when she passed by.

'I'm afraid that the room at the top is rather a mess. Some wine got spilt... across the wall. Could you change the bedclothes as well? As soon as possible.'

The girl gave her a cold little sideways glance. 'Yes ma'am I'll get onto it.'

'Is Mrs Landricam in the kitchen? I rather fancy oysters tonight.'

'Mrs Landricam has left your employment ma'am.'

'What on earth do you mean?'

'She didn't feel quite right working here anymore. She always got on with Mr Eden so...'

'How utterly ridiculous. Wretch of a woman! Well get someone else in. We... I must eat oysters tonight, lots of them.'

'Shall I arrange that before or after I clean the room upstairs?'

'I couldn't care less.'

A number of letters were waiting for her on her desk. They were mainly bills, some for hats and dresses she'd never even worn.

The last was a letter from Alfonso.

Darling Lucinda,

After our last meeting I thought it best to write rather than visit. We didn't part on the best of terms did we my sweet cherub? I hope you are well and getting some of this fine air; I often look out for you in the park.

Undoubtedly you will be pleased to learn that I have parted with young Betsey. Although I am well aware of your menacing thoughts about the child, she was really a rather sweet girl who had little use of an old man like me.

You are probably going to think that this is a begging letter; one that implores your forgiveness and the hope of reconciliation. And it is exactly that, in part. I do miss you my wife, and if for now I can live with even the faintest hope of coming back to you, then that is good enough for me.

But this letter has another purpose, the nature of which, however hard I try, I find impossible to phrase in a pretty way. When we last met you talked of an affair with the man from next door, this Tristan Whitestone. Lucinda, you know that although I have behaved brutally towards you of late, and am an ass for doing so, I still have your best interests at heart in my funny crooked way.

Since hearing that man's name from your lips I have made a few enquiries my dear. It seems he has some untoward habits; he is rather well known in one or two establishments in Soho. This in itself doesn't trouble me, it is a world we know rather too well ourselves after all.

One story has however 'awakened my senses,' shall we say. I can't really make head nor tail of it; it exists in a sort of rumour which circulates about the man. It first came to me by way of a girl at the theatre, Adelaide. Her sister worked out in India as a governess. It seems that there was some controversy out there to do with Mr Whitestone; something involving a woman, but not quite your run-of-the-mill affair. The woman got ill, I'm not sure how or in what way, but it prompted the involvement of the police and Mr Whitestone had to make a hasty departure.

I would have ignored the story if it hadn't been repeated by some military men I came across two nights ago. They were rather better for drink, home after a long spell in India. I threw Whitestone's name into the conversation and to my surprise it seemed to have a rather sobering influence on the gentlemen. They were loath to speak at first but after some encouragement soon blackened the man's name in language which made even me, old Alfonso, turn pink with embarrassment. The police were mentioned again but this time a love child also entered the story. I couldn't get much more out of them, but it was enough to send me home to my lonely quarters for the rest of the night, my mind reeling with worry for my dear Lucinda.

I have no doubt that your anger at my audacity regarding this matter will be immense. I envisage you now tearing this letter to pieces and flinging it into the fire – yes, I know you so well! And why on earth should you trust my word over his after all that I've done? Of course, I am well aware of that too. But I couldn't let this lie. I know how damaged you are and now I wish only for your happiness.

Your husband
Alfonso

The letter floated down to the floor.

What a clever man Alfonso was: to attempt to shatter her world with a piece of paper and then rob her of the pleasure of ripping it up afterwards.

She regarded herself in the mirror above the mantelpiece. 'Now, you're going to have a lovely long bath and then a nice walk in the sunshine,' she told her reflection. 'Sarah! Run me a bath!'

But when it came to lowering her body into the steaming tub, the sensation made the bile lurch up inside her. And when she lay back the water seemed to press down on her with its hot weight, her lungs struggling for space to move. She raised her arms and watched a network of rivulets trickle down her skin. It was sweat, not water. She could even brush it off with the side of her hand.

Her heart was beating far too fast. She began to sweat even more and then it felt as if all that wine she'd put inside herself over the past week was now seeping out of her skin: a film of crimson over her entire body, dispersing in the bath water and turning it pink.

She could see the newspaper headline already: 'Whitestone strikes again!'

'Look it's just wine,' she mouthed. 'I've been drunk for a week you see, it's JUST wine!'

She pounced out of the water. Who in their right mind sat in a sweltering pool of their own dirt on a day like this anyway?

The light blue dress felt just right. It had a yellow band around the waist which drew her in and made her feel slim and elegant and she had a straw hat which went rather well with it.

Out on the street she admired the image of herself as it shimmered across the windows of the houses. A young man walked by and tipped his hat at her. She beamed at him and he beamed back with surprised eyes.

She weaved in and out of the streets without a thought for where she was going, the sunlight filtering down through the holes in her straw hat.

Suddenly she was back at Druid Manor again, holding her father's hand and wading waist-high through a cornfield; minute mice flying from the terror of their tread. And then she was running across the pristine lawn towards her mother and brother, gripping onto the hat that she'd stolen from the trunk in the attic.

'What have you got on your head?'

Her mother's voice. She peeped up at the dappled rays poking through the brim and felt her fists dig into the alcoves above her hips.

'It was in the attic. Daddy says I look marvellous in it!'

The memory fell away and she came to a halt at the edge of a bustling road. Sweat was trickling down her spine but she couldn't strain her neck far enough to see if it had made a mark on her lovely dress.

Her head felt strange, like an empty bobbing cloud and when she faced forwards again the street seemed to undulate before her. There was a lamp-post nearby. She fell over her feet to get to it and gripped on as the pavement quivered beneath her.

Her insides turned to acid and she tried to swallow the bile back down. No... no, she couldn't ask Tristan about India. Definitely not.

'Can I help you?'

It was a man's voice. A carriage had stopped near her and from its door she glimpsed thin fingers on an outstretched hand. She fell towards it and it caught her, strong like wire.

When she woke up she could see a door with 36 on it through a carriage window and then Sarah was helping her inside. Her feet felt muffled, as if the nerves had been extracted from them with silver tweezers. She could taste chalk in her mouth. The front door was closing behind her but she turned to catch a glimpse of the edge of a purple cloak whisking itself into the carriage.

'Oh God it's you!' she screamed. Her voice felt hollow, it scratched against her throat and hot tears stung her eyes. She ran up and up through the house but behind her she could feel her father's presence, sad and groaning.

'Lead a pure life Lucinda. I've never touched a drink and neither will you. You're my little lass, aren't you?'

The door slammed his voice away. Face down on the bed she breathed in the beautiful silence.

The minutes and hours glided past with the changing hue of the sky. Her stomach grumbled hungrily. Perhaps she'd ask Tristan a question or two later, about India.

She blinked and in an instant the light seemed to have changed. There were a few clouds now outside, frilled about the edges with pale pink.

But hadn't they promised not to ask each other questions about their past? Although a promise meant nothing really. He would forgive her. She'd ask him as soon as he came in, and then they'd make love and drink wine and eat oysters all night.

It was almost dark when she heard the click of his door. A moment later he was in her room, a silhouette against the starless sky. She couldn't see his face.

He crept closer, a brooding shadow and she could feel every part of herself open up, reach out and drink him in.

'Come to bed,' she whispered. 'Don't ever leave me again.'

'I've brought you something, taste it.'

There was a clink of glass and then a single droplet of something sharp but warm landed on her tongue. It made her mouth feel all hollow and as soft as feathers. And then she felt her eyes closing, as if she were being beckoned into a beautiful dream. A hand reached down to her through rainbow colours, and she took it.

SERENA'S STORY

For the next few days I saw little of anyone in the house apart from Beth and Gladys. Beth and I made the most of the warm weather by spending much of our time in the park. Our base was Beth's favourite spot under the large shady tree we'd found on our first day together and we came bearing blankets, books and fat sandwiches prepared by Gladys.

Beth loved to lounge: stretching her small body out like a cat on the warm blanket. She listened intently to the stories I read her, watched me draw and played simple card games with me like pairs and snap. It was only when I tried to coax her to the playground that she began to frown; curling her small nose up into a tight button mushroom.

'It's too noisy over there.'

'But you can meet other children in the playground. Don't you want to play?'

'Not really. They don't like the same things as me.'

On the route between the park and Marguerite Avenue there was a nursery that sold bedding plants and water fountains and trees pruned into lollipops. I took Beth there to look for some small plants for my balcony. She skipped about over hoses and puddles whilst I made my choices: two dwarf rose trees and a lavender plant. And I bought a small bag of soil and three glazed pots to plant them in as well.

We heaved it all home and up to my room, squinting in the gloom after the brightness of outdoors. The house was quiet: the doors all closed and the atmosphere as still as a locked church. However, as we clambered noisily upstairs I got the unnerving sensation in my bones that we had a distinct audience; that they were all there, listening softly.

Arabella was definitely in. I could smell patchouli lingering in the air outside her office. Perhaps if we'd passed by a few seconds earlier we would have caught a glimpse of the edge of a scarf or her ash blonde hair disappearing around the door. And although the air felt so still, I began to hear the creak of a violin somewhere in a distant room.

I could almost feel their heat in the walls. And perhaps Seb was somewhere in there too. My fingers itched to test the door handles. I hadn't seen him since my first night, a whole three and a half days ago. I tried to squeeze the thought of him away and yet at the same time I looked out for him in every corridor and at each new turning in the stairs.

Up on my balcony Beth and I removed the plants from their old plastic pots.

'You'll do lots of nice things like this when you start school in September,' I told her.

'I don't think I'm going to go to school.'

She was inspecting some grains of black soil that had got between her fingers. It had smeared across her cheeks as well, transforming her into a wiry little chimney sweep.

'What do you mean, you're not going to go to school?'

'They don't think it's right for me.'

I lowered one of the lavender plants into its new pot and snapped off a stem.

'Here, smell this lavender.'

'Yuk, I don't like it!' She pushed my hand away. 'Smells like old people.'

'You shouldn't say things like that.'

'Why not?'

'It's rude.'

But she only looked confused.

'Hmmm, this is why I think you probably should go to school. Sometimes you just can't say whatever comes into your head; it might upset people. School teaches you things like that; how to mix with the world around you, as well as reading and writing and history...'

'But you can teach me all those things can't you?' she interrupted with imploring eyes. 'Grandma said you were clever and she got you here to teach me things like that so that I didn't have to go to school.'

'Did she?'

'Yes, of course.'

She smiled up at me but it was some moments before I could even try to force a smile back.

'Are you alright?' she asked. She was watching me intently now, the skin between her eyes all wrinkled up. I tried to shake off her words and stuck my tongue out at her as an answer, sending her into fits of giggles. It was nice to hear her laugh, she didn't do it very much but when she did it was infectious.

We pushed the finished pots up against the railings. They made the balcony look rustic and homely.

'Pretty as a picture, eh?' I said, patting her on the head. 'I know what, why don't we take a trip to Kew Gardens? They've got all sorts of wonderful plants there and great big glasshouses and lots of shady trees to sit under.'

A beam of light crossed the girl's face, instantly followed by a shadow.

'I'd like to but is it far away?'

'Um, not that far. We'd have to sit on a train for a bit to get there.'

'I better not then.'

'Why?'

'I'd probably get one of my headaches.'

By the time I managed to get all the soil off her, Beth's dinner was already waiting on the kitchen table: eggs benedict with hollandaise sauce in a china jug at the side.

'Tea?' asked Gladys.

'Yes please.'

I'd given up trying to make it myself.

'Do you know where that old fortress is?' Beth asked between mouthfuls.

Gladys cocked her head to one side, the teapot in mid-air. 'In the chest in the drawing room I think.'

'Great! Let's build it!'

'After you've finished,' I said.

She gobbled her meal up so fast that it gave her hiccups. '... you'll love it... *hup*... it's got gates... *hup*... and two armies and cannons... *hup*.'

The drawing room was full of evening light when we came in search of the fortress.

'It was Seb's you know. He played with it when he was a little boy and they were going to throw it away, but he gave it to me instead.'

I tried to cast a subtle eye across the sofas, empty this time.

'Here it is!' she squealed. 'Be careful though, it's heavy.'

It was. I heaved the old toy castle across the floor, my hair hanging hotly over my face until I came to a sudden bump against something behind me.

'Hello, how are you?'

I spun round to find Seb standing there looking highly amused. His shirt was crumpled, his skin blonde in the warm light.

'Have you settled in alright?'

'Yes, thank you. We've been going to the park a lot. I haven't... seen you...'

'And now we're going to play with the fortress!' interjected Beth, glowering up at us with her hands on her hips.

Seb's mouth twitched and suddenly he was on the floor beside her, limbs everywhere, clutching a fistful of soldiers. I drank in his long lithe body, his mop of dishevelled hair that my fingers ached to touch.

'You are still coming tomorrow, to Raphael's party, aren't you?' he asked with a sideways flicker of his eyes.

'Yes, of course. What time?'

'I don't know, eightish? Now men! Tear down those battlements!'

He launched his figurines at the fort, Beth fighting back by hitting each one over the head with a canon. One of his soldiers came hurtling towards me, and I retaliated by neatly dropping the castle drawbridge on his hand.

'Ahh! Girls don't play fair!'

Seb rolled over on his back in defeat and Beth jumped on top of him in a frenzy of giggles. As I laughed at the two of them my eyes landed on a figure watching us from the doorway. It was Arabella. She was holding a glass of wine and looked as if she'd paused there on her way to somewhere else. I tried to pretend I hadn't seen her, but I could feel her gaze like prickles and I watched her leave from the corner of my eye, stiff and straight-backed.

'Come on, let's clear up,' I muttered. 'Five minutes till bedtime Beth.'

Are you sending me away?

The words crossed through me like a shadow, although no one had spoken them out loud. Beth was gathering bits of the fortress up into her skirt and Seb was trying to mend a wounded soldier. I felt beads of sweat on my forehead; it was too hot in the room, the light had become as dense as amber.

Seb tossed the fixed soldier back into the fortress. 'I'll leave you to it then ladies, before I get even more battered. Oh... and I'll come and knock for you tomorrow night when the party kicks off if you like,' he added.

'Thank you.'

A little hand tugged at my sleeve and Beth's face smiled up at me, as pointed as an imp's.

'We won the battle!' she cooed.

'We've got some nice leftover beef tonight. I cooked it 'specially for Raphael.'

'Oh, I didn't know he'd already arrived.'

Gladys hurriedly laid out the plates. 'He got in a couple of hours ago.'

I felt my stomach gurgle. The air had finally cooled down enough for me to want to eat again.

'What is it that Raphael does exactly? Beth said he was an artist...'

Gladys screwed her nose up.

'That boy turned down a place at Cambridge to paint those horrible dark pictures.'

'What pictures?'

'Haven't you noticed them around the house? You'll find them soon enough.'

'Really?'

Gladys's disapproval was so intriguing that I was tempted to jump up and search for Raphael's paintings then and there. But my gurgling stomach had to come first, particularly when Gladys's sumptuous food was involved.

We chewed contentedly, the kitchen so quiet that it was impossible to guess who else was in the house. Its big old table and flagstone floor were beginning to hold a familiar comfort for me and after nearly a week I felt as if I was falling into step with Gladys's quiet company. But there was one tricky issue that I really did need to raise.

'Um, do you know how I could get a little time to chat to Arabella, on her own?'

Gladys's eyes briefly crossed my face but her expression gave nothing away.

'Is anything the matter?'

'No, not at all. I just wanted to speak to her a bit about Beth and her headaches. And school...'

Gladys stuck a large forkful of food in her mouth and chewed it rather vehemently.

'I'll find out when it's convenient for Mrs Hartreve to see you,' she said finally, putting her knife and fork precisely together as if to mark not only the end of our meal but also the end of the subject.

'Thank you... Can I help with the washing up?'

After being shooed out of the kitchen, I made my way as quietly as I could towards the front of the house. A mirror caught my reflection as I moved by, as sudden and fleeting as a passing ghost. The door to the drawing room was firmly closed now and I heard muffled voices behind it.

The library door across the hallway was wide open and I felt myself lured towards the soft glow of the room. Inside it was just light enough to get a reasonable impression of what hung on its walls, but almost every inch of space was crammed with paintings, photographs, framed certificates and all manner of artefacts. I picked a random spot and began to move round.

'Dark pictures... horrible dark pictures,' I murmured under my breath.

There was a sharp knock on the front door and I found myself freezing, as if scared of being caught in the act of doing something wrong. The drawing room door swept open and the tap of smooth leather soles moved across the hallway tiles to the front of the house.

'Evening,' came a voice from the street. 'Now I've got lovely dusters here, shoe polish, rubber gloves...'

'No thank you. Move on please.'

Edward's voice.

'I'm just trying to set myself up sir. If you look at these cloths.'

'I asked you to move on young man. Didn't you understand me?'

'I'm only doing my job!'

'Well perhaps you should go and find yourself a proper job.'

A second of incredulous silence.

'Fuck off you posh git.'

The door closed and the leather soles started to tap back

again. But as I let out a long breath they paused, almost as if Edward had heard me. I felt butterflies; surely it was alright to be in there? Wasn't it? The shoes seemed to scuff indecisively for a moment or two and then, quite suddenly, turned their pace directly towards the library. I stepped forward in readiness, but before I even had the chance to say something a long arm plunged into the room, grasped the doorknob and slammed the door shut leaving me inside.

As the shoes moved away again I cupped my hands over my mouth and laughed into them, although my heart was still beating fast. And then something that I hadn't seen before caught my eye: an imposing gilt framed painting of something very dark, so close to the door frame that the door must have masked it entirely when it had been open. I drew closer to it, waiting for the image on the canvas to emerge, but no, even up close the painting seemed to be entirely black. In the bottom right-hand corner two letters entwined themselves together in pale grey paint: RH. So this was one of Raphael's creations.

My eyes buzzed with peering at the thing. There had to be something more to it than black paint; like one of those optical illusions that demanded lots of intense staring to work them out. It wasn't a good light but yes, very slowly, some details in shades of lighter black and grey hues, rose up spirit-like from the canvas. They formed a silhouette in the centre of the painting, a human form it seemed but with limbs so elongated and frayed at the extremities that it looked grotesque. Up where the face should have been there was a blurred shape that looked like a giant yawn, or grimace. It made me shudder. I took a sudden step back, grabbed at the door and pushed it back up against the picture.

Back in the hallway the soft tones of a woman's laughter emanated from the drawing room. I retreated up to the first floor and wandered along the corridor past Arabella's office. At the end, behind a large fern on a pedestal, were a series of three paintings. They were just like the first: almost entirely black with the same haunting shape in various swooping poses in the centre. I brushed my hands up my arms. What sort of imagination would want to create these figures? Clearly whoever had hung them behind doors and plants had asked the same question.

Turning back out of the corridor another painting caught the edge of my eye. I hadn't noticed it before, probably because it was rather small and mounted in a dull rickety looking frame. But the painting itself was quite exquisite. Fine pencil strokes were covered in bright blotches of watercolour; playful and serious all at once. And the subject of the painting was the strangest looking man I'd ever seen. So strange that it left me with the uncanny feeling that I must have seen him somewhere before. He had a spindly body with a peanut sized head and was dressed in long wizard-like garments with a string of what seemed to be bottles and charms around his neck.

'So you found the painting of Walter then.'

I gasped at the voice. A young man in black was standing at the top of the stairs, watching me.

'Oh I'm sorry, did I scare you?'

'No, it's just that people always seem to be springing up on me in this house.'

'It's because of my mother's various ailments. We all learnt to move very quietly from an early age. I'm Raphael by the way.'

He came forward, and I recognized him instantly from the photograph I'd seen in Arabella's office. His face was long and considered, his eyebrows arched at the centre, conveying that same sense of surprise and sudden interest. It was a timeless, poetic face and now I could see why black and white had suited it so well.

'I know who you are, I've seen your photograph,' I said, taking his outstretched hand. 'I'm Serena, the new nanny.'

'Yes, everyone's been filling me in.'

'Have they?'

His eyes rested heavily on my face, so heavily that I had to look away.

'I... I actually came here to look for your paintings,' I stammered. 'Gladys told me they were all over the house.'

He brushed a lock of dark hair away from his forehead. 'Oh you'll hate them, everyone does.'

'Well I wouldn't say I...'

'No need to pretend. But this here is far more interesting. What do you think of it?'

'I don't know really. I think the man's intriguing – you called him Walter?'

'Yes. His name was Walter Balanchine. He was a nineteenth century mystic who worked for an ancestor of mine, the great Lord Hartreve.'

'Was he serious?'

'Oh yes, very. He was quite well-known in those days, especially in the East End where he lived.'

'But why would someone like your relative be interested in him?'

Raphael shrugged his shoulders, drawing his bottom lip in thoughtfully. 'We're not entirely sure. Lord Hartreve became a bit of a recluse in his old age. His wife died young, his son disappeared to Africa on a mission and his daughter Lucinda, well...'

'Well what?'

He looked at me again and this time I could see something flit within those dark heavy eyes: a tension, like a string suddenly being pulled tight.

'Lord Hartreve bought Lucinda this house,' he said slowly. 'She married a man he didn't approve of and then...'

'Yes?'

'Oh it's a strange story,' he answered. Somewhere in the house a clock chimed, and he glanced down at his watch. 'I'll tell you about it another time but unfortunately I've got to head out now. You're coming to the party tomorrow I hear.'

'Yes.'

'Well, I'm glad about that.'

He hesitated and then squeezed my arm briefly with his right hand. I could feel the warmth of his skin through my top and my cheeks coloured up in response. He smiled back, calculating my reaction, his eyebrows more quizzical than ever.

I turned my face hurriedly back to the painting of Walter again. An image of him wading through the Victorian East End in his billowing garments floated through my mind. How peculiar that he'd been linked to this family and what could the *strange* story about Lord Hartreve's daughter Lucinda have been about? But when I turned to speak to Raphael again I found myself standing there alone. He'd left as silently as he'd arrived, and through the shadows I just caught a glimpse of his dark hair sinking from view down the stairs.

I felt a sudden urge to call him back: ask about Lucinda, his paintings, maybe even the missing house next door... And yet something about Walter Balanchine's stern little face made me stop.

'They're all watching me you know,' I whispered to him. 'Eva,

89

Arabella, Raphael. Did you see the way he was staring at me just then? Now why do you think that is Walter Balanchine?'

I held my breath childishly for a response, for a little flicker of his watery eyes perhaps, but he stared on from his canvas at a point somewhere just beyond my left ear. What a shame, he seemed like the sort of man who would have had the answer to anything.

I ran my fingertips softly along the walls, up and up and over the bumps of door frames, conjuring the image of Lucinda Hartreve in my mind. Which of these rooms had she slept in all those decades ago? At Beth's room I paused to pop my head around her door. She was sleeping deeply, her breath as faint as moth's wings. Lucinda wouldn't have slept in here, no, not grand enough. And she certainly wouldn't have slept in my room, high above the tree tops.

Out on my balcony chair, with my sketchbook propped up on my knees, I tasted the sticky night air and watched Seb's face emerge once again from the end of my pencil. I closed my eyes and, drifting off, I could almost feel his lips touching mine. When I opened them again I was left with the hollow sensation of having been somewhere without realizing it. It was nearly midnight. Drunk with tiredness I stumbled to my bed.

I bought a new dress for the party.

'It's very nice,' said Beth when I tried it on for her. She was lying on my bed flicking through a magazine I'd bought. 'I like the floaty bits. Did you know there's a picture of Eva in here, in the society bit?'

'Oh really, I hadn't noticed. Are you sure the floaty bits don't make me look like a bride's mother?'

'No, more like a bride's fairy godmother.'

'Oh shit. Sorry, you didn't hear me say that word OK?'

The house buzzed all day with party preparations. Eva appeared intermittently, and a man in a Stetson flounced about the house barking out instructions to men in overalls – 'I want that sideboard out of here by ten. DO YOU HEAR ME!' The dining room furniture disappeared and a lorry load of new stuff wrapped in plastic was brought in.

'Why has he got so many earrings up one of his ears?' Beth whispered loudly to me, pointing at the Stetson man.

'Just to look a bit different I suppose. But you shouldn't point at people.'

'Must be awfully heavy!'

And she danced about the room with her head hanging to one side as if to empathize with his plight.

'Come on,' I said. 'Let's go and help Gladys.'

All the lavish preparations were beginning to make me feel rather nervous about the party, and particularly about my dress. By the evening my hands were actually quivering. The dress now looked even worse than it had in the morning. I put it on and then took it off again, standing in the middle of my room in my underwear.

The floaty bits were just wrong. I scrambled through my drawer for my nail scissors, the sudden thrill of destruction urging me on. In barely a minute the floaty bits were no more, and when I put the dress on again it was vastly improved.

I went to work on my face, the mascara brush dancing a jig in my hand. Just as I was surveying the end result in the mirror, a hammering came at my door.

Seb was wearing a skintight vintage looking purple suit, something half way between the Mad Hatter and a rock star.

'Like the dress.'

'Like the suit.'

'Do you? I found it in an old box. It's a relic I think.'

'How can you tell?'

He raised his eyebrows into the sort of smile which made me want to pull him into the room and slam the door behind us.

Downstairs the dining room had been transformed into a murky lounge bar with deep velvet sofas and black chandeliers. People were milling about everywhere, drinking cocktails and champagne and adorned in the sort of clothes that made Seb's suit look conventional. I squeezed to one side to make way for a woman in silver-sequinned hot pants and she swayed past us with the measured assurance of a supermodel.

'Great isn't it!' Seb enthused. 'Eva's friend Fabian did it all; he's a set designer. Look, he's over there if you want to talk to him,' and he pointed in the direction of the Stetson man who had now complemented his hat with a tight jumpsuit.

'No it's alright. He looks busy. Shall we find somewhere to

sit?'

Through the thick smoky air I spotted Eva. She was sitting in the corner of one of the sofas wearing a flapper style beaded dress. There was a glazed look in her eyes and she'd chosen a shade of deep maroon for her lipstick that made her mouth look like a bloody tear in her pale skin.

There was a big crowd around someone in the middle of the room. I craned my neck to try to see who it was.

'Hey,' Seb squeezed my hand. 'Meet Raphael.'

Something made me catch my breath as I was suddenly confronted with the two of them standing there together. They were about the same height, one fair one dark. Seb, with his purple suit and astonishing blue eyes, seemed to shine out next to Raphael, who was fully dressed in black like before. And yet one powerful glance from Raphael made me flush up with the oddest sense of having forged some sort of union with him: *we have secrets together*, it seemed to say.

'We met last night actually. I discovered Serena searching for my art,' he explained, musingly.

Seb looked alarmed. 'Oh you don't want to do that.'

'That's exactly what I told her. How are you getting on with Beth then?'

'She's just fabulous. Very mature for her age.'

'She's a tyrant,' laughed Seb. 'Beth knows more about what goes on in this house than all of us put together.'

A waiter sailed towards us with a silver tray and Raphael scooped up three glasses of champagne. 'Let's sit over there.'

We squeezed past the crowd in the middle and I caught sight of the person at the centre of it. Her head, wrapped turban like in a red scarf, was turned towards a group of young men. It wasn't...?

'Are you suggesting I don't know how to tango?' she burst out, sweeping her astonished eyes across the crowd around her. 'Robert, go and find some music!' A loud cheer rose up in response.

Yes, it was Arabella.

'This is quite a party,' I said to Raphael. 'You must have been away a long time.'

'About six months. I've been in Europe mainly, attending exhibitions and talks about art. I've just got back from Berlin actually. I went to see a display of Habsburg gems which was due to open there.'

'Wow, they must have been beautiful.'

'Yes I'm sure, only the exhibition never happened.'

'Why not?'

'The stones went missing in transit, stolen. An extremely professional job it seems.'

'God that's awful.'

The champagne bubbled on my tongue as we sat down. Seb was next to me, his leg just a tantalizing inch away from my own. He could have been chatting up any girl in the room.

'Why?' Raphael was studying me challengingly, his chin resting on the tips of his fingers beneath pressed together palms.

'Why what?'

'Why is it awful?'

'Oh! Because no one can appreciate those gems now. For all we know, they've gone forever.'

'How do you know they won't be appreciated? I would appreciate them.'

'But would you steal them?'

'Probably.'

'Cigarette?' Seb waved a packet in front of me.

Raphael shook his head and then fixed his eyes on me, so intently that I felt as if we were staring at each other through a tunnel. For a moment Seb's hand blurred out of vision. 'Most beautiful things are stolen; it makes them more captivating,' he murmured.

'Like Helen of Troy,' broke in a female voice that made me start. We all turned to find Eva standing before us. 'Hello Serena.'

But before I had a chance to say anything to her a hush suddenly fell across the room and then the slow-paced and almost eerie reverberations of violin music filled the air. The crowd dispersed as Arabella took to the floor, thigh-to-thigh with a young man.

We all pulled away to give them space; Arabella in her exuberance wasn't taking any prisoners and as she arched her body back and flung up her sickled neck to the man's lips I found myself squashed up against Robert.

As usual he was looking rather shy and uncomfortable, although I could certainly see why on this occasion.

'Hello,' I said. 'Lovely music!'

He shrugged his shoulders. 'Not really my sort of thing though.'

I glanced over to see his mother's face glide startlingly close to her partner's groin.

'Yes I can understand that,' I replied.

Across the dance floor someone was trying to push through the crowd. People shifted to either side with annoyed expressions. Over to my right Eva, Seb and Raphael had formed a disapproving little huddle. Arabella bolted across the floor, her turban coming loose and her hair tumbling across her shoulders.

'Look here,' said Robert, quietly. 'I don't really like to get involved in... family stuff, but none of them know what to do with you. Do you see? They've all got different opinions.'

I looked up into his pale face. 'What do you mean?'

'Nothing,' he shrank back. 'Perhaps you should leave... this house I mean. OK, just forget I said anything.'

The music stopped abruptly. Edward had appeared opposite at the front of the crowd, his lips set in a thin smile. I looked back at Robert, but he was moving away and now I was being pushed in the other direction towards Eva.

'We shouldn't have let her do it... and she's all tanked up as well,' I heard her murmuring to Raphael. 'Sasha's upstairs. He'll have a good probe whilst her tongue's loose no doubt. Yuk.'

Arabella curtsied to tumultuous applause as Edward led her gently away by the hand.

'We have to send that cretin back to Russia somehow,' replied Raphael. 'Can't your new man lend a hand, maybe they come from the same town or something?'

'Don't be silly.'

Eva turned and her eyes fell on me, narrowing at once.

'That's a very pretty dress,' she said through tight lips.

'Thank you.'

'Have you cut something off it?'

'No.'

Seb emerged from behind them, grinning broadly at me. 'Enjoy the show? Eva's not bad at the tango either, are you?'

Raphael smirked. 'She's too busy for all that now, eh? Spends all her time eating caviar with her new man.'

'Shut up darling,' said Eva, rolling her eyes.

Seb burst out laughing, Raphael egging him on.

'... So that's the black diamond he gave you eh?'

'He mined it himself no doubt.'

'In his lunch break probably.'

'Do oligarchs get lunch breaks?'

Gradually they squeezed a smile out of her and then even a laugh as she started to jibe back at them, their faces full of mock indignation. But I gave up listening to any of it. Around me the room began to buzz with white noise, and all I could think about was Robert's strange words, and the image of Edward escorting his wife from the room.

I nudged my way through the chattering groups in search of a silver tray, my shoulder brushing against a sweaty shirt front on the way. Above it a face like a West Highland Terrier glowered down at me.

'And who are you?'

He was in his thirties maybe, his lips shiny and moist; I could smell the drink on his breath.

'I work here. Sorry, excuse me.'

'You work here!' he exclaimed, grabbing at my hand. 'What, polishing the saucepans?'

'No, I'm a nanny.'

'Then shouldn't you be Latvian or something!' he bellowed.

'But I am. How did you guess? Was it my outrageous foreign accent?'

He looked baffled for a moment, and I snatched my hand back.

'Ah, there you are! Are you ready for your escort back to Latvia?' said a voice behind me. Seb's voice. Just the sound of it made my whole body soften like hot wax. 'I have a carriage waiting outside.'

I began to giggle and the man knitted his fuzzy eyebrows together in even greater bafflement.

'Come on,' said Seb, his lips soft against my face. 'Stop picking on the weak. Let's go to bed.'

His hand clasped mine and we let the noise of the party disappear into an underworld beneath us. My feet barely touched the stairs; up through the house together, my hand against the banister and then strumming tenderly up his spine. And then Seb, my Seb, stripping me of that bloody dress and falling onto my bed with me in his arms. I gripped his face between my hands and plunged through the deep blue water, no longer alone. And then I hid my face in his cool neck, my fingers buried in his hair.

He turned me onto my back, his body as gentle and enveloping as a shadow. I wrapped my arms and legs tightly around him until his skin felt like my own. He whispered my name and tears, happy tears, forged canyons down my cheeks.

That night I watched him sleeping next to me, his face even more carved and Aztec in the blue light and the sharp sweep of his ribs and hips beneath the white sheet. I pressed my back against his chest and his body curved itself around mine.

And then, much later in the night, just before the first haze of early morning, I think I had the strangest dream. A man came into my room. At first I thought he was Seb; the eyes were so similar, even in the shadows. But I could still feel Seb's body around mine and his breath on my shoulder. No, this was someone different and the sight of his gaunt shadowed face made my throat catch with the force of a stranglehold.

He watched me for a long time; his gaze all-consuming, and I screwed my eyes up tightly against him until I heard the brush of something leaving. But the image of his face stayed with me and then I remembered where I'd seen it before. Not in the kind beauty of my lover, but in paintings hidden in the quiet corners of the house; dark paintings that had turned my skin cold. The dream slid past, but even though I knew he'd gone I kept my eyes tightly shut until sleep returned again.

1892

It was the same as always. Her mother was wearing her linen nightgown, her hair plaited into two grey ropes hanging pendulously over her shoulders.

'Miranda darling, get me my medicine.'

She didn't like being in charge of mother. The medicine cupboard was so high up that she had to drag the biggest chair in the kitchen over to it and even then her childish legs could only take her so far, even on tiptoe.

She strained her arm towards the bottle with such force that she thought her ribs might tear apart.

'Hurry Darling!'

The voice was getting thin and watery; she smarted at its urgency and imagined the cracked lips through which it had travelled. Her hand fell on a bottle and she grabbed hold of it, her feet falling back flat on the chair and her heels just saving her from performing a clumsy backflip onto the stone floor.

The bottle looked alright; full of brown gooey stuff. And wasn't Mummy's medicine just like that, brown and gooey? She gazed up again at the cupboard, it seemed to have stretched even further away, and then back at the bottle.

'Coming!' she shouted.

Miranda let her eyes flicker open. The room seemed full of darting lights: sunshine dazzling her through the window pane. Something about her left cheek felt as if it didn't belong to her. She ran her fingertips along it and found a long bumpy crease where her face had been pressed against the cushion. The drawing room slowly came back into focus.

The sunshine was a surprise; just when she thought that summer had well and truly died. She stumbled to the window. Outside the wind had found a flurry of dead leaves. It scooped them up and then vomited them violently across the pavement, over and over again.

Today was Thursday. She tried to count back; had it been Saturday or Sunday when she last saw Tristan, his eyes red and his shirt collar ripped and stained? She gazed at the growing mountain of his correspondence on the table. From the top of the pile a fresh letter from Switzerland glowed whitely at her, their address on the front written in his father's hand.

There was a rumbling of wheels. A carriage passed her by, drawing to a halt outside Mrs Eden's. She cringed back behind the curtains and peeked out to see Mr Eden's expansive form emerge from the carriage door. His face seemed as benign as ever and from within his grey overcoat came the glint of one of his bold waistcoats: emerald green.

He knocked abruptly at number 36. No one opened. Then she heard the jangle of keys. They scraped and croaked about in the keyhole, one after another, but there was no sound of the door giving way. He muttered something under his breath and then suddenly the walls shuddered with the most almighty pounding. Miranda jumped away from the window, pressing her back against the wall.

'Lucinda, let me in! I want to help you!'

The pounding came to a halt as abruptly as it had begun and his retreating footsteps crunched back down the path. And yet there was no click of a carriage door, no hooves or sound of departing wheels. If anything his footsteps seemed to be getting louder again...

A determined rap now shook her own front door. Her fingers darted to her hair, the creased line across her face. Mrs Hubbard was approaching.

'It's alright, I'll open it. It's just an old neighbour of ours.'

'As you please.'

'Mr Eden! How nice to see you again.'

'Please excuse me. Am I interrupting anything?'

His eyes were moist and pleading. He seemed older than she remembered him, standing there alone on her doorstep.

'No, do come in. Would you like some tea?'

'Many thanks but no, just a moment or two of your time.'

He floated behind her like a large cloud into the drawing room, surprisingly soft-footed and rather dainty in the way he perched on the edge of one of the chairs.

'I'm rather concerned about the welfare of my wife, Lucinda. Have you seen her at all recently? Or perhaps her maid Sarah?'

'I have rarely seen your wife over this past year I'm afraid. She came for dinner some months ago but left with a headache. I used to see her servant girl quite regularly but well, now that I'm thinking about it, I haven't spotted her around for weeks.'

Mr Eden rested his chin in his neck. He looked as if he wanted to say something but wasn't quite sure how. She tried to focus on the gold button of his waistcoat.

'Is your husband at home?' he asked eventually. 'Perhaps he might have seen one or the other.'

'I'm sorry, but Mr Whitestone is working. I very much doubt whether he's seen them as he's rarely here. He works incredibly hard you know.'

He smiled kindly at her, his eyes soft and pleading again. 'I have a letter here for Lucinda,' he said, handing her a crisp white envelope from his inner coat pocket. 'It's rather important and I have a feeling that if I put it through her door it will simply sit there gathering dust. May I leave it with you? If you see her for any reason I implore you to give it to her.'

She glanced down at the envelope in her hand. 'How urgent is it? It is rather a responsibility.'

'I've often noticed you at the window. You sew there, don't you? I think you would be the most likely person to spot her if she is around.' He shook his head and stared down at the floor. His lip appeared to be trembling. 'My apologies, this is wrong of me. This is a very private matter, and I shouldn't be involving you.'

'No, no. Of course I'll pass it on if I can.'

But he still looked agitated, fidgeting about and unable it seemed to meet her eye.

'May I ask? Is your wife in danger of any kind?' she asked, quietly.

He scratched his head, scowled at the floor again, pulled all manner of awkward faces. The letter began to burn in her hands like a hot coal.

'I think she is mixing with a rather dangerous individual,' he replied. 'But it isn't my business to talk to you about this Mrs Whitestone. Please, please, don't let anyone else see the letter. And do contact me at the theatre if you see or hear anything. I'm so sorry I interrupted you.'

'No interruption at all, I'm sorry for your concern.'

As the carriage wheels groaned into the distance, she turned the envelope over in her hands. It was an innocent enough looking thing: light, small, no more than a couple of pages inside perhaps.

And just one word on the front: *Lucinda.*

She sewed at the window for longer than usual that afternoon, pricking her fingers at the merest hint of a moving hinge somewhere on the street. But no, no Mrs Eden. It was quite ridiculous really to expect to see the woman now after so long, just because that letter was smouldering away upstairs in her dresser drawer.

The light was starting to fail much earlier now. She retreated to her room and devoured some of Mrs Hubbard's home-made bread and butter under her warm bedcovers. There was no need to pretend to be busy at night; she could read novels until her eyes itched and drift off into sleep without having to move a muscle. Even now her eyes were closing down like shutters. Her book slipped to the floor.

Riawwwww. A wail. A screech like something inhuman. What time was it? Gone two o'clock in the morning. The room was full of shadows, she hugged her knees tightly under the blankets. *Riaaawwwww.* It was somewhere inside the house, as sharp as a blade edge cutting through the night air.

She had to do something, get help, but her body trembled at the thought of leaving her room. *Agwwwwwwww.* The bronze statue of Minerva glinted on her dresser. She grasped it and it felt cold and reassuring against the palm of her hand.

Out in the dimly lit corridor all seemed silent and still. She peered around her, gripping the statue so tightly that she could feel her knuckles turning white.

Suddenly there came the sound of a loud brushing jolt from downstairs, followed by something sliding across a floor. *Agh agh agh agh.* She panted for breath, her hand muffling her sobs. But her feet kept on, one trembling step at a time down the stairs, her shoulder pressed firmly against the wall and the statue now clutched against her chest.

'Oh, Tristan!' she gasped.

He was lying beneath her on the hallway floor. She couldn't see his face but he was breathing heavily, as if he were asleep, the clothes on him as tattered as a vagrant's. His shirt looked yellow, stiff with dirt. And near his foot was a hessian bag tied up with string.

Something in the bag began to move. It squirmed about, with

what looked like limbs extending here and there, struggling to get away. A... baby perhaps? She retched, clasping at her throat.

The squirming seemed to awaken Tristan. He raised his head for a moment and groaned.

'Damn blasted thing,' he slurred drunkenly. He drew his booted foot back a little and then fired it at the bag, sending it hurtling across the tiled floor. *Riiaaw riiaaw riiaaw.* The scream was coming from inside the bag, less piercing now, more of a whimper.

'Stop now!' she screamed.

'The blasted creature's good for nothing! Doesn't catch a thing,' and he scrambled across the floor towards the bag, his fist poised for attack, a clump of sinew quivering in the air.

The blow was short; over so quickly that it was hard to say whether it had actually happened at all. But Minerva was smiling up at her from the ground and one of her slender hands was slightly bent. Tristan's eyes were shut firmly; she could already see a surly looking mound of blue rising up at the side of his forehead and scarlet where the skin had broken.

She picked the knotted bag open with shaking fingers. 'Don't worry little thing, it's over now.'

Her hand landed on soft fur. A ginger cat, no longer a kitten but still young with green marble-like eyes.

'It's alright.'

Its silky fur was warm against her lips.

'Would you like some milk? You're too thin little thing. Where did he find you? Here, let me take you to the kitchen.'

The cat clung to her as if it instantly recognized a friend and once down on the kitchen floor it squirmed ravenously towards the saucer of milk she gave it, one of its back paws dragging along behind it like a spare part.

'Ah I see you still want to live. That's very good.'

But that leg looked bad. She rifled round for something to set it: there were some bandages in the cupboard by the door and a small wooden spatula that would work as a temporary splint for the night.

When the animal had licked the saucer clean, she lay it carefully on the kitchen table and eased the shattered bone back into place. It watched her with listless but unblinking eyes, too exhausted to object.

'I thought you might fight me on this little thing but you're being very good. I used to have a cat like you when I was a girl. It was a very naughty cat though, always getting into trouble and it broke its leg too. I watched them fix it, just like this. All better again. Now, I'll take you upstairs with me, but I need to get my statue back first.'

Tristan was still lying exactly where she'd left him in the hallway. She crept past him back upstairs, the cat clutched under one arm and the statue under the other.

'You can sleep here on this cushion. Look, this is my bed, I'm not far away. Good night Minerva. It's a rather good name for you, don't you think? You're a strong little thing, aren't you?'

By the morning the cat was curled in a tight ball at the end of Miranda's bed. She ruffled its fur gently with her fingers and caught sight of herself in the mirror. Her skin was pale but she looked quite calm, not shaking at all now.

'Breakfast time little cat, come on.'

Downstairs, Tristan had gone. The hallway echoed with emptiness and she felt as if she was standing on its cold tiles for the first time again, a stranger in her own home. An ugly looking stain caught the corner of her eye. It was comma shaped: a flaky, bloodstain on the wall at the bottom of the stairs. A little further up there was another similar mark, and then another. She shrank back and hurried on to the kitchen, Minerva purring softly against her chest.

'Now what are you bringing into my kitchen?' groaned Mrs Hubbard.

'A perfectly civilized young cat. I've called her Minerva, isn't she lovely?'

'What's wrong with its leg?'

'I think she must have been attacked. I found her on the street last night making the most awful din.'

'I don't like creatures in the kitchen.'

'Think of her as a friend then. Would you mind feeding her? I need to see to something upstairs.'

The comma shaped mark laughed at her in the hallway again. She chipped at it with her thumb nail and it fell away leaving a dirty tea coloured scar on the wall behind. She pictured him crumpled and staggering up the stairs, half blind with pain, touching his head, brushing his bloodied fingers against the wall.

Was this really the same lithe energetic man she'd married? The man who'd once, only once, held her close to him. On that glorious day she'd pressed her ear against his heart, listened to all that young blood surging through him, full of promise and her absolute belief.

'We're getting married. Tristan's proposed!' she'd proclaimed in their tatty old parlour and her father's chest had puffed up with pride. For the first time in her memory he had tears of happiness, for her, in his eyes.

'He's a fine man, your Tristan Whitestone,' he'd said. 'A man of business, a man of the future! You've done well.'

'Am I forgiven then Daddy?'

And he'd smiled warmly and moved his head in a way that was neither a nod nor a shake but felt comforting nonetheless.

The blood stains went up and up through the house. Gradually they got fainter until they were barely apparent at all, but she could still spot them; even the merest fleck glared out at her like a beacon. And then when they'd disappeared altogether she kept on going, up to the little servant's door at the top.

The unlocked door swung open to an empty room. It was a bleak and chilly cell of a place with bare walls and no furniture at all apart from Tristan's desk. A jacket of his had been tossed over the back of the chair. She buried her face in it, breathing in the scent of his cigars. A neat pile of papers sat on the otherwise empty desk. The one on the top was untouched, entirely blank. She turned it over and then the next and the next, but they were all also quite bare.

Her mouth went dry. She hugged her arms around herself and then her fingers edged back to the papers. Over and over, one empty page after another. No work, nothing to show for all that time he spent up here, until the final page shone up at her. And in the centre of that page a single sentence floated in the desert of white.

I have warned you before. Keep your snout out of my affairs. TW.

Her body swayed from side to side like a pendulum. She lurched away from the desk, her shoulder slamming against the balcony door. It didn't jam like it used to and she flew out against the railings, gulping like a stranded fish at the cold air.

It was starting to rain and yet she couldn't bear to go back in. It was only when the drops grew heavier, drenching her clothes and her hair, that she finally turned. But something, a glimmer of white languishing in a puddle on Mrs Eden's adjoining balcony, suddenly made her stop. She crouched down and eased her hand through the iron railings to pick it up: the remains of one of Tristan's cigarettes.

The crumpled cigarette floated in a puddle in her palm. It was a brand she would have recognized anywhere, Tristan's favourite, with a brown scalloped pattern across the edge that even the grimy puddle had failed to eradicate. She crushed the soaking remains of the tobacco between her fingers and let it drizzle back down to the ground.

Her skirts were so sodden with water that she had to heave them up to her hips to climb over. The railings felt slimy and she didn't dare look down but she was over in seconds, a trespasser suddenly, hovering at the edge of Mrs Eden's balcony. Just a mere soggy step more and she'd be able to look in through the window.

'Wake up. Lucinda, wake up! Look, look at my head! Have you got anything for it? You must have something in this filthy fleapit.'

She twisted her neck slowly and tried to focus on the jumble of blue and red at the side of Tristan's face.

'What happened?'

Her tongue felt like a large piece of raw meat in her mouth, not part of her at all.

'I'm not sure.'

Outside the sky was grey and billowing. It was raining heavily.

'I've just had the strangest dream,' she said. 'A woman was standing on our balcony looking at us. I think she rose up out of a lake, dripping wet. I know her face, but I can't remember, she looked in pain...'

'Shut up! Do you really think I want to hear this? I'm the one in pain... go... do something.'

'Alright, alright. Stop shouting at me you blasted man. Look, I can barely walk.'

Her legs felt like soft butter when she raised herself.

Something dark and slithery shot out from under the bed and into a heap of dirty linen in the corner of the room.

'You know, I think that could quite possibly have been a rat. Where's our cat gone?'

'I got rid of the thing, it was useless. Didn't catch a single mouse.'

'No, probably because the rats got there first. We have to do something, hire a new maid to sort all this mess out.'

'Interfering busybodies. Get on with it Lucy, you're leaving me to die!'

Her leg brushed against something cold and wet: an overflowing chamber pot lapping at her shin. There was a bottle of gin on the dresser with just a little left swilling about at the bottom. She filled her mouth and pushed the bottle into Tristan's hand.

'Here, have the rest of this. Something to start with.'

Beyond the room the house was so murky she could hardly see, and she nearly went flying where the carpet had come loose. More scampering: little claws everywhere, scratching against wood. She felt like a small girl again, creeping through her parents' house in her nightdress. *Mummy I can't sleep. Can I sleep with you?* Down, down, so many stairs she no longer knew where she was. But then there were cold tiles beneath her feet and, yes, her own front door.

The image of the lady on the balcony came back again. How agonized she'd looked, and with a face so wet you couldn't tell if it was water or tears. She must have fallen in the lake, the one at home, just like when she was a little girl and her father had plunged his arm in and dragged her out.

Lucinda dragged her eyelids apart. She was now lying on the hallway floor. The cold tiles stung her through her nightdress and she heaved forward, the gin from earlier reappearing across the floor in a honeycomb pattern of bubbles.

She staggered up, tried to open the front door, but it was locked. And the door frame appeared to be gleaming in some way. Gradually the gleaming dispersed into a series of gold smears all around the door and then the smears began to take shape, transforming into... what was it? Padlocks. Thirty, forty of them maybe, although it made her eyes buzz to count.

Quite the most curious thing she'd ever seen. She heard a faint giggle, her own, and then the joy drained out of her in an instant. It was Walter Balanchine, up to no good most probably;

hatching some outlandish plan with her father. Or perhaps Alfonso seeking revenge for not taking him back. Tristan would be outraged.

She limped into the drawing room, as dark as midnight with the curtains tightly closed. Behind the heavy fabric were yet more padlocks, and this time even thick nails in the frames to make sure the windows wouldn't move an inch. Tristan must learn about this, immediately.

Back on the stairs, her knees groaned as she tried to lift her heavy feet. And then the memory of Tristan's poor old head suddenly came back to her. She knocked her forehead with the palm of her hand. Too much gin. Too much gin and wine and that other thing that Tristan kept giving her that made her feel so lovely and sleepy.

She scrambled towards the door with the stained glass panel. No gleaming Bacchanalian faces now, no light from within to soak through the coloured glass. This room was the blackest by far. There was frenzied rustling inside; something brushing against her nightdress.

The shutters swung open easily enough but behind them were yet more padlocks and nails. The sudden glare of light made her blink. Dust motes hung uncertainly in the air and the room looked as tired as Alfonso's face when she'd last seen him. She steadied herself against the back of a chair and peered around until her eyes landed on his old bureau. The small box was still inside it, under a pile of dog-eared newspapers. It was an old tea chest really, with rather pretty zigzag marquetry.

The next flight of stairs felt as steep and perilous as the face of a mountain. Soon she was on her hands and knees, struggling to move an inch and a moment later Tristan was carrying her up into their room.

'You've been gone for hours.'

'Have I?'

'What's in the box?'

'Oh, something you'll like. It was Alfonso's.'

His face seemed pleased by its contents. He removed the bamboo pipe between two fingers, skillfully lighting and moulding the opium before lying back to smoke.

'You've done this before.'

His laugh made the joy rush into her again. But something

urgent was tugging at her. 'Ah! I've just remembered what I wanted to tell you. A terrible thing has happened downstairs my love.'

'And what might that be?'

'We've been made prisoners. There are padlocks and nails in all the doors and windows. Who could have done such a thing?'

He inhaled deeply. There were hollow caves in his cheeks and his eyes were glazed and milky.

'I did.'

'You did what?'

'I locked us in.'

Her mouth opened but no words came out. She felt pain and saw that there was blood underneath her fingernails. Her palm was bleeding.

'Why?' she whispered.

'It's for your own good. Look what happened last time when you ventured out on your own. That servant of your father's might have kidnapped you.'

'But he didn't.'

'I can't have you wandering about by yourself. You're in my protection now.'

'I... I haven't left the house for days.'

'Months actually.'

'Oh my God.'

The room began to move around her in soft circles, like a carousel warming up. She gripped her stomach, it felt swollen. The room got faster and faster. Padlocks. Nails. And then the ceiling came crashing down towards her. She gripped the bedclothes, forcing her body down down into the mattress until she thought she might come out through the other side.

'No! Help me! Help me please God!'

The ceiling kept falling, fast then slow then fast again but never quite reaching her.

'Help me please, please. Alfonso, why did you leave me?'

Tristan's face was leaning over her, a laughing blur. She lunged out at it, her knuckles ripping into flesh.

A man's sobs. Tristan was curled up in a tight little ball on the bed next to her. He was naked; his skin almost transparent where it stretched across his ribs.

'Why are you crying?'

'Because you hit me.'

His sobbing was like a bubbling stream, as weak as a little boy.

'Where? Where did I hit you?'

But his face was locked in his arms. He flinched at her touch.

'You needn't worry. I won't hit you again.'

He peeked out at her, a child behind a parent's legs.

'Are you sure?'

'Yes. I am your prisoner after all, aren't I?'

And finally he unravelled his body, easing her softly into his arms, tucking her head into his neck.

'Darling Lucy, you are not my prisoner. You are a beloved jewel in a vile, stinking world. My darling, my beautiful Clementine. Let me keep you to myself.'

'Who is Clementine? Why did you call me that?'

'I didn't my love. You're hearing things; you must be tired after all your adventures.'

'I am tired, but I doubt whether I'll ever sleep again.'

'Would you like some of your medicine?'

'Yes... I think I would.'

She parted her lips and two small droplets slithered down her throat like smooth pearls, magically cooing with the promise of dreamless sleep.

The next time she woke it was night. Tristan was beside her, sitting bolt upright in the bed, the moonlight catching at the knotted rope of his spine. He seemed so vulnerable, like a hunted fox.

'What troubles you?' she whispered.

'Dark thoughts.'

She moulded her body around him. It heaved beneath her, dreadful and lonely.

'My poor man, you've been hurt.'

He clutched at her wrist and the thrill of his touch sent a shock of light through her. She gripped her thighs tightly about him, smothered his shoulders with her hair and her kisses.

'Don't leave me,' he groaned.

'No. I'll never leave you.'

'Thank you. Thank you Clementine.'

SERENA'S STORY

'We prefer to keep Beth at home. She has the protection of her family here.'

'But it's only school. Surely that's a safe enough environment.'

Arabella smiled at me in the way that nurses smile at mental health patients.

'Beth is an unusual little girl. Very sensitive and special as I'm sure you've gathered. She finds it hard to make friends with other children and they don't particularly warm to her.'

Beyond her shoulder the Bacchanalian revellers were bright with evening sunshine, the colours almost garish. And from through the open windows the scent of the climbing rose washed dreamily across my face.

'I do understand, but perhaps we should at least try.'

Arabella threaded a bangle between her fingers, her eyes fixed on the floor as if in deep consideration.

'Beth gets headaches,' she murmured softly.

'Yes I know.'

'We find that they can be prevented if we keep her close and familiar.'

'I see. Have you taken her to a doctor?'

'I've... spoken to various experts.'

Experts. The word came through shining teeth; the 'p' in the middle not quite spat but as precise as a rattlesnake's tail. I shrugged lamely, 'If there's anything I can do to help.'

She dissolved into big smiles.

'How lovely of you to offer. We will be getting all the various school materials in due course. Simple reading books, and so on. Perhaps if you could assist her with these?'

'Yes, of course.'

'And I'm so glad that Gladys set up this meeting because I wanted to ask a favour. What are your plans for Christmas?'

'Um, I don't have any right now. I usually spend it with my aunt but I think she's quite keen to go away this year.'

'Fabulous! We always spend Christmas at Druid Manor, the Hartreve family seat in Wiltshire. You've probably heard of it. Edward's brother, the current Lord Hartreve, lives there with his family. The place is a mess as they have no idea how to look after it but it's a lovely house and I wondered whether you'd like to join us. Beth is the only child and sometimes gets a little bored, I'm sure she'd love your company. And it's also a charming place to spend Christmas.'

My mouth burned with the one question I wasn't able to ask: would Seb be coming too? Christmas in a big old country house with Seb would be just perfect and if anyone could sneak an invite then he could.

I stole a glance at the photograph of Raphael on the wall. He looked back at me with bemused interest, like the hero of a silent film.

'I'd love to come. Thank you for asking me.'

'Excellent!'

Down through Arabella's window the climbing rose had totally consumed the wall at the end of Marguerite Avenue; a cascade of blushing pink blooms.

'I think you have the best view from this room, of the rose.'

'Yes, glorious isn't it. I see how much you admire all the beautiful things we have here.'

My neck burned beetroot.

'Oh I didn't mean to embarrass you my dear! On the contrary, I've been quite taken by the way you've adjusted to us... We wouldn't want to lose you.'

'I've no intention of going.'

There was a sudden knock, and Robert twisted his head around the door.

'We have to go. I'm on in two hours and have to get warmed up.'

Arabella shot out of her chair, tossing a pashmina around her shoulders. 'Must scoot!' she cried back at me as they raced downstairs together.

I hovered on the landing, waiting for the sound of their footsteps to disappear, and then backed away, up to my room. Beth's bedroom was empty; she was still out with Raphael. I dashed past it, up the last staircase to the top, stroking my hair back as I reached the final step.

'You're three minutes late.'

Seb was already lounging on my bed, his shirt half unbuttoned.

'Well I couldn't exactly excuse myself because I had someone waiting for me in bed upstairs. She's my boss; some of us have to work for a living.'

'How do you know I don't work for a living?'

'Do you?'

'Can't say I'm afraid. If I told you I'd have to kill you. Is Beth back?'

I peeled my clothes off.

'No. Anyway she's Raphael's until tomorrow morning.'

'I love your afternoons off.'

'So do I. Hey I was thinking, why don't we try to go away together somewhere for a couple of days?'

'What's wrong with here?'

'Nothing really, just all the sneaking around I suppose. We could do what we liked if we went away. What do you think?'

'Maybe.'

'Oh and you know what, Arabella's asked me to join them at Druid Manor for Christmas. Do you know it there?'

He didn't reply and his face went all straight and serious, as if the usual jokey humour had all at once been sucked right out of it.

'What's wrong? Isn't it nice there?'

'Oh it's a lovely old place. Full of happy memories.'

'Then why don't you come too! We could sneak along creaky corridors to each other's rooms in the night.'

'I can't. I... have to spend Christmas with my father.'

'OK, I'll tell Arabella I can't go either and I'll join you.'

'No. It's miserable with him and besides, if you've already said yes to Arabella then you shouldn't back out. Beth will love having you there.'

I felt myself sink down into the bed like a deflated cushion. Images I hadn't even been aware of yet came crashing down around me: the perfect country Christmas, snowball fights with Seb on the lawn, curling up next to him by a log fire.

He stuck his lower lip out at my glum face like a toddler and I couldn't help but grin back at him.

'Anyway,' he said. 'Why the hell are we talking about Christmas? It's summer! I'm in your bedroom, the sun is shining, the air smells of jasmine...'

'Ahhh, so it is jasmine! I was wondering about that. Smells wonderful.'

'I'll bring you some of the flowers.'

His eyes were astonishing. So blue it felt as if I were being carried away by their gentle current.

'I love your eyes. I've never seen eyes like yours before. Have I told you that yet?'

He drew me towards him, tantalisingly close.

'Many many times. But do you know what I love about you the most?'

'Oh don't tell me.'

'Why not?'

'I'll get all self-conscious about it.'

'Well I'm going to tell you anyway.'

'OK.'

He drew a line with his finger from the curve of my right hip up to the bottom of my ribcage.

'It's this bit of skin here. So smooth and impossibly warm.'

I cringed away. 'No Seb, you're joking right?'

'Why?'

I swallowed. 'Because that's where my scar is, silly. I hate the bloody thing.'

He bent closer and examined the long silky line that cut down through the right side of my torso.

'I genuinely hadn't noticed it until now,' he murmured.

'You're a very good actor.'

I tucked the bed sheet around myself. The scar still made me wince, even after all these years. I closed my eyes and carefully squeezed the thought of it away again, compressing it right down to the smallest speck. It was a process I'd got good at over time; so good I'd nearly forgotten about the scar's existence altogether. Nearly. But before I knew it Seb had pulled off the sheet again and was kissing the old wound with a softness that was almost painful.

'Can I tell you something?' he said. 'It's taken me such a long time to learn this, such a long time, but it's absolutely true. Sometimes people just don't notice things. Their lives don't stretch out enough to allow everything in I suppose, particularly the stuff that might upset them. We all do it; it's a natural instinct to cringe away from pain or suffering. And sometimes people begin not to see such things at all. They can stare them in the face and gaze right through them. It softens life you see. No scars, no pain. I'm sorry.'

'It's alright, better to see me for the nice things. I prefer it that way.'

'I love you,' he said, kissing me warmly on the cheek and then tilting his head up at me.

'I love you too. Hey, wait there. Don't move.'

'Why?'

'I have to draw you, just like that.'

'What? Again?'

In the morning Seb had gone. I had a blurry memory of him leaving some time during the night, kissing me on the shoulder before disappearing. The morning sunshine shot spears of light across my ceiling and a feeling of warmth, like rich golden honey, rose up through my limbs.

I threw on a light summer dress and padded downstairs barefoot, the soles of my feet relishing the cool wooden floors and bristly carpets along the way. Robert was in the kitchen, leaning against the counter with a piece of toast in his hand. I hadn't seen much of him since the party but whenever I did his strange words that night came back to me like a niggling little tick.

He was talking to a man at the kitchen table. I recognized him from the day of my interview in Arabella's office. Sasha.

'Good morning,' said the man with a bird-like nod of the head. His Russian accent was deep and round and his body was similarly spherical. In fact he was so round that I think he could only have rolled himself into the patched tweed suit that stretched about him. I thought back to the way Eva and Raphael had spoken about him at the party.

'Hello,' I shook his hand. 'We met briefly once. I'm Beth's nanny, Serena.'

'Yes, I know,' he said, turning straight back to Robert. 'So when do you leave?'

'On the fourth,' Robert replied. 'We'll be performing at two concerts in Vienna before moving onto Salzburg.'

I sat down quietly at the table, trying not to intrude anymore and Robert seemed to throw me an apologetic glance.

'Ah, Vienna! One of my favourite European cities. I lived there once you know, for two years when I was completing my studies.' Sasha twitched his head about and waved his little arms enthusiastically as he spoke.

'We're not going anywhere if percussion doesn't get it right.'

'Surely they're not all that bad.'

'They have no concept of the piece. And just when I think we've turned a corner, they play like baboons!'

It was hard not to giggle at an angry Robert, particularly when the subject of his rage was drum and cymbal players. I grabbed a piece of toast from the toastrack on the rather mucky looking table and plunged a knife into some melting butter. Of course, it was Gladys's day off. That explained why they were down here, making a mess of her usually spotless kitchen.

Sasha clasped his little hands about his protruding stomach. 'Well you must upbraid them then for their failings, over and over again if you have to.'

'I do! God, I even trashed their instruments once.'

I spluttered laughter into my toast, fighting back the crumbs as they battled hard to surge down my windpipe. But Sasha shook his head sombrely, 'No dear Robert, no. This is not the way to approach the situation. I have seen this time and time again at the Moscow Conservatory: musicians getting, how shall I say it, hot under the collar during times of artistic crisis. I have been brought in on many occasions to deal with such issues, yes silly old Sasha here...'

'Pasha!' came Beth's voice suddenly, breaking him off mid-speech.

She flew through the doorway and, quite ignoring the rest of us, climbed straight up into Sasha's arms. He balanced her on the small space on his lap that his stomach allowed for his knees and patted her hair contentedly.

'Ah my little Bee. Look, I have a small present for you in this little box in my jacket here.'

'Amethyst crystals; my favourite!' she squealed. 'I'll just put them in my room. Thank you! Hi Serena.'

Beth squeezed back out of the room past Raphael who was leaning languidly against the inside of the doorway. He was wearing his customary black: a T-shirt with faded jeans and there were deep shadows under his eyes.

'Coffee?' I asked him.

'Yes, please.'

'Oh it's Raphael. What a treat for us all to have you here,' interjected Sasha with a smile that almost purred. 'We should all have coffee together then. In the drawing room.'

The mugs rattled threateningly against the tray as I teetered across the drawing room floor. Robert and Raphael were standing by the mantelpiece whilst Sasha appeared to be holding court before them, gesticulating wildly with his arms as he spoke. Raphael seemed distracted, moody even, staring down at the carpet and saying nothing.

I put the tray down on the coffee table and then caught sight of the couple, entwined in each other's arms on the sofa. They didn't even seem to notice I was there.

Eva was wrapped around Seb like a cat. She was wearing a fuchsia pink evening dress and tired make-up, as if she'd only just got in from a party and Seb was lying with his head in her lap, utterly at ease. It was like a painting. The two of them looked so painfully exquisite lying there: Eva a model of sculpted diffidence and Seb like a beautiful young boy, his face a picture of idleness and innocence.

I stepped back shakily and my leg knocked against the table. Seb started and then smiled up at me. 'Hello!'

Eva arched her neck as well to look. 'Oh, you're here.'

'Eva!' chimed in Sasha, barely before she'd closed her mouth. 'And there I was thinking you were asleep.'

He scurried towards her, closely followed by the others.

'Thanks for the coffee,' said Raphael quietly with a long grateful glance.

'I haven't seen you for a while my dear girl,' Sasha continued with a look at Eva that lingered a little too long. 'Although I did have to go to New York for some time. Always coming and going, coming and going.'

He stepped forward to help himself to a biscuit, thankfully obscuring my vision of Seb and Eva together. 'But for now I intend to remain in London for several months. I have much work to attend to with Arabella. Your mother is a cruel taskmaster. I have found myself travelling to the British Library for her already twice this week...'

He edged to one side bringing Eva back into view and I felt my eyes widen. She was sitting bolt upright now and her usual demure demeanour had been replaced by a grimace. The skin around her mouth had even turned a greenish hue, as if she was going to be sick.

I tore my eyes away from her and found Robert and Raphael just staring vacantly at the floor. Seb was also sitting up now, unusually quiet and still although he kept looking over at me with long sideways glances. I ignored him and his face drooped down with a hurt look.

Sasha was still talking, now about Arabella's Africa projects it seemed:

'We have to grapple with the heart of the problem, go out there if needs be. I have many connections with the royal family of...'

The room had become sticky and unpleasant. I ached to leave but couldn't quite drag my bruised limbs away. Seb wasn't even trying to look at me now. Sasha scooped up another biscuit.

'Now, on a different note,' he exclaimed, posturing towards Eva again as a grin tweaked at the corners of his mouth. 'A little bird told me that our young princess Eva here cannot sleep without an arrangement of lilies by her bed.'

There was a long dramatic pause as he wiped his moist lips with a handkerchief. 'When I observed a vase of wilted blooms in her room yesterday, I took it upon myself to ensure that our fine lady's sleep is secure for at least a few more days. I hope the flowers I chose are to your taste.'

He made a little bow that would have been amusing if it hadn't seemed quite so lecherous and she seemed to turn even greener.

He sidled up to her, breathing heavily by her ear. 'And furthermore, I was wondering whether to ask you to play Beethoven or Bach today, Robert. But it is such a fine morning outside! Am I correct in thinking that Eva would hate both in this weather? She would much rather have Mozart I am sure.'

Eva stood up without a word and walked stiffly out of the room, our eyes meeting for one brief moment.

'Ah, she doesn't look well!' said Sasha in response, biting into his biscuit with thick yellow teeth. 'I will check on her later to see how she is.'

My own mouth went dry as I watched the small crumbs sticking to the tip of his tongue.

He now turned to Robert and they launched into a new line of music themed discussion, but Raphael was still staring at the carpet. Only the shimmer of a nerve along his jawline gave away something of what he was feeling.

I leaned towards him. 'Can I ask you a question?'

His eyes met mine; they were so dark that I almost backed out.

'Go on.'

'Why did Beth call him *Pasha* in the kitchen earlier?'

Raphael produced a wry sort of smile. 'It comes from her old baby name for him, *Papa Sasha*. She just amalgamated the two words over time... unless he did it for her.'

I slipped quietly out of the room to the now empty kitchen. Some clean glasses were drying by the sink and I grasped one of them, holding it under the tap until the water frothed up to its brim.

The image of Seb lying there with his head in Eva's lap loomed up at me from the bottom of my glass. Even when I screwed my eyes up it ran on, repeatedly.

'Serena.'

I jumped so violently that the glass slipped from my hand, crashing against the porcelain sink into countless spinning shards.

'No, don't!' I cried.

Seb was moving me away by the shoulders, poised to plunge his hands down into the sink. The air went thin.

'It's OK,' he said. 'I'll clear the pieces up.'

'Don't, please.'

I pushed his hands away and yelped at a stab of fire in my thumb. Almost in slow motion, it seemed, a sliver of crimson dripped into the sink and exploded like a firework in the puddle of water around the plughole.

'Oh Christ.'

'It's alright, ' he mouthed, pressing his own thumb down on the wound. 'It's just a tiny scratch. You don't even need a plaster.'

His tender voice felt like an echo; his other hand squeezed my side.

'No, no... you're right. It's just, I'm slightly phobic.'

'Phobic of what? Of blood?'

'Oh no, of broken glass. It's stupid really.'

'No, it's not stupid at all,' his blue eyes seemed more piercing than ever. 'It's perfectly reasonable. Go away, go for a walk. When you get back it'll all be gone. Don't worry; I'll make everything go away.'

I found my way to the front door, breathless and practically falling over my own feet as I pushed myself forward. Outside it was easier and I speed walked down the street to get away. Around the corner I bought some cigarettes from an off-licence and lit one immediately. I felt my lungs relax and fan out with the smoke. Less than a month in Marguerite Avenue and I was hooked on those bloody things once more. My heart began to beat at its normal pace again, the sunlight combing warm fingers through my hair.

But still that image of Seb lying in Eva's lap looped in and out of my head and then it jumped to Beth climbing onto Sasha's knee and that revolted look on Eva's face.

Papa Sasha.

I watched the smoke curl up into the air. So, was that the answer then? Was Sasha the father of Eva's child?

I tried to picture how it must have happened, how maybe Sasha had sneaked up on her one night in the discreet upstairs corridors of the house. Perhaps she'd allowed him out of juvenile rebelliousness, perhaps he hadn't given her a choice. I shuddered at the thought of those small hands running themselves over her young body. But if that really had happened, then what on earth was he still doing in their house?

The growl of an approaching engine cut through my thoughts. A great black motorcycle, utterly incongruous with the quaint road I was walking along, prowled up behind me. I paused to let it pass, stubbing out my cigarette, but instead it pulled up right by my side onto the pavement.

A shock of fear swept through me and I instinctively felt for my money, my phone. But as soon as I locked eyes with the driver, a strange, almost guilty laugh rose up in my lungs instead.

'Where did you get the bike?' I asked.

'I borrowed it from somewhere,' Raphael replied. 'Hop on.'

I gingerly took the crash helmet from him and climbed onto the back, my heart suddenly beating very fast, my body acutely conscious of how close it was to his. I wrapped my arms around his waist and the bike sprang into action. Before I knew it we were tearing down the narrow streets, the lines of his shoulder blades an inch from my cheek.

I lost track of where we went. We crossed the river over the Albert Bridge and we looked back at it through the quiet hum of

Battersea Park. We left London and flew like an enraged wasp down the A roads and onto the motorway, dancing past the cars and playing chicken with the lorries.

I gripped tightly onto Raphael now, my eyes closed for much of the time, the sharp air stinging through us. But the closer I held him the more dangerous it felt until I was quite convinced that any moment we'd take our fall, our bodies skimming across the black roads together and under the black tyres of the traffic around us.

But at last we slowed down and I found myself back in the quiet streets of west London again, slaloming elegantly through the stream of traffic. I felt a slowing down of senses, like at the end of a funfair ride: the feeling of relief saddled with a small but undeniable yearning for more.

Only minutes later we were back where Raphael had found me and he stopped to let me go. I unlocked my arms, the heat of his body still in them, and slid away from him. He didn't look round. As soon as my feet touched the pavement he fired up the engine again and sped off. I watched him disappear and wondered for a moment whether our adventure had really happened at all.

When I got back to the house Beth was waiting for me in the kitchen.

'You've been gone ages!' she cried.

'Sorry.'

'It's alright, you're going to give me an art lesson now.'

'Am I indeed?'

I went over to the sink and checked inside; not a glass shard in sight.

'Yes, look I even got your pencils down from your room.'

'Hmmm, I can see that.'

I sat down with her and we both began to draw: Beth a rather impressive castle equipped with turret and drawbridge and me the rounded torso of a man.

'You like Sasha, don't you?' I murmured.

'Oh yes! He says he's going to write a book about me and make me famous.'

'Really? Why?'

'Because he says I tell him interesting things. But I'm not allowed to tell him about you.'

I paused and looked up at her. She was concentrating on her

castle, colouring it in with dark pink spaghetti-like squiggles.

'Look, shade it in like this, softly on the side and then we'll use a black pen to outline bricks on top... What can't you tell Sasha about me?'

Her hands suddenly flew to her mouth. 'Oh nothing!' she shrieked. 'Forget I said it, please.' She buried her head back over her work, shading feverishly.

I looked down at the drawing I'd begun and before I knew it the torso had acquired short little arms and legs and then a bird-like head sprouting out of the neck. The cheeks came out all puffed-up and swollen and the eyes set in a sort of stupefied plea. I added a little red to the cheeks, some pearls of sweat around the neck and the forehead.

'Has Sasha gone now?' I asked.

'He went up to Eva's room just before you arrived to see if she felt better.'

My stomach churned over. I finished the face off quickly, adding a pursed, choking mouth and the remains of a biscuit flying out from between his lips.

'Um, I'm just going to get that pen for you. You'll be alright for a few minutes won't you? Start on the sky when you've finished that.'

Eva's room was on the second floor. I hadn't had any need to go there before, but now as I approached the heavy door with the drawing of Sasha folded in my hand, I was filled with the shaky sensation of stepping over an invisible boundary. The sound of a soft murmuring voice, Sasha's, came to me from behind the door. It was impossible to hear what he was saying, but he seemed to be talking endlessly, rhythmically even, and every so often the sound of Eva, whimpering, seemed to cause him to pause.

I stepped back, the drawing rustling in my hand.

'No!' screeched Eva, suddenly. 'Can't you just leave me alone!'

His voice grew faster, as if he was appealing to her and then there was a loud shattering jolt, like something being knocked over: a vase perhaps, or a lamp. I jumped and raised my hand at the same time, knocking urgently at the door. There was a stunned silence for a moment and then the quiet pad of feet. The door eased open. Eva's face appeared, her mascara running down her cheeks.

'Hello, I'm not disturbing anything am I? Oh Sasha it's you in there is it?' I said, craning my neck. 'Fancy bumping into each other twice in one day.'

Eva moved aside a little and Sasha appeared behind her, fury quivering at his nostrils.

'It's just that I have something here for you,' I said, handing Eva the folded picture. 'Something I've been working on. I thought we could discuss it. But only if I'm not interrupting...'

We both glanced over at Sasha. He brushed the sides of his hair back with sweaty palms, readjusted his jacket and released a sober little laugh.

'Then I will leave you to it ladies,' he said under his breath, marching briskly between us and away.

Relief seemed to flood into Eva's face as soon as he was gone. She wiped her eyes with the back of her hand but when she opened the picture of Sasha she only smiled thinly.

'This isn't your business,' she murmured.

'What is that man doing in this house?'

She gulped back. 'Look, you have no place here. Leave us... please. Before something awful happens.'

'What on earth do you mean?'

'Just go. Go!' she groaned, pressing her head back against the door, fresh tears streaming down her face.

I turned away, but before I'd reached the end of the corridor she called out to me again.

'Serena!' My drawing was raised up in her hand. 'May I keep this?'

'Of course.'

And she smiled back at me through her tears.

I climbed up to my room, the vague memory of having promised to get a pen somewhere at the back of my brain. Pushing my bedroom door open with my shoulder I closed my eyes and ran my hands down over my face. And then a movement, from somewhere in the room, rippled over me. It was no more than the merest flutter of air, but enough for me to know that Seb was there without even having to look.

He was by the window, an untidy bunch of small white flowers clasped in one hand. I could already taste their pungent scent.

'Jasmine from the garden,' he said. 'I hope you like them.'

'I'm sorry about earlier. I've always been terrified...'

'You don't need to explain.'

'Oh God, oh God!' I murmured.

'What's wrong?'

'What's wrong? I don't know where to begin!' I tried to steady my voice, swallow back the tears.

'Well I do. Why did you ignore me downstairs earlier?'

'Are you quite serious? You and Eva, curled up together like a loving couple!'

He tossed the flowers on my bed, clenching his fists. 'I don't understand why you keep going on about her. There's nothing between us; she's my friend.'

'But you looked so... in tune with each other.'

'She's my friend,' he repeated, his voice trailing slightly.

He gazed trustingly into my face and every hurtful word I wanted to hurl at him just seemed to fall away.

'I saw Eva... just now,' I whispered. 'She told me to leave this house in case something awful happens. Robert said I should leave too, on the night of the party. I'm beginning to think I should take the hint.'

He pulled me towards him and I clasped myself tightly against his chest. And when I closed my eyes I heard voices from my childhood in my head, gentle voices I hadn't heard for such a long time.

'When I'm close to you,' I whispered. 'I feel as if I've returned to a part of myself I thought I'd lost. It's like coming home I suppose.'

'Then stay here, this is your home now. Don't listen to them. I'll look after you. I'll make sure that nothing ever hurts you again. No more broken glass to run away from. OK?'

'OK.'

At some point that night I woke up quite suddenly with the sensation that I was being watched. Somewhere, in the corner of my consciousness, I saw a figure slip away, so slight and subtle that it almost must have been a dream. I looked over at the balcony window but there wasn't a flicker of movement, only baking, lifeless air.

Seb was breathing rhythmically beside me but it was too close in the room for me to fall back to sleep. I stumbled downstairs to the bathroom and washed my face and neck with water. It was no good though, even the water felt warm. It ran down my face in clammy trickles and seemed to turn to vapour before even reaching the neck of my thin nightdress.

Further down the house it got cooler and more comfortable and I felt as if I could breathe again. I caught my pale reflection in a mirror and found myself smiling back at me.

Down at the bottom an enticing wave of fresh air caressed my face and arms. It was coming from the conservatory at the back of the drawing room – its door leading out into the garden had been left wide open.

Outside the air was almost drinkable, full of dew and damp leaves and the scent of jasmine. It was more than tempting to curl up on a bench and spend the rest of the night outside. I reached out, inspecting the petals of flowers here and there. There weren't a great many plants: a few shrubs down the sides in terracotta pots and some shady trees at the end. But no jasmine.

'What are you doing out here?'

I peered into the darkness for the voice but saw only shadows. But then came a sharp scraping sound, the strike of a match, followed by a flame which metamorphosed into a round orange spot suspended in the night air. I moved towards it and the spot became the end of a cigarette. Closer still and Raphael appeared. He was smoking on the bench in the garden's far corner.

'I could ask the same of you.'

'Well I am having a smoke.'

'And I'm looking for jasmine.'

'Here, join me.'

I perched next to him.

'How's the motorbike?'

He shrugged his shoulders. 'Don't even know where it is now.'

I pictured the vast black machine dumped in a wasteland somewhere, waiting to be vandalized or stolen. Clearly its job had been done, as far as Raphael was concerned.

I took a deep breath of the luxurious night and peered up at the back of the house. It seemed to be gleaming down at both of us in reply.

'What do you think of this place, my home?' he murmured softly.

'I think it's beautiful.'

He chuckled. 'Why?'

'Because it is a home I think, a real home. It's hard to be lonely in a place like this.'

'And is loneliness something you do well?'

I swallowed hard but didn't answer.

'Well I'm buggering off in a few minutes. Going back to Europe.'

'Beth will miss you. Does she know you're leaving?'

'Oh she's used to it.'

'When will you come back?'

'Probably at Christmas. I hear my mother's invited you to Druid Manor, will you still be with us by then?'

'Oh you're not going to tell me to leave too are you?'

He gazed at me unblinkingly and a chill ran up my arms. His long intelligent face seemed to ripple with tension and his eyes had turned jet black, like deep bruises. They made me want to back away but somehow I found myself drawing closer to them instead.

'No,' he said eventually. 'I very much think that you should stay.'

He turned away and suddenly without his gaze I felt as if I'd lost something I didn't even know I was looking for.

'Before you do go, I want you to tell me about something,' I said.

'And that is...?'

'I want to know about the missing house.'

He paused. 'What do you mean by missing?'

'Oh you know what I mean. The fact that this is number 36 but the one over there next to us is 32. When I tried to ask your parents about the missing number in between they gave me different stories, which makes me think that neither of them are true. And, the strangest thing of all is that Beth seems to think that there is a 34. She pointed it out once.'

His eyes found me again; tunnel black. I peered through the shadows and they stretched around me, so tender and consuming that everything on the periphery of my vision began to diminish. Our faces were so close now that I could feel his breath.

'Look over there,' he said. 'What do you see?'

I tore my eyes away from him to look over. 'A fence, separating your garden from number 32. A few pots. The wall sticking out from the extension next door.'

'And that's exactly what you should see. There is no missing house. Listen to me,' he said in a low hushed voice. 'When something scares you, when you see the ugliness of life, just pretend it's not there. It's for the best; it's what we do. We lock up sickness and disease in institutions; we keep it off the streets. We chop up slaughtered animals into segments and wrap it up until it becomes nothing more than *meat*. We cover up our own imperfections, give ourselves new faces. Because who wants to see the other side? Not me, not you.'

'Seb told me something similar. But the way you say it scares me.'

'And so it should.'

'You're all watching me, aren't you? I don't understand why.'

'Look, go back in.'

'Do you think I should leave, really?'

'I'm not sure whether you can.'

I felt his hands gently circling my waist. He was raising me up onto my feet and my legs felt shaky, as if I was half asleep. I raised my hands and felt his warm face against my palms. His mouth moved towards mine.

'What have you done to me?'

My voice sounded far away.

He stopped and moved his lips away so that they brushed against my hair.

'Go back to bed,' he murmured. 'I'll see you at Christmas.'

I found myself walking back across the garden and a vision, so beautiful, appeared before me that I heard myself cry out with surprise. Butterflies. They were glowing white, stark and fluttering against the night air. I rushed forwards, my hand outstretched, but just as I got to them a sharp spear of pain tore through my left side.

I'd collided with something: an old crumbling wall that couldn't possibly have been there before, rising up nearly to my shoulder. I reached up to touch the fluttering wings above it and as my fingers fell upon them they turned into petals; white jasmine petals tumbling over from the next garden and intoxicating enough to make my mind swim.

I snapped off a small cluster of buds, but the world was becoming blurry. My feet danced sideways, sleep was drowning me, and the flowers had turned back into quivering butterfly wings. It took every last shred of energy to drag myself back up to bed, my eyes sore and throbbing and the jasmine buds crushed in my hand.

1892

The plant had quite taken over. If she let it grow anymore it would be eating up the windows in another season. Miranda grappled the thick foliage away with her left hand and plunged in with the shears. A volley of dead leaves shot out at her, straight at her eyes and mouth.

'Ah, fighting back are you?'

Above her the sky was already gun-metal grey with evening gloom. Soon it would be time.

The pruning caused an awful mess. She raked the twigs and branches onto the pile in the middle of the lawn. It would make a good bonfire.

'I wish you'd get a gardener to do that.'

Mrs Hubbard was standing on the doorstep wearing the thick blue shawl she'd made for her.

'Oh I love it. It gets my blood pumping, makes me feel alive.'

'I suppose you miss the country.'

'Yes... I suppose I do in a way.'

'Now are you sure you want me to go home so early?'

'Yes yes of course.'

'I've left some cold ham and bread out.'

'That's marvellous, thank you. Now go home to those sons of yours!'

Mrs Hubbard returned to the glow of the drawing room and the forced smile fell from Miranda's face like a lead weight. When it got too dark and cold to go on anymore she finally edged inside. In the mirror a smudged and dirty face stared back at her; there were even a few bits of broken twig in her hair. And yet her skin was glowing. Just over an hour to go. She hurried upstairs.

In the warm bath she rubbed her body as thoroughly as possible with a new bar of soap. When at last she was properly clean, she dried herself briskly and peered into her wardrobe. Her navy dress would do. She liked the snake of buttons which ran all the way up the middle and the rather pretty V-shaped neckline. She scraped her hair back, adorned it with a black silk hairband and examined herself in the long bedroom mirror.

'Gosh, I look like I'm going to a funeral.'

But for once it felt rather pleasing to look at herself. Dark colours suited her, they seemed to give her chin more of a chance.

She paused motionless as the sound of gentle footsteps moved past her room. They faded away and disappeared behind a closing door, the key murmuring in its lock.

Downstairs she brought the food into the dining room. There were three place settings, just as she'd requested. Only the wine was left to prepare. She took a long, deep breath. Her heart should have been pounding, her body should have been shaking, but she'd never felt so calm and still in her life. What would Jane think of her dull little sister now?

'Look, I've tidied up your room Jane! You see, all your pretty ribbons set in a pattern, just like a rainbow.'

She must have been twelve or thirteen at the time. Jane had glanced about her, eyes alert and her face all pinched and suspicious looking, as if she could hear a strange sound but wasn't quite sure where it was coming from.

'I'm here. Here!' Miranda had cried. 'Look I tidied up your room whilst you were out.'

'Oh it's you! What are you doing here? Get out of my room at once!'

A clatter of footsteps came down the stairs. Miranda positioned the wine carefully at Tristan's place setting and took her seat. The clatter crossed the corridor; the door swung open.

'Where is he then? Not arrived yet?'

Tristan looked better tonight. He'd shaved and was wearing some clean clothes for once. But his skin wasn't good and the whites of his eyes were a sort of carnation pink.

'Oh good. I'm glad you remembered to come,' she said quietly.

He raised his lip in a churlish sneer. 'Of course.'

'Your father must be running a little late. Won't it be pleasant to see him again after all this time?'

'I very much doubt that.'

He knocked the wine back in one mouthful as if he needed the courage. She filled his glass again.

'What a funny thing to say dear.'

'Look, I'll tell you now before he does. Things aren't going too well with the company.'

'I had read in the papers that the business was suffering a

little.'

'More than that. We're probably going to have to sell this house. I'll stay on in London to sort things out and you can move to the country if you like.'

His eyelids suddenly drooped down and he threw his head back as if to wake himself up, taking another large gulp of wine.

'Are you alright?'

'Yes... Fine. Tired that's all.'

'Oh that's a shame. You must be working awfully hard up there.'

'There's a lot to do.'

His cheeks were drooping now; he hiccupped loudly.

'Is there anything I can do to help perhaps?'

'No. You wouldn't understand. This is an awful messsss...'

His eyelids drooped again and this time he collapsed forwards, knocking into the table and landing with his head face down on his plate. She gave him a small prod and his arm fell limply to his side.

'Yes it is a mess. You're quite right about that.'

She dashed to the door, locking him inside the room and then ran quickly, quickly up the stairs, past her bedroom door to the small spare room at the end of the corridor.

'It's Mrs Whitestone. We're safe now,' she whispered, tapping gently.

The door edged open. Mr Eden's face was so pale that it almost glowed up against the gloomy interior.

'Is he sleeping?'

'Yes, that powder you gave me worked quickly. I just hope it lasts.'

'I know, although I was assured it would take hours to wear off. Here, let me give you back your key.'

'Have you got the lamps?'

'Yes they're in here.'

'Let's light them then. No time to waste.'

Miranda brushed past him but Mr Eden continued to hover by the door.

'I don't know how to thank you for this,' he murmured.

'Then don't.'

She lit the first lamp and the room glowed up into life, revealing fat beads of perspiration on Mr Eden's forehead. His heavy jowls seemed to be quivering and he must have sensed her look of pity because he lowered his head and glared at the floor. She lit the other lamp.

'Come on, let's go,' she said, urging his arm forward towards the stairs.

'How did you get him to come down in the end?'

'I forged a letter from his father saying that he would be visiting from Switzerland to talk about the state of the business. It was easy, I just reused the envelope from a real one. I'm glad I opened that; Tristan's father isn't happy. The company's falling to pieces because of him.'

'I'm so sorry for you then.'

'Oh I don't really care about the money.'

They were nearing the top of the house. Mr Eden was breathing heavily behind her although his footsteps were almost soundless. The stairs grew narrower and narrower and the light from their lamps glowed around them in a golden sphere. At last they reached the small closed door at the top.

'Locked,' she whispered, gripping at the handle.

'It's alright. If I may...'

She squeezed herself against the wall as he inserted two slim metal prongs into the lock. With a bit of jolting and shifting the door suddenly swung open.

'Well I am impressed.'

'I've led a colourful life.'

'Yes I can quite believe that.'

The balcony door was also locked but Mr Eden opened it in even less time. He followed her outside, cramming his hefty body into the small space next to her on the balcony.

'Here, let me help you,' he said, offering her his hand and politely looking away as she hitched up her skirts to climb over.

She landed on the other side without a sound but he cast a worried eye over the railings.

'Are you alright?' she asked.

'Yes, just feeling my age.'

'Look, there isn't a keyhole on the outside of her door, just these sacks leaning against it. Hopefully it's unlocked. Let me go in first. You follow when you're ready. Just remember to be prepared for this.'

'I only hope it's not too late,' he whispered.

She could feel her heart pounding. 'Oh God, so do I!'

She heaved the heavy sacks to one side and the door opened easily. At once the stench hit her: putrid sweat and vomit and vermin.

Mrs Eden was lying on the bed. Her eyes were closed and she was quite motionless. Clutching her handkerchief over her nose Miranda touched the woman's arm with the back of her hand. It was hot. She gazed at her protruding stomach. There was the sound of a step behind her.

'She's alive, at least.'

Mr Eden was shaking and retching violently.

'Come now, Mr Eden.'

'I never thought. Or imagined! My Lucy!'

His wide body heaved back and forth with sobs, his grief filling the room.

'I know.'

'I've never seen squalor like it,' he went on.

Miranda held the lamp up to the walls. There was thick yellow mould in places and brown stains. Beneath her feet the floor was covered in droppings. Rats. Lucinda was also filthy, her hair matted into one solid lump and her nightdress wet and stained and stuck to her skin in places. She was so thin that she looked like an emaciated child, barely recognizable.

'Yes. It's quite appalling. I don't want to spend a moment longer than I have to here. Let's go downstairs and see if we can find a way out.'

She caught hold of his hand and he followed her limply down the stairs like a sorry old dog.

The rest of the house smelt better than the room at the top, but however hard she forced her handkerchief into her nostrils the smell of effluence seemed inescapable. On the first floor they passed a company of rats and she cringed against the wall. They slunk sulkily away, barely bothering to break into a run. And then the sight of the front door crept slowly into view.

For a moment she could go no further, as if her heart had stopped beating altogether. Mr Eden groaned next to her.

'This is the work of a madman.'

'Yes,' she murmured.

It had an almost mythical quality, like some sort of outrageous device from a Greek tragedy. She tried to count but quickly gave up. How many padlocks could possibly be attached to one single door frame? And there wasn't even any order or reason to them; they clung to the wood in the most haphazard way and some of them even hung from the centre of the door and in the walls like limp afterthoughts with no purpose to them at all. For the first time she felt her knees buckle under her. She took a step backwards and breathed hard.

Mr Eden disappeared into the drawing room.

'It's the same in here! We could always smash through the windows I suppose.'

'No, it will cause too great a disturbance. Is the carriage there?'

'Yes.'

'Then we'll lift her over the balcony and carry her down through my house.'

He took her elbow with a firm but comforting hand. His company at least felt reassuring; there was no need for words or excuses, just a beating urgency to leave and be done with it all.

Mrs Eden was still lying motionless in her bed when they returned. There were no blankets or clothes to wrap her in, even though it was so cold. Empty bottles were strewn everywhere and there was one rather odd looking little bottle on the bedside table, made from bluish glass and half filled with something medicinal looking. She sniffed the contents and hot tears immediately pricked up into her eyes, tickling her nose until she sneezed. Aniseed, mixed with a potent smoky flavour of some sort. She slipped it into her pocket.

'If you carry her, I'll climb over to the other side and you can then hand her to me.

Mr Eden nodded and leant down tenderly.

'She's as light as a feather,' he murmured. Her swollen belly stretched tightly under her nightdress and she let out a faint whimper.

Miranda was back over in a second and he lifted his wife into her arms like a baby. He was right, she was terrifyingly light; she could quite easily have carried her by herself.

'Now put the sacks back please,' she told him. 'And we must try to lock the other doors again. He mustn't know we came through here.'

'It shouldn't be a problem.'

But locking the balcony doors again was no easy matter; he was shaking so much that the metal prongs slipped hotly in his hands.

'Keep calm now Mr Eden, it's nearly over.'

The minutes groaned by with the length of hours. What if Tristan were to wake up now, beat the door down, discover them stealing his lover away from him? She gulped until her throat hurt.

'Done!'

'Well done. You would make a first class thief! Now just one more to go.'

'I'll have this one fixed in a second.'

Mrs Eden whimpered again in her arms; it was impossible not to crush her a little on the narrow stairs leading down from the room. Her eyelids fluttered briefly but remained closed.

'All secure, he should never guess we've been up here,' he said. 'Let me take Lucy again.'

'Yes do, but we must tread carefully; these floorboards do squeak so.'

They tiptoed softly down the stairs with their burden. On the first floor landing all still seemed quiet and motionless.

'Wait here with her, let me just make sure.'

She edged down the last staircase and pressed her ear to the dining room door. Not a sound.

'It's clear. He must still be asleep.'

Outside the carriage waited silently. Mr Eden clambered across the threshold, shoulders drooping wearily despite the weightlessness of his load. Streaks of sweat forged diagonal marks across his cheeks. Or were they tears? He seemed to have shrunk into himself, as if the exhaustion had suddenly taken over. His eyes swam and he was shaking again.

'Come with us, to Dover at least,' he pleaded. 'She needs female help and I didn't dare hire a maid. Only for a night or two...'

'I can't. It would be wholly inappropriate.'

'Please, I beg of you. You are far stronger than me. I... I can't do this on my own.'

She stared deeply into his pleading face. It was an odd sensation, to be needed so desperately; like a sudden tingling in a previously lifeless part of her body.

'Put her in the carriage and wait for me around the corner. I'll be there in fifteen minutes.'

'Thank you. We'll be waiting.'

She clasped her hands against her hot cheeks, the doors

around the hallway gaping back at her like questioning mouths. Time was ticking fast. She dashed into the drawing room and scribbled a quick note:

Jane is unwell. Must leave for a few days.

And then she raced upstairs. There was an old bag at the top of the wardrobe in her room. It smelt of dust but was big enough for a few things: a change of clothes, an extra nightdress for the patient, clean gloves, her hairbrush and a pair of sewing scissors.

She carried it down and then unlocked the dining room. The door glided open; there was Tristan, exactly where she'd left him with his face down in his plate. She poured the remaining wine from his glass and the bottle into the plant on the dresser and left them both next to him.

Around the corner of Marguerite Avenue, the carriage was waiting ahead of her. Mr Eden's silhouette loomed up from the pavement. He was talking to a small figure next to him, a raggedly dressed boy it seemed. The boy started at her footfall and scampered off.

'What were you doing?'

'He's going to put a rock through Lucinda's drawing room window. Make it look as if she escaped all by herself. No harm in making a noise now that we're safe.'

'Safe, yes,' she heard herself reply.

But as she climbed into the carriage something made her dart her head back to look behind her. Something or someone. Surely she'd felt it sweeping across her spine; a pair of keen eyes in the shadows perhaps? It made her shudder. But no, there was nothing. Nothing to see at all but stone walls and trees and shadows.

The doctor slipped out of the room like a ferret. Even his hair was smooth and shiny.

'She's extremely ill, in desperate need of nourishment although I doubt whether she'd be able to hold much down at the moment. You say she was being poisoned?'

'I think so.' Miranda reached inside her pocket for the bottle she'd found by Mrs Eden's bed. 'This is what I found.'

He sniffed at its contents with a twitch of the nose.

'I don't know it, but it's strong whatever it is. Make sure she never goes near it again.' He hesitated. 'You know she's with child. Several months gone.'

Mr Eden nodded. 'Tell me doctor. Has she any chance of surviving this?'

'I honestly can't say.'

'What can we do for her?'

'I'll give you something for her pain, of course. But my primary concern is her malnourishment. Treat that and she should make some sort of a recovery. Now, regarding my payment.'

'Of course.'

'Please excuse me,' said Miranda.

She needed to get away from the two men. What sort of a doctor was he anyway, asking outright for money like that? The man was so slippery it made her flesh creep.

Mrs Eden's breath came in soft whispers from the bed. She looked better now in the clean nightdress, but her hair was still filthy, splayed across the pillow like a piece of stranded seaweed. It was a far cry from those tendrils that had caught Tristan in their web on the night of the dinner party: beautiful shining things adorned with peacock feathers. She lifted the dirty lump of hair up with the tips of her fingers and let it fall back down with a muffled thud. It was no use, nothing would save that hair now.

The sewing scissors she'd packed were small but sharp and surprisingly easy to force through the solid clumps. In no time at all the hair was all gone and Mrs Eden re-emerged as a young boy lying against the pillow. But her face really was exquisite and without the hair it was far easier to see the sloping curve of her cheekbones, too hollow, but as pronounced and fine and symmetrical as a carving of some great ancient deity.

'How well has all this beauty served you?' Miranda whispered to her.

Her eyes flickered open.

'Do you know who I am Mrs Eden?'

'Yes. The lady on the balcony!'

Her voice was as dry and grating as coarse sand.

'The lady on the balcony? So you saw me that day. I am Tristan's wife, Miranda.'

She winced her eyes and then they filled with tears.

'Tristan.'

'We think he might have been poisoning you. You were

trapped in that room for months.'

'But I loved him!'

'I know.'

She took her dry hand.

'You need to drink. Can I give you some water? It will help you... and the baby.'

This time her eyes widened, so enormous that they turned her face into a skull.

'What baby?'

'Didn't you know – that you're carrying his child?'

Her face puckered up into what looked like a silent cry.

'Could I have some of my medicine now?' she asked in a small, childish voice.

'What medicine?'

'The droplets.'

Miranda tried to force her shoulders into a confused shrug.

'I'm afraid I don't have any droplets. What about some water or a little tea instead?'

But Mrs Eden just sobbed and groaned, arching her back repeatedly as if she was in pain.

'Is something hurting you? Mr Eden!'

The door swung open and he raced over to the bed, his face ashen.

'She's been asking for that medicine, she seems to be in some distress.'

'Let me sit with her. Oh my sweet dove – your lovely hair!' He brushed a tear away with the back of his big round fist. 'Please, go to your room and get some sleep now Mrs Whitestone. You look tired.'

'But not as tired as you. No I'll stay here.'

Mrs Eden's groans gradually decreased into whimpers until she fell fast asleep again. Miranda felt herself yawning and collapsed into the chair by the bed. A blanket appeared miraculously across her knees.

'Thank you.'

Her head flopped back against the chair and darkness rushed in. But it seemed as if only a second had passed before she felt orange brushing against her eyelids once more. The light that crept in through the flimsy curtains of the inn room was thin and watery; it was early. Two large eyes were staring back at her from the bed.

'Where have you brought me?' Mrs Eden whispered.

'I'll tell you if you agree to drink a little water.'

She nodded slowly and Miranda drew her up by the shoulders, forcing a pillow behind her head. The action reminded her of something, an old memory that pricked like needles.

Mrs Eden sipped at the water like a kitten, flinching as it moved across the deep red cracks in her lips.

'Now tell me.'

'We're staying in a small inn near Dover. Mr Eden and I brought you here because you were in danger of losing your life. We did it secretly, at night, and as soon as you are well enough your husband will be taking you abroad to recover.'

'And Tristan?'

'He doesn't know. We did it whilst he was sleeping. I think it would be best for him not to know where you are.'

She seemed to be staring at her hands. They were clasped together, a jumble of bones and joints. They were resting on her stomach and tears began to stream down her face.

'There was some medicine. Tristan gave it to me.'

'Yes I know. You were asking for it last night.'

'Please PLEASE find it!'

'I don't have it. I think it was a poison of some sort.'

'Oh help me!'

Her bony body began to convulse. Miranda reached towards the bed but Mrs Eden lunged back at her, her fingers screwed up like claws and her eyes bulging from their sockets like a madwoman. She grasped Mrs Eden's wrists with all her strength but instead of having to fight her off like some enraged tiger, the woman simply dissolved beneath her touch, as weak and defenceless as a dying moth. She collapsed against the pillows and within seconds was breathing steadily, fast asleep again.

Even in this condition, Mrs Eden was still so mesmerizing; Miranda couldn't tear her eyes away from that pale but beautiful haunted face. The door opened and Mr Eden stepped in.

'How is she?'

'Sleeping. She's very very weak.'

'I've brought you some food and some news as well. A nurse will be arriving from France tomorrow morning. She can take over Lucinda's care and then transport her back across the channel with me. I don't want anyone else in this country knowing about her, the news could easily get back to your...'

'Husband.'

'Yes.'

'So you only need me until tomorrow then.'

'You don't have to stay...'

'I will. As ugly as this situation is it soothes me somehow to know that I've done something right.'

'But you never did anything wrong! You've shown more kindness and selflessness through all of this than I thought was humanly imaginable.'

'Stop, before you make me cry,' she croaked. He was smiling so kindly back at her. 'Now you said you had some food.'

'Are you hungry?'

'Famished.'

Mrs Eden slept for most of the day. Whenever her eyes flickered open Miranda did her best to feed drops of water and weak tea into her mouth. The night drew in and her breath grew deeper and steadier as she slept. Miranda lit candles, ready to see the night out in her chair by the bed. At three o'clock in the morning Mrs Eden finally woke up.

'How are you feeling?'

'A little hungry I think.'

'That's good. Here try this small piece of bread.'

She bit off a tiny morsel and shifted it drily around in her mouth.

'Why are you helping me?'

'I'm not sure.'

'Do you pity me?'

'In a way. Nobody deserves such treatment, although your behaviour was as despicable as his at first.'

'I just wanted to be happy.'

'By stealing another woman's husband? Do you know nothing of how to behave in decent society?'

She murmured a soft laugh. 'I am a product of *decent society*.'

Miranda reached forward to take the bread away, but Mrs Eden grasped her hand.

'It's alright, I'm not going to attack you again. May I ask, do you have a mother?'

'No.'

'What happened to her?'

'She was ill. Someone gave her the wrong medicine and she died.'

'So we both missed out then. Mine died too, because she was bored and lonely. I think, if I survive, I would be a rather disgraceful mother. Don't you agree?'

'It's not for me to say.'

'You would be a very good mother, Miranda.'

She looked so beautiful again, her eyes as soft and trusting as a baby's. Miranda stroked her dry cheek and she fell asleep beneath her hand.

The morning came with grey clouds and drizzle. It was time for her to leave, pack up her things and put on the few fresh clothes she had remaining. In the mirror new lines had gathered like ripples in a stream around her eyes. They looked like friendly lines though; perhaps there was a funny sort of beauty to her ugliness after all.

A short time later she heard footsteps in the corridor. Mr Eden's familiar face suddenly filled the doorway and then from behind him a small neat looking woman with dark hair hurried in. The woman nodded courteously and perched in the chair by Mrs Eden's bedside. Her chair. She caught at a lump in her throat and left quickly.

Mr Eden's broad back led her downstairs and out onto the narrow street. She hadn't ventured outside since their arrival and after the sick-room the cold fresh air hit her face like a sharp slap of icy water. A carriage was waiting. Her hand slid into his palm.

'Thank you so much,' he said.

She felt her chin tremble.

'I'll take her to Paris, we have some friends living on an old farm just outside the city. But I think it's for the best if we don't remain in contact. I hope you understand. It's for her safety and yours.'

'Yes of course.'

'One last thing. When I first came to you, looking for my wife, I gave you a sealed letter for Lucinda. It contains information about your husband's past. Please do read it. I implore you to read it! Of course it's your decision what to do, but I advise you to remain as far away from that man as possible.'

He gave her a small bow and her eyes blurred as the carriage moved away. Soon she could see nothing but the shimmer of his waistcoat, radiant with turquoise and blue; just like the peacock feathers she'd once seen in his wife's hair.

The journey home was long and tiring. It was impossible to rest; the carriage jerked her bones about too much and her body felt cold and shivery. There was a blanket but its bristles scratched at her and it seemed to give no warmth at all. Her feet had turned into icy blocks of granite. She screwed her eyes shut and tried to summon up the memory of warmth.

Italy. Their honeymoon. Orange trees and the sparkling sea and those delicious almond biscuits which they'd found in their hotel room. People had smiled at them when they'd arrived; she'd even taken hold of Tristan's hand, clasping onto it stubbornly.

Their hotel room had been smaller than they'd hoped for, but with a stunning view and the sea lapping against the rocks below. As a child she would have imagined mermaids sliding blissfully through the small triangular waves.

'Shall we perhaps take a rest darling?' she'd asked, her face turning scarlet.

'No, I'm fine. This room is rather small don't you think?'

'Yes, but so pretty and how wonderful to be able to look out at the sea.'

She'd raised her hand falteringly towards his shirt collar.

'Well it's far too small for me. There's an empty room next door, I think I'll go and see if I can get that one for myself.'

'If that's how you feel darling, then we'll both move together!'

'No, you seem to like it here. I wouldn't want to spoil that for you.'

The journey had been strained and unloving enough but she'd felt sure that things would change once they arrived. She was wrong. She'd come to Italy with nothing but the shell of a husband. The real man had stayed somewhere behind and that absence had suddenly sucked every last trace of warmth from the lovely air. She'd felt as cold then as she did now, shivering in the back of a carriage. An entire marriage of separate bedrooms and closed doors.

'One day I will have a house with no doors or locks inside it at all,' she murmured softly to herself.

At last the carriage rumbled down Marguerite Avenue and

then, once again, she was peering up at her home. Her body ached to turn around and run away.

'Hello.'

The voice seemed to have come from the direction of a cluster of charms and small coloured bottles hanging from a chain. They glinted against a backdrop of purple velvet: beads with evil eyes, feathers, a silver skull and little bottles, green and orange and blue, with delicate silver tops, all hanging jumbled together.

She followed the chain up and up until she found a small face at the top crowned by a halo of wispy hair. Of course she knew the face well. She'd seen it enough times on its way next door, but never close-up like this.

It was a very small face considering the extreme dimensions of the body beneath it and lined like a walnut, the eyes black pinpricks with barely any eyelashes to frame them at all. But although it was an ugly face, it was in no way threatening and it gazed down at her with a rather worried looking expression, as if she were the one who appeared to be at odds.

'Hello,' she replied. She wobbled a little and for a moment his face split into two identical twins.

'Are you alright?'

'Yes, just very tired. I've been looking after my sister, she's ill.'

'I'm so sorry. My name is Walter Balanchine. I'm a friend of Mrs Eden's father.'

He nodded in the direction of Lucinda's house. The front door and windows had all been forced open.

'I believe she was your neighbour,' he went on. 'You do live at 34?'

'I do.'

'Yes. I've often seen you sewing in the window.'

He edged towards her and she found that she couldn't move her legs. The bottles around his neck became even clearer; they contained powders and liquids.

'May I ask what it is that you do?' she said.

'Yes, of course. I mend broken souls.'

He was watching her intently, those tiny eyes of his drawing her gaze into them. She couldn't bring herself to look away. She didn't want to. It felt so comforting, as if he'd leaned forwards suddenly and cupped her tired head in his hands.

'All those things around your neck. Are you a doctor?'

'Of a sort.'

'Then perhaps you can help me with something.' The bottle of poison hugged her hand from inside her pocket. 'Find out what this is, please.'

'Of course.'

'My name is Mrs Whitestone.'

'But I shall call you Miranda.'

'How did you know that?'

'Your eyes told me. You clearly need some rest, it's a long way from Dover. Go inside and I'll come back soon.'

'Yes... How did you know I came from Dover Mr Balanchine?'

'It was a good guess. But please, call me Walter. Rest now, as I said I'll come again soon.'

With a blink he set her free and her legs felt full of blood again, strong enough to walk up to her front door, climb up to her lonely old bedroom and slide open her dresser drawer. There inside was the envelope with *Lucinda* written on the front in Mr Eden's hand.

SERENA'S STORY

'Come on Beth, you've got to be scared of something!' Seb exclaimed from across the dining table.

'Nooo,' she nibbled on a breadstick. 'I can't think of anything.'

'Not even monsters?'

'Or large bloody wounds oozing with blood?'

'Robert! Don't terrify the child on her birthday!' said Arabella.

'Noooope.'

'As I was saying... everyone's got a phobia,' continued Edward. 'Beth just hasn't discovered hers yet. I have one.'

'Do you dear?' Arabella looked around the table with stunned eyes. 'I never knew.'

'Yes, I do: the sound of two pieces of polystyrene squeaking against each other. Makes the hairs on my arms stand on end. I have to leave the room.'

'Goodness, after all these years of marriage I never knew. But does that really count as a phobia?'

Robert smiled authoritatively. 'I would say so. It's not unlike the fear of fingernails scratching the surface of a blackboard. Doesn't bother me, but spiders do.'

'Boring!' bellowed Edward. 'Spiders, snakes, I've heard it all before. Anyone got something more interesting to add?'

'Serena's got a good phobia,' said Seb quietly.

An array of expectant faces landed on me.

'Do I?' I stammered. 'I wasn't aware of one.'

'Yes you do: broken glass. You hate broken glass.'

'Is that true?' Edward asked.

'Yes, in a way. It makes me want to cry when I see it, or be sick. I don't know, one of the two.'

'Broken glass, that is a good one,' he mused. 'Well you win, a round of applause for Serena.'

They all began to clap heartily and I tried to make a gracious bow.

'That's a very pretty necklace Beth, is it new?' asked Eva.

Beth was wearing a delicate little Celtic cross around her neck which I hadn't seen before either.

143

'Yes! Raphael left it here for me for my birthday. I've been waiting all this time to open it. Aren't I good?!'

She blinked softly at us all with her innocent blue eyes and Seb began to laugh, so infectiously that in a moment we were all laughing too.

'Ah! Am I interrupting anything?' came a voice. Sasha was standing in the doorway, his eyes fixed on Eva.

'Can I keep my necklace on tonight?'

I tucked the blanket under Beth's chin. It had turned cold and I could hear rain scratching at the windows. 'Yes, I suppose so. But take care of it. It really does look very special.'

The pendant rested in the small cave between her two collar bones: a thin spider's web of silver crafted into a cross with a ring around the centre.

'Night night darling. Happy birthday.'

I tiptoed down the stairs. Gladys would be sorting out the kitchen and, as we'd planned Beth's birthday meal together, she could at least let me help her clear up for once.

When I reached the first floor I noticed that Arabella's office door hadn't been shut properly. A well of light from the room scorched across the corridor carpet and up the wall, just brushing the edge of the painting of Walter Balanchine on the opposite side. Although the picture was bathed in shadow I could still detect the vivid hues of his wizard-like garments and the cluster of trinkets around his neck. The picture drew me closer.

'Why do you do this Mummy? First you let that bastard in and now her! They love her you know, how are we ever going to get rid of her?' It was Eva's voice, coming from Arabella's office. My feet glued themselves to the spot.

'How on earth could I have known what she'd be like?'

'You shouldn't have employed anyone in the first place! I told you time and time again not to let a stranger in.'

'Beth needs looking after, and some sort of an education.'

'And couldn't we have done that?'

'Hardly. You know how busy I am and you wouldn't have a clue. Serena's bright.'

'Well thank you very much. And you know Sasha's at it again: threatening me one minute, his hands all over me the next. He says he'll go to the tabloids.'

'Oh dear, really? And I thought I'd been keeping him busy with my Africa stuff for once.'

'Oh screw your Africa stuff! He's been going on about Raphael again and the Burnside money. What the hell am I to do? I'm still the only one in this house who doesn't pander to that bloody man but I don't know if I can take much more.'

'Keep them close darling. It's the only way.'

'How bloody close do you intend him to get! I can feel his breath on me MOTHER, right now. It's so real I could vomit. And just remember, if you hadn't kept Sasha quite so *close* in the first place, then he wouldn't have found out all this stuff about us.'

There was a biting pause before Arabella spoke again, now in a slightly shaky voice. 'I am aware of that, darling. Sometimes we cannot help but fall into our mistakes; you know that too... But even if we talk about it until we're blue in the face, the main thing to remember is that still, after all these years, Sasha has remained perfectly blind to it all. And that's all that matters.'

'But *she* isn't, which is even worse. And to cap it all you've asked her for Christmas! Is there no escaping her?'

'Keep them close darling. God, the door's open.'

I heard footsteps and dived back, pressing my body into the recess of the next door along. In the corner of my eye I saw Arabella poke her head out and look up and down the corridor. She slammed the door shut and muffled footsteps moved away again.

I waited for a minute and then made my escape, down into the light of downstairs.

Keep them close.

It was like that old saying: *Keep your friends close and your enemies closer.* Is that what Arabella had meant?

My feet carried me to the kitchen but Gladys soon saw that I was no use to her there.

'Go to bed, you look ill.'

She was right. I must have looked like a zombie shuffling around behind her in a haze, putting things in cupboards and then taking them out again for no reason. I mumbled an excuse and left, taking solace in my sketchbook.

Eva's face appeared before me from my pencil for the first time, her gaunt cheeks hugely exaggerated, her eyebrows arched in anger. But when I drew her eyes they peeked out at me, soft and sad. I had wanted to fill them with wrath, hatred, anything ugly and cruel and yet instead they welled up with tears.

That night Seb took me in his arms. I ached to tell him about what I'd heard but couldn't face fighting about Eva yet again.

'Thanks for organizing this evening. Beth thought it was great, she loves you. I love you,' he said.

'Do you really mean that?'

'I wouldn't have said it otherwise.'

'I think I'm trying to live in a world that isn't my own. Is the bubble going to burst soon?'

'No. Does that mean you don't love me?'

I could see lines of agitation, panic even, on his face.

'You know I do. I can't remember a time when I didn't love you.'

I pressed my forehead against his and we fell asleep together, but in the morning he was gone.

The internet café was just off the high street. I found a quiet place in the corner and drank bad coffee from a polystyrene cup. The first thing I searched for was *Burnside money*, just as Eva had said it.

A few old articles about a Lord Burnside popped up at the top, but most of them now led to nowhere and had lost their content. One, however, from a financial bulletin and entitled, *Where did all their money go?* still remained intact. This Lord Burnside it seems had masterminded some sort of rogue pension scheme, swindling all sorts of poor people out of their life-savings before disappearing to South America. I scrolled down the entries but found out nothing more.

And then I tried *Lord Burnside* and *Hartreve* together. As the results came up I almost took a large bite out of the cup I was sipping from. Again, the articles were mainly old and lost, but the titles alone were enough to throw a great big spotlight over Eva's past. *Lecherous Lord Spawns Hartreve Baby*, was the first. It was dated five years back, coinciding perfectly with Beth's birth. *Lord Cradle-Snatcher Gets Heiress into Trouble*, was the second. The next article came up with a picture of Eva on it, looking particularly young and winsome in black and white. The journalist described her teenage pregnancy as the *undisputed* result of an affair with her father

Edward Hartreve's acquaintance Lord Burnside. Eva was described as a *spoilt, rich brat*, who had snubbed *loony* Lady Burnside's repeated efforts to clear her husband's name. It finished with the lines:

> *So, how did the mysterious Lord escape the country with the police hot on his heels? Not with the help of Edward Hartreve, that's for sure, or any of those poor old pensioners he screwed over either. But clearly Lord Burnside still has friends somewhere, South America better watch out.*

I swung back in my chair and read it over and over again. I'd been wrong about Sasha being Beth's father then, if these articles were to be believed. But Sasha was clearly involved in this somewhere along the line. He'd been threatening Eva about the *Burnside money* after all. Could this be something to do with those dodgy pensions? Where had Burnside's money ended up?

I looked at my watch. Jessica would be arriving soon to visit me, I didn't want to be late. But there was one more thing I wanted to look up before I left. Even his old-fashioned, funny sounding name made me want to smile when I typed it in: *Walter Balanchine.*

This time the result was quite literally breathtaking. I felt a buzzing in my ears, excitement and astonishment all cocktailed up together. This was how detectives must feel when they're onto a good lead, or explorers at the gateway of a newly discovered tomb. There at the top of the page I read:

> *Discussions on 'Walter Balanchine and the Art of Hypnosis,' a lecture by Sasha Apostol.*

I let the cursor hover over the word *Sasha* for a moment and then clicked.

The link led to a lengthy dialogue on an academic chat room about hypnosis. In spite of its title the discussion seemed to focus only briefly on Sasha's work, citing him as an *esteemed lecturer* and Walter Balanchine as a... *colourful East End character born to eastern European parents, an early devotee to the art of hypnosis and the act of disappearance.* And yet further down, in spite of Sasha's apparent academic prowess, he was criticized for... *not having yet uncovered enough material to reveal more about his subject. Perhaps he will go on to find something more meaty about this elusive Victorian mystic.*

That was all. I grabbed my coat and dashed out onto the

street; definitely late for Jessica now. It had turned chilly and with every gust of wind leaves with sad faces floated down about me. I squinted my eyes and tried to imagine this man Walter Balanchine, in his funny wizard-like clothes, kicking up the leaves along the London streets before me. Perhaps he had Lord Hartreve by his side, or his daughter Lucinda.

Sasha seemed to know an awful lot about the Hartreve family. Enough to threaten Eva with in his creepy lustful way. But the one thing he didn't seem to know enough about was this man, Walter Balanchine. Was this what he was *blind to*, as Arabella had remarked? Is this what he really wanted? But the thing that made no sense at all was why I was such a threat as well.

I could see Jessica already standing on the doorstep as I approached the house.

'Hello!' I called, jogging up to her.

'There you are! I knocked but no one answered.'

'That's funny, I thought Gladys was in. Beth's been taken out to buy clothes so it's probably just us. Oh it's so lovely to see you!' I gave her a great bear-hug. 'Come on in. Sorry I'm late, I was at an internet café messing around.'

'What happened to your laptop?'

'Oh, I sold it to buy some canvases. Too lovely to resist.'

'Typical! Ah, you're wearing the peony brooch I gave you.'

'I wear it all the time.'

Now that we were inside I hugged her again. I could smell the familiar scent of home on her clothes: lavender mixed with a sort of generic washing-up aroma. I felt a sudden surprising pang.

'What a glorious house,' she murmured as I pulled her into the drawing room.

'It is, isn't it? Come and take a seat.'

'Isn't it extraordinary that there isn't a number 34?' She collapsed into one of the deep sofas. 'I almost thought that this house didn't exist and I'd fallen on the wrong Marguerite Avenue.'

Good old Jessica to notice. 'I know. I had that problem too the first time.'

'Is there a reason?'

'I don't know... there's all sorts of stories. Maybe it was war damage.'

'But these roads didn't suffer, all the houses are Victorian and pretty much intact. I could try and find out the real reason.'

'How?'

'Oh census records, old documents, a bit of digging about. Remember that old genealogy course I did?'

'When you found out that our ancestors were a bunch of no-good criminals?'

'Yes,' she said, bubbling up with laughter. 'It was fascinating though. I loved it!' Her laughter simmered down and she gave me a long, thoughtful glance. 'So what's changed with you?' she asked softly.

'What do you mean?'

'You seem different. I hardly hear from you. Either they're working you like a slave or you've met someone.'

'Not a slave, no. Beth is lovely, very old for her age. Her mother Eva's a sort of society princess, too busy partying to have much to do with her. She's going out with a Russian oligarch at the moment apparently, although I haven't met him. The whole family's a bit eccentric.'

Jessica's eyes glistened. 'So it must be the other thing then, that's changed you.'

'What other thing?'

'You've met someone.'

My cheeks went hot and I tried to look away.

'Oh I was right!' she exclaimed, clapping her hands together.

'Yes. But I wasn't going to tell you about him yet. It's early days and... a bit tricky.'

She gave me a pursed smile and nodded slowly.

'Well I hope he's nice.'

'He is.'

'And good looking.'

'Very.'

'And has a good job.'

'Um... yes.'

'He sounds lovely. I can't wait to meet him.'

I tried to say something back in agreement, but the strangest feeling of emptiness in my stomach, as if the best party ever was coming to an end, suddenly stopped me.

'Jess,' I said in a quiet voice, glancing for a moment at the door. 'Would you really be able to find out something about the house? You know, about the missing number next door?'

That evening I still felt too tied up by my own thoughts to take much notice of Seb when he came to my room. He kissed me with eager lips, tried to pull me towards him, but then let go when he felt my resistance.

'What's the matter?'

'Nothing.'

'How did it go with your aunt?'

'Alright. I told her about you. She asked a few questions, one about whether you had a good job.'

He paused, his eyes lapping at my face.

'Look,' I faltered. 'I know that you don't work. And that you don't like to be questioned about... anything really. But don't you think it's odd that I have no idea what you actually do?'

'I don't do anything.'

'Then where do you go when you leave this room every morning? Surely you must go somewhere, do something?'

'Serena, where is all this coming from? One meeting with your aunt and now you're badgering me. You've completely changed in one afternoon!'

His face looked grey suddenly, tired and almost haggard. I felt the urge to comb my fingers through his hair, draw myself closer to his cool skin.

I'm sorry, I whispered in the recess of my mind and his answer echoed instantly back to me.

It's alright.

'There just seem to be so many secrets in this house,' I murmured.

'Don't worry about secrets.'

'I do when they cause a person to hate me.'

'Who hates you?'

'Eva.'

He rolled his eyes and threw back his head. 'Oh I wish you'd just stop!'

'How can I when she's desperate to get me out of this house?'

'What's wrong with you?'

'There's nothing wrong with me. I overheard something the other night. They see me as a threat here, either to be got rid of or kept close. I don't know, do you? There was stuff about Sasha and Raphael and money, and me all wrapped up in it. God, it makes me feel sick! Seb, please, just take my side. Help me, do something.'

I waited for him to reply but got nothing.

'Look, maybe you should go for tonight,' I said, disappointment grating through my voice. 'I think I need to be alone.'

I turned my back to him, praying at the same time that he would come to me, put a hand on my shoulder, explain it all away. But the gamble didn't pay off. Instead I heard his footsteps move back towards the window in quiet retreat. A second later I knew he was gone.

In the empty room a bubble of loneliness seemed to grow instantly around me. When eventually I managed to lie down on my cold bed it moved with me. It got in the way of my blankets and laughed at my attempts to sleep.

Beth glared down at her new dress again for the fiftieth time.

'I really don't want to go.'

'I know.'

'No, you don't understand. I really really don't want to go.'

My temperature was rising. 'Listen, it's only a birthday party. Children need to play with other children, particularly at parties. Now, we're not far from home, nine houses away to be precise and I'm sure this little girl is very nice.'

The door swung open and a woman in tight white trousers with smiley white teeth grinned at us.

'So you must be Beth from down the Avenue!' she declared.

Beth offered up her confused, wrinkled up nose expression in response.

'Thank you so much for inviting us. Here's a present for Fifi.'

Beyond Mrs Seddlescombe's shoulder a tribe of children in bright party clothes were running around chaotically and doing handstands against the wall.

'Oh thanks, do come in. Will you be staying with Beth or would you prefer to pick her up later?'

Beth shot me a glance, her eyes huge and frightened looking.

'I'll stay for now, if that's alright.'

The house was so different from 36. Although its size and shape felt almost the same, it had been more recently decorated in glacial pastels and designer furnishings. A flat screen television peered blankly from the drawing room wall and speakers in

STEPHANIE ELMAS

undisclosed places blared out Disney music as children jumped up and down stuffing sweets and marshmallows into their mouths.

Beth teetered listlessly in the middle of it all and my heart ached for her. She didn't even try and play with the others and they seemed to sidestep her, as if she were someone's rather uninteresting older sister whom nobody could be bothered to talk to. Then a woman in lots of pink nylon and a pair of wings danced into the room brandishing a plastic wand.

'Hello my little fairies! Who's coming to play in fairyland?' she cried.

'Meeeee!' came a unanimous chorus and a tide of children rushed towards her, sweeping Beth along with them. Suddenly they were all gone.

The glossy-eyed television smirked back at me and I stuck my tongue out at it. The music had stopped in this room and was now whining on in another part of the house. A crushed biscuit teetered on the arm of a chair.

Two whole weeks of nothing. Two whole weeks without Seb. I must have drawn a hundred pictures of him in that time. Not the laughing carefree face I knew but expressions of hurt, loss, emotions I didn't even know he had until they appeared like magic through the end of my pen. I kept trying to build a brick wall in my mind, somewhere to push even the thought of his face behind, but those blue eyes just jumped right back out at me every time. I studied my hands, tried to bend my fingers. Every muscle ached.

'Can I have a word with you please, Miss?' boomed a voice.

I looked up to find Mrs Seddlescombe marching through the room towards me. At the end of her outstretched arm Beth was being dragged along by the wrist. The woman's white smiley teeth had completely vanished.

'I've never seen anything like it.'

'I'm sorry?'

Her lips appeared to be quivering with anger.

'Corporal punishment? In fairyland? I have an entire room of crying children in there. I mean I know you're only the nanny but someone must have put ideas like that into this child's head.'

Beth was staring down at the floor, her hair straggling over her face.

'She's... not all that used to other children. I'm so sorry. We'd better leave.'

152

'I should think so. Good Lord! I... I have to get back to them all now.'

Finally she unleashed Beth's wrist and almost ran out of the room.

Beth and I said nothing about it on the way home. I couldn't bring myself to tell her off and, after all, it was my fault for forcing her to go in the first place. When we got back Sasha was slouched in the drawing room reading a newspaper.

'Pasha!' whimpered Beth, the tears finally flowing.

'What is it my little bee?'

She rushed into his arms, burying her face in his neck.

'We had a bit of a bad time at the party,' I said, scooping up the newspaper which he'd tossed to one side. 'The children didn't take to each other too well.'

'Now now, you just tell Papa Sasha everything and he'll make it better. Don't you cry my little bee, don't you cry.'

I needed a cigarette. I escaped the room for the bench in the garden, still clutching the newspaper that Sasha had been reading. It was folded into quarters, one side covered in fragments of sports news and the other framing an article with the headline: *Burglary at the V&A*. I began to read:

A valuable collection of antique Celtic jewellery has gone missing from archives at the Victoria and Albert Museum in London. As the pieces have not been displayed for over a year, staff at the museum cannot be sure of when the items actually went missing. They might have been stolen weeks, or even months ago, making it extremely hard to track down the thieves. The collection, consisting of many rare silver crosses, is one of a kind...

I drank the words in again: *antique Celtic jewellery... rare silver crosses...* and remembered that little cross nestling in the dip between Beth's collar bones. Raphael's birthday present to her.

The last time I'd sat on this bench had been that night with Raphael. The memory of those dark, bruised eyes shot through me, and those lips coming dangerously close to mine.

I looked over at the fence separating the Hartreve's garden from next door and the rendered side of the extension which jutted out behind it. Had I really seen a wall there instead; an old wall cascading with jasmine petals? Or had it been a dream?

I tossed the end of my cigarette away and went indoors. Beth and Sasha had both disappeared from the drawing room. The house felt deserted.

Most beautiful things are stolen; it makes them more captivating.

Raphael's words on the night of the party, when he'd told me about the missing Habsburg gems. I pictured us on that motorbike again, inches from catastrophe and yet glorious in our moment.

I climbed two steps at a time up to my room and found it again at the bottom of a drawer: the cluster of jasmine buds I'd picked that night. They were a little yellow and wrinkled up from the way I'd crushed them, but dry now and still sweet-smelling nonetheless. No, it hadn't been a dream.

Darkness fell. Beth's room was empty and it was nearly her bedtime. Further down Arabella's office door was closed with no light emanating from behind the stained glass window. All of them seemed to be gone. I trudged all the way to the bottom of the house. The drawing room and the library were empty too.

And then suddenly I heard a quiet step behind me. Two cool hands swept around my face and covered my eyes. I knew their touch instantly.

'Seb.'

'We're alone. Edwards's taken them all out to cheer Beth up.'

'I thought I'd lost you.'

'Come with me.'

My body tingled at the thought of him standing behind me. He coaxed me forward and I walked blindly into what felt like the direction of the dining room.

'OK, ready?' he asked.

'Ready for what?'

'For this.'

He took his hands away and I gasped out loud. The room was full of coloured paper lanterns, and the candles inside them cast kaleidoscopic rays of light across the walls of the room.

'Do you like it?'

'It's magical. A real fairyland.'

His face was pink and blue and yellow in the light.

'I feel like Alice in Wonderland.'

'Does that make me the White Rabbit?'

'No, more of a Mad Hatter.'

I pulled his arms around me and kissed him. The touch of his lips after so long brought tears to my eyes.

'Come on let me pour you some champagne. And look there are smoked salmon sandwiches and chocolate cake. All your favourite things!'

My head was spinning with happiness.

'I've got a present for you as well,' he said. 'I've been thinking hard over the past weeks about what I can do to prove how much I love you. It's silly really but here we go.'

He retrieved a flat leather pouch from his pocket and emptied it onto the table. A few old coins and two photographs slid out face down.

'Ah, here it is!' he said, flipping one of the pictures over. It was a photograph of Eva and Raphael.

'I don't understand,' I muttered.

'I've carried this photo around with me for years. These people are very special to me, like a family,' he said thoughtfully. He gazed at their faces, a deep groove forming between his eyes. He looked haggard again, just like on the night of our argument, as if he'd suddenly gained fifteen years in as many seconds. Then, with a sudden fluid movement, he whipped away a nearby lantern and held the photograph to the exposed flame until it had burned and smouldered into nothing but a curl of ash.

'Why did you do that?'

'The other week, when we argued, you said that you wanted me to take your side. Well, I have now. You're the most sensational thing that could have happened to me.'

The lanterns flickered and their glow felt like treacle against my skin.

'You didn't have to burn the picture for me.'

'Well it's done now,' and all the light flooded back into his face again. 'Right, is there anything else you'd like to discuss before I rip all the clothes off that fabulous body of yours?'

'What about the sandwiches? Could get messy.'

'Bugger the sandwiches.'

'Actually there is something else.'

'Damn.'

'It's OK, won't take a second. I just wondered who that other picture was of?' and I nodded my head at the other photo that had fallen out of the leather pouch.

He handed it to me. It was a black and white portrait of a woman and extremely old judging by the austere, high-necked gown she was wearing. She looked middle-aged, not particularly attractive with a rather weak chin, but she had soft, benevolent looking eyes and there was something pleasant about her smile and the agreeable way she confronted the camera.

'Who is she?' I asked.

'Her name was Miranda White. A rather special person in my family once.'

'Why do you carry it around with you?'

'Because I've always admired her. She has a lovely face, don't you agree?'

'Yes, I know what you mean.'

'Don't ever stop loving me. Don't ever lose faith in me,' Seb implored when our bodies came together that night.

'No, of course not. Why do you sound so scared?'

'I never want to let you go, that's all.'

We held each other so tightly that it hurt and I made a silent promise to myself to stop prying. Stop bothering him with questions.

I fell into a groggy champagne-fuelled sleep, although at first I kept trying to wake myself up, over and over again, just to check he was still there. When at last sleep took hold of me properly, I dreamt of jasmine and piano music and the smell of home. But then, just like a house of cards tumbling to ruin, my dreams suddenly fell apart and turned into a painful nightmare. It started at my throat, a dead-weight pressing down relentlessly. It seemed as if I was drowning and I tried to push myself up to the surface, my arms frantically thrashing about. And then it moved down to my chest, so heavy that my lungs seem to shrivel up beneath it.

I heard wheezing, sleep fell away and all at once I found myself choking and spluttering, flat on my back in my bed. And yet somewhere through my noise I could hear voices. I rolled onto my side hugging my chest, lapping the air back into my lungs. My eyes were streaming but through the tears I thought I could see Seb talking, no arguing, with someone: a figure at the end of my bed. The room was so dark, but Seb's movements seemed jerky and agitated.

'Seb?' I gasped.

Two pairs of luminous eyes fell on me, like cats in the night and a scream rose up in my throat. The figure dissolved into darkness but I'd seen enough to know that it was him: the same man who'd watched me in my bed when Seb and I had first slept together. There was no mistaking the shadowy, grimacing subject of Raphael's paintings.

And then Seb was sitting on the bed again, stroking my face.

'Are you alright?'

'That man, was it him? I think... I think he was trying to strangle me. It must have been him, where is he?' I clutched my hands around my sore neck.

'What man? What are you talking about?' Seb drew his brows together with a confused look.

'The man you were talking to just now, at the end of my bed.'

'You've had too much to drink darling, and look, you've been a bit sick in your sleep. That's what you were choking on. Have some water, does your head hurt?'

'Yes, it aches,' I fell back against the pillow.

'Don't worry my love, there's no one here, apart from me of course. You must have been dreaming. Look, lie here, where it's clean, and go back to sleep.'

1892

Backwards and forwards, slipping and sliding. A little scrape at the crust to brush off the excess left on the knife. Then smooth out the excess, slipping and sliding again. Eyes locked in concentration, hand jerking yet determined.

'Gracious, soon the layer of butter will be thicker than the toast itself.'

'Yes.'

Tristan dropped the knife as if it were a hot coal, snatching up his cup of tea instead. But half its contents was already slopping about in the saucer and some began to dribble down onto his lap.

She looked over at the clock. 'It's half past nine dear. You should have left for work half an hour ago.'

'Absolutely.'

He sprang up from his seat but then hovered in the middle of the room scraping his unkempt hair back with his fingers and looking lost.

'Did you hear a voice?' he said.

'No.'

'Then I'll go right now. Wouldn't want to be late!'

His abandoned teacup tremored in its mucky puddle as he slammed the door behind him.

'Have a lovely day.'

The orchids on the windowsill had started to bloom. Miranda stroked their petals to try and steady her nerves. He'd be here soon.

One of the corners of the letter in her pocket prodded at her thigh like a stern finger.

My Darling Lucinda, I am writing this letter with such heaviness and concern for you...

Those lines were beginning to plague her.

You see I have heard more news...

No, it was ... *some more news...* surely?

Her fingers sneaked down towards the envelope; its edges were beginning to feel rather fuzzy.

Read me! It begged constantly. *Read me again, just to make sure!*

'Oh very well. But this is the last time today and then I'm shoving you in the fire!'

My Darling Lucinda,

I am writing this letter with such heaviness and concern for you. You see I have heard more news about this man Tristan Whitestone, news which has alarmed your old Alfonso immensely.

But first and foremost WHERE HAVE YOU GONE my dear Lucinda? No one has seen nor heard from you in these past months. The house is dark... empty I think. I am sick with worry for you my darling, sick with worry. And now I shall explain why.

It took some digging to find him, a man by the name of Hughes living in a quiet spot out by Epsom. A newly retired policeman, still deeply tanned and accustoming himself to the cold life back at home. He'd been in India for the best part of twenty years and he knew our man out there, Tristan Whitestone, only too well.

'I'd never seen anything like it, in all my professional life,' he told me, with a sombre shake of the head. But it took several bottles of rum to get him going, not that he drank them then and there. Oh no. 'Keeping them for my missus,' he said. 'When her chest plays up in the winter.'

Clementine Mandeville. Has your Mr Whitestone ever mentioned this name to you my Lucinda? She was a high ranking Bombay wife, auburn haired, extremely beautiful and a woman with a 'playful eye,' according to Hughes. Read what you will into that.

Her affair with Whitestone caused nothing short of an earthquake in that tight colonial circle. 'I'd known him for going for the local girls many a time but never one of his own, and certainly not another man's wife! Thought he was cleverer than that,' were Hughes's precise words on the subject.

But people's fury, it seemed, gradually withered to a mild concern when reports of Mrs Mandeville's condition and whereabouts became more and more hazy. Eventually news began to circulate that an English woman was being kept in one of the slums. This was when Hughes was brought in in a professional manner.

'I found her all locked up in a filthy hovel. Had to break the door down to get in. Oh it was a dreadful sight, she was that thin! Delirious

with something in her blood and a tiny baby by her side.'

I could detect paleness even beneath his ruddy tan as he recounted the story.

Mrs Mandeville died Lucinda! And Whitestone escaped without her testimony or a trace of evidence holding him accountable. A clever fellow after all. Oh this man is not safe. Where are you now? I will make one last attempt at delivering this letter and then, if I have not heard from you within a week, I too will turn to the police. Please forgive me, but you are and always will be at the forefront of my concern.

Alfonso.

'There's a man at the door asking for you,' said Mrs Hubbard. 'A very peculiar looking individual, I'm not sure if he...'

'It's alright, I've had a note from him. He's a sort of doctor. Please don't be alarmed.'

Walter Balanchine swept into the room, his broad-brimmed hat tucked beneath his arm. He looked even taller indoors, like a circus character on stilts. He eyed the letter in her hand and she slid it back into her pocket.

'Thank you for agreeing to see me Miranda and my apologies for it having taken me so long. The potion you gave me was a rare one but I think I can tell you something about it now.'

'Oh no, I must apologize for handing it to you in the first place. I'm rather embarrassed... I was very tired that day. Exhausted in fact.'

'Would you like to sit down?' he said.

'Oh yes please! Although shouldn't I be asking you to do that? Um, do you drink tea?'

'Generally not.'

He had an appealing voice. Rather soft, with a vaguely effeminate London slur, but there was something foreign mixed up in it as well. Hard to tell from where. Green was clearly his choice of colour today: green suit, green sweeping cloak and a green emerald pinned into his tie. When he sat down even an expanse of green stocking poked out from beneath one of his trouser legs. He wasn't really a man at all; more an exotic sort of bird, ugly and beautiful at the same time.

'May I ask you a personal question?' she said.

He raised his eyebrows in response.

'Why do you dress like that?'

'Like what?'

'Like... well. And where exactly do you come from?'

'From East London. Limehouse. But my family were immigrants, from the other side of Europe.'

'Limehouse. I've never been there, although I have never been anywhere much.'

'Then let me take you. You will find it very different; people from all over the world land-up there.'

'I hear there are opium dens.'

'Yes. I could take you to one of those as well if you prefer.'

'Oh goodness gracious no!'

If only they could drink tea or eat cake or something. It would take the emphasis away from his eyes a little which were so intense that she felt quite stripped to her bones.

'You will find nothing in an opium den half so noxious as the substance in this bottle,' he murmured. And as if by magic the bottle of poison she'd handed to him on her return from Dover appeared in his palm. It made her start to see the thing again.

'What is it, a poison I assume?'

He placed it carefully down on the table with long white fingers.

'Before I tell you, would you mind me asking how it fell into your possession?'

'I'm afraid that's a private matter.'

'Did it belong to your husband?'

'I...' She had to look away.

'Don't worry. The reason I ask is because this bottle contains a barbiturate from India; a place your husband knows well. Its ingredients are awfully rare. You call it a poison and I suppose you are correct. In small doses it stimulates the brain causing drowsiness and compliance. But in an experiment I conducted only three small drops of the concoction managed to kill a rat. I daresay a couple more would kill a human.'

'How do you know about my husband Mr Balanchine?'

'Walter, please.'

'How do you know about my husband Walter?'

'I have been observing him for the past three weeks since your return. He leaves the house in the morning, shaking and hollow eyed and returns in the evening half conscious.'

'You've been spying on us!'

'I have no real interest in your husband apart from any involvement he might have had with Lucinda Eden. This routine of his seemed to have started with her disappearance. She is still missing and although I am striving hard to find her, her father is dying with grief. He is my dear dear friend; quite a damaged soul, rather like you in a way. Yes, I see the pain inside you! You try to make it invisible, make yourself invisible, but I see it there, smouldering away.'

He leaned towards her, his eyes heavy on her face.

'Has something awful happened in your life? I see so much sadness in your lovely face.'

Suddenly her hand was in his and their faces were barely an inch apart. Was he going to... to kiss her?

'Please don't. This is hardly fair, please,' she stammered.

'You're not ready to speak yet, I can tell that.'

'Tristan has an awful lot of problems... It's alright though, his father is travelling back to England and he's going to bring some sort of specialist to make him better.'

'But you're not so sure that anyone can help him.'

'I didn't say that, did I?'

'Do you feel in any sort of danger?'

'I don't think so.'

'Promise that you'll come to me, when the time is right?'

'But why would I...?'

'Promise.'

'I promise.'

He cupped her chin, so caressing, as if he could read her mind through the blood vessels in his hands.

'Here is your bottle. You know what it contains now. Be brave with it.'

All afternoon the bottle and the letter brushed against each other in her pocket. The two of them jolted and rustled and antagonized each other so much at the fortnightly church hall meeting, that she could barely string a sentence together. And, rather like two unruly children, she felt the need to check on them constantly: to twist the rim of the bottle with her fingers, just to make sure that it was still closed, to stroke the furred edges of the letter during her stroll home.

And to make matters worse the extraordinary Walter Balanchine now simply refused to leave her thoughts. She'd watched him for so long and now the portrait had miraculously come to life, leaving her with both a yearning and a deep bubbling fear that ran hot and cold though her body at the same time.

As she approached her house a young couple appeared before her outside number 32; their new neighbours presumably. They were closely pressed up together on the threshold, furniture and boxes cluttering up the pavement. The vision made her pause for a moment. He was young and handsome, quite tall, and he was looking down at his small wife with eyes that seemed to say, *Look at our new life together. Look at our new home!* In return she raised her hand and brushed his cheek with the edge of her glove. Such a small gesture but enough to reveal what was in her heart.

'Oh thank you for feeding Minerva.'

Mrs Hubbard let the cat slide down from her lap to the kitchen floor and Miranda pretended to look away. It had become an unspoken rule not to acknowledge how fond the cook and the animal had become of each other.

'I've just passed the new young couple moving into 32. They look awfully pleasant.'

'Yes, Mr and Mrs Bone.'

'Gosh, rather an unfortunate name. News travels fast though, how did you find out about them?'

'Oh the cooks' network,' she chuckled. 'I suppose you won't be needing me anymore today.'

'Is it six o'clock already? No, please do go home and rest.'

Her pulse started galloping immediately and the bottle and letter in her pocket met in a collision. But Mrs Hubbard remained fixed at the kitchen table; showing no sign of putting on her coat at all and appearing as if she had something she rather needed to get off her chest.

'Now please don't think me overly bold in saying this,' said the cook. 'But aren't you taking too much upon your shoulders at the moment?'

'What on earth do you mean?'

'Well all the housework, that's what I mean! Dismissing all the staff, apart from me. Is it quite fitting for a lady like you to clean upstairs, scrub floors? And you hardly let me do a thing anymore.'

She raised a handkerchief to her eyes.

'Dear dear Mrs Hubbard. Please don't take this the wrong way, it's awfully difficult to explain... I come from a frugal family you see, we always mucked in with the work. It's quite natural for me to scrub baths and so on. And we have no children, just me and Mr Whitestone rattling around this big place.'

'But I do worry about you so.'

'No really, you needn't. Let me help you with your coat and take some of that almond cake home with you. Here you go! No time to lose before it gets too dark and cold.'

'Thank you Mrs Whitestone.'

'No, thank you. And why don't you take Minerva home with you, look she's trailing your feet already.'

'It's the cake she's after. Come on Puss.'

The pounding came only fifteen minutes after Mrs Hubbard had gone.

'Tristan!'

He flopped forwards through the door, just teetering on his feet and a long crimson stain in the shape of a 'V' covered his chin and the front of his shirt.

'What on earth's happened to you this time? Have you been attacked?'

His top lip arched up into a scowl, a red cavern appearing where his two front teeth should have been.

'Good grief, they've knocked your teeth clean out! Was it a brawl? Are you alright?'

'Shhhhhut up woman.'

She sidestepped his lunge and he went flying across the hallway, belly-down. A rainbow of blood glistened up from the floor.

'Come on, let's take you to the sofa.'

It was barely any effort at all now to drag him into the drawing room. She'd mastered the technique of hoisting him up under the arms and pulling him along like a sack of potatoes. She'd have to add another sheet to the sofa first though, what with all the blood and goodness knows what else by the end of the night.

And then the sobbing began, the hardest thing of all to bear. It turned him into a little crumpled up ghost of a person. Not menacing at all, just hideously pathetic.

'What are you crying about tonight?'

'I'm so lonely.'

The words whistled and gurgled between the gap in his teeth.

'We're all lonely.'

'Where did she go?'

'I'm not sure whom you're talking about. Clementine or Lucinda? Or some other woman I don't even know about yet?'

'They all leave me!'

'Because you persecute them dear.'

'You wicked old hag!'

He punched forward with his fist but her hand struck neatly against his jaw before he reached her, the sound of the blow striking through the air like a whip.

'Aaaagh!'

'Now enough of that. You know better than to hit me if I'm to tolerate this behaviour.'

He hugged his knees into himself, rocking back and forth; an innocent child peering out at her with bewildered blue eyes.

'What have you been drinking all day?'

'Rum.'

'Have you eaten anything?'

He shook his head.

'Are you hungry?'

'I can't feel my legs but there are daggers in my mouth. I'm so lonely.'

'Yes, I know. Will you sleep?'

'No. Lonely. Lonely.'

'Please, just STOP repeating yourself! I can't bear it anymore. Don't you think of anyone else? Does it not occur to you that I am lonely too? That I've been lonely every day of our life together? I thought the world of you when we met. I saw you as my saviour. I would have done anything for you! And this is how you repay me. This is my marriage: sweeping up your blood and vomit, clearing up your mess. Lonely? Let me teach you about loneliness!'

'Stop bawling witch!'

'Oh a new name for your list! Only I seem to be the witch who is keeping you alive at the moment, in spite of all your best efforts!'

'Perhaps I want to die!'

'Is that so? Then let me help you along the way. Do you

recognize this bottle? You should do, you've done enough damage with it yourself after all. Lie back, taste what's inside. Just three drops can kill a rat, or so I've been told. How big a rat are you then?'

His eyes grew like saucers, but he didn't fight back. On the contrary, he seemed to be opening his mouth a little, beckoning the poison in.

... *Be brave with it.* Is that what Walter had meant? One... two... the drops slipped onto his tongue like little luminous pearls. He didn't flinch at all, just stared straight back at her in a blue haze.

Three...

Enough to kill a rat now.

'I've done this before you know my darling husband. I killed someone once, by accident. That's when my life ended.'

Four.

Her hand was shaking; a grey blurry cloud swept in front of her, eliminating everything apart from two blue circles. Mad eyes. Evil eyes. The bottle screamed in her hand. She hurled it into the fire and in a moment Mr Eden's letter followed it, scorching and crackling in the flames.

'You're staining me as well,' she murmured as the flames died down. 'You're turning me into something evil like you. How could you be so cruel?'

But there was no response. His eyes were closed now and thankfully she could just hear the murmur of his breath.

'Miranda, it's been a long time.'

'Yes. How is Switzerland?'

'Cold. May I introduce Dr Blythe. He's come down from Scotland especially to see my son.'

Dr Blythe was an average looking individual, although having to hover in James Whitestone's aura perhaps made him look even more average than he would have done otherwise. He was of an average height, average build and had light brown receding hair of an almost identical shade to his tweed suit.

'Thank you for coming doctor, you seem to be highly recommended.'

'I'm very pleased to hear that, I only hope that I can offer some sort of assistance.'

'Oh I doubt it, but we ought to try I suppose. What a

charming accent, are you from Edinburgh?'

'Ah no, the Highlands.'

'Oh how beautiful! What a lovely long way from here. Would you like to see my husband right now? He's in his bed. I'm afraid I've had to tie his hands to the bedstead for the purpose of this visit to stop him from running away or attacking anyone.'

Mr Whitestone emitted a deep strangulated cough, the corners of his mouth crumpling up as if he'd just bitten into a rotten piece of meat. Tristan really did look a lot like him. She'd forgotten how much over the past few years. Although James Whitestone seemed taller, stockier than his son, or was that just because Tristan had withered up so dramatically over the past weeks? Nevertheless, he was a handsome man still for his age. Rather a dashing figure in his foreign looking suit.

'Um, may I have a quick word with my daughter-in-law in private? We have a few details to catch up on,' he said, turning to the doctor.

'Yes of course.'

Even the sound of the doctor's departing footsteps and the way he politely urged the door shut behind him seemed moderate and considered.

'Are you quite well my dear?' James Whitestone asked her in a quiet voice. His eyes were staring fixedly at the mantelpiece rather than at her face.

'That's an awfully difficult question to answer, considering.'

'This house,' he seemed to shudder. 'What on earth made you buy it?'

'I'm not sure I understand what you mean. Marguerite Avenue is highly sought after, what could possibly be wrong with it?'

'I... I don't know. It seems very dark; I almost walked right past it outside. Blythe had to direct me in. Odd. But anyway, moving on... you are fully aware that my son and I have never been close.'

'Yes.'

'And that by handing the London side of the company over to him and moving away I was attempting to wipe the slate clean, give him a fresh start to prove himself for once.'

'Is that how you see it? You weren't just simply washing your hands of him?'

'I beg your pardon?'

'You were aware of his history at the time, I presume? His misadventures in India? It's alright, I know about it now. I'm not the same naïve little child who walked down the aisle.'

'I...'

He gaped at her with such a stunned expression that she might as well have hit him in the face.

'Was he always like this? I mean when did you first discover your son's true nature?'

He shrugged, brushed a bead of sweat away from his forehead. She'd been so in awe of him in their former brief meetings, but now she could feel the fear in him: in the way he stepped from one foot to the other and looked impossibly large and suddenly rather uncomfortable in his foreign suit.

'He was always an awkward boy,' he muttered. 'Slippery. Used to get up to all sorts of odd things.'

'Like what?'

'Oh I don't know... hankering after the maids, going into the woods. He liked to catch animals, string them up before killing them and so on.'

In one lucid moment Lucinda Eden's face came back to her, drawn and wretched, half dead against the pillow.

'If I had such a son,' she said. 'I think I would have thought twice about allowing him to marry any woman.'

'Now look here young Miss. I will not take such impertinence from you. How dare you speak like that to the man who's given you everything you've got!'

'No, you look here. I would sacrifice every stick of furniture in this house for a man who was capable of treating me decently. Would you like to see him now, your son? Dr Blythe!'

The doctor was already waiting for her at the foot of the stairs when she reached the hallway.

'He's just up here. I'm afraid he has difficulty speaking as he lost some teeth in a brawl several days ago and the wounds have since become infected. I fear that the infection has spread around his mouth in a rather horrifying way.'

'Have you sought medical help?'

'Oh yes. It was a disaster; the man ran screaming from the room when Tristan attacked him. Perhaps you could help... now do excuse me, I have to lock him in you see.'

The key to his room hung on a chain around her neck and her

fingers fiddled the clasp in her hairline.

'That does it. Now do come in, as I said I've tied him down.'

Tristan's body lay still and straight on the bed. His eyes appeared to be half closed: two glassy sickles of blueness skulking beneath his lids. His feet poked out, bare and marble-white beneath the nightgown she'd forced on him. They were so slim and bony and the veins in them wound up over his ankles like bobbly worms.

James Whitestone slipped in through the doorway after them.

'Tristan, open your eyes dear. A man has come to see you, to help you. His name is Dr Blythe.'

Not a flicker. Not one ripple of a sinew, tightening of a muscle.

'Mr Whitestone, I have come all the way from Scotland to see you. Now, I believe you to be awake at the moment. Is that true?'

Not a sound. He barely seemed alive, his body so long and stiff, drawn out like a piece of string on the brink of snapping.

'Enough of this, wake up son!'

A floorboard creaked and the father pushed himself past the doctor towards the bed. 'You're being downright insolent lying there like that.'

Tristan's eyes snapped open.

'I really don't think this is appropriate Sir...' implored the doctor.

'Of course it's appropriate. He's acting like an infant! I give him everything and look at the sod, look at him!'

Tristan blinked at her, the hurt in his face as brutal as broken shards of glass. And then his mouth gaped open, strings of puss and blood-stained spittle connecting his two jaws, criss-crossing the cavern inside.

'OUT! Ouuuuuuut!'

The shriek didn't sound like his voice at all. It didn't even sound remotely human; just a mass of fear and hatred and despair all mixed up together.

The two men jumped away from the bedside, grasping at each other's shoulders. For all his experience Dr Blythe looked quite ashen.

'Ge...t out!!'

'Stop him screaming Miranda. Stop my son from screaming.'

James Whitestone was clutching at his throat as if he was being strangled, his back pressed up against the wall.

'I'm afraid I can't. You'll have to leave.'

Tristan's screams were turning into high-pitched gurgles. His feet and head thrashed against the bed as a pinkish froth collected in the corners of his mouth.

'Then I will. This is quite, quite repugnant.' And Tristan's father scrambled along the walls to the door, Dr Blythe following a few paces behind him with a sort of hesitant shuffle.

'Tell me Doctor. Are you here to treat my husband or my husband's father?'

The doctor paused, his cheeks had turned pink. 'I... I think that our presence has troubled your husband greatly. I'll try and be back in the morning with a dental practitioner and some sedation. This is, quite rare I think. My apologies for now.'

She looked down from the window as the two figures retreated along the pavement outside, their coats hugged about them like two churlish crows. A fog was descending; you could see the grey line where it was squashing the clear air down lower and lower into the road.

Tristan's screams had petered out into a whimper, his feet now flopping down exhaustedly against the bed. The infection was spreading from his mouth: a series of purplish circles were now forming around his chin and making their way down his neck.

'How long were you going to keep this a secret from me?'

She jumped at the sight of Mrs Hubbard, standing in the doorway.

'Oh... I'm so sorry! With everything going on I'd quite forgotten you were here.'

The cook walked over to the bed with small calm steps and cast her eyes down the length of Tristan's body.

'I suppose you'll want to leave our employment now. And I quite understand. Although I do hope you know how much I've appreciated, loved, your company and good faith.'

'He was never good enough for you. Do you realize that?' asked Mrs Hubbard, turning to her with soft eyes. She removed her apron and wiped the froth and sweat away from his mouth. 'I've watched you trying to please him now for far too long. Come, let's smooth out these bedclothes, they're all creased. That's it, here we are.'

'You're not scared? Repelled by him?'

'No more than I was when he was fit and handsome. Now

you look exhausted, far too thin and pale. Go and lie down. I'll watch him for a bit.'

'Oh! Thank you. I really don't know what to say. I never imagined...'

The room seemed to sink, submerging itself in water and suddenly she was clinging to Mrs Hubbard and sobbing until every muscle in her body ached.

SERENA'S STORY

Seb's misery was palpable even from behind the upstairs window. I tried a feeble wave and then pressed my head back against the smooth leather seat of Edward's Jaguar, closing my eyes to the sound of the engine as it purred its way down the street.

'It's only Christmas, just a few days. I'll be back before you know it.'

How many times had I tried to reassure him with those words?

'Yes I know. I just get so lonely though.'

'Then come with us!'

'I can't.'

Our sombre parting seemed to have killed Christmas before it had even begun and I could feel my mood tuning itself into the dank, rainy atmosphere of the morning. Only Beth's perpetual chatter and buzz from the next seat prevented the gloom from swallowing me up entirely.

'Druid Manor was built by Druids, did you know that?' she said, fidgeting like a fractious cricket.

'Really?'

'Yes really!' she leaned over to inspect the peony brooch on my coat lapel with loving fingers. 'They put all these great big stones on the ground and then it grew up from them as if by magic!'

'Is that true?'

'Not entirely true,' came Edward's voice from the front. 'The story behind the name is still a bit of an enigma really. There are some ancient stones in the foundations of the building, you can see some of them in the cellar, but the house was far likelier to have been named after a rather eccentric ancestor of ours who had a long white beard and dabbled in pagan rituals. He was quite a character; parts of the house had to be more or less rebuilt after he died in the mid-nineteenth century because he let it fall into such bad disrepair.'

'Rather like your brother darling,' murmured Arabella next to him. Edward didn't reply.

The journey seemed to take longer than I thought it would,

probably because as the miles clicked away I could feel the ever-growing distance between me and Seb settling heavier and heavier on my shoulders. Even though he was off to spend Christmas with his father, all I could do was picture him in the house in Marguerite Avenue, lonely and pining at the window.

We left the motorway and drove for nearly an hour down country lanes until Edward suddenly swung off to the right through a pair of gates marked *Druid Manor – PRIVATE*. The single track went on for some minutes, rising up and up towards a dark mound in the distance and getting narrower all the time as if the fields on either side were encroaching in on us, threatening to swallow the car up whole.

The mound in the distance began to take shape, sprouting chimneys and windows and pillars and yet more windows. It was colossal. And in its circular driveway there appeared to be a black spike, jutting out just in front of the long colonnade of pillars that made up the façade. We edged closer and finally the fields withdrew sulkily. The spike turned into Raphael.

'Where's Eva, Mum?' he asked, pulling Arabella's door open. He didn't look at me and I felt an irritating knot of disappointment in my stomach.

'Oh, she's coming tonight, I think. Robert's got some church thing this afternoon, so the two of them are coming down together after that.'

'She's dumped the oligarch.'

'Yes, I read about it in *The Times* colour supplement. Have you lost weight dear?'

'I don't know, probably.'

A pleasant looking middle-aged couple in wellies came out to greet us with at least five dogs of varying sizes at their heels.

'Darling Fiona!' squealed Arabella, pressing the fakest of fake looking kisses into each of the woman's cheeks. 'How lovely to see you!'

Edward and the man patted each other's shoulders in a fond and hearty sort of way. They were the same height and shared that tall, straight-backed physic; you could tell they were brothers.

'So you are still with us then,' said Raphael, suddenly standing quite close to me.

'Of course, where else would you expect me to be?'

He brushed his hand softly down my arm.

'May I introduce Lord and Lady Hartreve to you, my aunt and uncle.'

'Come now, none of these formalities!' laughed the lady. 'Rupert and Fiona please. And you're Serena, aren't you? It's very nice to have you here and is this really Beth! Haven't you grown young lady.'

The grand hallway of Druid Manor was easily large enough to have contained my aunt's house. It was lined with marble and had the sort of staircase that Cinderella might have escaped down when she lost that crucial glass slipper. The walls were adorned with grand portraits of bewigged nobles bearing remarkable resemblances to their dogs and an immense chandelier swooped down from the ceiling, crowning it all.

But as my mouth gaped open in admiration, I also took in my first breath of the damp air circulating about the place. It tasted of mushrooms and I felt myself shiver despite the fact that I still had my thickest winter coat on. The place was freezing, colder than outdoors, and horribly damp. Beyond the twinkling bulbs of the chandelier, ribbons of plaster were curling away from the ceiling and an ominous brown stain loomed above the arched window over the stairs. Arabella's comment in the car came back to me; the house really was in a sorry state.

'Let's take these bags up,' said Fiona, coming up to me. 'I'll show you to your room.'

The upstairs corridors smelt even damper than the hallway and glimpses into rooms showed a mismatched collection of old furniture.

'Where's Estella and Olly, Auntie Fi?' asked Beth.

'They're just doing the rounds on the estate. They'll be with us shortly.'

'They're our cousins,' said Beth with big confiding eyes.

'I know. You told me in the car. Twice.'

'Now this is your room, Beth's is next door. Do come in, I hope you'll be comfortable here.'

We were summoned to lunch soon after with the cousins. The dining room felt warmer than the rest of the house; it had a huge baronial fire full of crackling logs and as everyone milled about the room I inched towards it, tripping over several basking dogs on the way. The flames melted my fingers and the new warmth edged silkily up my arms towards the rest of my body. Seb would have loved this. I could picture him at the centre of it all, teasing Beth, hurling bread rolls across the table.

'Lunch is served! Everyone find a pew!' hollered Edward. He seemed more jovial and at ease than I'd ever seen him and he'd already changed from his city clothes into tweed trousers and a rough Pringle jumper, just like his brother. The look suited him; not quite a uniform but more like his natural state of being. He was at home.

In contrast, Arabella seemed to have done the opposite. She looked even floatier and more chiffony than ever and must have been freezing, although she didn't show it.

'You'll find there's an awful lot of dog hair on that chair. Try this one,' she mouthed at me with exaggerated lips. 'Now Olly, you sit next to me. I want you to tell me all about your fascinating line of work. What is it that you do again?'

'I'm a qualified chartered surveyor now,' said the ruddy-cheeked, rather shy cousin.

'How interesting! And I'd always hoped you'd be the one going into the money-making side of things.'

At the other end of the table Beth was giggling away with Estella, Olly's sister, and all around the family began to eat and chat away together in high spirits. Only Arabella stood out, winding her fingers along the yellow silk scarf around her neck and looking at Olly as he spoke with a smile that seemed to threaten to rip his throat out in one fell swoop.

Beth disappeared after lunch with Edward, Rupert and the cousins.

'It'll give you time to unpack dear, although come back to us soon!' said Arabella.

I wandered back to the grand hallway, feeling rather like a trespasser after visiting hours in a stately home. Seb must have been with his father by now. I tried to imagine the two of them together but got nothing, although with my eyes closed I could just about feel the touch of his mouth on my neck.

'So what are your first impressions of the Manor?'

'Oh, I didn't see you!' Raphael was leaning against the banisters, half in the shadows. 'Um, it's beautiful, very grand. A bit cold though.'

'Yes,' he smiled, his eyebrows raised comically. 'Things can get almost arctic here. You have to pile the jumpers on, although my mother never bothers and always catches cold. The secret is to acclimatize yourself to it slowly, one of the reasons I arrived a day early. If you have a moment I'd like to show you one of my favourite rooms here.'

He led me back past the now empty dining room and through some doors into a lengthy network of corridors, clearly not in use anymore. Again the damp smell was much worse here; there were no windows and all the doors along the way were firmly shut. It had seemed impossible to feel any colder than I'd been already been but my teeth were now chattering. It was also becoming increasingly dark: few of the existing light sockets had bulbs fixed into them and some were just wires sticking out of the ceiling.

'Where are you taking me?' I asked and my voice sounded surprisingly small. 'It's like a maze in here!'

'Then you've sort of hit the nail on the head. Look,' he opened a door to his right and nothing but a flaky brick wall sat behind it.

'Are they all like that?'

'No, some of them lead to rooms, some to other corridors. But many of them are fake like this one as well. Now hang on, I always get a bit lost here. Let me concentrate. Where's good old Seb when we need him?'

'Does Seb know it here?'

'Better than anyone. He didn't tell you about the library I suppose.'

I felt a stab of annoyance and disappointment. 'No.'

'OK, we need to turn right.'

It got really dark now. Raphael took the lead, brushing his hand against the wall and testing the light switches when they came his way. I didn't break the silence. His head was stooped as if he was thinking his way along, following some sort of instinct. In the dim light he seemed like a monk, padding along a cloister. I could just make out the curve of his shoulder blades, and I thought about the way I'd pressed myself against them on the back of the bike. I'd followed him that time as well, blindly putting my life in his hands.

'Found it!' he gasped, suddenly halting by a large pair of doors.

'Thank God.'

176

'Sorry, I think I took a couple of wrong turnings. It's been awhile. When I was a child, I knew it inside out. Here we go.'

The doors groaned apart and the room lit up before me.

'Wow!'

The sight instantly sparked off a memory, something my mother had shown me long ago:

'Look at this little flower. It's called a hellebore.'

'That's nothing special,' I'd replied to her. It was just a timid little bell of a thing, brown and innocuous, staring down at the ground.

'Try turning it upwards darling. Look inside the flower.'

And when I did I'd found myself gazing into one of the most elegant and perfect things I'd ever seen; a circular explosion of pink and purple.

I turned to Raphael, my mouth gaping. 'I... it's unimaginable! How did we get here?'

'This library stands at the centre of the house. It's the heart of it, if you like,' he answered, his voice echoing.

The room was completely round, but so large that every shelf that lined its interior walls must have been crafted to the most subtle of curves in order to slot perfectly into place. And in every segment of shelving sat hundreds, if not thousands, of books.

Instead of windows there was a spectacular glass domed ceiling which, even in the overcast winter gloom, lit the room up like a stage. Hardly any furniture occupied the central parts of the room; there were a couple of heavy wooden desks and a few easy chairs scattered about here and there, but little could have done justice to a space of such extreme proportions. And yet somehow it was able to exist quietly out of view, almost impossible to find.

'I can't get over it. No one would ever guess that it was here.'

'That's what's so interesting, isn't it? You see it was built entirely for that purpose.'

'What do you mean?

'Some things just don't want to be seen by anyone who looks in their direction,' I could hear the excitement in his voice. 'They can be right in front of your face, you can walk past them, around them, within their very shadow, but unless they want you to see them, you just don't notice.'

'We walked miles to get here though.'

'Not really. You might not have realized but most of the

corridors we walked along just wind and turn in on themselves. In fact the glass roof of this library is only a few feet away from your bedroom window.'

'It can't be. I would have noticed it. My bedroom looks out onto nothing but sky and a brick wall.'

'Yes, you're right, because the angles are all wrong. And none of the other inner-facing rooms look out onto it either. The library simply doesn't want to be gaped at by any old person.'

'You speak about it as if it were a living thing.'

'And who says it isn't?' he asked. I could see the tension in his eyes again: the urgency, the tight string poised to snap. 'Don't you believe that buildings have a life of their own?'

'Whoever built this place must have been a master craftsman of some kind. A famous architect.'

'No he was nothing of the sort. He was a man called Walter Balanchine. I've spoken to you about him before I think, the first time we met.'

Walter Balanchine. That name just kept cropping up again and again.

'Sasha would be very interested in this place then,' I said, treading carefully. 'Isn't he some sort of expert on the man?'

'Sasha would cut his right hand off to come here,' he answered in a voice so dry that it set my teeth on edge. And then he suddenly smiled up at me, as if shaking the subject of Sasha off. 'We're lucky we still have this place actually. A large part of the Manor, including the library, threatened to cave in on itself a few years ago. Subsidence.'

'It must have cost a fortune to repair.'

'Yes... luckily we were sort of, bailed out, at the last minute so to speak.'

I gazed around the room; it would have taken weeks, months to do justice to the jungle of books and manuscripts and endless artefacts that had been crammed into the library walls. No part of its circumference had been left bare and where the shelving ended it was replaced by drawings and paintings and mounted shotguns and stuffed birds in cases and a thousand other things.

'It's like Marguerite Avenue, but on steroids.'

'Yes, you're absolutely right about that!' he laughed.

But one large oil painting did draw me closer; it seemed only natural at first as it was bigger and more imposing than anything else in the room. And yet there was something more to it than that, a funny sort of magnetism about it that made me breathe a little faster with every approaching step. The beautiful girl at the centre... I knew her, I'd seen her before. Somewhere. I couldn't tear my eyes away from it.

'It's beautiful, isn't it? My favourite painting in the house,' said Raphael. He'd followed me across the room and I could actually feel his presence on the back of my neck. 'It was commissioned in the 1870s by an unknown artist.'

There were two people in the painting: a middle-aged man and the young familiar woman sitting on a horse. The man, who was standing at the horse's head with the bridle in his hands, was broad-chested and stocky and looked as if he would have been far more comfortable sitting on the horse himself. He had large grey whiskers and a rather arrogant, bulldoggish expression on his face.

But the girl's eyes shone out so piercingly from the painting that it seemed as if she was staring straight at me. She had tints of red in her hair that were set off by what must have been a very smart riding habit, and she sat mounted on the lovely chestnut horse as if she owned the world and despised everything about her at the same time.

'The great Stephen Hartreve,' said Raphael, breaking the silence. 'The man in the painting. This was his room, it was built for him.'

'And the woman?'

'His daughter, Lucinda.'

'Lucinda Hartreve, the one who lived in Marguerite Avenue?'

'Yes,' he whispered.

'You never did tell me about her.'

'What do you want to know?'

'I feel as if she's a person I was familiar with once but need reminding about. Don't you think she's laughing at us all in this painting, as if everything's a big joke?'

'Yes, you've got a point. I suppose that nowadays we would label her as nothing more than a rebel, but she was called far worse in her time. Lucinda and her father parted on bad terms. She ran off with the wrong man when she was quite young and eventually had an illegitimate child with someone else. Lucinda was her father's favourite, he had a son as well who went to Africa as a missionary and died there. That's why the inheritance eventually came to our side of the family.

Lucinda was the apple of her father's eye: strong-willed, a good horsewoman and very much admired for her beauty. After she left, Stephen retreated into himself. His wife had died many years before and he started to go mad rattling around Druid Manor on his own. And so he got Walter to build this library for him. He wanted something large enough to contain everything he might ever need to keep him occupied and yet so private that he should never be bothered by anyone.

As he got older he spent more and more time here. He was drawn to its discreet grandeur; he loved the novelty of being able to disappear into it as if by magic. In fact invisibility became quite an obsession for him; you'll find a whole section on it in this library, along with books on ghosts, the occult and so on. One wouldn't associate a man like that with such subjects, but his daughter and, her legacy, changed him I think. He started to look inside himself until it became an obsession.'

'It's so sad, a good story though. You seem to know a lot about him.'

'I have excellent sources.'

'What happened to Lucinda?'

'Ah, that's not a good story. But we should go, I expect Beth will be back by now and I have a number of things to do. Do you remember the way back?'

'No.'

'Well let's hope I do then!' he answered with a low laugh. He reached out, drawing me from the painting with his hand.

Eva eventually arrived with Robert late into the evening. They pulled up the driveway in a glimmering Aston Martin and we all assembled outside to greet them.

Olly stroked the bonnet of the car with an adoring hand. 'Like the motor!'

'A present from the oligarch, just before she jilted him,' said Raphael.

'Didn't he want it back?'

'No,' replied Eva. 'I think he'd already forgotten about it.'

'Couldn't you have strung him on a bit longer then, got a few more pressies out of him?'

'No.'

I trailed behind as the cousins swept into the house chattering loudly, and when no one was looking I disappeared upstairs. In my bedroom I peered through the window into the black night air. Slowly the outline of the brick wall that shielded my view of the library roof began to take form. It seemed impossible that that gigantic glass dome was only a short distance away, when all I could see was a patch of jet black sky and the silhouette of a crooked mound of ugly bricks. A secret library, hidden so cleverly from the world's eyes. My spine tingled. And poor old Stephen Hartreve, withering away in that vast place, alone and heirless. What did happen to Lucinda in the end?

I woke up the next morning to the glare of bright sunshine and the clamber of animated footsteps running along corridors and up and down stairs.

'Serena!' my door burst open, and Beth came flying onto my bed. 'It's the Christmas Eve treasure hunt, get up! Oh they're always so brilliant, Grandpa and Uncle Rupert do it for us and you've got to come too. Oh please, please!'

'Calm down!'

'I'm trying to, I really am, but I can't breathe. You will come won't you?"

There were bright red circles in her cheeks and her eyes were sparkling with excitement.

'OK, let's get dressed.'

Seven of us eventually congregated in the grand hallway for the beginning of the hunt. I was surprised to see Eva there, joining in, dressed in a thick fur coat. She seemed to be avoiding my gaze. Raphael was there too.

'We have to look for the first sign,' announced Estella, sombrely, and Beth squeezed my hand until it felt as if most of the bones had been snapped in half.

'Look, old Harold's got it!' Robert exclaimed, dashing over to a suit of armour in the corner. A rolled up piece of paper had been tucked into the mouthpiece and was only made discernible by the dangling end of the red ribbon that tied it.

'Uh, I thought that was blood dripping from his mouth!' cried Beth.

Olly unleashed the clue and read from it with great pomp and gravity:

> *Seek that which takes us up and over*
> *Close to the place with the four-leaved clover.*

Everyone paused in deep concentration.

'Estella once found a four-leaved clover in the bottom field,' murmured Raphael.

'Yes you're right,' cried Estella. 'I was just thinking that. It was years ago and Daddy helped me press it under lots of books in the library.'

'The bottom field it is then!'

The bottom field turned out to be a muddy bog. I squelched across it ahead of everyone to try and keep up with Beth who squealed triumphantly through the air,

'Look... *up and over*... the clue's on the stile over there!'

'Well done!' I shouted, beaming at her success.

She looked ready to explode with pride and clutched onto Olly as he read the next clue:

> *See the smoke above the great pane,*
> *Find the place from whence it came.*

'Oh that's easy,' said Eva, casually lighting a cigarette and hugging her coat around her. 'The *great pane* must be the stained glass window on the side of the east wing.'

We trudged back through the mud and found it soon enough: a massive stained-glass window set in the far side of the house depicting saints and angels and writing in Latin. Nestling on the roof above it was a cluster of six chimneys, only one of which was emitting a curling wisp of smoke.

'Now all we need to find out is which room that chimney belongs to.'

'It has to be the Rose Room,' concluded Estella.

But when we arrived, sweating and breathless in the shabby old parlour of that name, we found nothing but an untouched hearth that hadn't been used for a decade. Seconds later the scroll was found tucked away under the stone mantelpiece of Rupert's haphazard office next door.

Find me safe in the turtle dove's wings
Close to the place where tonight the parish sings.

'Is there a midnight mass tonight in the local church?' I asked gingerly.

Raphael smiled. 'Well done, it's just on the edge of the estate. Let's go!'

I could feel my face colour up with the glory of my small success and my heart fluttered in spite of myself. As we marched back across the estate, breathing steam clouds into the air, I thought back to all those Christmases with Jessica: the endless telly, the dry roasted turkey breast and the inevitable game of draughts to break things up a bit. I swallowed hard with shame at thinking about Jess like that, but it felt so glorious to be part of a real family for once.

The old Norman church rose up like a pile of building blocks by a side entrance to the estate. To get to it, we had to walk out through stone gates and around a small and picturesque lodge cottage that guarded them to the right. Now all we needed to do was find a turtle dove.

'Shall we go inside the church, maybe there's a statue or something?' suggested Estella.

'No, they're not in the church. They're *close* to it.'

'I've got it!' shrieked Beth suddenly. 'It's the wooden carving in Miranda White's house!'

'What wooden carving?'

'The one that sits on the kitchen dresser.'

'Let's go and have a look then, I know where the key's hidden,' said Olly.

I felt myself pause, my eyes locked on them in dumb amazement. The group ran back to the lodge cottage by the gate.

Miranda White

I knew that name already of course. She was the woman in the old photograph that Seb carried about with him. He'd described her to me as a ... *rather special person in my family.* Yes, that was it. They even shared the same surname. But now, it seemed, she was connected to the Hartreves as well...

By the time I entered the old and deserted building, they'd already found the next clue, nestling in some wooden wings in a lumpy Victorian carving of two turtle doves.

'Why do you call this place Miranda White's house?' I asked, not even sure if anyone was listening.

'Because a woman of that name once lived here, a long time ago. No one has ever lived here since.'

It was Eva who spoke, with a soft and almost loving voice. I gazed back at her.

'But Seb once told me about her...'

'Oh just be quiet,' she hissed through gritted teeth, her face turning to stone.

'Why? What are you hiding?'

'Just go away,' she gasped.

'Why?'

'Please God! I keep trying to tell you and you don't listen. It's only going to get worse if you stay.'

I stared back at her face so hard that it started to turn into zigzags. And then my feet began to retreat, clumsily, almost tripping over myself, and as soon as I got out of that place I began to run, fast across the fields, swallowing back my every instinct to scream out into the wintry air until I was far enough away not to be heard.

'Serena!'

The pounding of sprinting feet was suddenly catching up with me, hunting me down. I pushed my legs harder until they burned but my pursuer was too fast. A hand pulled me by the shoulder, spun me round. It was Raphael.

'Leave me alone!'

'Why?'

'Because I have to get away from, all of you! I don't belong. I shouldn't be here. Eva keeps telling me to go, but she won't say why.'

He peered back at me, his face pale and riveting in the cold air, drinking my words in as they came tumbling out of me, half crying half shouting. 'And now Miranda White! Who the hell was she, really? I've seen her picture. Seb doesn't tell me anything about himself you know. It's all bloody secrets!'

'OK, calm down,' he said. All that running had made his dark eyes fill with water. He still held me by the shoulders, the warmth of his hands bearing down on me. 'You want to know about secrets. Fine, I'll tell you. But you have to tell me something first.'

'What?'

'Tell me about you. Why are you different?' His hands edged down my arms, squeezing them tenderly but firmly. His eyes devoured my face.

'I don't have a clue what you're talking about.'

'You can see things Serena, things that you shouldn't,' he said, urging me closer towards him. 'I keep trying to work out why. It's all I ever seem to think about... Tell me, has something awful ever happened to you? Have you ever been in great danger? Injured perhaps...'

'No, stop talking!' I squealed, shrugging him off. 'And get your hands off me!'

I pushed him away and marched on through the mud, but he came back again.

'Don't do that,' he shouted, anger suddenly splintering through his voice. A thrill of ecstasy tore up my spine at the sound of it, and I hated myself for it immediately. 'I want you, you know,' he yelled. 'And I have a habit of getting what I want.'

He grabbed at me again and drew the back of my head towards him, pressing his mouth against mine. Every instinct urged me to push him away again, to lash out, belt him hard across the face. And yet for one brief moment, as if I barely belonged to myself, I fell right back into him, like a tumbling pack of cards into his warm inviting mouth.

But, as I kissed him back and drew my fingers through his dark hair, the gentlest touch rippled across my skin. My eyelids fluttered closed and I felt the soft caress of arms, Seb's arms, entwining themselves around my body.

I pulled back, gulping hard, guilt and fear washing over me like freezing rain.

'No! NO!'

I kicked him in the shins until he yelped out and then I ran, unstoppable now, faster than I'd ever moved in my life with the wind wailing around my ears.

They call it adrenalin: the thing that fires human beings up, but it's much more than that. I saw it more as a kind of burning magic that pulls you up and out of disaster and sweeps you along with invisible strings. It had saved me once before, on the worst day of life, and here it was again, giving me a free ride back to the house, to my locked bedroom and the safety of my bed.

1893

The room was pitch black, and yet she could still see the outline of the moving figure. It came closer towards her bed: round shouldered, looming.

'Lucinda are you awake?'

'Yes, I was never asleep.'

The scratch and flutter of a flame sparked up, and Alfonso's face bobbed up and down in the air, surrounded by a halo of light.

'We have to leave my cherub. I'm so sorry.'

'No, not again!'

'I know, but we really have to go. There are two men this time. I've seen them drinking downstairs three times now. Franz says they converse in English when they think that no one else is listening. We can't be too careful.'

A sob lodged itself in her throat. It was becoming so difficult to breathe.

'Where are you taking me now?'

'A train leaves in an hour for Leipzig.'

'Soon we'll run out of land to flee across. This child will be born in the middle of the ocean.'

'Nothing of the sort darling, nothing of the sort. I'll summon Claudette to pack your things, and Franz will help to get us on the train.'

Outside a fresh blanket of snow had made the world white again. Plumes of steam exploded from their mouths and the horses danced about on the spot, kicking down through the snow to the hard cobbles in protest. There was no method of lying or sitting with any degree of comfort anymore, so she pressed one side of her ribs flat against the carriage wall and squeezed her eyes shut.

'When I open them again I'll see the train. And the train will have a bed. And I won't have to move from it for a long time,' she told herself.

But at the station the railway line was empty, speckled all over with stones made white and furry by the snow.

'It must have been delayed,' she heard Franz mutter to Alfonso. His mouth was half concealed by a thick muffler, but his round red cheeks still stuck out over the top. If she squinted a little she could squash his face to look like someone else. Yes, that was it, all round and rugged – Daddy. And if she raised her top eyelids up a bit she could lengthen the face out, make it slimmer. Tristan.

'Monsieur Eden, Madame is fainting again I think!'

'Wait, I'm coming.'

Darkness.

Am-ber Am-ber Am-ber Am-ber

'Madame, you are awake now?'

Claudette's round face appeared over hers, her eyes as small and dark as two raisins plopped on top of a nice pie.

'Where are we?'

'On the train, you can hear it? It came two hours late, but we have a cabin now.'

Am-ber Am-ber Am-ber

'Where is Alfonso?'

'He found a bed, in another part of the train. You want me to find him?'

'No, let him sleep.'

Through the carriage window the white world glared back at her. It was snowing again; the small flakes attacked the glass, slamming their heads against it in a bid to get in. Nothing but white. If only they could have gone south.

'Aaah!' A blade of pain shot up through her pelvis.

'Are you alright Madame?'

'Yes... I think so. Just the baby, moving I think.'

'Lie back, change your position.'

She fell back against some cushions, but a burning sensation now came up from her chest into her throat.

'No, it's no good, I need to sit.'

'And you need to eat Madame! You are still so thin.'

'No no, I have no appetite, you know that. Just hold me up and I'll rest. That's it, thank you.'

Sleep came in flurries now, just like the snow, with cold biting memories that made it easier not to sleep at all. *Ah.* That pain again, like a sudden dagger pushing up through her. And the tiredness was hurting too, sitting on her eyelids, urging them down into sleep...

'Who are you?'

'I work for your father. My name is Walter Balanchine.'

'Haven't I seen you on stage? You were staring into people's eyes, hypnotizing them. You made a caged gorilla disappear.'

'Yes, that's one skill I have, among others. I rarely perform to the public nowadays.'

He was like a scarecrow with a little shrivelled head. The sight of him had made her feel mildly nauseous.

'Did my father send you?'

'Yes he did. He wanted me to give you this. It's rather a lot of money as you can see.'

'And I'm to have it in exchange for what?'

'The removal of your husband.'

His face hadn't moved an inch.

'What are you suggesting? Has my husband something to be scared of? Is murder one of your many skills?'

'No. No one would get hurt. But I could certainly make your marriage disappear. Documents, records. I could even make the world believe that you were never married in the first place.'

His eyes had stroked her. Beckoning. Urging. There was beauty in there, in all that ugliness. It came from his eyes. It had almost made her want to...

'Get out of my house!'

'I will come back. Your father has asked me to be persistent.'

'Come back as many times as you like, but I'll have nothing to do with you. And tell Lord Hartreve that he won't succeed in buying his daughter for all the money in the world.'

'Ha!'

'Are you alright?'

'Yes, fine. Just a bad dream. Where's Claudette?'

'Sleeping.'

Am-ber Am-ber Am-ber

Alfonso was holding her hand. He had lost weight; his neck now hung down over his collar in folds of empty skin and his face had a mottled, withering pallor, with rings as dark as charcoal under his eyes. She'd wished him dead once, but never would she have imagined that it would happen like this.

'You have the document still?'

He patted his jacket where the inside pocket was. 'Of course, although I'm sure it won't be necessary.'

'Tristan's spies. Have we fooled them?'

'Well they're certainly not on this train. I've been up and down checking. We'll be safe in Leipzig.'

'We were safe in Paris. We were safe in every other place along the way. Oh!'

'Are you alright dear?'

'Yes, it's nothing. I just feel so weak, that's all.'

'If only you'd eat.'

'I don't have the stomach for it. You know how sick it makes me.'

'Then rest now. Just rest.'

Ambeeer Ambeeer Ambeer

The train was grinding to a halt and there was sunlight on her face now. Perhaps they'd travelled somewhere warm instead by mistake. She forced herself up on one elbow, her stomach so heavy now, like a great boulder strapped against her.

'Oh, more snow! More damned snow!'

The train finally stopped; there were busy voices outside. She tried to heave herself up further, but her arms felt ready to snap. And what was that on her legs? They felt sticky. Gosh, they were soaking.

'Claudette!'

The door swung open, but Alfonso's head thrust itself around the door instead.

'We've arrived. I've called for a carriage and I'll carry you out now.'

'Yes, but put as many blankets around me as you can. I'm awfully cold.'

The stickiness was making her legs itch.

'I need a bath,' she sobbed.

'We'll go straight to an inn.'

'Aaaah!'

It hurt to be picked up now and there was that dagger again, digging even deeper than before and this time twisting a little, just making the pain last that bit longer.

The inn was the worst they'd been in yet. The walls of her room were covered in brownish lined paper that made her eyes itch and the air was filled with the smell of stewing meat from the kitchen below. She retched into her handkerchief but the effort of it hurt her body even more.

'Claudette, you must change my clothes,' she gasped. 'My legs are all wet.'

The maid carefully unbuttoned her dress. It hurt to be touched but the young woman was an expert now at sliding off her garments with the least possible fuss.

'Your petticoat. It is soaking Madame.'

'Yes I know. Please let's not talk about it.'

'But I think it is important. The baby, are you in pain?'

'I am always in pain. Just let me sleep.'

The woman on the balcony was getting wetter and wetter. And her face... all that agony locked in one expression.

'Can I help you? Why are you so wet? Have you fallen into the lake?'

'Do you know nothing of how to behave in decent society?' she asked through the glass door, with eyes so sad.

'I fell into a lake once, I nearly died.'

'You stole my husband.'

'Yes, but it's alright, because I'm going to give something back to you. I've planned it all. I'm going to make you happy.'

Her eyes opened. 'Aaaaaaaaah!'

'The baby is coming Monsieur. You must go and find a doctor.'

Claudette's back was turned away from her, but she could see fear in the woman's bent posture, in the way she wiped her hands repeatedly against her skirts.

'Why can't you help her? I thought you'd done this before!'

'I have, many times. But Madame is so weak, I am afraid for her.'

The brown lines on the walls sprung into zigzags. 'Oh Jesus Christ, Lord, not again!' And there it was, no longer an invisible blade but a clawed hand now, reaching down towards her from the sky... 'No!'

Too late. It plunged headlong into her stomach, gripped at her intestines and screwed them into mush between its talons. The sound of her own whimpers curdled in her ears. If only she had the strength to scream. She clenched her feet and hands, trying to force the pain into them for as long as it attacked her.

The claw retreated, gone to lick itself clean before coming back for more.

'The medicine, please, just a drop... Tristan knows where it is.'

'I have no medicine, Madame. A doctor is coming. I think your baby is in the wrong place, let me sit you up, it will help.'

'Noooooo!'

The claw came back snarling. It plunged and plunged, blood dripping, ripping her to tiny shreds.

'I... I'm dying!'

'No Madame no.'

Over and over again it came and each time it took part of herself away, burying it deep underground, lost forever.

A man was suddenly bending over her. He had a lined face, glasses, and a mournful heavy jaw that was mouthing something to her in a language she didn't understand. Too late.

The claw had a face this time, a face with beautiful blue eyes.

'I loved you so much.'

And it smiled softly back at her. It kissed her on the mouth with the most caressing lips she'd ever touched and then it plunged straight in. Daggers, scraping and sliding her insides clean. The lower parts of her body were exploding beneath her. Nothing to do now but let it happen.

She was sinking backwards, water was streaming up her nostrils.

'I'm in the lake again. I've fallen in the lake. It's alright, Daddy will save me, just like he did last time.'

She peered up through the green water but no one was there, no silhouette reaching down towards her this time.

What was that? A baby's cry?

And then darkness.

'Hello, Mrs Bone I believe? My name is Miranda Whitestone, I live next door. Do forgive me for not having introduced myself sooner. My husband has been ill you see and I've been rather taken up with looking after him.'

The pretty woman was all blonde ringlets and saucer eyes. She was wearing a pale blue bonnet and a cape to match, an unexpected slice of spring against the grey winter air.

'How lovely to meet you. It's funny but I didn't think that anyone was living next door. I knew it was being decorated and that the previous occupant had left...'

'Oh yes you're right, but that's number 36! I live at 34, next to you.'

Mrs Bone jerked her head back across her shoulder towards the houses, her delicate eyebrows knotted together.

'I'm sorry, I think I must have got a little muddled. I...' Her lips toyed with a polite smile but she still seemed confused, looking back and forth at the houses again.

Miranda tried to smile back. 'I hope you're settling in well. It's a lovely road.'

'Oh yes! We're so happy, it's such a blessing to be married!'

'Yes. Please do excuse me. It was very nice to meet you.'

Inside Minerva dashed up to her, squeezing her purring body against her ankles.

'Hello lovely Puss. Where's Mrs Hubbard, in the kitchen?'

The shopping was getting rather heavy, cutting a line across the palm of her hand.

'Ah, fresh tea. How do you always know exactly when to make it?'

'Too many years of being a cook I suppose.' Mrs Hubbard eyed the shopping bag. 'You got everything you needed?'

'I think so. Bandages, yet more disinfectant. And some ointment that's supposed to help but goodness knows. Is Dr Blythe still up there?'

'Oh yes, doing his electricity business on Mr Whitestone. Silly waste of time if you ask me.'

The warm tea caressed her throat. 'I met Mrs Bone outside, for the first time. She seemed to be confused about who I was, thought she lived next door to Mrs Eden's house.'

'I wouldn't concern yourself about her, she's still on her honeymoon as far as I can tell. Have you seen how they walk along together, all wrapped up in each other's arms as if they'd got stuck like that!'

'Must be nice to be so in love.'

'Hmmm.'

And yet Mrs Bone hadn't been the first to show some confusion about the house. Tristan's father had said something odd

about it too, about how he'd almost walked straight past it at first.
And he'd said that it was *dark*. Dark? It had had a fresh coat of
white paint only last year. And its windows glimmered far more
cleanly than most in the road. The bottom of her cup stared up at
her. Dark.

Dr Blythe was already tripping downstairs with his case as she
began dragging her feet up to Tristan's room.

'Any luck doctor?'

He smiled thinly. 'Time will tell. He gave me a fair old fight
today,' and he turned his head to reveal an angry looking scratch
along his right cheek.

'How did he achieve that? I thought we'd tied him down
securely this time.'

'Oh he has his ways. I'll be back first thing to check on him.'

Tristan's eyes were wide open when she tiptoed in, but he was
staring at the ceiling. He seemed to be tied down well enough,
although the new shackles were clearly making his ankles sore: the
skin had gone red and flaky where they had been rubbing against
them.

'He's shaved your head again. That's good, it'll be easier to put
this ointment on. It's a new one, I've been told it doesn't sting.'

'I hate you,' he snarled.

'I hate you too. Come on dear.'

It was hard to know where to start. The infection had now
spread across the top of his head, down along his shoulders, over
his chest and nearly to his stomach. It was mainly yellow and
pustular, almost green in some places; an expanse of volcanic
bubbles where the skin had once been. Hard to recognize the man
beneath it at all.

She reached for their secret flask on the top shelf. Tristan's
mouth was already open, waiting for it obediently, and when the
brandy trickled in he slurped away at it, grunting like a famished
wolf. When it was her turn she swigged more than a modest
mouthful and let it swish about it in her mouth until it was almost
numb.

'Mooore!' he groaned.

'Oh go on then, open your mouth. But don't tell the good
doctor because you'll get me into trouble alright?'

However hard she tried to rub it in, the new ointment seemed to do little more than sit in puddles on his skin. He scowled and yelped beneath her hands, thrashing about with his mouth as if he was trying to bite her. All that thrashing made one of his sore ankles far worse. It began to bleed angrily, the shackle digging into the wound.

Perhaps if she unlocked it, just for a minute or so, then she could wrap a bandage quickly around the sore area. His wrists were well enough tied down, as was his other foot.

The key to the shackles was in a dish on the window sill. She sneaked it into her hand without him noticing and then she prepared the bandage and something to wash the wound with, waiting for him to calm down.

His shrieks petered out into small grunts as his body settled. Soon he was quite still again, flinching only occasionally with nothing more than the mildest of spasms.

Click

The metal hinge sprung open around his ankle. All calm. Her hand remained steady but she could hear own short sharp breaths as she ran the wet gauze back and forth over the wound. Still not a twitch. The bandage unravelled itself to the floor, enough to wrap a mummy in. She drew it round and round the ankle and reached for the scissors on the table. But as she did so the bandage came loose and suddenly she was all fingers and thumbs, trying to do two things at the same time.

Ping

The scissors crashed to the floor.

Tristan's foot approached her face like a battering ram. She screamed, began a hasty retreat, but not fast enough for a clean break. The flame of his blow swept through her shoulder and she hit the wall with her other side.

'Mrs Hubbard! Help!'

His heel punched away at the air, the force of his body pulling the mattress up. The entire bed was shifting towards the window.

The door swung open. 'What's happening!' Mrs Hubbard cried, 'Where's his shackle gone?'

'I unlocked it for a minute, just to wrap his ankle up,' she panted back.

'You should know better than that by now. Are you alright?'

Her shoulder was throbbing but she could still bend and flex her arm with little difficulty.

'Yes.'

'Come on then, let's sort him out.'

For a small slim woman, Mrs Hubbard had a surprising degree of strength in her. She poised herself at the thrashing leg as if it were a wild creature that needed grappling by the scruff of its neck and then, when the moment was right, she dived in with both hands, thrust the limb back down on the bed and sat on it.

'Bitch! Evil evil bitch!' spat Tristan.

'Yes yes, I know. Quickly, put the shackle on.'

Miranda snapped it firmly back around his leg. She was still panting fast and the blood was lapping warmly about in her shoulder. It would be blue by the morning.

The key to the shackles burned in her hand; she almost threw it back into its dish.

'You'll be alright tonight on your own with him?' Mrs Hubbard asked, brushing her apron smooth.

Tristan had gone rigid again, his eyes now squeezed tightly closed against them.

'Of course I will. Thank you.'

'No more untying or unlocking. However much pain he might be in?'

'Absolutely not. I promise.'

'I've prepared a tray for you downstairs, I'll be off home now. You must try hard to sleep tonight.'

'Yes I will.'

She collapsed into a chair. Sleep wasn't any good. It just brought nightmares and that awful moment on awakening when the world feels fresh and new, and then real life suddenly comes screaming in through it all.

'Miranda,' said Tristan.

His voice almost sounded normal again.

'Let me talk to you.'

His eyes looked alert for once, not glazed but vibrant with blueness like they used to be.

'What is it?'

'Unlock me tonight and I promise I won't harm you again.'

'How stupid do you think I am?'

'Unlock me tonight and you'll be rid of me forever.'

The moon was brighter than usual. It lit the street, reflecting against the frost, almost fooling her into thinking that it was a sunny day outside. Tristan was sleeping deeply now; the escapade with the shackle must have exhausted him.

And yet she couldn't quite bring herself to make that journey back to her own bedroom. She'd watch him for a few more minutes, just to make sure. The key to his shackles lay safely in its tray. She picked it up, solid and cold. It felt even safer in her hand.

A draught swept down the fireplace with a dull whoosh that sent the shivers up her. She pulled a blanket up around her neck and curled up in the chair. Her shoulder was throbbing like distant thunder. It would be stiff in the morning.

Her eyes flickered closed for barely a second when all at once her chair seemed to be swept away from beneath her... she was tumbling, hurtling down. She landed hard, although it didn't seem to hurt, and a moment later she was back in her chair again, yawning and digging her fists into her eyes.

'I have to go to bed,' she groaned.

Tristan looked so harmless lying there. Not a twitch. Nothing more than a mound of foul-smelling meat under a blanket. He was rotting. He always had been, even when she'd first fallen for that handsome face. Mrs Hubbard had seen it, perhaps Jane had as well. She was the fool, along with that woman in India and Lucinda Eden of course. Where was Lucinda, now?

'I'm here.'

'No!'

'Don't be scared. Tell yourself you're dreaming.'

She was wearing that sapphire blue dress again, the one she'd worn on the night of the dinner party and peacock feathers glimmered in her hair.

'You're beautiful again!'

'I know, that's what happens when you die. Give me the key.'

'Which key?'

'The one that you're guarding so faithfully.' Lucinda nodded towards her clasped hand, her lips so plump and red, set in a cupid's bow of a smile. 'Well if you're not going to give it to me then I'll just have to take it for myself.'

Swish swish. The silk dress brushed against the floor towards her, bathing her face in its blue shadow and Lucinda's neck rose so poised and swan-like above it. The key slid out from her palm.

'What are you going to do with it?' she whispered.

Lucinda twisted a silky tendril of hair with her fingers and then tucked it back up behind the feathers.

'I'm going to make you happy. Close your eyes. Go back to sleep.'

Swish swish. The train of her dress slithered towards the bed like the tail of a magnificent blue dragon, the back of her neck white and faultless. No wonder he'd wanted her so badly.

'Ouch!' her shoulder creaked with pain, far worse than she'd imagined it might be. Morning light washed over her face, and she raised herself up in the chair. She tried to rotate her shoulder carefully in small circles; it was enough to make her grit her teeth together.

Mrs Hubbard was probably preparing breakfast downstairs. She had to get Tristan cleaned up for the doctor, but unravelling herself from the chair was no mean feat. Her ribs appeared to be pounding as well, probably from when she'd knocked them against the wall.

'Time to wake up! Tristan? How are you today?'

Gone.

The pain stopped. Her heart stopped. The room went white. Gone.

And then, in a vast wave, everything came gushing back in. The bed. The four shackles lying empty. The key, idly tossed aside in the middle of the sheet. Her blood flying through her veins.

'Tristan!'

Her feet thundered down the stairs, the skin on her palm sparking against the banister.

'Tristan!'

She collided with something.

'Dr Blythe, it's you! You have to help me, Tristan's escaped. I fell asleep and he must have got hold of the key. It was lying in his bed.'

His bag landed with a thump on the floor, he clutched at her arms.

'When did it happen?'

'I don't know!'

'Did you unlock any of the shackles after I left yesterday evening?'

'One yes, but I thought I'd locked it back up properly again. It was on his ankle, how could he possibly have escaped from that?'

'Because he's clever. I've seen it before.'

'Aaaaaah!'

The shriek came from the kitchen.

'Mrs Hubbard! Quickly Dr Blythe, quickly!'

The cook was standing stock-still in the middle of the kitchen floor, her fingers clenched tightly in her apron and her face like ash.

'Where's Tristan? Have you seen him, where is he?'

Mrs Hubbard uncurled her hands slowly and raised a pointed finger towards the larder. Its door was hanging open.

'It's the place where I hang the game from,' she stammered. 'He used an old piece of rope, on one of the hooks in the ceiling.'

Just within the entrance of the cold little room two feet dangled in mid-air, long and blue now and one ankle bandaged up.

Mr Fairclough's office smelt of leather and wood polish. Its ceiling was higher than the room was wide and its long windows were set so far up the walls that it was impossible to see anything through them apart from clouds. It seemed as if the entire room, and everything in it, had been stretched upwards, including Mr Fairclough himself.

'Mrs Whitestone,' he said with a solemn voice, elevating his long angular body from behind the desk. 'My deepest condolences. I really do wish you had let me come to you.'

'I am well aware of that, but I prefer to be out of the house as much as possible. Keeping busy is the best thing for me.'

'Naturally.'

Miranda fought back a tickle in her throat. It really was a very dry room, and Mr Fairclough a very dry sort of man.

'Now that the funeral is over with I wish to discuss two urgent matters with you,' she continued. 'Naturally there will be much more to consider presently, but at the moment I have some pressing concerns that simply can't wait.'

'Of course,' replied the lawyer. 'How can I be of assistance to you, Mrs Whitestone?'

'Ah, funnily enough you have just unconsciously fallen across the first point which I intended to raise with you: the issue of my name. I would rather not be known by that surname, Whitestone, anymore you see. I never really liked it in the first place!'

Mr Fairclough raised his eyebrows.

'From this point on I would prefer to be known as Miranda White. It's not my real name, I know, but it feels comfortable. So from now on I would much rather be referred to in all manners by my new name, Mrs White. I'm sure I can leave the whole legalistic side of that in your capable hands.'

Mr Fairclough raised his eyebrows even further. He seemed to be about to speak but then scratched a private note down with his pen instead.

'The second reason for my visit concerns the house in Marguerite Avenue. I want to get rid of it, as quickly as possible.'

'I see. You would like me to assist you in its sale.'

'Absolutely. There's very little money left and I certainly don't need to live in anything so large and ostentatious. It also carries with it some very painful associations.'

'Why of course it does. Now that your husband has gone.'

A ray of sunlight fell across the desk revealing a swarm of dust motes spiralling through the air.

'If only it were that simple,' she replied. 'If only it were that simple.'

It was nearly evening by the time she made it home from Mr Fairclough's office. A familiar figure was standing in the doorway of number 36. She'd already spotted him from some way off; he was wearing vivid purple today.

'I heard about your husband,' said Walter Balanchine with a solemn face.

The windows of Lucinda Eden's house were open; the sashes had been freshly painted.

'The house looks as good as new.'

'Lord Hartreve has given it to his nephew's family. We've done our best with it, it was in a deplorable state.'

'Mrs Eden went to France. I think I can tell you that now.'

His eyes looked dull and sad. He nodded. 'Yes I know, I followed you to Dover that night. I had men tracking her across the Channel but her husband was too canny for all of us. They kept moving on and on until we finally found her in Leipzig.'

'What condition was she in? Well I hope?'

He shook his head this time. 'They found her in her grave. She's dead.'

'Oh no!'

'She died the same night as your husband. Isn't that strange?'

Miranda crept rather than walked back into her house, her gloved hands clutched at the base of her stomach. The hallway seemed to have got larger for some reason and the natural daylight just wasn't getting to it, even when she did leave all the doorways to the rooms open.

'I'm back now,' she murmured into the still air and a shadow swept across the floor, making it even darker.

'Home again.'

SERENA'S STORY

I woke to a pitch-black room. The Manor was quiet, the hallways empty. Downstairs the lamps had been turned down low and nothing was stirring in the drawing room apart from the twinkling lights on the Christmas tree. But a bit further along, just past the dining room, the low murmur of voices wafted towards me. A pool of light flooded out from beneath the kitchen door. I pushed it open.

'Hello! How's your headache?' asked Raphael. His eyebrows were raised in interest but his face was unfathomable. They were all playing cards around the hefty kitchen table.

'Oh... much better I think. Is Beth alright?'

I directed the question at Eva, but her eyes twitched instantly away.

'She's fine,' Raphael answered. 'We put her to bed a while ago. Wild with excitement about tomorrow of course. Hey, are you going to come with us to Midnight Mass? Mum's staying behind so you don't need to babysit.'

'Really? Alright then.'

Arabella was gazing glassy-eyed at me from across her cards, Edward scratched his nose thoughtfully and played his hand.

It's a funny feeling, only the mildest tingling up the spine. But sometimes you simply know when a group of people have just been talking about you behind your back.

Venturing out into the night we were all so bundled up in coats and hats and scarves that it felt as if I'd been incorporated into a gang of thieves. The black air tasted of hay and wood smoke and I stuck close to the crowd, just in case Raphael tried to approach me again. But he didn't seem that interested in coming near me, pacing on ahead instead, entrenched in black. You'd hardly even know that he was there.

The fuzzy whiteness of the lodge cottage gradually came into view. I couldn't keep my eyes off it. As we passed it by I brushed my hand against the old stone walls. They left a dry chalky residue on my fingertips. The cottage fell behind us and a moment later the church door sucked us in.

The church was almost full and our party had to split up to find seats. There was just enough space for one person to squeeze in right at the back and I grabbed it. The priest looked even colder than the rest of us: he had a number of scarves wrapped tightly about him and a bright red nose which he mopped with a yellow-looking handkerchief.

'Good evening everyone and a very Happy Christmas to you all', he began, wiping his nose again solemnly. 'Before we begin our midnight service there is something very sad that I am compelled to draw your attention to. As many of you know, the painting of Jesus feeding the five thousand on the east side of the nave has been a beautiful and constant part of our St. Mary's life for more than three hundred years. Unfortunately, only two days ago, it went missing.'

A unified gasp travelled across the congregation. Heads turned and necks craned to catch glimpses of the empty patch of wall.

'Yes, I can see the shock in your faces. It is a very sad thing. Very sad indeed. If anyone knows anything regarding the whereabouts of this precious object, then please do not hesitate to speak to me about it, in confidence, at any time. Right, let us move on and remember that this is Christmas: the glorious celebration of the birth of Christ. Please turn to page number 34 in your hymn books for *Hark the Herald Angels Sing*.'

Standing almost right at the front of the congregation, and next to Eva, I could just about see the back of Raphael's head, bobbing from side to side with the force of his singing. A sickening feeling rose up from my stomach - I was already itching to get out and by the time the closing notes of the hymn had faded away, I was back in the night air, on my own.

The walls of Miranda White's house were old but solid. It was a charming little place, almost Hansel and Gretel like, with wooden gables and oversized chimneys. Who had this woman who once lived there been; a servant maybe to the Hartreve family?

Scrambling around the cottage in the darkness wasn't easy and the back walls were heavily overgrown with nettles and brambles. But I just managed to cling on with the tips of my fingers to the edge of one of the window frames at the back, pulling myself across.

The windows themselves were clear, and the faint glow of the church just hinted through from the bay at the front, bathing the entire interior with dappled light. All the internal doors must have been left open although, as far I could make out, there didn't seem to be any doors hanging from the frames at all.

There was nothing else in there, just the faint outline of the wooden carving I'd seen earlier in the day.

The sound of singing piped up again from inside the church:

'In the bleak midwinter...'

Yes it was rather bleak, and cold. And if I stayed out any longer my nose was in danger of turning as red as the priest's.

'Oh it's just you Serena.'

Arabella was hovering in the hallway when I tried my best to slip back in through the Manor's vast, creaking doors. Her voice seemed flat, quite sapped of its usual chirpiness, and for the first time I noticed that there were cracked lines around her lips. Her lipstick had bled into them and the rest of her make-up looked caked and old.

'Yes, just me! Are you alright?'

'Oh fine.' And then she smiled sadly. 'This house doesn't agree with me I think. Too many chills... and troubles.'

Her eyes looked moist, she wobbled a little as if she'd been drinking.

'Try and get some sleep. It's gone midnight now, and we're supposed to forget about troubles on Christmas Day.'

'Really?' She tilted her head towards me appealingly; uncannily similar to Beth.

'This family of mine,' she chuckled at last and walked away as if I'd disappeared from sight.

The next morning a large thud at the end of my bed prized me out of sleep. It was accompanied by a:

'Gloooooooooooooooooooooooooooooooooooria! Hosanna in excelsis!'

'What *are* you wearing?'

Beth looked twice her usual size, wrapped up in every dress, jumper and cardigan from her suitcase as well as tights, leggings and a shawl of Arabella's which she'd tied sari-style about her on top of everything else.

'The heating's given up in my bedroom. I nearly went blue.

Hey, it's Christmas! Now who does this look like? "Ding Dong Merrily on High..."' She sang it in a way that made her eyes bulge and her neck look as if it was trying to eat her chin.

'Very naughty!' I laughed.

'But it's just like Uncle Rupert isn't it? Go on, say it is.'

'Yes, you're very clever. But don't do that in front of anyone else. Shall we go and see what Father Christmas has brought for you?'

Present unwrapping was accompanied by a chaotic breakfast fry-up.

'Attention all! Who's for sunny side up and who's for easy over?' yelled Fiona from the kitchen.

'Isn't it *over easy* Mummy?' Estella laughed. She was pulling on a new furry hat from Eva. 'Oooh lovely, I'm not taking this one off today.'

Everyone dashed about with tousled hair, kissing and thanking each other. All apart from Arabella, who remained slouched in a chair wrapped up in a kimono and hugging an untouched mug of coffee to her chest. She looked dazed and hungover.

'A present for you,' said Raphael, handing me a bottle shaped gift, wrapped up in red paper.

'Thank you. I always like receiving books at Christmas.'

'Oh I'm glad. Just make sure you don't get drunk when you're reading this one.'

He clasped his hands behind his back as if to reassure me that he wasn't coming any closer.

'Sorry about the other day, I was wrong to force you like that.'

He was the young man in the black and white photograph again: charming and rather captivating. Not the man on the motorbike, or the one who'd chased after me the day before.

'OK. But don't do it again.'

'Breakfast is served!' announced Edward, striding in in his brand new apron. It had a picture printed on the front of it of a turkey sunbathing on a tropical island whilst balancing a cocktail in its wing; a present from Beth. 'I don't know why you're all laughing at me! I think I look extremely handsome in this.'

After breakfast the morning sunshine suddenly slunk away

behind foreboding clouds. Droplets of rain began to spatter at the windows and the shadows loomed in.

'Damn, the heating's failed altogether now,' said Rupert, marching in, hands frustratedly on hips. 'Can't make the bloody thing start up again.'

'And how much will that cost us to fix?' asked Arabella through tight lips.

'Arabella,' said Edward in a voice heavy with warning.

Rupert pretended not to have heard. 'I'll get as many fires going as I can,' he said, hurrying out again.

As the morning wore on, Arabella's mood seemed to have become infectious. Before long Robert, Eva and Raphael were also sitting despondently in chairs, hugging layers of clothing around them.

'What's that?' I asked Beth.

She was curled up under the Christmas tree, flicking through a new book she'd been given, tongue poking out to one side.

'It's my Christmas present from Pasha. He's been trying to find this book in English for me for ages because I always liked the story so much when he told it to me.'

'What's it called?'

'*Papa Sasha and the Little Orphan Children.* It's about this man who helps all the poor children in Moscow. We think it's a funny story because he's got the same name as Pasha, I mean Sasha. Our Sasha!'

'Is that why you started calling him Papa Sasha, Beth, because of this story?'

'I think so. He liked me calling him that so much that he started giving me presents for it. So I carried on! And then the two words got mixed together into Pasha.'

The door suddenly opened and we all looked up as Aunt Fiona wandered in with a worried expression on her face. 'Looks like the oven's on the blink too,' she said quietly. 'Anyone ever barbecued a turkey before?'

For the first time in hours Arabella calmly rose to her feet, left the room and slammed the door violently behind her. After a few moments of stunned silence Raphael went too, followed by a more hesitant looking Edward, a pipe clutched between his teeth.

'Shall we go and make some sandwiches?' Estella asked Beth. 'I think we could all do with a bite to eat.'

'OK.'

They left and I disappeared quietly from the room for a wander in a bid to keep warm.

Great Christmas. Suddenly the dried up turkey and mindless television watching with Jessica felt heavenly. Once again I relived yesterday's scene with Raphael; it came back to me like a dull tooth ache. I could still feel the imprint of his hands on me and those words that turned my bones even colder than they already were:

You can see things Serena, things that you shouldn't.

I hugged myself, the air had gone stale. Where was I exactly? I'd been wandering through the corridors, too busy to pay much attention to which way I'd been going. The air had turned dim and even when a set of light switches turned up they did nothing when I flicked them on. Most of the light bulbs had blown or weren't in the sockets at all.

A door appeared to the right. Its brass handle felt cool and sticky; unpolished and unused. The door swung open and a brick wall stared back at me.

A faint throbbing started in my ears. I turned back from where I came, trying to retrace my steps, but there were so many turnings and if anything it was getting even darker. I grappled with shaking hands along the walls for light switches. Nothing. Just darkness and damp old plaster walls, so soft that I could actually squash dents in them with my fingers.

But then, in the distance, came the sound of voices. I shuffled in their direction and they got louder. It was a woman talking mostly, at great speed and almost shrieking at times. Closer still and I realized it was Arabella. The outline of another door floated towards me. I dived for its handle and a room appeared.

'It's fucking ridiculous! Those country bumpkins, screwing up the inheritance, that idiot son of theirs making a mess of it all. Raphael, you were born to run this place, why don't you see that? You have the brains, the authority, the bearing. Why are you wasting your life? How you could have shown your face at that church last night... I just don't know. '

She was yelling so hard at Edward and Raphael that they hadn't even seen me enter. I'd come into a sort of double length drawing room that narrowed into an arch at the middle. They were right at the other end, Arabella thrashing her arms about with her back to me and the other two on either side of her. I turned to go but found myself hovering instead. Just the idea of having to return to that darkness, that dank maze...

There was an old winged armchair just within reach. It was facing away from them, easy enough to curl up in and hide until it was all over.

'Why don't you just sit down Mum, calm yourself a little bit.'

'I don't want to sit down! I want to wring everyone's bloody necks! I've worked so hard to bring Olly round, so hard, but all I get is that idiotic shrug of his! Everyone knows they're fools, and parasites at that.' She turned to Edward, her finger pointing challengingly at his chest. 'When you got that Burnside money, risking EVERYTHING to get that man out of the country, then what did you all do with it?'

'We stopped the house from falling down,' murmured Edward in a deep voice.

'Yes, for the next ten years or so, before another chunk of it starts to give way. What a stupid waste! DO something with the place, make some money! Turn it into a hotel, a museum, flatten it, I don't know... or just bloody sell it and save us all one great big headache!'

'This house is not ours to sell,' he replied in long drawn-out words. 'It belongs to the family, of which Olly will be head one day. Not Raphael. Druid Manor is part of our legacy and it will remain private.'

'Well if that is the case then surely Raphael is the only one bright enough to pull it off. Just think of the sense of purpose it would give him. If only you could make a stand, for once in your life Edward!'

'Stop trying to change things all the time, pushing your way around as if you were born into this family!' Edward's voice was getting louder now, brimming with frustration. 'You're too indiscreet, I've always warned you about that. Trying to change everything...'

'Change can be for the better Edward and God knows this family needs a bit of freshening up.'

'Freshening up? Is that what you call it? And does that extend to dragging all these strangers into our lives? What a success that's been!' he snarled. 'It's been bad enough having to tiptoe around that Russian for all these years but now you've brought this young woman in too!'

'It wasn't healthy for Beth to live in so much isolation.'

'But Beth is not a healthy little girl, is she?'

There was a cold pause. Strange, but I could feel them all shudder. My hands found their way across my mouth, but the tears had already sprung into my eyes.

'Serena won't last.' Arabella's voice was calmer now, more measured. 'If we sack her she'll make a fuss. She's still too in love with him. Let her get tired, fed up with it all and just watch her closely in the meantime, stop things from getting out of hand. I'm sure that then she'll just... melt away.'

'Well let's hope so!' Edward bellowed back. 'Let's hope she's not just like our frustrated academic, trying to sell us to the world. And have you seen the way he watches Eva now? Revolting!'

'Raphael, please leave us.'

'Yes Mum.'

There were footsteps, the sound of a door creaking shut.

'Why did I marry you?' Arabella asked in a quavering voice.

'I thought it might have been for love.'

She laughed faintly. 'If I'd known then what I know now...'

'I warned you that there was a legacy.'

'If only we could LEAVE Marguerite Avenue.'

'Out of the question. It's my home, it always has been, it's part of our history, the people we are. And now it's Beth's home.'

'It's a prison.'

'I... I simply don't understand you Arabella. You were so happy there for so many years.'

'Yes. Until I saw what I'd really let myself into. Until it started to destroy our children. Do you think they had a normal upbringing darling? Look at them all now, trying to escape into their funny little worlds, not living real lives at all. Raphael's getting worse and worse.'

'Let me deal with Raphael.'

'Ha! You always say that but nothing ever gets better does it? God, do you know how many times I've toyed with the idea of just burning the damned place down?' she laughed.

'Don't be disgusting.'

'You're disgusting darling, you've wrecked my life. No more of this, I'm off.'

'Off where?'

'To try and get bloody warm, what do you think?'

'Arabella...'

It had stopped raining outside. Patches of watery blue blinked from behind the grey clouds, lighting up a sheen of dew, or frost maybe, across the grass outside. I unravelled my body from the chair and left the now empty room from the same end as where Edward and Arabella had been standing. It brought me out into one of the central corridors of the house and then back into the grand hallway. Robert was there, buttoning up his coat.

'Oh hello. You don't happen to know where Beth is do you?'

'No idea,' he stammered. A fresh crop of spots had sprouted up on his neck. He caught me staring and wrapped his scarf around them self-consciously. 'Off to play the organ now in the church for a bit.'

'Have fun. Oh Robert!'

He paused.

'The thief who stole the painting from the church. I think I know who he is. Should I be scared of him?'

Robert swallowed uncertainly, toying with his long hands.

'You should be scared of a lot of things,' he mumbled quietly, making for the door before I could reply.

I found Beth in the kitchen.

'Fancy a walk? It's stopped raining now.'

'Alright. You'll have to follow me though, there's something I want to show you!'

It felt so much better when we got out of the house. Beth skipped about ahead of me, her wellies splashing and squelching in the newly sodden grass. We passed through some ornamental gardens with old roses cut back into prickly stumps and animal-shaped box hedges now badly frayed at the edges. The paths were cracked and caked with slippery wet leaves and curtains of ivy had crept up walls and statues, robbing them of all shape and identity. Beth pulled me through a gate in one of the hedges, so innocuous that I had to stoop to get through.

'Wow, a lake!'

'Yes I know, it's wonderful isn't it?'

Another hidden gem in this sad old place.

We found a flat stone on the bank to perch on. It was damp but our coats were thick enough. Beth found pebbles and we tried to skim them across the water. *Plip. Plop.* Most of them refused to cooperate, sinking straight down to the bottom.

'A little girl almost drowned in here once,' she said thoughtfully.

'Really? How do you know?'

'I'm not sure. I think I suddenly just realized it one day when I was talking to Sasha.'

'Does he help you remember things?'

'Sort of. He always speaks to me in this nice soft way, like feathers. Sometimes he looks in my eyes and my brain feels a bit funny. Raphael says I mustn't let him do that, that it's called hippo, hipon...'

'Hypnosis.'

'Yes that's it. Raphael can do it too, he learnt it from a special book in the library. I try not to let Sasha do it but then he's so nice and I... I don't mind really,' but she screwed up her forehead in a troubled sort of way. 'AND he's writing this book about me, which is so exciting, so I can't help but tell him things, like the way the little girl nearly drowned in this lake. I'm going to be famous!'

Her eyes were suddenly so huge and innocent that it hurt just to look back at them.

Beth is not a healthy little girl.

If only I hadn't heard those words. It was true: sometimes it was better not to see, not to know.

I hugged her to me, her little head pressed close to my chest.

'I'm sure you will be famous, in your own way. But don't get too excited about it now.'

We squelched our way back to the house and Estella came tripping up to the door to let us in.

'Dad's fixed the electrics! So there'll be warm radiators and turkey on the table!'

Arabella sailed past in the background, a nearly empty glass of wine in her hand. She'd changed into a red dress with lipstick to match. Her hair was tied back in a chignon. She was ageless again.

'Hello darlings, did you have a nice walk?'

'Yes thanks.'

'Good good,' she smiled distractedly, sliding around a door.

I got away from them as early as I could that evening. All that forced hilarity: the champagne drinking, the cracker pulling, their unrelenting attempts to catch each other under the mistletoe, left a sour taste in my mouth. It now felt as if I'd been away from Seb for months and when I tried to picture that pining face at the window I now found only blurred images and sometimes, even, a cruel grimace at the centre of a black painting.

I fell into a restless sleep, the events of my stay racing through my mind with such vivid cruelty that I gripped my blankets until my knuckles hurt. And when I sank into even lower, mournful dreams, a figure, Raphael, crawled into my bed.

I tried to hold back at first, my limbs rigid, my heart racing. But when his body enveloped itself in mine it was impossible to resist him. This time my fists clutched at handfuls of flesh, urging him closer to me, his breathlessness in my ear, the taste of sweat on my tongue.

I threw myself up, bolt upright in my bed.

No one.

There was no one else in the room apart from me and the frenzied sound of my own breathing. Slowly I unclenched my fists and grasped my sketchbook. In the half light of my table lamp Seb appeared before me, more sad and gaunt than I'd ever seen him, his eyes fixed in an urgent plea.

Just as I was finishing the final strokes of the picture something scraped against my bedroom floor, near the doorway. I stiffened at the thought of a mouse, but when I gingerly turned to look, I discovered something white lying there instead: a note. I unpeeled myself from the warmth of my bed and opened it.

Dear Serena,

When I apologized to you this morning I was utterly sincere and I feel I owe you a rather better gift than the one I've already given to make up for things properly. You talked about secrets, well here is one that very few people have ever had access to.

It's an enormous volume, I've learnt so much from it over the years. It really has benefitted me immensely. But as you have little time left here I suggest you just read the introduction. It's enough to give you an insight.

Oh, I forgot to tell you where it is. Look out of your window. It'll give you a clue and then close your eyes, follow your instincts. You have more hope of finding it than most people.

*Good luck and I trust that you won't tell ANYONE about this.
I'm leaving tonight so you won't be seeing me here again.*

Raphael

His handwriting was small and jagged, as if a spider had written the words. I rushed over to my window, drawing back the curtains and looked into the night. On the other side of the glass the brick wall outside glowered back at me. I could see it quite clearly; it was almost like a London night out there, not particularly dark at all. There was no moon to light things up, but even so it was an orange sort of glow, like bright lamps turned up to the sky.

The library.

Only the big glass dome of the library, properly lit up, could reflect so much light.

Fear and excitement pumped through my veins until my body felt hot, even though I could see my breath before me. Druid Manor was sleeping now, so dark that I didn't need to close my eyes, although I did anyway. I followed my instincts, just as Raphael had instructed and gradually the air turned cooler about me, the smell of damp stronger in my nostrils. My fingers skimmed against the crumbling plaster and across the occasional light switch, but I didn't even bother trying to turn the lights on. And with every footstep my journey suddenly seemed to make more and more sense, as if I'd walked it a thousand times, knew the route as well as the lines on the palm of my hand.

When I opened my eyes the library's double doors rose up before me and shafts of light beamed invitingly from around their edges. *Come in*, they seemed to say. *Come and hear some secrets.*

The first thing I saw inside was Lucinda's face in the portrait, grinning straight back at me like before.

'Hello Lucinda Hartreve,' I murmured, half expecting her to answer back.

A round table had now been placed in the middle of the room and on it lay a book that looked like a big old dictionary. It had a brown leather cover, hardly embellished at all apart from the title and the name of its author on the front.

Disappearance and the Art of Hypnosis by Walter Balanchine.

The pages, some as thin as tracing paper, smelt of dust and history. My fingers were shaking so much that I could hardly bring myself to turn them. On the first page it read:

This book is dedicated to my dear friends, Lord Stephen Hartreve and Miranda White.

I scooped the book up as carefully as if it were a newborn baby, sat down with it, cradled in my lap, and began to read:

I have been accused of performing magic many times in my life. From the unruly children who battered me and broke my bones on the streets where I grew up, to the audiences who have sat open mouthed with wonderment at my theatrical exhibitions. But I tell you this, the magic around us, in the natural comings and goings of our daily lives, is a thousand, nay a million times more phenomenal than anything I could ever conjure.

They say I can make things appear and disappear. Well yes I can, not by spells but through the manipulation of the mind. So skilled am I in this craft that I can make almost anything happen for the person who wants to believe it, or the person who looks deeply enough into my eyes. And I will discuss this art later in my volume. It is something that can be learnt through rigorous training.

But how did I learn it? I hear you ask. In truth I did no more than take heed of the world around me. I watched what others refused to see. I loved and admired what is beautiful but studied with equal vigour what is ugly and displeasing to the eye. This magic you all speak of is everywhere! And in our world things appear and disappear about us all the time. Let me help you, reader, to learn how to take notice of this natural occurrence and harness its power in your own way.

I will begin with a story. A melancholy story about a little girl called Miranda. This is what happened to the dear little creature:

Miranda's mother became ill. She took to her bed for more than a year, white with fatigue and groaning with pain. The family acquired medicine, although it was of little use, and kept it in a high cupboard.

One day young Miranda was left alone to nurse her mother. The woman was in a particularly troublesome state and called to her young daughter to administer her medicine. The child had some difficulty in reaching the high cupboard where the potion was kept. She was scared of falling, of breaking her bones against the hard stone floor. But she reached as high as she could and found the bottle, or should I say 'a' bottle which she felt suited the purpose.

Little did Miranda know that this bottle was certainly not her mother's medicine; that it contained a ruthless poison that ripped through the woman's stomach within minutes and left her a corpse.

Miranda's father and sister were naturally distraught by the untimely death of the woman they loved and together they agreed that, as a form of punishment, young Miranda should be completely ignored by everyone for an entire year. Even the servants, who cherished the little girl's sweet nature, were threatened with dismissal for breaking this rule. And so the little girl was left quite alone to her misery and wretchedness.

The year passed slowly and as each day went by Miranda became further and further entrenched in her desolation, until even her skin began to look grey and unhealthy. Gradually she started to forget what it was like to be noticed and spent so much time on her own that any form of human contact became quite terrifying to her. When strangers approached her she shrank away from their company, as if their sympathy was too painful to bear. Even outsiders stopped talking to her; they sensed the fear in her eyes and in her stooped, pale little frame.

It was a year and a half after her mother's death before her father and sister even realized that Miranda's sentence had been well and truly served. But her family had got so used to ignoring her that it seemed quite unnatural to bring a sudden halt to the habit. She continued to spend most of her time alone or occasionally in the company of kind servants.

As the years went by Miranda's family began to find her presence in their lives so faint that at times they barely found it possible to see her at all. In their hearts they liked to believe that she had vanished altogether. But she was there all the time, wilting and pining in the background and one day, quite suddenly, she was a woman: a woman with strength and courage, married off to a despicable man and left to grapple with the evils that life threw at her. So courageous and so quietly beautiful.

Now reader, what do you think of this? Did magic make the little Miranda disappear? Or was it her family's disgust and contempt that imprisoned her in her own guilt and forced her out of their lives...?

The introduction ended like this, with a question mark. I shivered: my teeth were chattering and I noticed that my fingers had turned blue. I had nothing on but my nightdress. My arms were so rigid with cold that it was a struggle just to put the heavy book back in its place on the table.

On the wall by the double doors more than a dozen brass light switches saluted up at me. One... two... three. I flicked them off, one after another, gradually lowering myself into darkness like a diver sinking down into the blue. When the last light went out I closed my eyes and felt for the door handle. It felt better not to try and look at all when there was nothing left to see.

1893

Yet another carriage scraped to a halt outside. More furniture for the new inhabitants of number 36 no doubt. At a safe distance from her bedroom window, Miranda glimpsed down at the street below, expecting to see a wardrobe or perhaps a piano wobbling across the pavement. But no, a lone carriage was waiting down there instead, and a dark figure of a man was unfolding himself from inside it.

She squinted down and realized that the emerging figure was her lawyer Mr Fairclough. And then the edge of a petticoat brushed against the carriage door behind him, the gloved fingertips of a woman's hand reaching out for the lawyer's assistance.

Miranda's hands sprang up to her cheeks. She raced to her dressing table to inspect her blotchy skin in the mirror. Her dress was awful and her hair was in such a state: greasy at the roots, dry at the ends. She scraped it back as far as it would go but it still looked frightful.

A knock came at her bedroom door, and Mrs Hubbard entered looking rather hot and flustered.

'You have some visitors.'

'Yes, yes I saw them through the window. I have to do something to this face of mine!'

But Mrs Hubbard seemed to hesitate, as if she was trying to find the right words for something. 'Rather an unexpected guest...' she murmured.

'I know! All very unexpected. Please see to them, I really must sort myself out now.'

The door groaned shut and Miranda was left alone with her face in the mirror. Her skin had always been pallid but now increasing colonies of speckled marks seemed to be moving in, along with small veins like cracks of red lightning in her cheeks. And the purple rings beneath her eyes didn't help matters.

'What's become of me?' she whispered to her reflection. But the mirror seemed to be in an unforgiving mood today, looming closer and closer towards her like a magnifying glass, stretching her face to double the size. The veins in her cheeks multiplied, toxic red now, uglier and uglier. And then the shadow fell behind her.

It was so dark and sudden this time that a spasm shot through her and a yelp escaped from her lips. The mirror had turned black, a gaping cave-mouth; she could barely find her face in it at all.

'Please... not again. Leave me alone for pity's sake!'

She scraped the stool back beneath her, away from the dressing table, away from the mirror, the palms of her hands clutching against her chest. She screwed her eyes tightly shut: one... two... three... and then slowly blinked them open.

The mirror was white and watery again, all gone. Nothing left of the fear but the sound of her own rapid breathing.

When she entered the drawing room, the lawyer was standing there alone.

'This is most unexpected,' she said, moving towards him. 'I thought you came with a guest...'

'Ah yes, in the other room Mrs Whitest... White. I wanted to take the liberty of speaking to you alone first. My apologies for coming without warning, it is rather an urgent matter.'

'I do hope it's good news - something about the house? Do tell me you've found a buyer at long last.'

Mr Fairclough lowered his head and made a sort of brief gurgling sound with his throat.

'Um, I'm afraid...' he answered, casting his eyes along the full length of the room and drawing his eyebrows together in such a serious sombre way that they were almost in danger of touching in the middle. '... I'm afraid to say that the sale of your house is not the reason for my visit today; it is proving to be something of a problem.'

'A problem? Why, what are people saying?'

'As I have not been directly involved in proceedings it's difficult for me to judge accurately. But news has come back to me that, for some untold reason, people are keeping away and the few who have visited have been rather, how can I put it, disturbed.'

'Disturbed?'

'They say that the house is shadowy, that it harbours an atmosphere of, unrest? I can't explain...'

'There's no need, no need at all. I quite understand.'

The lawyer coughed into his hand, flicking his eyes across the room again, the corners of his mouth arching down.

A funny sort of cry, like a low wail, met her ears. Minerva

perhaps, grappling at the door. Although it didn't sound at all like her.

'Excuse me for a moment,' she said. 'I'm not quite sure what that strange sound is.'

'No, don't go. Please. I think I am the one to explain that to you. The sound that you have just heard lies at the cause of my visit today. I think you should probably sit down for this... Not two hours ago a young Frenchwoman by the name of Claudette Chauvin was delivered to the doors of my offices. She was accompanied by a lawyer I know well, a Mr Barrowman who has been acting on behalf of a former neighbour of yours. Mrs Eden.'

Just the sound of that name, spoken out loud was enough to turn her cold.

'Miss Chauvin has been rather emotional since her arrival. She's endured a long journey it seems, with something of a burden to take care of. And yet she refused to disclose anything at all about her circumstances to me until I could convince her of one thing.'

'And what was that?'

'That your late husband, Mr Whitestone, is dead.'

The sound came again, a soft innocent cry like a baby.

'It is now that I should probably give you this letter. It was written to you, although unsealed, by the late Mrs Eden shortly before her death and will, I think, explain everything. I will leave you to read it in private.'

The letter was written on cream paper. The last time she'd seen that rushed scrawl it had been on a torn piece of magazine: Lucinda's response to that fatal dinner invitation.

Dear Miranda

May I call you that now? You nursed me so kindly that I feel an unexpected closeness to you.

If you are reading this letter then it means that your husband and I are both dead. Because that was the agreement you see, that Claudette couldn't possibly come to you until you were well and truly rid of him. How I hope and pray for this happy circumstance!

I have harmed you Miranda. I am so sorry. But please let me give you something in return that is more precious than anything I could ever dare possess for myself. The child, my child, that I made with Tristan in all my folly!

I feel it moving every day inside me, dragging his heels along my sides – yes, I'm sure it is a boy! And in spite of all my feebleness he is strong, stronger than me!

Alfonso gets angry with me. He has fooled himself into thinking that I'll live through this, but I know better. I have been watching myself fall apart. I am a dead woman already.

You lost your mother, as did I. And those bitter holes in our worlds have shown us how necessary a mother is to a child's life, my child's life. But a mother should not be an ignorant fool like me! Heavens no. She should be someone like you who is strong and forgiving. Someone who still endures in spite of all the wretchedness and ghastliness around them.

Take him. Please take him and love him and do whatever it is that you must to make him happy. Until now I have made all the wrong decisions in my life. I trust you to make the right ones.

Lucinda

The soft wail reached her again; its sadness pulled her towards it, growing ever louder, bouncing petulantly against the walls of the hallway.

Motherless. Motherless! it seemed to say.

The door handle opposite turned and the lawyer appeared, his expression as sombre and downcast as before.

'You have read the letter?'

'Yes.'

'This is a most unusual set of circumstances. If you would like to take some time to think then I could arrange...'

'That won't be necessary. It is all quite legal?'

'Yes, I have the documents. Mrs Eden summoned Mr Barrowman to Paris during her time there although the child was later born in Leipzig. She was most exacting apparently, specifying that the child should remain in Miss Chauvin's care until he could be handed over to you on your husband's demise.'

'He?'

'Indeed. She had a son. She named your late husband as the father. You know she died on exactly the same day as Mr Whitestone, just a matter of hours before him it seems. Strange.'

Swish swish

The sound of that dress brushing against the floor came

whispering back to her and the sight of those peacock feathers, glinting in all that lovely hair...

'Oh, it's not quite so strange,' she replied. 'Not really I don't think. Alfonso Eden, where is he?'

'Abroad still. Miss Chauvin says that his wife's death weakened him considerably. He's a broken man it seems, unwilling to move from where she left him. He couldn't even bring himself to look at the child apparently.'

The wail came again: *Motherless! Motherless!*

'Well I will look at him. Right now if you'll excuse me.'

The Frenchwoman was patting and rocking the small parcel feverishly in her arms. It was the same small dark woman who'd come to nurse Lucinda in Dover on that cold morning. She rushed towards her.

'He will not settle Madame,' she said, putting him in her arms. 'He is usually quite content, I don't know what it could be!'

'Is he hungry?' asked Miranda; the bundle seemed impossibly light.

'He will not eat. That is also so unusual for him.'

She drifted towards the window, the small red face screaming up at her in protest, eyes tightly shut.

'I will leave you for now Mrs White!' came Mr Fairclough's voice, raised to make itself heard above the wails. 'But before I go I would like to leave one suggestion in your mind. It is a bold one, but in light of your financial circumstances, one that I should at least make an attempt at. Mr Whitestone's family...'

'I will hear nothing of them.'

'Indeed, but please do listen to what I have to say. I am aware that Mr Whitestone's family have hardly been forthcoming in their support of you so far. Lucinda Eden however was, as you might know, a Hartreve. They are a wealthy family, with a large estate in Wiltshire, and although I understand that there were difficult relations caused by Mrs Eden's marriage, there was once a close bond between her and her father. Lord Stephen Hartreve is commonly known as a strong-minded man, but he has also displayed a capacity for enormous acts of charitable generosity in the past. He could be a valuable friend to you and the boy.'

'I am afraid that such a proposition is simply unimaginable. I will manage. We will manage.'

'I see. Please then accept my apology. And do remember that

as your lawyer my interests are only in your well-being. If, for example, you have any difficulties remaining in this house, then a solution must be found...' his voice trailed off. She didn't even need to look at him to know that those sharp eyes of his were once again sizing up the room around him.

'Yes, I do understand. And thank you for your concern.'

The baby punched at the air with his red knuckles.

'Does this place make you cry little man? Sometimes it makes me cry as well,' she murmured to him, gently kissing his hot smooth face. He stopped wailing quite suddenly and looked straight up at her with eyes so achingly familiar, that in a moment she was as smitten as that very first day when his father had taken her hand and smiled, just as if it had been love at first sight.

'Like beautiful pools of crystal blue,' she whispered, as he stared up at her unblinkingly. 'And you seduce the world with them just like Tristan did, don't you? But we won't let you be like him. Oh no. Not like him at all.'

The baby yawned like a young lion cub and gradually, in her resolute arms, fell into a deep and exhausted sleep. For two hours she held him in the warm glow of the window.

'You see, I am your slave already little man. And we've only just met!'

She spotted her in a moment, not far off on a bench.

'She's over there, I can see her. Are you sure he's warm enough?'

Mrs Hubbard raised her eyes to heaven. 'He has three blankets wrapped around him. You should be worrying yourself more about him being too hot!'

Two blue eyes winked up at her from the perambulator. It was no good, she just had to lean in and kiss those soft cheeks one more time. A toothless grin beamed up at her.

'How he loves the park! Alright. One circuit should do it; I don't want too much time with her. Then bring him over to us.'

Jane had found a place to sit under a large oak tree. She was wearing a thick brown coat, far too warm for a day like this, and her mouth was fixed in a solemn pout.

Miranda waded slowly towards her through the grass. Her sister appeared to be looking in her direction but showed no hint of recognition. Closer and closer, just yards away now, and still she didn't even blink or move a muscle in that resolute face. Walter Balanchine's words came flooding back to her:

I see the pain inside you! You try to make it invisible, make yourself invisible, but I see it there, smouldering away.

'Hello.'

'Oh it's you,' said Jane, refusing to meet her eyes. 'I didn't see you coming.'

'Yes I know. Thank you for meeting me here.'

'Rather more appropriate to have met at the house I think.'

'Actually no. The house is not the best of places to be in at the moment. I am trying to sell it. It was disappointing that you were unable to come to Tristan's funeral.'

That did it. She had Jane's full attention now: eyes round, lips trembling.

'Did you really expect me to attend the funeral of a lunatic suicide?' she spat.

'He was my husband.'

'A vile individual.'

'Yes. But my husband, your sister's husband, nevertheless. And now I've been left in an awful predicament. I have no money and the house won't sell.'

'What do you mean it *won't* sell?'

'It revolts people, turns them away. I really can't explain it. But I have a child now to care for as well.'

'A child! I had no idea.'

'He's not mine. Tristan had an affair with our neighbour Mrs Eden. She bore him a son and when they both died she left him to me. I am responsible for him now.'

It was almost possible to feel sorry for Jane at that moment. Her astonishment was such that she actually spluttered and all the taut muscles in her face suddenly slumped down.

'Are you out of your mind?' she gasped.

'No. Mrs Eden was very badly abused by Tristan. I think you might be aware of his history in that respect. I helped her escape from him and now that she's gone the child needs a mother.'

'There are other family members.'

'But he has been left to me!'

Jane's mouth hung open. She raised her hands as if she were about to grab her by the shoulders and Miranda felt herself slink back an inch.

'Please, lower your hands. Please. My sole intention today was to meet you in an open and honest way. Because we have never really been honest with each other, have we? I have been punished all my life for a wrong I never meant to commit. I now find myself with no money, a home that has become wretched and a child to care for. You are my only relative, and although we have never been friends, I am asking you outright whether you have any space in your heart to help me.'

Jane's eyes glistened. Could there be tears there or was it just a ray of sun glinting back at her? Beyond her sister's shoulder Mrs Hubbard was approaching, the wheels of the perambulator sluggish in the grass. He was probably sleeping now, his downy head resting peacefully against his pillow. Happy sleep. Not like at home.

'Look. They're coming now, just behind you, my cook Mrs Hubbard and the baby. You can hold him if you like. He only seems to cry at home, as if it hurts him to be there. I think his father...'

'Be quiet!' The tears had gone, or perhaps they'd been nothing more than a passing sunray after all. 'Of all the things you've done over the years! All the ridiculous behaviour.'

Mrs Hubbard was almost with them now. She was red in the face, puffed out with all that pushing.

'Are you telling me that you won't help?'

'I... I cannot.'

She bowed her head, eyes cast firmly down.

'How very sad. And after all these years you still struggle to look me in the eye.'

'That's simply not true!'

'Yes it is. Goodbye sister; from now on you won't even need to ignore me ever again, because I'll be gone. But I have one thing left to say to you. Just one last thing. If our roles had been reversed in this life I would never, NEVER, have treated you in such a heartless despicable way.'

'But Miranda...'

'Goodbye.'

Her feet felt surprisingly light as she walked away. Answers, even the most unwanted ones, were still better than lingering questions. In the corner of her eye she could see the bent shame in Jane's curved back.

'How was your walk?' she asked, beaming at Mrs Hubbard.

'Ah, there's my boy! Lost in happy sleep. Let me kiss him gently.'

The sound ribboned in and out of her sleep. Her body felt like rocks; so tired that she doubted whether she'd be able to run from a blazing fire if she had to. And there he was once more, gliding through her dreams. Walter Balanchine...

'Do you feel in any sort of danger?'

'I don't think so.'

'Promise that you'll come to me, when the time is right?'

'But why would I...?'

'Promise.'

'I promise.'

The sound came to her again, lulling her out of the tunnel, wishing her awake... but Walter pulled her back towards him, with those eyes that could read into her soul. He'd taken the old nightmare away, replaced it with himself. All was jewel coloured in her sleep now: bright emerald green and amethyst, and the tinkling of trinkets hanging from a chain.

'Promise that you'll come to me, when the time is right?'

'I promise.'

And then that sound yet again; that familiar, painful wail. She drew her limbs back through the tunnel, heaved the great boulders off her eyelids.

The baby was punching at the air when she got to him: fists red and hot, his small head streaked with sweat.

'Oh I'm sorry, I'm sorry my darling. How long have you been crying? I'm just so tired, you cry so much here...'

In her arms the wail simmered down to a pathetic whimper. He stared up at her pleadingly, as if he were desperately trying to tell her something with those watery blue eyes of his.

'What is it little man? If only, if only you could just tell me!'

Her arms felt bruised with carrying him; her shoulders pounded with knots and strains. How many hours had it taken to get him off to sleep? Four? Five? And now awake again, with rings under his eyes and hers.

'You sleep everywhere except here. You laugh and smile everywhere except here.'

The first light of day trickled in from between the curtains, casting spike headed shadows across the floor.

'I'll get you some milk now,' she murmured to him. 'And

perhaps some water to clean that sweaty head of yours. Just wait for me here, you won't even notice that I've gone.'

But as soon as his body touched the mattress of the cot again, his fists curled, his little back arched up and his lungs let loose a cry of double the previous force.

'Two minutes,' she stammered, dashing out of the room and flying downstairs to the kitchen. 'Two minutes!'

She raced across the hallway, almost tripping over herself as something seemed to brush against her. Just a gust of cold air but it made her shiver. It was so gloomy down here, like wading through a grey cloud. She could hardly see a thing.

The crying was a distant noise now, even fainter when she got to the kitchen. The floor was icy against her bare feet and she moved hastily, preparing his milk and putting it on a tray along with a glass bowl of water to mop his sweaty head. But then, quite suddenly, the crying stopped. She closed her eyes and took a deep breath as relief sank in.

The warm water slopped about in the bowl on the way up and as she walked along the corridor to his room. Hadn't she left his door wide open? It was almost closed now, tricky to pull back with the tray in her hands. And he wasn't asleep. She could now hear him murmuring in short sharp tremors:

'Ah... ah... ah.'

She had to balance the tray carefully and then wedge her foot in the door to open it again. The bowl of water slopped about even more. 'Ah... ah... ah.' The door swung open.

Do you feel in any sort of danger?

Walter's voice came roaring back through her head again almost before she saw it, standing there.

'Ah... ah... ah.'

Motherless. Motherless.

The shadow hung over his cot, its spine like a long knotted rope. And on the mattress beneath it a small fist punched at the air.

An explosion roared beneath her. The shadow began to turn, its spine-rope bending with the grace of a cat. Her eyes fell down to the splintered tray on the floor, to the bowl of water now smashed into a thousand shards of broken glass, the bottle of milk rolling to a standstill in a ridge between the floorboards.

'Aaaaaaw!'

His mew was like a tortured animal.

'When will you stop?' she cried. 'They're always quite defenceless, aren't they? Your victims.'

The broken glass was barely visible on the floor, as deadly as black ice.

'I thought I loved you so very much, once...'

She took one cautious step with her naked foot. A tearing sensation slithered along the bottom of her heel. She lifted it and something wet dripped down between her toes. She took another step closer.

'Aaaaaw!' came a small strangled wail.

The knotted rope bent double, its head swooping down into the cot.

'Get out!' she screamed and the glass crunched beneath her naked feet as she threw herself forwards. 'Leave us alone Tristan! Leave us in peace!'

The spine wavered, his great mouth gaped back at her as she plunged through the darkness, cold claws scrabbling against her skin. She tasted blood, her own, and threw her fists back at him.

Promise that you'll come to me...

All she could hear was Walter's voice ringing in her ears. She grasped the child up into her arms, wailing in frenzy against her neck, and at once the darkness seemed to shrink away: smaller and smaller into nothing but the brush of scurrying footsteps retreating across the floor. Gone.

She threw a few things into the same bag that she'd taken to Dover.

'Right. Try not to look at this little man,' she said.

But the baby watched intently from his position on her bed as she drew the shards of glass from her feet with tweezers and bound the wounds with torn strips from an old petticoat. There were deep scratches on her cheeks and neck as well, she could feel them with her fingertips. But she didn't dare look at herself in a mirror, not yet.

'We're going now. This blanket should be warm enough for you.' And she scooped him up, grasping the bag with her other hand. 'We're leaving this godforsaken place forever.'

The grey gloomy cloud of the downstairs hallway seemed to be spreading up the stairs. She plunged down through it, the precious bundle tightly in her grasp. Something soft like fingers strummed across her shoulder blades.

'Don't touch me! I'm not afraid of you Tristan. Do you understand?' she screamed into the air, hugging the child even closer. A petulant whine rose up and then fell away behind her.

Her feet were throbbing now. She flung the door open and fell out into the street, the cold air stinging her face. As Marguerite Avenue flowed into the distance, each step felt as sharp as knives. The bandages on her feet began to squelch with blood, and yet she found herself smiling all the same and then actually laughing out loud.

'I'm free! Look at us little man, we're free!' she cried out.

A woman in black was approaching, a basket on her arm and the outline of a neat bonnet against the white morning sky. Gradually her face came into focus, peering back at her in criss-crosses of disbelief.

'Mrs... White... are you quite alright? Why look at your face! What's happened to you? And you can barely walk!'

Mrs Hubbard dropped her basket and dashed towards her.

'It's alright. I'm so glad you're here, I didn't think I'd see you again.'

'I came early to help. Thought you'd have a bad night of it.'

'And that I did! But it's over now. We've left and we're never going back again.'

A soft purring body suddenly pushed itself up against her leg. 'And it looks like Minerva's joining us!'

Mrs Hubbard's jaw twitched. Her eyes wandered down the road towards the house and then back to her again.

'So you've finally left,' she murmured. 'That place is a scourge of a house if you ask me...'

'Not healthy for a young baby.'

'Not healthy for anyone. Well,' she said with a shrug. 'Then I'm coming with you.'

'Oh surely not! You have your sons.'

'They don't need me. Big grown men. You're my family now. You and the young gentleman here. Come on, lean on my arm, that's it. Slowly slowly.'

'I am so fortunate to have met you. How can I ever thank you?'

'You could start by telling me where we're going.'

'Oh, of course. We're going to a place called Limehouse, to

find Walter Balanchine.'

SERENA'S STORY

I heaved my suitcase up the last few steps and rammed the door open with my shoulder.

'Welcome back.'

Seb was sitting on the edge my bed, pale faced and scruffy.

'How was your Christmas?' I asked.

'Lonely. How was Druid Manor?'

'Lonelier.'

He fidgeted with his hands. There were dark circles under his eyes. Neither of us seemed to be able to say anything. I began to unpack, my art things first, pulling open the drawer where I kept my hundreds of sketches.

'Oh my God!' I cried.

'What?'

'My drawings, they've all gone.'

I brushed my hand against the bare wood at the bottom of the drawer and then began pulling all the other drawers open as well, rummaging under bits of clothing and anything else inside. 'No they've gone. Gone. Who could have taken them? Do you know?'

Seb had stood up, his shoulders seemed thin and hunched. He shrugged them.

'I have no idea.'

The fire rose up inside me. 'Even if you did, you wouldn't tell me would you?'

He shook his head. 'You've changed. I knew you would.'

'No I haven't, I'm just... tired. Sorry.'

And I really was. In a moment my anger fell away again and left me with exhausting hollowness. I wanted so much to tell him about it all, before he had another chance to speak, but the words just jammed in my mouth. Instead I took him in my arms, gripping on as tightly as I could. He smelled of home and love and of being loved, his cheek nestled on the top of my head.

His hands moved down to my waist, pulling my top up and over my head, running his fingers down the sides of my ribs. And then, kneeling down, he found the scar on my side with his lips. I shivered at their touch, knotting my fingers in his hair and drawing him closer and closer still.

There was a letter waiting for me in the kitchen when I went down later.

'How was your Christmas?' I asked Gladys as I ran my finger under the seal.

'Passable!' she replied. She was feverishly whipping life into some egg whites at the kitchen table.

The letter was from Jessica.

Dearest Serena

I hope this gets to you before Christmas. I've been rather rushed getting ready for my cruise. If not then I hope they treated you well at Druid Manor. Is this our first Christmas apart?

I'm writing because I've uncovered a few interesting things about that street you're living on. You asked me when I came to look into the cause of the missing house next door. I had a rummage through the archives (you can see that I've included some photocopies of various census records in this letter) and this is what has emerged:

It appears that in 1891, number 34 Marguerite Avenue was very much in existence. It was occupied by a seemingly childless couple called Tristan and Miranda Whitestone. Number 32 was owned by a family named Smithson and 36 by a couple called Alfonso and Lucinda Eden.

Now, the strange thing is that when you get to the census of 1901, there's no record of 34 or the Whitestone couple whatsoever. A family by the name of Bone is now living at 32 and your house, number 36, is by then inhabited by Hartreves: Charles and Virginia Hartreve and their three children.

I've been through every manuscript and rotting piece of documentation I can find, but there is NO evidence of 34's existence after that time. There are various records relating to the Whitestones from before then: their marriage certificate for example and documents appertaining to Tristan Whitestone's profession. He was in India for a while but then returned, under a dark cloud it seems, to run his father's business in London, which went into liquidation just a few years later. All records relating to his later movements and eventual death seem to have miraculously disappeared. His wife is nowhere to be found either.

All a bit of a mystery isn't it? I've mulled it over again and again and although this sounds rather dramatic, I can't help but think that someone has actively tried to make it all disappear. I've looked everywhere

*I can think of, but this particular little slice of Kensington history just
seems to have been lost forever. So there you go. Perhaps it would interest
your hosts to pass on this information, or then again, it might be better to
let sleeping dogs lie. I'll leave that one to your discretion.*

Much love,
Jessica

I picked up a pencil and began to dawdle on the back of the
torn envelope.

'Gladys?'

'Yes.'

'You've been working here a long time, haven't you?'

'More years than I can count.'

'What do you know of the house next door?'

She brushed the egg white off the spoon with her forefinger.

'You mean number 32?'

'Yes of course... there is no other house, surely?'

She raised her eyebrows and began to remove her apron.

'It's owned by the Herberts, or something like that. They're
never around. She's French and they spend most of their time over
there. Before them there was old Mr Bone.'

'Bone?'

'Yes. He inherited it from his parents, the youngest child and
only son of an endless stream of children. I don't know how his
mother did it, silly little blonde thing!'

'You speak as if you knew her.'

She patted her hair, hurrying to the door. 'He lived well into
his nineties, old Mr Bone, and then the house got sold out of the
family. Is that the time? I've got all the unpacking to do and the
washing. You don't know how long it takes to get that damp Druid
Manor smell out of those clothes...'

As soon as she was gone I dropped the pencil and picked up
the census copies that Jess had included with the letter. The 1891
record sat on top and I scanned the list of names until my eyes
landed on hers, Miranda Whitestone, in thick black handwriting.
Surely this was the same Miranda White? She'd been married to a
man called Tristan, and Lucinda, the rebellious young woman I'd
seen in the painting, had been her neighbour. But the second
record, ten years on, bore no number 34 on it at all.

The door swung open and Sasha walked in.

'Good afternoon. I trust you had a good Christmas with the family,' he said, pursing his lips into a tight little smile. 'I've been looking for young Beth, do you know where she is? Upstairs in her room perhaps?'

The hairs on my arms stood up. 'Yes she is, but she's rather tired and we have unpacking to do. Sorry.'

I snatched up my things and dashed out, passing Edward on my way up the stairs. His face looked sullen and hard, like a prison wall. He nodded at me but said nothing. Somewhere in the house there was a large thud.

Upstairs Beth was lying on her bed with three pillows over her head.

'What are you doing?'

'Eva keeps arguing and slamming doors. It's driving me mad!'

Just on cue a mighty slam from below shook the walls of Beth's room and up drifted the muffled sound of voices barking at each other in high-pitched tones.

'Do you know what's going on?' I asked her.

'Oh there's a big article in one of the newspapers about Eva's ex-boyfriend today. There's stuff about her in it too and she hates it when it's brought up.'

'How do you know?'

'I listened to her on the phone with Raphael.'

'Beth!'

'Don't be angry! I do it all the time.'

'And that's supposed to make things better?... Look, I tell you what, let's go to the park. We'll kick some leaves about and get some fresh air and hopefully by the time we come back it'll all be over.'

'Alright then. But I want to bring my new scooter.'

'Good idea.'

We meandered through the grey streets together, Beth scooting on ahead and the winter sky so low that it threatened to devour us. I had hoped it would feel better to be back in London, but the city was dead, its usual busy crowds still locked away consuming the dregs of Christmas leftovers.

We passed a small newsagent with an *open* sign in its door. A pile of newspapers was stacked up in the window.

'Beth!' I called. 'Come back and I'll buy you some sweets.'

'Oooohh, yummy!'

I found the article whilst she was deliberating over the pick 'n' mix. It was on the second page of one of the tabloids:

Oligarch Flees Home After Police Enquiries

It was Eva's ex alright, not that I'd ever met him, but there was a picture of her standing right next to him bang in the middle of the article. He was rather handsome: blonde and tall and she was sipping a glass of champagne under a big floppy hat. There were several lines about Eva:

> *... pictured here with his on-off partner Eva Hartreve who has a rather shady history of her own. Born into good English aristocratic stock she set tongues wagging a few years back with a teenage pregnancy: a result of dallying a little two merrily with one of her father's friends, Lord Burnside. Is it 'Ten Lords A-Leaping' in the Christmas ditty? Well this Lord leapt all the way to South America, leaving his wife a miserable recluse in her Richmond shack. Society darling Eva Hartreve sure knows how to pick them. A close source has also indicated that there might be something even more to this cosy Burnside Hartreve relationship. Is such a thing possible? And could it carry the stench of dirty money along with it? Stay with us as the story unfolds.*

A close source. Oh God, Sasha really was honing in on them now.

'You found it then?'

I started and felt my face turn a guilty red as two blue eyes gazed up at me.

'Found what?'

'The article. The one that goes on about that silly Lord. They've got it all wrong you know.'

'What do you mean?'

'He's not my daddy.'

I scrunched the paper closed. 'Then who is? Do you know?' I asked her in a voice that barely sounded like my own and instantly made me feel sick at myself.

The blue eyes blinked back at me. 'Sorry, I can't tell you. I've always promised not to tell anyone. But I thought you'd guessed?

Maybe it's true...'

'What's true?'

'That sometimes people can't see what's right under their noses.'

I put my hands on her shoulders and squeezed them softly.

'I'm sorry I asked you.'

'It's alright. Can we buy the sweeties now?' she shrugged me off. 'Look, I've chosen all my favourites and some of yours too.'

When we returned to the house, Sasha was loitering in the hallway.

'Hello!' cried Beth.

'Yes yes, hello there,' he answered through gritted smiling teeth. 'Now run along to the kitchen. Run along.'

I followed after Beth as she trotted away but his arm snatched out at me, grabbing my elbow towards him so hard that I winced. He drew his face close to mine; I could see the moisture on his teeth.

'I have your picture,' he whispered through them.

'Oh! So *you* took my drawings. How dare you! I want them back.'

He drew his eyebrows together and fished something out of his pocket.

'I don't know what you mean about drawings but this is what I have,' he muttered.

In his hand I saw the torn envelope that Jessica's letter had come in. I'd dawdled a picture of Seb on it; his mouth and his eyes so sad.

'You left it, in the kitchen. I want... I need to speak to you about this,' he said, his eyes flashing.

I backed away from him across the hallway. 'Not now.'

'Then when?' he snarled, but there was a hint of desperation in his voice.

'Not now. I don't know when.'

A flock of seagulls skirted up into the white sky and then fell back down again, eyes bent on a catch. I couldn't see the river behind the houses but I could smell its closeness in the air: damp and onerous.

She wasn't in. I knocked on the door once more - nothing.

The seagulls soared up again, screaming into the sky. Then something moved behind the smoked pane of glass at the top of the door; the fuzzy silhouette of someone's head.

'Hello. Is that Lady Burnside?'

'Who are you? Why are you disturbing me?' came a clipped, queenly voice from the other side.

'My name is Serena; I've come here to speak to you about the Hartreve family.'

'Didn't I tell you people to go away?'

'No, please hear me out. I'm not a journalist...'

'I don't care who you are, goodbye.'

'Please, I'm only asking for a few minutes of your time. I work for the Hartreves; I'm actually employed as their nanny. Here, this is my contract of employment with them.'

I prodded the piece of paper through the letterbox with my finger.

There was a moment of silence, then the rustling sound of my contract being snatched up.

'What are you doing here?'

'I've... I've come to tell you something. And also to find out anything you might know about the family. I know you were once good friends. I've become involved with one of them you see... and there's something I need to tell you. But you have nothing to worry about, really. I have no more interest in speaking to the press than you do.'

The door creaked open and a lined, once handsome face, looked me up and down.

'Come on in then if you must. But only for a minute or two.'

Lady Burnside's conservatory looked out onto the river. It was furnished with large wicker chairs, their cushions faded by too much sun. She sat opposite me, bolt upright, with her fingers firmly interlocked in her lap.

'So which of the family members are you sleeping with then, not Edward surely?'

'No.' I wanted to shrink back into the cushions. 'It's Sebastian, Sebastian White.'

She raised her eyebrows so that they nearly disappeared into her helmet of sprayed hair. 'Never heard of him.'

'Really? He's a close friend of the Hartreve children,

practically grew up with them I think.'

'Well clearly not in my presence then! I would have known him, we were often in the house.'

'Oh...'

'Look,' she said, with an agitated shake of the head. 'I don't believe in small talk. You came here for a reason, which you have so far failed to explain, and I will not permit you to waste too much of my time discussing those people.'

I felt myself getting smaller and smaller in my chair. 'Of course. This is all very awkward for me but I suppose I came to tell you that I don't believe your husband is the father of Eva Hartreve's child.'

She seemed to freeze, stock still, so noiseless that my thumping heart echoed even louder and then she threw back her head and unleashed a shrill laugh.

'Is that all?' she cried out. 'I could have told you that my dear. Martin only left the country because he'd swindled one too many people out of their life savings. And besides, he was too busy bedding Arabella at the time even to notice her precocious pain of a daughter. You seem shocked, didn't you know? Oh yes, Arabella Hartreve was so bored and frustrated by her marriage that she must have slept with half the House of Lords by the time that ghastly little Russian academic came along.'

'Sasha?'

'Yes! That was his name. He seemed to have an almost hypnotic effect over her, goodness knows why. We called him her Rasputin.'

'Did she ever explain why she let him into their home, what he was doing there, apart from... well, you know?'

'Only once, although it was a load of old rubbish if you ask me.'

'No, please tell me. I desperately want to know.'

Lady Burnside drew her brows together. Her face was softer now, tired-looking, as if just the mere effort of talking about the Hartreves exhausted her.

'Oh...' she shook her head. 'If you must know, but then you really should leave.'

'Of course I will. I promise.'

She clenched her hands back together again.

'Arabella had had too much to drink one night. We'd been

playing cards and she'd lost badly, which never went down well with her. I took her off to bed but she kept on calling out for the man, Sasha.

"'Be quiet, Edward will hear!'" I kept telling her.

'But she didn't seem to care less: "Sasha's going to take the ghosts away," she kept saying. "He's going to heal us!"'

'Oh the gibberish that came out of that woman's mouth! All sorts about how she could never be mistress of her own home, that it was destroying their lives... I don't know. But what I do know is that that man, Sasha, was a nasty piece of work who had no intention of helping Arabella Hartreve with whatever her problems were. He had ambition stamped all across his face that fellow. Ugh, covers me with goose bumps just to think of him.'

She stopped talking. I felt her eyes on me but I couldn't meet them. Beyond her shoulder through the conservatory windows the river pondered on, slowly heaving itself towards London. The seagulls had abandoned it now; there wasn't even a boat in sight.

'I know that look. They've got under your skin, haven't they?' she said quietly and her gaze drifted somewhere far away. 'They're a cruel bunch. Edward helped Martin, but for what price? All that money, just to prop their crumbling old house up... And still they keep that rumour about the child alive without him being around to defend himself! Martin might have been a crook and an adulterer, but he would never have touched a young girl like that. A word of advice: get out of that house before things turn nasty.'

The tears filled my eyes and the looping river suddenly sprung up into a tight concertina.

'Ah yes, I forgot! Lover boy. What was his name again?'

'Sebastian White,' I whispered.

By the time I got back from Richmond it was early evening, and a haze of drizzle met me outside the tube station. I turned my collar up and ploughed on through it. Close to Marguerite Avenue an area of the pavement had been cordoned off with yellow tape. There were flashing lights and several policemen stepping gingerly through smashed glass on a shop floor.

It was a small antiques shop that sold old maps and globes. The frazzled looking owner was standing in the middle of it all, wringing his hands, shaking his head, trying to answer the policeman's questions. I fled to the other side of the road, my pulse beating time to my quickened pace.

'Hey, I was beginning to get worried about you. Where *have* you been?' Seb pulled my coat off as soon as I got inside, brushing the rain from my cheeks with his hands. 'Guess who's here.'

'Raphael?'

'Yes! How did you know?'

'Oh, just a hunch.'

He smiled, tenderly pressing his fingers against the base of my spine to urge me towards the drawing room.

The lights in there were dim, the carpet warm and soft against my feet after the harsh winter pavement. Raphael was stretched in one of the sofas, a glass of whisky cupped in his hand, and Beth was curled up as usual in her favourite chair, like a small cat.

'Hello you, have a good day?' he asked. His tone was so familiar. It was as if I'd seen him just that morning, maybe shared a pot of coffee and read the morning papers over the kitchen table. But his face told another story. It was full of secrets, our secrets.

'Umm, sort of,' I replied.

'Serena guessed you were back,' said Seb.

'Really? How did you do that?'

'It wasn't hard. You left your calling card.'

His dark eyes seemed to hesitate on my face. 'Where?'

'At that small antiques shop down the road.'

'Right, she's clearly lost it,' laughed Seb. 'Come on Beth, there's nothing for it but to tickle the insanity out of her!'

The two of them pounced on me, tickling until I fell squirming under them onto the carpet. Raphael looked on with a faint smile, but something that looked like fear tugged at the corners of his face, and I saw that familiar tension tighten in his eyes.

I ate in the kitchen as usual that evening with Gladys. When Beth finally came in from the family meal, she scrambled onto my lap, yawning loudly.

'I'll put her to bed tonight,' I said.

'Are you sure, it's your day off isn't it?'

'I don't mind. You must be exhausted and they're all so excited about Raphael coming back.'

The laughing voices were echoing all the way to us in the

kitchen.

'They're setting up a card game already,' she tutted.

She rested her little head against me on our way up the stairs and I wound my arm around her. 'Are you OK?'

'Yes. I've just been bothered a lot today.'

'By what?'

'Voices. They've given me a headache. You see that lady?' she came to a halt. 'She lived here once.'

'What lady?'

'That one there, can't you see her face?'

Her finger was pointing high up into the cornices, just beneath the place where the wall met the hallway ceiling, and a moulded bust peered back at us with a disdainful smile that I'd have recognized anywhere.

'That's Lucinda Hartreve, isn't it?'

'Yes, although she became Lucinda Eden. Her husband's face is over there.'

In the cornice behind us another bust gazed down. He had a large, avuncular face, almost broken in two by his widespread grin.

'He left her alone here,' continued Beth. 'She's the one I hear crying sometimes.'

'Are you sure about that?'

'Of course I am.'

'You need some sleep young lady.'

I ruffled my fingers through her blonde mop, half dragging her up the rest of the way.

Why hadn't I noticed the faces before? Lucinda had been smirking down at me the entire time, and I'd never even thought to look up to find her there. They were everywhere I went, those two women: Lucinda and Miranda. Almost as if they were barely dead at all. Ghosts.

By the time I got back down the card game was in full swing and the drawing room thick with smoke.

'Come on boy!' hollered Edward, poking Robert in the ribs with the mouthpiece of his pipe. 'A three? Surely you can do better than that!' The brandy he was drinking slurred in his voice.

Seb wasn't there, but Sasha was. He cornered me instantly.

'We haven't had our conversation yet,' he murmured hotly in my ear.

'We have nothing to say to each other.'

'You will speak to me or...'

'Or what? Are you going to start threatening me too, as you do with this family? I know all your dirty tricks, just to serve your own interests. Walter Balanchine's dead and buried, just leave it alone.'

He gaped at me with surprise.

'You know about Balanchine? You, the nanny?'

'Yes,' I answered, my blood rising with a sudden urge to hit this man where it really hurt. 'I found a book of his at Druid Manor. Something about disappearance and hypnosis.'

'You found this?'

'Yes I did.'

He brushed some beads of sweat from his brow. The fine veins in the whites of his eyes throbbed with excitement.

'I have spent much of my professional life studying this man,' he whispered hurriedly. 'He was a genius, you have been very fortunate to come across this book. Nevertheless, I cannot believe that you just found it.'

'Sasha!' It was Arabella. 'Come and help me out darling, I'm losing miserably!'

'Yes my dear!' He rearranged his features into a smile and offered her a small salute across the room. 'Here is my card,' he whispered hurriedly. 'Come to my office. I'll make it worth your time.'

'Sasha!'

The whole table had stopped playing now. They were all staring at us.

'I am coming! Ah yes, I see you are in a lot of trouble.'

It was impossible to sleep that night. Instead I listened to the soft whispering of Seb's breath and watched on as old memories flooded towards me through the darkness; bolder and brighter and larger than ever before.

She was there almost every time I closed my eyes: her curved back, straining beneath the old T-shirt, her hands so busy patting down fresh black soil.

'Mum!'

She'd pause, begin to turn, just a hint of a profile coming into view and then the image would start to crack up, blurring the colours until they ran in muddy, stinging streaks.

Long after midnight a sudden beam of light came rushing in from under my bedroom door: it was the single lamp that lit the narrow staircase up to my room. Beth most probably, wandering around half asleep and looking for some company. I crept downstairs, but she was safely huddled up in her bed, her face still and tranquil in the throes of sleep.

'Hello.'

I jumped, my hands flying to my mouth. Raphael was standing right behind me.

'I'm sorry; you didn't hear me coming?'

'Oh my God, you scared the life out of me! How could I have heard you coming when you don't make any noise at all?'

He was wearing black trousers and an old shirt with the sleeves rolled up; fully-dressed as if night and sleep mattered little to him. I noticed for the first time how slim his arms were, all sinew and muscle, the blue veins like streaks of lightning in his skin. Those thin arms had grabbed me once; how surprisingly strong they were.

'Can I have a word with you, in my room?' he murmured.

'Can't it wait until tomorrow?'

'No.'

'Alright then... Did you switch that light on to get me up?'

'Yes.'

I'd never been in Raphael's room before. It looked out towards the back of the house and had very little in it apart from a bed, a small table cluttered with objects, an antique wooden wardrobe and numerous paintings propped up against the walls all around the floor. In the dim light some of them just looked like canvases painted jet black, presumably his own stark creations, but there were many more: portraits, pictures of buildings, even a humble impression of a jug of wild flowers.

'Take a seat,' he said, offering me the edge of his bed. 'Would you like a cigarette?'

'Thanks.'

I could see even more of the paintings from this angle. One of them looked like a portrait of Beth set on its side. The edge of another small painting poked out from behind it, chipped and old, embellished in shades of gold and brown. Raphael was watching me; his pale face lingered in the corner of my eye.

'Why do you want me here?'

He didn't move.

'I'd like to know what you meant earlier, about me leaving a *calling card.*'

The gold and brown painting caught my eye again. I could just about see the edge of a man painted in the middle of it, his head crowned by a halo.

'Every time I see you, your arrival miraculously coincides with news of a robbery: Habsburg gems, Celtic jewellery not dissimilar to the necklace that you gave Beth, the painting in the church, the small antiques shop. And who knows where that bike came from! It's what you do, isn't it? You're not an artist at all; you're a thief.'

He laughed gently, a sad laugh. 'Has anyone ever told you that you look like an elf? Actually in this light you're more like a beautiful slender fairy. You're not quite real, are you Serena? And you're lonely, really lonely. We're so alike in that way. Let me take care of you.'

I turned my face away from him. The haloed figure was holding something silver in his right hand: a fish. And the figure was Jesus, feeding the five thousand. I swallowed hard, summoning up the strength to carry on, willing myself not to look him in the eye.

'I could threaten to tell your parents, but they already know don't they?' I said.

'How well you've come to understand my family.'

'Why do you do it?'

'Because I can. You found the book in the library? Read the introduction about poor little Miranda? I've read the whole thing. I've been studying it all my life. Balanchine was a genius you know. He understood the susceptibility of the human mind and he harnessed it! That little man in the antiques shop earlier, he was there the whole time, never even saw any of his stuff go until it was too late.'

'I don't think that Walter Balanchine wrote that book to train thieves.'

He pulled something from out of his pocket and cupped it in his hand. I raised my chin to see. A cross, similar but larger than the one he'd given Beth nestled there in the coils of its chain. It was intricately engraved and a red stone glinted like a dark, knowing eye from its centre. Raphael drew a tender finger across it.

'I'm not a thief. I just like to have beautiful things about me.'

'I could call the police right now.'

'But you're not going to, are you? You want something else.'

'Yes.'

He let the cross slide gently from his hand onto the table and then moved closer. His expression was calm, measured, and I raised my eyes to meet his.

'Take me there,' I whispered and his gaze rushed through me like an electric charge. My fingers twitched, I raised my arms towards him. 'Take me to the house next door.'

I could barely feel the pavement beneath my naked feet. Raphael's arm was around my shoulders, propelling me softly on, turning me to face back towards the row of houses. Something had changed.

It felt so subtle, like the smallest adjustment to a much loved face or an old family photograph; barely discernible at all but enough to turn the familiar into something entirely alien. Number 36 was just as it was, nestled at the end of the row against the old brick wall. But the house before it was whiter than the one I knew. It had pots of orchids growing behind the drawing room windows and on the door two brass numbers shone out proudly in the moonlight: 34.

The arm around my shoulders tightened. 'Come on.'

The door wasn't locked; it fell open with a single stroke and inside the air tasted of wretchedness. Its putrid haze filled the rooms like a grey cloud, smothering the antique furniture, the chandeliers, the threadbare curtains and moth-eaten carpets. It stung my eyes so that they filled with tears but Raphael's arm drew me on and I floated through it all, mouth agape, a century of dust clinging to the soles of my feet.

The walls felt cool and firm against my fingers, no less real than the house I lived in right next door. He led me to the dining room, its table set with plates and glasses, as if awaiting a dinner party. And on the wall there hung a portrait of a young couple. The woman gazed out of it with anxious eyes, her mouth and chin slightly askew as if she might have needed some convincing to sit for the painter. Miranda.

But the man next to her. Oh God, I knew those eyes so well.

'Tristan Whitestone,' came Raphael's voice.

'Miranda's husband.'

243

'Yes. He had an affair with Lucinda Hartreve, Mrs Eden. And then he imprisoned her up in that room where you sleep now, pregnant with his child.'

'Did she survive?'

'Only just. Miranda saved her, helped her escape. But childbirth finished her off. She left the baby, a boy, in Miranda's care and they went away.'

'What happened to Tristan Whitestone?'

His breath quickened into small gasps. 'Tristan Whitestone has never really left.'

We glided up the stairs, passing gaping corridors filled with closed doors, the grey air washing around our limbs. Raphael's touch kept me hostage; we moved as one and when his heart began to beat faster and his body began to tremble a little, then mine followed suit. I couldn't speak, I couldn't move, I couldn't breathe without him.

Right at the top of the house there was a room like my own; a lonely little turret with nothing more than an empty desk inside and glass doors leading out onto a balcony.

'Just like your bedroom next door, isn't it?'

'Yes it is,' I whispered.

His mouth brushed briefly against the back of my neck. I felt his hands glide over me and my back arched in response.

'This can be our room if you like, for now,' he said.

'What do you mean?'

'You wanted to come here so badly. Well now that you've finally made it, you should stay awhile.'

Our lips met and, just like in the dream, I felt my hungry hands grasp hold of him, ripping at his shirt, as if I were incapable of doing anything else. The haze grew up around us; a whirlwind of grey, stinking fumes.

But even though my body ached for him and I felt my limbs wind themselves around his, a cry rose up in my throat from somewhere deep inside.

'Seb!' I yelled with all the strength I could summon, although my voice came out as nothing more than the faintest whisper.

He drew away from me, his eyes incredulous, aching with hurt and rage. I began to cry.

'Seb?' he spat, holding me at arm's length like a rag doll. 'Do you really think he's going to help you?'

His face blurred through my tears.

'Seb... who destroyed my sister's life, ripped her world apart as well as the rest of the family. Has he ever done anything to help us? No! Then why the hell would he help you?'

He slammed me against the wall, urging his hard body against me: lips cloying against my face, hands reaching between my thighs. 'I've got you now.'

'No!' I mouthed. 'Please.'

'You know... you have to be my best prize yet,' he murmured breathlessly in my ear. His eyes were blacker than ink now, blacker than the darkest cave. 'Did you know that? Did you know? I told you once that I have a habit of getting what I want.'

I whimpered inside but, as he smothered my helpless body, the growing haze suddenly surged up behind his head. It spread out like a great hand, its fingers just discernible, flexing to the ends of their tips.

'Not this time,' I whispered back.

The hand curled its fingers and slammed down over him, sending Raphael tumbling to the floor and dragging me down close behind. My ribs turned to fire as they collided with the ground and Raphael's head bounced against the floor until there was blood and his eyes were closed. When I turned to look up a scream filled my throat once more, crying out loud and shrill this time like a blade of glass severing the haze.

The face came towards me, its gaping mouth like a deep well. I dug my nails into the floor, my teeth chattering through my cries. It pressed itself against my cheek, the putrid mouth oozing down my neck.

'I'm so lonely,' it murmured, in a deep droning scar of a voice. 'So lonely.'

The eyes were agonizingly blue, its nose a dark recess that began to run down the length of my body, sniffing me in like a hungry wolf.

Next to me Raphael stirred. I shifted my head closer to him.

'Help me!' I implored through my sobs.

As he tried to raise himself up the face loomed forwards again, snarling through the darkness and sweeping me aside.

'No, no!' Raphael screamed. 'I thought you'd be pleased. I've got her now. See, I'm just like you! Don't you understand?'

I grappled backwards into a corner, hugging my knees up into my chest against the hard floor.

The mouth shrieked with fury and Raphael began to whimper. 'You have her then, if that's what you want. I thought you'd be pleased...'

But up came the clawed hand again. And then the air filled with the thunderous roar of glass smashing and Raphael's shrill screams as his body plummeted into the dark night air. I buried my face in my hands and all turned to whiteness.

1893

Another turning, now left, now right. The doors on either side watched their quiet march as candles in the walls flickered obediently to their passing. Walter's back lurched on before her, cloaked in a dark shade of gold that looked brown in the dim light: a monk in his cloister. Only the contents of the small tray he was carrying cut through their silent journey with its gentle clinking sounds.

Her hands were freezing cold in spite of the spring day she'd left outside.

There were no windows here, only closed doors and the smell of wax. No possible connection to the world beyond. Her heart fluttered at the thought of her boy, waiting out there for her with Mrs Hubbard.

At last his lurching back came to a halt before a pair of doors. He lowered his chin towards her, smiled thinly.

'Are we here at last? I cannot believe that we are still in the same house!'

'Yes.'

'I am – perplexed. Who would ever have thought of such a thing?'

'Me.'

'Walter... I don't think I can!'

'Now now. Look at me, look carefully. There you go. When you came to my lodgings you asked for my help. You put your trust in me. Would I ever abuse such a precious thing? Would I Miranda? This is the best and only way, I promise you. Hold onto your bravery; he won't do anything to hurt you. Even though he can appear brash, he is a kind and gentle man. Have faith in me, please. Do come in and try not to be dazzled.'

He clasped her hand and drew her into the room but the light inside nearly knocked her back into the corridor. She screwed her eyes up as tightly as they would go without closing them entirely.

'If you would remain here for now, I will just have a few words with Lord Hartreve first,' Walter murmured.

She edged back against one of the walls, hands outstretched, and gradually eased her eyes open so that the full extent of the room blossomed into view. It was a mammoth, circular library crammed with all manner of collections and crowned with pane upon pane of glass. How on earth was it possible for such a place to exist within that murky warren of tunnels out there?

'Walter, is that you? I must have nodded off,' muttered a shaky old growl of a voice.

'I am sorry to disturb you,' came Walter's softer tone.

'Never mind, never mind. What time is it?'

'Gone two o'clock in the afternoon.'

He was over at the far side of the room, huddled up and almost unnoticeable in the depths of a winged armchair. His whiskered face looked mottled, his hair just a few remaining strands and there must have been three or four blankets wrapped around his knees.

So this was the man whom Lucinda had so despised: her father, Lord Hartreve.

'Have you brought me some tea?' he barked.

'Yes sir.'

'Bring it over then. I'm parched, positively parched.'

But Walter seemed to be in no hurry. He strode casually over to a small table some distance away, lowered the tray upon it and then proceeded to haul the table and its contents together across the room to his master.

'Good gracious, surely there must be an easier way?' grumbled the old man.

'In fact, no.'

'Really? Astonishing.'

He gathered the tea up into his shaky hands. Just beyond his chair there was a large painting on the wall, so vibrant and energetic that it seemed to beckon her towards it. The man in it was clearly Lord Hartreve himself: younger, stronger and far more bullish looking than the frail figure in the chair now. And there was Lucinda as well, sitting on the horse beside him. Beautiful young Lucinda with all that hair, laughing at the world around her.

'You have a visitor sir,' said Walter, taking the man's hand fondly into his own.

'What are you talking about? You know that I don't see anyone.'

'I do know that, but you will make an exception today I'm sure. And she is already in this room. Your visitor is a lady called

Miranda White.'

'Miranda White?'

'Yes. And she is of the utmost importance. This I know will come as a great shock to you but Lucinda's child, the baby she was carrying when she fled to France, has survived. And Miranda is his legal guardian. She came to me in London for guidance and I have brought her here to you. They seek your help.'

The old man fell forwards, wheezing loudly. In spite of his apparent feebleness, Walter had to use both arms and enough puff to turn his cheeks red to grapple him back into his chair.

'This tincture will sooth you sir, take a little,' he said and like a baby Lord Hartreve drank directly from one of the small phials about Walter's neck.

At last, when his breathing had slowed down again into soft regular gasps, Lucinda's father whispered something to Walter. Walter patted his shoulder with a reassuring hand and glanced over at her.

'Lord Hartreve will see you now. Please do come over here.'

Her legs quivered beneath her.

'Stephen Hartreve is a kind man.' Walter had said it over and over again.

'But he will hate me! He will turn me away.'

'No. He will do what is right by his grandson. You must trust me. Please.'

Lord Hartreve seemed less frail at closer quarters. Although he was hunched down and too thin for a man with such a sturdy frame, his eyes still glistened brightly and as soon as she tiptoed closer they fell on her like a hawk.

'So you claim to be in possession of my grandchild?' he growled.

'That is correct.'

'How do I know that you're telling me the truth?'

'I have it all here: a birth certificate and letters from Mrs Eden to her lawyer.'

He grasped at the papers, leafing through them one by one, his hands now as steady as a young man's.

'You have the child here?'

'Yes, outside in the care of my cook who has become a close friend. I also have a personal letter from your daughter, if you'd like to read it.'

He took the crumpled letter with tender fingers, his eyes devouring every line and as they reached the end they filled with tears. His hands began to shake again.

'You nursed my Lucy!' he whimpered.

'I did, for the first few days until her husband was able to find her a proper nurse.'

'Sit down Mrs White,' he sighed, all that sternness suddenly retreating from his face. 'Now, explanations,' he continued softly. 'You call yourself Miranda White. Have you changed your name from Whitestone?'

'Yes, I changed it shortly after my husband died; it suits me better I think. I believe that I've endured enough associations with that man.'

His eyes widened. 'And yet you were able to forgive my daughter her... dalliance with him?'

'Quite frankly, if I may be blunt, I was horrified by both of them at first. Please forgive me when I say that I disliked your daughter thoroughly for her behaviour. But my husband Tristan was a foul man and he treated her in an abominable way. He trapped her in one of the rooms of her house, drugged her into senselessness. I couldn't allow it to go on; no one deserves such punishment.'

'So you are the woman Walter told me about. The woman who helped her escape from him?'

'I am. I tampered with Tristan's wine one evening, sent him off into a deep sleep, and Mr Eden and I smuggled her out. We took her to Dover, but she was so weak that I agreed to stay until the nurse came.'

'And what was she like then, my Lucy?' His eyes filled with tears again.

'Muddled, weak, astonished to discover that she was even carrying a child. She seemed to think that she would be a bad mother.'

'Then why didn't she come back to me? I would have cared for her! Why on earth did she leave my grandson to you?'

'You've read her letter, she seemed to trust me. Forgive my forwardness, but although your daughter conducted herself with great exuberance in her lifetime, I think that she was in truth a very troubled soul. We both had the misfortune of becoming involved with a despicable man and I think that, for her at least, this formed some sort of perverse bond between us.'

Lord Hartreve made no reply. His expression was fixed towards the floor, his chin nestled within clasped fingers.

'I have one final question,' he said at last. 'If my daughter left her son to you, then what are you now doing in my house?'

She breathed deeply; this was the moment she'd been dreading.

'Just tell him the truth Miranda.'

Walter's last words when the carriage had drawn to a halt before Druid Manor's stark walls.

'He'll think I'm mad.'

'Perhaps. But I will support you.'

She leaned forwards towards the old man. 'This is a very hard thing for me to explain.'

'I imagine that few things could be more difficult to say than what you have already told me.'

His voice was soft and coaxing, nothing like the growl she'd first heard.

'Yes, you are right, absolutely right. You see, first of all, I have no other suitable place to go. Tristan's family have turned their backs on me and my sister too, who is my only close surviving relative.'

'Presumably you have some money and property of your own?'

'A very small amount of money. In the last few months of his life Tristan frittered most of our fortune away. I have the house, but it is becoming somewhat of a burden.'

'I don't understand.'

'We lived next door to your daughter, in Marguerite Avenue. As you know the houses there are rather fine, the envy of many I believe. But since my husband's death in there, something about our home perturbs people. In spite of all my efforts I cannot sell the place.'

His eyes narrowed. 'Have you a more precise explanation for this odd resistance? Surely a man's death cannot be enough to render a property abhorrent to the entire metropolis?'

'You would be surprised.' She glanced at Walter who nodded gently for her to go on. 'Sir, you may never wish to see me again after you hear what I am about to say. It is perhaps in vain that I implore you for some level of understanding of my plight, but I'm doing so nonetheless. My husband Tristan Whitestone died by his own hand in the kitchen larder of our house. My cook discovered his body, but I saw it too: he was smiling, in fact grimacing would be a better word for it.

'Ever since that ghastly episode, I have been plagued by regular and increasingly vivid visions of him within the walls of my home. At first I truly believed that my superstitions were overcoming my grasp of reality and even now, when I hear myself saying these words, a part of me still feels as if I'm doing my own sanity a disservice. However, when I discovered that he was not only haunting me but also persecuting his defenceless child, a baby I now love as my own, I finally became convinced of the truth.

'There is a vile and haunting aura in that building that revolts and terrifies everyone who moves within its shadow. I would rather live in the workhouse than spend another night of my life in there and as proof I am handing over the keys of my home to you now. Confirm my words for yourself, take the house, I never want to see it again. I have nothing left but the love I bear towards a small boy and the hope of your guardianship.'

Lord Hartreve regarded the keys beneath his heavy brows and said nothing for a long time. 'I've witnessed many things in my rather long and tortuous lifetime,' he answered, finally. He was breathing heavily again, struggling it seemed to speak coherently. 'You must understand that I too am haunted by ghosts; most human beings are, although few are willing to admit to such a thing.

'What you have said is indeed shocking and somewhat sensational and yet I still feel as if I'm in the presence of an honest, if not bruised and distressed woman. I doubt whether you have descended into the realms of lunacy yet!'

He smiled at her with such reassuring warmth that her heart melted towards him.

'Walter will look at your house; he understands the way this world works far better than I do. But in the meantime, for both our sakes, let's not talk about this again for awhile.'

He pulled himself up and out of his chair, clenching his fists firmly together behind his back as if to separate himself physically from the subject.

'When was the last time I left this library?' he called out. 'Two, three years ago?'

'Closer to four,' Walter replied.

His legs shook uncertainly and then he tottered forwards as if about to turn head over heels. She dashed towards him, grasping hold of his arm.

'Ah. Thank you... There is a small lodge cottage on the estate. It's a little rundown, but Walter will arrange for its refurbishment. You can live there if you like.'

'Are you, are you quite sure?' Her hand squeezed his arm tighter.

'Yes, I am.'

She peered deeply into his honest watery eyes and suddenly it felt as if the bright beams of light from the roof above were filtering right through her, filling her with warmth to the tips of her fingers, the ends of her toes.

'Words cannot express my thanks. If I can ever repay you for your kindness...' she faltered.

'You can indeed. You can repay me with immediate effect.'

He hobbled on towards the doors, her hand still wedged tightly in the crook of his arm.

'Anything!'

'Well introduce me to my grandson then. He is the only thing I now have that's worth leaving this library for.'

'Of course. Nothing would make me prouder.'

The glow of sunset had set the fields on fire. The air was at its loveliest at this time: still full of the day's warmth but cool enough to breathe and so clean and golden. Two silhouettes appeared against the skyline, rather like a tall grasshopper and a squat little ant with a walking stick.

It would perhaps be better not to tell Mrs Hubbard that they were already on their way. She was panicking enough as it was about the garlic and the raspberry flan and the flour on the floor. She'd greet them out here first, talk things over in the fresh air before taking them inside.

Then later, if she could get him on his own, she'd tell Walter about her swims in the secret lake. It was surely the closest thing to heaven to glide through that pure, silky water each morning when the rest of the world was still sleeping apart from her and the dragonflies. And if he knew about it then maybe he'd join her one day...

The silhouettes had doubled, tripled in size, Lord Hartreve moving almost like a sprightly young man now that he had the comfort of his new stick by his side. They paused to circle around something lying in their pathway: a small furry mound as orange as the sky.

'Minerva! Oh you lazy cat,' she murmured. 'Always sprawled out somewhere as if the estate were your own.'

Walter was clutching the folds of his crimson coat about his legs with one hand. In the other he clasped, what was it, a bouquet of flowers?

She pressed her eyelids closed. It wasn't enough just to breathe this air, she had to feel its fingers on her skin as well. Skin that felt softer and plumper than ever before.

'Good evening! I trust you're well!' Lord Hartreve cried out, saluting her with his stick.

'So well. And our boy has a new tooth on his bottom gum. I found it this morning; he hasn't complained one bit about it. Ah peonies, my favourite flowers. Thank you so much Walter!'

She pressed the fluffy blooms to her face. 'Heavenly.'

'He's a very brave boy my grandson. Never complains. I still haven't seen him cry properly, did you know that?' he asked, turning to Walter.

'You have mentioned it, several times.'

'Mrs Hubbard's been making all manner of things for us with some of the new ingredients Walter's been showing her. I think she's rather flustered about it all so I've left her to it for a few minutes.'

'Ah excellent!' Lord Hartreve patted his stomach. He was refilling that portly figure of his again and looking more like his old portrait in the library with each passing day. 'Is it to be that exquisite mousse again with, what were those things in it?'

'Cardamoms.'

'That's it!'

'No, it's a raspberry flan. And she's put some of the wild garlic into a hotpot. I don't know how Walter managed to persuade her to do that. We've had the windows open all day with it.'

Walter bowed his head with a smile. 'It'll keep the chills away. Strengthen you all for the winter.'

'Tell me, how was your visit to London?' she asked, her lip trembling a little beneath the question.

A dark cloud passed across Walter's face. 'It was... illuminating. Perhaps we three should sit down for a few minutes before we bother Mrs Hubbard?'

A small dry cough rose up in her throat. It was still there in her lungs, that grey cloud. The golden country air hadn't quite killed it off yet. Sometimes, when she closed her eyes, that smile, that... grimace, flashed back at her against her lids.

'You visited the Whitestone property?' Lord Hartreve's voice was low and hushed.

'Yes.'

'And what state did you find it in?'

'Desperate.'

'My nephew Charles and his family have settled into Lucinda's place?'

'Yes.'

'And how do they regard the house beside them?'

'They do not appear to notice it, very few do now.' Walter's brow wrinkled and he solemnly drew his bony fingers through his hair. 'My Lord... as Miranda knows well, that house positively groans with the pungent aroma of wasted life. I've never encountered such a sorrowful place before!'

'Is that so? Is that so?'

'I have brought many experts there now, some have refused even to go in. It seems to be the loneliness in the air that horrifies them the most. Several leading occultists have already failed to notice the building at all.'

'Your power is immense; I knew you could make it all go away!' cried Lord Hartreve.

'Oh it isn't me. No. It is revulsion that seems to blind them. Even I have walked straight past the place without realizing on several occasions.'

'Have you seen... him... there?' The words scratched drily against her throat.

'Yes.'

Walter bit deeply down into his lip, turning it white. 'I have witnessed the wretch several times now. He stalks the corridors, lunges unsuspectingly through mirrors and weeps like a child in the darkest corners. He has begun to speak to me as well: muttering constantly about his loneliness and yet grinning through his tears in a most disconcerting way. He even attacked me on one occasion.

I was quite fascinated by him at first but now I've reached a stage where I no longer want to see. Yesterday I found myself collapsing out of the front door in a bid to escape the vileness. It has a peculiar way of latching onto you, drawing you in, sapping you of strength.

I'm afraid that for the sake of my own health there is little more I can do. Misery is consuming that house and before long no unsuspecting individual will even be aware of its presence at all.'

The sun was sinking low now. Two hares sprinted and played at bullying each other at the far end of the meadow.

'Your world is too complex for me,' murmured Lord Hartreve at last. His cheeks had drained to white.

'I'm afraid that we are all forced to share this world you speak of,' he replied. 'But most human beings are simple and optimistic beasts; they don't want to interrupt the mechanics of their day-to-day lives, or sully the innocence of their outlook with visions of pain and lunacy.'

Lord Hartreve laughed gently to himself. 'And I think that I'm beginning to understand why. Why should I strain my already old and fading eyes with the stuff of nightmares, when I can so easily gaze at beauty such as this in my own back garden?'

'Is that you, Mr Balanchine?'

The shrill voice cut through their reverie like a welcoming firework – it was Mrs Hubbard, calling from the cottage behind them. And then her face suddenly popped up in one of the windows, framed between two potted orchids. Miranda smiled gratefully at her. The cook's usually tidy hair had come quite loose with all her flustering and her cheeks had turned scarlet in the heat.

'I need your expertise! The rest of you can wait a few minutes.'

'At your service.'

But Lord Hartreve clutched onto Walter's arm before he could leave. 'One more thing. Did you take care of the other business?'

Walter nodded, his eyes soft and reassuring.

'I've eliminated every document I can find sir: death certificates, birth certificates. Everything that might possibly link the boy to his father.'

'Well done. Well done.'

Miranda watched Walter lope off towards the cottage with a lighter spring in his step than before. Perhaps he'd needed to unburden himself of his dark story, make space for the golden light to fill him.

The countryside seemed to suit him just as much as it did her: his figure cut against the landscape like a reminder of a bygone era. He'd have fitted in well with the Druids who'd once populated this place. She could just imagine him, gathered up with such a company around a blazing night fire, his face lit up by the glow and his eyes as tender and searching as ever across the flames.

She turned to Lord Hartreve. 'May I ask, how on earth did a man like you fall into the company of Walter Balanchine?'

A low laugh escaped from between the old man's lips and then he shook his head heavily.

'My family had all more or less abandoned me,' he began. 'My wife died, my son went overseas and my daughter, well, you know that ending. I have strived all my life to be good, to serve my family and my tenants well. In return however I've received nothing but derision and strife. I turned to the church and was greeted by empty words, fawning priests and the undeniable absence of God. So, rejecting the ghastliness of the world about me, I turned in upon myself and commissioned the building of what I have often described as my cocoon, my library.

'I had heard tales of Walter's brilliance for some time: *The Conjurer of the East End* as he was known. After some difficulty I eventually tracked him down in a London opium den, where he lay glassy-eyed and inebriated on a filthy divan. I walked away, thinking that I'd never see him again, and returned straight to my club where, as I was told on entering, I had a visitor. And there he was, waiting for me, freshly shaven and with his wits about him.

'Walter's ways have never failed to astonish and confound me, but he gave me my library, as well as his friendship and love. He is a faithful and true servant and has done more to convince me of the innate spirituality governing our world than any man of the cloth. He is my family, just as the two of you are now.'

'And you are mine,' she said. 'I would never have believed that happiness had a place left for me until I came here.'

'Come on in, dinner is served!' Mrs Hubbard's face rose up from between the orchids again. 'And the young Master's awake and gurgling for his tooth inspection.'

'Then we cannot possibly leave him waiting, or your good self!' Lord Hartreve laughed heartily. 'Now help an old man up, take me to my boy.'

Walter was balancing the baby in the crook of an unnaturally angled arm as they squeezed into the cottage.

'Don't breathe!' exclaimed Mrs Hubbard. 'In case the garlic suffocates you. I never thought I'd find myself cooking with such a thing.'

'It smells marvellous. Hello my little man, shall I take you now?'

Miranda squeezed the child's soft body against her, burying her lips into his cheek. Walter rolled back his shoulders; he seemed relieved to have his arm free again, although he still watched the child intently. And when those round blue eyes met his he clutched onto them so heavily with his gaze that the poor little thing suddenly stuck out a quivering bottom lip.

'You're scaring him!'

'My apologies,' he murmured. 'I just find the child a little puzzling, that's all.'

'Puzzling!' chimed in Lord Hartreve. 'I'll tell you what puzzles me: the fact that all the inner doors of this cottage seem to have unhinged themselves and run off.'

Miranda felt herself go pink. 'Ah, let me explain. You see, I just don't like the things – doors that is. I've always said that one day I'd live in a house without any doors in it at all, and well, here I am.'

'Extraordinary! And what in heaven's name is this?'

'Oh, you've spotted my new carving, the one I was telling you about. The carpenter in the next village finally finished it.'

Lord Hartreve's eyes bulged up at the thing. 'Rather crude, isn't it?'

He was right. It was far larger than she'd expected and it did swell out rather lumpily above the small mantelpiece.

'And I thought you'd wanted kingfishers?'

'No, I changed my mind; the turtle doves are so much more peaceful. I know it's crude, but I like it anyway. The last few months have taught me that I am a simple person at heart, that I desire nothing more in life than a small corner of peace. Being here has brought me untold happiness and we all know what a rare and precious thing that is.'

By the time the two men had left the sky was deep blue velvet and glimmering with stars.

'Like one of Walter's cloaks, don't you think?' she murmured to Mrs Hubbard.

'Hmm, never thought a man would teach me how to cook.'

'And it really was so delicious. Thank you.'

The temperature had dropped just a little; a few goose-pimples had risen up on her arms, but she couldn't bear to drag herself inside just yet. Somewhere behind her she could feel the presence of the little church beyond the cottage, prodding up at the sky with its pointed steeple. She'd found it impossible to pray there; it filled her with so much more warmth to look out like this in the other direction instead, towards the fields. The horizon was her altar now, the grass her pew.

'Come now, let's go in,' urged Mrs Hubbard. 'You'll catch a chill out here. Come and watch the boy sleep. He's as peaceful as I've ever seen him.'

A single lamp in the corridor was enough to fill the entire cottage with a soft glow. She bent over the crib, stroking his feathery hair with her fingertips.

'I never thought I'd see him sleep like this. Not in his own home anyway. We did the right thing, didn't we?'

'Oh yes Mrs White,' and Mrs Hubbard smiled down from the other side with a face so full of love and patience that it made her want to lean across the crib and embrace the woman then and there.

'You know, I'd very much like it if you started calling me Miranda. Formality doesn't really work out here and you're the closest and dearest friend I've ever had.'

Mrs Hubbard started slightly at the words and began to untie her apron with hurried fingers.

'Oh dear, have I embarrassed you? I hope not. And I've made you cry!'

'Not at all!' She brushed her apron hurriedly across her eyes. 'It would be a pleasure to call you by your true name, Miranda. But you must do the same as well. Please, call me Gladys.'

The baby sighed gently in his sleep, flexing his fingers in the air before burrowing his head to one side against the pillow.

'He's our boy now, isn't he, Gladys?'

'I'd follow him to the ends of the earth. I think I already have!'

She laughed under her breath, reaching for Gladys's hand across the crib.

'My little man! Our little man. Our Sebastian.'

SERENA'S STORY

'I'm going to Sasha tonight.'

'No, don't please.'

Their voices were quite clear although I felt as if I was miles away from them, on the other side of a mountain range, listening through the pure air. I tried to force my eyelids apart.

'Look, she's stirring,' said Eva. 'I better leave you two together.'

'Try to change your mind,' came Seb's low voice.

'Why? What have I got to lose now?' she yelped back and the image of a lost wounded fox swam through my mind. 'He's already started talking to the papers. They'll have a field day with this and so will he... God knows what he might tell them about Raphael now. If I go to him, just once, then maybe he'll leave my family alone, with all our pain. We need *some* privacy.'

I winced through the glare of the light and found her drawn face staring right at me.

'You know he won't do that,' Seb answered.

'She's awake now... I'll see you later.'

I heard the muted click of a door closing. To my left I saw the outline of windows with curtains on either side and a patch of sky. It looked remarkably like my room.

'Hello. You're back.'

I turned my groaning neck to discover a blur sitting on the edge of my bed. Slowly it turned into Seb.

'What happened?' I croaked.

'It's alright, you're safe. I came when I heard all the noise and got you out of there. You've been asleep for ages.'

I listened to the sound of my own breathing, calm and rhythmic like waves, and then a sudden needle of fear clawed its way into my guts.

'And Raphael?' I whispered.

Seb's face went dark. 'No. He's dead.'

My head began to throb. I felt Seb take my hand and kiss it softly with his cool lips.

'I want to be alone,' I said, closing my eyes to him.

When he was gone I slowly eased my creaking body off the

bed. Every bone felt as if it had been removed and rearranged and I gripped the bedpost at first to find my balance. My room looked sparse, all my belongings gone apart from a few clothes flung onto a chair in the corner.

When I could feel the warm flow of blood moving around me again I put the clothes on and ran my fingers through my dishevelled hair. In the mirror my face looked hollow and pale and different somehow.

Downstairs the air felt silent but inhabited. I reached Arabella's office and her door was open, the Bacchanalian revellers urging me in. She was in there, staring out of the window with her back to me, a large butterfly clip clasped in her hair. She glanced over her shoulder at the sound of my step, drank me in with swollen eyes and then turned her back on me again.

'You know I knew it wasn't normal, living here as we do, but I never quite predicted this,' she said in a quiet and considered voice.

'I'm sorry,' I murmured.

She laughed softly. 'Oh it's not your fault. It's this stinking goddam place. That ghost, thing, whatever you care to call it, feeds off fear. And my Raphael had plenty of that.'

'So you're awake at last then!' bellowed a voice I barely recognized.

I jumped and turned to find Edward looming in the doorway, red cheeked and glowering like a drunk.

'Now get out,' he spat. 'Hurry up, your things are downstairs.'

I tried to back away from him. 'Can I at least say goodbye to Beth?'

'No you certainly cannot!'

'The girl's done nothing wrong,' said Arabella, calmly.

Edwards's fists curled up into punches. 'Oh no. No! Only led my son to his death. And who let her in this house in the first bloody place?'

He grasped me by the shoulders, forcing me out of the room.

'It's not my fault!' I yelled as he pushed me forwards down the stairs.

'I never want to see you in my house again. Do I make myself clear?'

My face felt livid. 'You don't understand! He tried to... to...'

A small face from somewhere between the banisters blinked back at me like a scared shadow.

'Beth!'

'There is no Beth,' snapped Edward's voice. 'Take your things and get out of my house.'

A rectangle of light appeared as the front door swung open. Edward forced me through it, his knuckles firmly wedged into my spine and then my bags followed, one by one, strewn like pieces of rubbish across the pavement.

The door slammed shut again behind me, black and glossy and impenetrable. I lowered myself slowly onto the step. A box of art pencils had exploded from one of the bags. They lay around my feet, flashing their bright colours up at me from the grey stone. I picked them up carefully and put them away.

'Are you alright?'

I looked up to find Robert staring down at me from the pavement. He was wearing a long grey coat, his hands thrust deeply in his pockets.

'I've been thrown out of your house.'

'I can see. I did try to warn you.'

'Yes, I wish I'd listened. I... I don't know what to say.'

He looked away for a moment, squinting into the cold air. 'My father's very angry,' he murmured, his voice wavering. 'He's blaming *everyone* at the moment. Sorry. Can I help you?'

I raised myself to my feet and we glanced up at the house together. A curtain twitched in an upstairs window, Eva's room.

'Yes you can,' I said quietly. 'There's one small thing that I can do for your family, if you'll let me. I need you to get something for me first though, from Raphael's room. Would it be possible, do you think?'

The card Sasha had given me was for an address in Bloomsbury called The Machen Institute. I plunged headlong between the buses along Tottenham Court Road and then into the quieter back streets.

The Machen Institute was an austere thirties building squashed between two much nicer Victorian ones. I hurried up the three flights of stairs to Sasha's office. His door was at the end of a musty corridor: *Sasha Apostol* it said on a yellowing piece of card in a metal frame.

When I knocked his face appeared from behind the door with

a clinical little smile.

'Ah, you've made it. Come in. I have to say that your phone call was most unexpected in light of recent fascinating events. I thought you would be needed by the family. Please, take a seat if you can find one.'

He was wearing his usual tweed suit and a mismatched checked shirt underneath which had seen better days. He'd also oiled his hair into thick shiny strands across his head.

'I've stopped working for the Hartreves. You won't be seeing me at the house again.'

He raised his eyebrows. 'That surprises and saddens me. I have much to tell you that you would find interesting, I think.'

'And for what in return?'

He didn't reply but turned instead to a pile of papers on his desk, rifling through them with purposeful fingers.

The office was crammed with bookshelves on all sides. I squeezed myself between two piles of dictionaries onto a small sofa by the window and scoured the room for a hiding place.

The bookcase to my right jutted out from the wall quite a bit. I craned my neck and discovered a good three inch gap above the old skirting board between the bookcase and the wall.

'Here, take a look at this,' he said, suddenly brandishing a piece of paper and thrusting it into my hand. 'Walter Balanchine, shortly before his death in 1939. This image actually appeared alongside his obituary. He was in his mid-eighties.'

It was a photocopy of a black and white photograph. The man in it had little more than a skull of a face and long wispy white hair. His deep-set eyes were fixed far away, as if he were peering at the horizon. It was an ugly, yet perversely beautiful face, something from a different world or an ancient era even.

'Who was he, exactly?' I asked.

'A mystic, a visionary, a madman. At the age of seven he was arrested by the police for purportedly turning a local publican into a rat; at twelve years old he had a stall in Limehouse selling miraculous cures for anything from gout to gangrene. In adulthood he acquired clients from across the country and, indeed, from all over the world: pitiful and lonely souls who leaned upon him like children and lived in awe of his miraculous abilities. Lord Stephen Hartreve was one of them.'

'Was Balanchine famous?'

'In a sense. The Victorians craved spirituality in many forms as the nineteenth century wore on. Darwin, among others, had done his best to upend religion and men like Balanchine offered hope to the disenchanted... But now,' and he paused, dragging his palm across his oily head. 'Enough of my chattering and time for you to tell me something.'

He sat down and pulled his chair up close.

'What do you want to know?' I asked.

'Why don't we start with that book you found in Druid Manor? Where did you come across it exactly?'

'In the library.'

He breathed deeply. 'The great library itself! And who took you there?'

'No one.'

'I don't believe you. You would never have found it on your own. Was it young Beth? It must have been, tell me.'

'Why are you so interested in Beth?'

He strummed his fingers slowly across his thigh. 'Surely over these past months you've come to realize that Beth is... not quite normal for a child of her age?'

'That sounds a little dramatic. She's very bright of course, her head is bursting with thoughts and ideas like any young child.'

'Thoughts and ideas! Ha! Listen to me. I know everything there is to know about the Hartreve family and that child has told me things that...' he stopped himself.

'That what? What are you trying to say?'

He gave a low laugh. 'Things that she couldn't possibly have invented.'

The air hung between us like a heavy velvet curtain.

'You know, the introduction to Balanchine's book was very interesting,' I said, breaking the silence. 'Haunting really. It was about a little girl called Miranda.'

'Miranda? Really? What did it say about her?'

'Oh, she had a terrible childhood. She poisoned her mother by mistake and was punished for it for so long that an awful thing began to happen to her.'

'And what was that? Tell me.'

'No, not yet. You tell me about Beth first.'

He jumped from his chair, frustration flexing through his fingers. 'This is a silly game, a stupid game that you are playing!' he snapped, wiping his forehead with his sleeve. 'Alright... She sees things, hears voices.'

'What sort of voices?'

'Voices of the past, if you must know.'

'I don't believe you.'

'You don't believe me?' he laughed loudly.

'No. Why should I?'

I glared at him and his nose flared up into a snarl. He snatched at a file on his desk and tore another piece of paper from it.

'Take a look at this. You'll recognize Balanchine to the right. It's a satirized image of him with a young companion, drawn around 1910.'

The cartoon depicted the two men walking shoulder to shoulder along an urban street. There was a caption underneath: *Beauty and the Beast.* Balanchine had been sketched with a grimacing scowl, devil horns and the pointed end of a serpent's tale poking out from beneath his cloak. His companion was a young sharp-suited man about town, with fashionably floppy hair and a face I knew better than my own.

The image swam before my eyes. I wanted to touch it, draw my finger across the lovely face and yet my hand flinched back at the same time. Sasha leaned in close; the acrid smell of his sweaty skin in my nostrils.

'That young man you see in the picture was believed to be the illegitimate grandson of Lord Stephen Hartreve. He was brought up almost in seclusion at Druid Manor, but as a young adult returned to what was once his mother's home, by then resided in by some cousins: 36 Marguerite Avenue. London loved him of course and soon the idle tongues of friends and family told the world that this was the son of the notorious beauty Lucinda Hartreve.'

'What happened to him?'

My voice sounded small and bruised.

'Ah, now I was hoping that this was something you could tell me!'

He waited but I made no answer.

'One day,' he continued. 'Not a year after the young man's arrival in London, he simply vanished and no one has seen him for a hundred years until I showed this picture to young Beth. She must have been three at the time, no more. "That's Sebastian," she told me in that little voice of hers. "He's always here. He's funny!" I already had my suspicions of course; Arabella, stupid miserable woman that she is, was simply a treasure trove of information in those early days, but it was the child who confirmed it all. Oh! And when she looked deep into my eyes, such a sweet innocent voice came out of her.'

He wiped his lips with the back of his hand and then his eyes sparkled. 'But now, now, I have something even more!' he said, unfolding a piece of paper. It was the torn envelope from Jess with my drawing of Seb's face scribbled onto it. He dropped it into my lap, padded softly over to his office door and locked it with a small key which he then dropped into his pocket. 'Speak.'

I held the picture of my lover tightly in my hands. I couldn't take my eyes off it.

'Beth didn't take me to the library on the first occasion, Raphael did,' I murmured eventually. 'The second time, when I found the book, I really was alone. I seem to be able to find and see things which I shouldn't... As I've already told you, I read the introduction about Miranda. Her family chose to ignore her as a punishment and gradually she disappeared, just like the house I think.'

'What house?'

'34.'

'So you noticed.'

'Of course. The missing house fascinated me right from the start...'

'Yes!' his excited tongue flicked out as he sat down again. 'That house is the key to it all. Balanchine's greatest feat. And every day I feel, I know, I am closer to discovering it!'

'Why?' I asked.

'It baffled me for a long long time. How could it have disappeared? What happened to the couple who once lived there?'

'Miranda and Tristan Whitestone.'

'You even know about them, as well?' his face filled with something that looked almost like admiration.

'I do. Miranda changed her name, brought Lucinda's child to Druid Manor.'

'Yes yes,' he said hurriedly, suddenly gripping my hand. 'But Tristan... where did he go? When and where did he die? I'll tell you!

Just last year, about the time that you joined the household, I finally unearthed the truth.

'I was reading the newly-discovered journals of a fascinating Scottish psychiatrist of the time by the name of Blythe. In a chapter dedicated to the causes of suicide, Blythe wrote about the case of a man called Tristan Whitestone of Marguerite Avenue. He describes the man's hideous decline, his wild ramblings regarding the loss of his mistress, his despicable treatment of his wife and finally the eventual discovery of his body in the kitchen larder of their house.

'The date given to the commencement of Whitestone's mental decline closely coincides with the secret disappearance of his neighbour Lucinda. As soon as I put these dates together I knew that I had found the true father of Lucinda's child. Lord Hartreve would not have enjoyed being associated with such a scandal and that's where Balanchine wove his magic. The man eliminated it all: birth and death certificates, legal correspondence, even the house itself.'

He sat back and loosened his collar, breathless with his own brilliance.

'You've got it wrong,' I uttered.

'What do you mean?'

'Walter Balanchine might have eliminated many things to save the Hartreves from scandal, but he didn't make that house disappear. When I read the story about Miranda's childhood, there was nothing contrived about her invisibility. People just couldn't stand seeing her misery anymore, her loneliness. I think the same thing happened to the house. Goodness me, in spite of all your delving you really don't know that much about Walter Balanchine after all, do you? 34 Marguerite Avenue is still very much there, disguised by nothing but its own cloud of sadness.'

'How do you know?'

'Because I've been there myself.'

'You've been there? It really does still exist?'

'Yes.'

His face went rigid. 'Then take me there. Take me to the house.'

'Why would you want to go to such a place?'

He jumped from his seat, every sinew and muscle so taut that he looked ready to climb out of his own skin. 'Do you have any idea what I... we... could gain from such a discovery? We could tell the world!'

'And what would that do to the family, to Beth?'

'No harm would come of Beth! She's my prodigy, practically my own child. I would turn her into a sensation.'

'I wonder what Eva would think of that.'

He drew his tongue across his lower lip. 'She'll learn her place, eventually. You just leave Eva to me.'

'That's what I'm most afraid of.'

He threw me the same look as when we first met on the threshold of Arabella's office: his face crunched like a fist but this time ready to punch.

'You like her, don't you?' I said slowly. 'All that aristocratic beauty: those long legs, that youthful body. You can barely keep your hands off her. Do you really think she'd give in to you?'

He broke into a small laugh. 'How naïve you are. There are ways of persuading people into doing things, didn't you know? And the Hartreves can be bought. I have proof of that.'

'Your plans would destroy them.'

'Oh they're already destroyed, you don't need to worry about that. And even so, what does it matter at the end of the day? Eh? A few casualties at the expense of such an extraordinary, momentous find?'

'Even if you do tell the world, you might just be laughed at. They'll call you a crank.'

'Absolutely not! I have too much evidence and enough credibility to make myself heard. All you have to do is take me to the house.'

I stared back at him, into that sweaty covetous face and thought of Eva. I saw those little hands of his fondling her white skin, his breath heavy, panting even. I saw the tears in her eyelashes as they closed together.

'Take me to the house!' he commanded, urging me from the depths of his eyes.

'Alright, yes I will,' I heard my voice say. 'Now unlock that door please.'

'Do I have your word?'

'Yes, but I want to go back alone first, just to say goodbye to Beth, to Gladys...'

'Gladys? Who is she?'

I drew in a deep breath. 'Meet me in two hours on Marguerite

Avenue.'

'Do you swear? I'll find you if you let me down.'

'I swear that I'll be there in two hours. Unlock that door.'

He turned to the lock, fumbling with the key and in one swift movement I did it. I drew the small package from my pocket and slipped it behind the bookcase, balanced quite comfortably on the thick skirting board. Sasha opened the door and I brushed past him without another word, my legs trying not to run.

Outside the air was thick with fumes and clouds. I wiped my hand against my top, the memory of Sasha's sweaty palm still engrained in my skin.

There was an empty phone box up ahead, littered with cigarette butts and exotic dancers' calling cards. I pulled the door open.

'Hello... yes, I'd like to report the discovery of a stolen item... a Celtic cross with a red stone, from the Victoria and Albert Museum... you'll find it in the office of Sasha Apostol in the Machen Institute in London... he's there right now. No, I don't want to give my name.'

My shadow was long and lean by the time I was back on Marguerite Avenue. The houses had turned grey against the sky, their blinds pulled down, their curtains drawn, the climbing rose on the wall at the end nothing but a naked brown rope. I hunched my shoulders up against the cold. A gust of wind swept the leaves and dust up from the road.

I was ten years old again, my grubby school shoes slipping on damp leaves. My mother was at home in the warm glow, worrying why I was a little late, poised to tell me off whilst hugging me at the same time as soon as I stepped in through the door. And we were all ignorant of what was waiting for us around the corner. The minibus sleeping its last night in the big hollow coach station. Three tickets to a London show sitting in my mother's handbag.

I stopped abruptly, my hand pressed firmly against my scar.

'Leave me alone,' I whispered through clenched jaws.

But as I began to move cautiously again, the glint of gold shimmered in the corner of my eye. When I turned towards it two brass numbers smirked back at me: 34.

I am here. I've always been here, they seemed to say.

And somewhere, perhaps deep inside myself although I wasn't

quite sure, I felt the beginning of a beat. It sounded like a distant drum or the rhythmic pounding of a heart.

As I walked up to the house the beat seemed to pause for a moment, as if unsure of something, and then it started up again, a little louder this time. The door fell open with the softest touch and closed behind me. I could hear my breathing quicken, my eyes adjusting to the gloom as the final rays of light teased the dank air with small white prongs.

I wandered through the hallway and the sound grew stronger again. I stopped abruptly, turning to look around me. Where was it coming from? Something had changed in its rhythm as well. Listening carefully I realized that a second beat had joined in; a second pounding heart echoing the first. And, almost as an accompaniment, my own pulse quickened as my knuckles clenched and I carried on.

In the dining room the table was set as before with plates and glasses, as if awaiting a dinner party. I looked up at the portrait of Tristan and Miranda and scooped up one of the wine glasses from the table. It looked so delicate, its pattern woven around the bowl like frost on a spider's web.

In a sudden flash an image swept through me, the two beats strengthening yet again. I saw skin: a woman's neck, a fine bead of sweat trickling down between her breasts. I felt myself gasp and clutched the glass tighter.

'Would you like a drink?'

I jumped at the voice. Cold fear sliced through me as my eyes scanned the room for its owner. At the end of the table sat a lone figure in black.

'Raphael!'

He peered back at me, the handsome poetic face I'd first seen in the black and white photograph now barely recognizable. There were jagged tears up one side of his face and his hair was matted with blood. He seemed to have diminished, hunched and hollow now, the loneliest creature I'd ever seen.

'So you live here now, as well,' I murmured, trying to control my voice.

He smiled sadly, his lips etched with cracked purple lines. 'You saw it just now, didn't you?' he answered. 'You can hear it too.'

'Hear what? What do you mean?'

'The beating truth. It's upstairs you know. Or are you too scared to face it?'

I glanced down at the glass I was holding between my shaking hands and felt Raphael's gaze edge towards me like a dark veil, its feelers probing softly at my skin. My eyes shut for a moment as they lapped against me like soft kisses.

'It's alright, you don't have to go there. Come to me,' came his voice.

My muscles began to give way. I felt my feet stumble. He opened out his arms.

'Come to me.'

The black waves washed over my body, drawing my head in last of all. I saw Seb in the distance; his beautiful eyes blinked back at me with tears and the drum beats stormed in my head. The image of the woman came to me again. Her lips this time, blood red. I heard her moan with pleasure and I cried back, mutely.

And then somewhere, somewhere within the pounding and the horror, came the softest, most meagre flicker; a white shadow, not bright enough for a flame. I reached towards it and its whiteness merged into a limp little bell of petals in my hand.

'Look inside the flower,' came my mother's voice. 'Look inside...'

I lifted its small head and from within the humble petals a dazzling light shone out at me, so bright that the force of it threw my head back and sent fire through my limbs. And as I lurched away from Raphael I crushed the palms of my hands together as tightly and irrevocably as I could.

The fragments of the wine glass chimed as they met the floor.

I felt my face go white and waited for the pain. But nothing came; nothing other than cool serenity. My hands were clean. Not a drop of blood in sight.

'Look,' I whispered, raising my hands to Raphael. 'Nothing.'

He seemed to recoil, fear etched in his face and I began to move away, suddenly breaking into a run.

'No!' he screamed through tearing lips.

'I'm stronger than you!' I cried back at him, 'and I'm not scared anymore!'

I raced through the hallway and up the stairs, the haze diminishing before me at every footfall. The beats grew stronger the further up I went and now the visions of her came to me thick and fast: her fine white skin, her haunted face and his lips slowly moving up her neck. My throat choked with sobs but I had to go on. I had to see the truth.

Their heartbeats pulsed as one now, drawing me to the final corridor upstairs. And yet I could see them in my mind before I'd even found the room. His arms drawn tightly round her waist, their bodies perfectly and exquisitely in tune.

'Seb!'

Two pairs of frightened eyes darted towards me as I stood shivering and crying in the doorway, hugging myself with lonely arms.

'Seb,' I moaned again.

Eva uncoiled herself from him, her half naked body horribly gaunt. Seb stepped towards me but I cringed back and he halted, hurt searing through his face.

'Why?' I sobbed. Their betrayal ached like a gushing wound.

He drew his fingers back through his hair, trembling as if he was barely able to speak. 'You didn't want me anymore,' he finally uttered.

'That's not true. Be honest, you've been with her all this time, haven't you?'

'No,' he shook his head. 'Not until now.'

'Really? Well what about before then?'

Eva leapt forwards. 'Don't you ever stop?' she snarled as Seb grabbed her arm to hold her back. 'Always searching, probing, digging up what isn't yours to find. I warned you to keep away. I warned you to leave!'

'So that you could have him.'

'No!' she screamed. 'To protect *you*. To save you from this!'

Seb hung his head down low. A tear glided down the angle of his cheek and I felt myself crumble.

'I don't understand,' I whimpered.

'Yes you do,' she snapped back through gritted teeth. 'Just face it. We don't have to tell you anything, it's there already. You tell us. Go on! Who is this man you are in love with? What is he?'

My arms fell limply by my sides as he raised his head up again; his blue eyes were the colour of agony.

'A ghost,' I answered.

'And who is Beth's father?' came her voice again. 'Who made my fragile little girl who should never have existed, never been born?'

He looked ready to fall apart and I ached to hold him, more than ever before. 'You Seb, you.'

'And what do you have to do now?' she demanded.

Her face suddenly came between us, poised like a bullet ready to aim. She was barely breathing.

'I have to leave.'

I can't remember exactly how I got back to my old room: running, stumbling, clutching my aching stomach up the final flight of stairs and across the balcony to my barren bed. I'm not sure how long I lay there, torn apart by misery, knowing that there would be no Seb to greet me that night, no eyes to lap me up, no eager hands to rid me of my clothes.

At some point my eyelids flickered closed and I drifted into dreams: my mother in the garden, patting down the soil, her back always turned away. And the reflection of my young face in the bus window; a smiling ghost looking back at me from the motorway beyond.

'Serena,' came a voice; the same voice that was still ringing in my ears from earlier. 'Serena.'

Cool slim fingers were interlocking themselves with mine. A body was curling up against me, its white face gazing down.

'Eva!' I plunged upwards through my sleep, up and out into the air again. 'What are you doing here?'

'Sshh. Don't be afraid. I'm... I'm not going to yell at you anymore.'

'Where's Seb?'

'Still next door. Lost and drowning in his misery.' Her mouth looked nearly purple in the moonlight. 'I just heard what you did... to Sasha. Robert told me about how he got that cross for you and then Sasha rang my mother from the police station, fuming with rage about some meeting he'd missed with you. She told him never to come back here again. At last! You tried to protect us from him, didn't you? You tried to protect me, and Beth!'

'Yes.'

Her face trembled. All the anger and pain of our last meeting seemed to have sapped everything from her. 'Thank you. Thank you so much.'

I sank my head back into the pillow. 'It's alright. At least no one will believe anything he says anymore. I think he got off lightly though, he wanted me to take him to the house.'

'Oh God!'

'His grand plans for Beth were hideous. She's delicate enough as it is...' I swallowed hard. 'What will become of her?'

Eva's eyes were wide and sad. 'We honestly don't know, only time will tell. She isn't a normal little girl. We never thought that such a thing as Beth was possible, when we fell in love.'

'Eva?'

'Yes.'

'Why did he come to me when he's always been in love with you?'

She laughed deeply, toying with my fingers in her hands.

'Because I've tried my best to reject him, over and over again.'

'Why?'

'Because,' she paused. 'Because I have a life! Seb is someone who's always inspired love. It makes it all the more tragic. Miranda, the woman who brought him up, loved him more than anyone ever could. But it wasn't enough to keep him safe. I have loved that man from childhood. He's my very first memory and I know that he'll be my very last.'

'What happened to him when he came back to London from Druid Manor?'

The moonlight drained away and her face fell into the shadows. Her fingers unthreaded themselves from mine. 'The country wasn't enough for a young man like that,' she said eventually. 'He wanted to know where he really came from and once he was old enough to find out for himself then no one could stop him. Lord Hartreve sent his assistant and Miranda a faithful cook as his guardians, who both swore to protect him and to bring him home safe and sound when he'd seen enough. But once Tristan got his son back he was never going to let him go again. He trapped him there, forever.'

It was so dark I couldn't see her at all now, although I could hear the soft sound of her breathing.

'Why is it that I was able to see into your world, right from the start?' I asked.

'We've never come across anyone else like you before. Raphael was fascinated, mesmerized by you. My brother was an obsessive person... such a sad, dark soul.'

She stopped and swallowed hard, fighting back the tears. 'It took my own mother years and years to find out what really existed around her. That's when she stopped being happy. You saw it all straightaway. You seem to have something special... I think that only Seb can explain that to you. He truly loves you, you know that? You have to go, but say goodbye to him first.'

I shrugged. 'I'm leaving tomorrow. I can't stay here any longer. But I would like to say goodbye to Beth, properly. Do you think I can?'

'She'll be waiting for you in the morning... and one more thing, before I leave.'

'Yes?'

I felt something heavy land in my lap. My fingers fell on rough paper.

'Your drawings,' she said. 'I took them from your room when you left for Druid Manor before me at Christmas. They're so beautiful. I sent them to a friend of mine in Paris, an illustrator. He wants to meet you. His address is on that parcel.'

I felt my throat choke up. 'Thank you,' I stammered. 'I... I wish that we could have been friends.'

'I know. We can, in a funny sort of way. Just promise that you'll live your life, for both of us, and I'll always be watching from a distance. Do you promise?'

'I promise.'

And a gentle parting kiss brushed against my lips.

1911

'My boy! Take me to my boy!'

The icy pavement crunched beneath her feet as she fell into Gladys Hubbard's arms.

'I can't. That's why I summoned you to London – thank goodness you came! He's been gone for days now. He's somewhere in there,' and Gladys nodded back at the house behind her. '... We just can't see it to let ourselves in!'

The air was dense with freezing fog. The cold had crawled right through Miranda's fur coat during the journey and then deeper and deeper into her flesh. And now that she was here, in the presence of that house once more, it felt as if even her bones had turned to ice and nothing would ever make her warm again.

Was it really still standing there after all these years? The place she'd hoped and prayed never to see again? The brass numbers, 34, gleamed down at her.

'God help me.'

The world smeared into whiteness and her knees seemed to dissolve beneath her. But before she could tumble into the ice, two firm hands clutched at her elbows from behind. They scooped her up again, cradling her with their loving strength.

'Oh Walter! Wasn't it enough for him just to live in his mother's house, spend his time with his cousins? Did he really have to wander into the darkness? Why didn't you stop him? You promised, both of you, to protect him.'

Walter had become so gaunt that his skin was now translucent; the angular bones in his face threatening to sever right through.

'We did as much as we could,' he murmured. 'We tried to keep him away, but we are not that powerful my darling. He saw the house right from the start and fate seemed to draw him inside.'

'Then I will draw him back out again. I'll drag him out of that repugnant hell-hole if I have to! Just follow me.'

The icy pathway shattered like glass as she scrambled to the door and hurled it open. The grey cloud within reared up at the sight of her but she waded on into it, squinting through the haze with stinging eyes at something lying on the floor ahead: the body of a young man.

'Oh my boy!'

Walter rushed ahead, collapsing to his knees. He brushed the frost from the man's lips and pressed his ear against them.

'It's no good. He's gone.'

'My darling son, my baby. He's taken you away from us. Tristan's got you now, hasn't he?'

A shadow passed between them, slipping over the banisters and up into the house beyond.

'Oh, is he gone? What have I done? Is our Seb really dead? Is he?' yelped Gladys, staggering towards them with her hand clutching at her chest.

'Yes he is,' whispered Miranda. 'It's not your fault. It was his fate, just like Walter said.'

She cradled his head up onto her lap. His skin was as smooth and faultless as it had ever been. His eyes, which were still open, were as blue as the sky on a bright spring day. Even in death he was beautiful.

'Oh my chest, I can't breathe!' Gladys gasped. She crumbled down, wheezing and spluttering onto the cold floor.

'Oh, help her!' Miranda yelled.

Walter snatched a small bottle from around his neck and tried to force it into the struggling woman's mouth, but with one final wheeze her body suddenly slumped down in stillness, her eyes gazing unblinkingly up at them.

'No!'

The walls echoed her shrill cry straight back at her.

'There's nothing left for you now Miranda White,' they whispered.

'Nothing left. I have nothing left.'

'Yes you do.'

A pair of arms gathered her closely in, pressing her ear against a chest filled with a warm and beating heart. Walter.

'You still have me,' he said.

SERENA'S STORY

'I want to give you something.'

'What is it? Oh, your peony brooch!'

Beth's eyes glinted up at me.

'There you go. It looks just lovely on you.'

She patted it contentedly against her chest but then suddenly wrinkled up her forehead.

'That means you're leaving, doesn't it? That's why you've brought me to the park, to our favourite place.'

I huddled up next to her on the blanket. Above us the great tree wove a mesh against the sky with its branches. No leaves yet, just the merest buds like emeralds glinting down at us.

'Yes. I'm so sorry.'

Her chin wobbled slightly. 'Is it because I'm different from other children?'

'Oh God no. No! Beth you're wonderful, don't ever change. It's nothing to do with you at all.'

She nuzzled her cheek against my arm and I squeezed her close, blinking back the tears.

'Will I see you again?'

'Of course darling. I'll write to you and you can visit me when you get older.'

'But you won't come back to the house?'

'No.'

'I'll miss you.'

'Me too. Come on let me take you home.'

We grasped hands and pulled each other up.

'You're freezing!' I cried. 'Where are your gloves?'

'I don't like gloves.'

'Then I'll have to warm you up.'

And I rubbed her hands between my palms as we made patterns along the dewy grass, back towards Marguerite Avenue for the last time.

Gladys was vehemently polishing in the hallway when we got in and the mournful notes of Robert at the piano stroked the air from the room next door.

'Look at my brooch,' said Beth to Gladys. 'Is there anything to eat? I'm hungry.'

'You'll find fresh bread in the kitchen.'

My heart turned a somersault as she scuttled away. I was back at the beginning again: standing here with the smell of wood polish and baking in my nostrils, the sound of the piano drifting by.

'I'm leaving,' I said.

'Yes I realized that,' Gladys replied; her voice already seemed far away. 'I'm surprised you stayed so long.'

'You'll take care of Beth, won't you?'

'I'll love her as my own. Just like I've always done. Good luck dear,' she squeezed my arm. 'You're right to leave. Go and live your life to the full, you're wasting it here...'

She looked away, brushing her wrist across her eyes.

'Thank you for everything. I think I'm very lucky to have known you.'

But she was already hurrying off, half way back to the kitchen, her apron tied firmly in a knot in the middle of her back.

'Edward and Arabella are in the drawing room if you want to see them,' she called behind her.

The drawing room door was half open. I cleared my throat to speak; a few well-rehearsed words ready on my tongue. But when I peeped in at Edward and Arabella sitting there, gazing silently across each other's heads like two empty husks, I backed quietly away.

My hand slid smoothly up the wooden banister for the last time. Up in the cornice Lucinda's moulded face watched me leave. The sound of Robert's playing fell behind me and I nodded a farewell to the painting of Walter Balanchine as I passed by.

Up in my room the parcel with all my drawings in it lay sitting on my bed. I tore off the French address, put it in my pocket and wrote *For Eva* in its place.

Just as I was turning to leave there was a small click behind me, followed by the familiar sound of the balcony door swinging open. I smiled to myself as if I was already looking back at a vision in my memory.

Seb barely moved. His hair was a mess. He wore tatty jeans and an old crumpled shirt hugged his slim body. But the graceful angles of his face, his blue eyes and those lips were as delicious and beautiful as ever.

'You've got his eyes you know,' I said quietly. 'Tristan's. Just like in that painting of him. But your face is much kinder than his.'

'I am nothing like that man,' Seb replied.

'And yet you're trapped with him now, aren't you? Because you couldn't keep away.'

'I was so young; his loneliness appalled me, terrified me! And he dug his claws further and further in until it became impossible for me to leave. I stopped eating, stopped breathing...'

'You lied to me about Eva.'

'I lied to you about everything, I had to!' he came towards me cringing, hands outstretched, shoulders slumped; pain scarring every gesture. 'What else was I supposed to do? Scare you away with the truth when you'd only just walked into our lives?'

'Oh God, I loved you so much!'

I fell towards him and he drew me close, burying his face in my hair. And with his touch the bright colours of a forgotten memory suddenly burst forward through the darkness.

At last she turned to face me: my mother with her grubby old T-shirt sticking to her sides. Her cheeks were full of sunshine and her eyes sparkled as she dropped the pink bloom into my hand. A peony.

'I have to ask you something,' I said.

'What?'

'Why is it that I can see you, and Gladys, and now the house? What's so special about me?'

His fingers reached down to my waist, slid up beneath my top and traced the scar I'd carried with me for so long.

'You were there in the bus with them that day, weren't you? When your parents died? That's how you got this scar, from all that glass smashing about you when the bus veered into the shop window.'

As the words came out of his mouth the scar burned hot beneath his hand.

'How did you know? I've never told anyone,' I groaned.

'No. And I doubt whether you've ever truly faced it yourself. But there had to be some reason why you were so scared of broken glass.'

The memories surged back in. Unstoppable now. Unshrinkable. My own private fortress crashing down around me.

'A great shard of it went in,' I tried to swallow back the tears.

'Freezing cold and boiling hot at the same time. I fought my way out of the wreck alone, with the glass still inside me. It took hours for them to stitch me up in the hospital. I lost so much blood...'

'And whilst you were lying there you stared right into the face of death, didn't you? After that the world changed forever. You stumbled on through life like a lonely ghost, seeing everything around you for what it was. All that had ever been beautiful was gone.'

'Until I came here,' I sobbed. 'Until I found you!'

'But it's too late for me. Leave this place, please, before I try to stop you. Don't throw away a second chance.'

He lifted up my chin and our mouths touched with a kiss that gently melted into nothing. When I opened my eyes, he'd gone.

We have all lived with ghosts at some point in our lives. They've embraced us passionately in the darkest hours, made us laugh and cry when we are lonely and at our most vulnerable. But there also comes a time when we have to shut the doors of our past behind us and venture back into the world with new skin. And although I lost a part of myself forever when I walked away from Marguerite Avenue, it also felt as if my heart was finally beginning to beat with fresh blood again. Second chances really do exist. It was time for me to live.

The End

ACKNOWLEDGMENTS

I would like to thank my family and friends for their unfailing encouragement over the long period of time it has taken me to write this book. I am also so grateful to hhb agency for being a powerhouse of support, know-how and empathy throughout this process. Thank you Heather Holden-Brown, Elly James, Celia Hayley and Claire Houghton-Price. Celia, I could not have made The Room Beyond what it is without your editorial skills. I would never have found hhb agency without the help of Clarissa Dickson Wright. Thank you for pointing me in the right direction. My heartfelt thanks go to Jennie Rawlings for her beautiful cover design. Finally I would like to acknowledge my husband Alpaslan and mother Jarmila for reading all those rewrites and always encouraging me to follow my dream. This book is for both of you.

ABOUT THE AUTHOR

Stephanie Elmas was born in Hong Kong to an English father and Czech mother but spent most of her childhood in Bristol. She studied English at university in London. She has worked as a head hunter, taught English in Japan and returned to university to complete a Masters in Victorian fiction. It was here that she developed her interest in the dark dangerous world of Victorian sensation writing. Stephanie now lives in a chaotic house in Surrey with her husband and three highly energetic but wonderful children

REVIEWS

If you have enjoyed my writing, I would be very grateful if you wrote a review on Goodreads and/or Amazon. Reviews and social networking sell books and, as a new author, I would appreciate your help. My success as an author will come from the quality of my writing and my readers' support.

COMING UP

The Curious Life of Walter Balanchine
(working title)

During the writing of The Room Beyond I fell so in love with the character of Walter Balanchine that I felt he deserved a story of his own. And so my next novel plunges into the labyrinthine alleyways of the Victorian East End to find Walter in his youth. It is told through the eyes of Tom Winter, Walter's old workhouse friend, and how together the two men turn a simple conjuring show into a mystical sensation that will rock the very pillars of London society.

Stephanie Elmas